P9-CBH-411

FARMHAND
ROB GUILLORY'S

VOLUME 1
REAP WHAT WAS SOWN

Created, Written and Drawn by
ROB GUILLORY

Colors by
TAYLOR WELLS

Letters by
KODY CHAMBERLAIN

Graphic Design by
BURTON DURAND

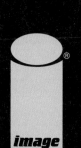

IMAGE COMICS, INC. • **Robert Kirkman:** Chief Operating Officer • **Erik Larsen:** Chief Financial Officer • **Todd McFarlane:** President • **Marc Silvestri:** Chief Executive Officer • **Jim Valentino:** Vice President • **Eric Stephenson:** Publisher / Chief Creative Officer • **Corey Hart:** Director of Sales • **Jeff Boison:** Director of Publishing Planning & Book Trade Sales • **Chris Ross:** Director of Digital Sales • **Jeff Stang:** Director of Specialty Sales • **Kat Salazar:** Director of PR & Marketing • **Drew Gill:** Art Director • **Heather Doornink:** Production Director • **Nicole Lapalme:** Controller • IMAGECOMICS.COM

• **Deanna Phelps:** Production Artist for FARMHAND •

FARMHAND, VOL. 1. First printing. January 2019. Published by Image Comics, Inc. Office of publication: 2701 NW Vaughn St., Suite 780, Portland, OR 97210. Copyright © 2019 Rob Guillory. All rights reserved. Contains material originally published in single magazine form as FARMHAND #1-5. "Farmhand," its logos, and the likenesses of all characters herein are trademarks of Rob Guillory, unless otherwise noted. "Image" and the Image Comics logos are registered trademarks of Image Comics, Inc. No part of this publication may be reproduced or transmitted, in any form or by any means (except for short excerpts for journalistic or review purposes), without the express written permission of Rob Guillory, or Image Comics, Inc. All names, characters, events, and locales in this publication are entirely fictional. Any resemblance to actual persons (living or dead), events, or places, without satirical intent, is coincidental. Printed in the USA. For information regarding the CPSIA on this printed material call: 203-595-3636. For international rights, contact: foreignlicensing@imagecomics.com. ISBN: 978-1-5343-0985-2.

DEDICATION

For my family.

———

Special thanks to John Layman,
Ross Thibodeaux and David Harper
for the encouragement.
And thanks to April Guillory
for all the love.

CHAPTER 1

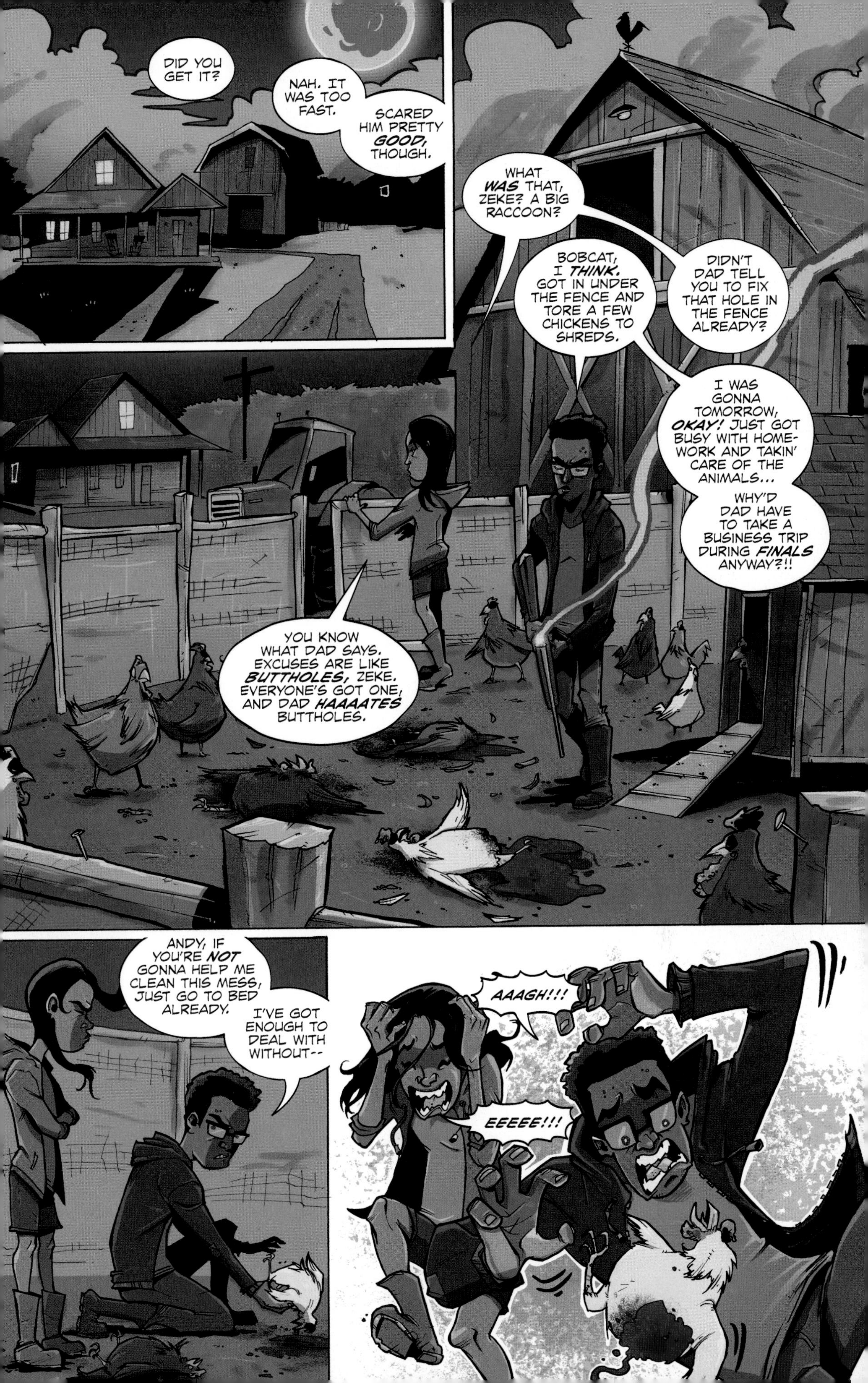
DID YOU GET IT?
NAH. IT WAS TOO FAST.
SCARED HIM PRETTY GOOD, THOUGH.
WHAT WAS THAT, ZEKE? A BIG RACCOON?
BOBCAT, I THINK. GOT IN UNDER THE FENCE AND TORE A FEW CHICKENS TO SHREDS.
DIDN'T DAD TELL YOU TO FIX THAT HOLE IN THE FENCE ALREADY?
I WAS GONNA TOMORROW, OKAY! JUST GOT BUSY WITH HOME-WORK AND TAKIN' CARE OF THE ANIMALS...
WHY'D DAD HAVE TO TAKE A BUSINESS TRIP DURING FINALS ANYWAY?!!
YOU KNOW WHAT DAD SAYS. EXCUSES ARE LIKE BUTTHOLES, ZEKE. EVERYONE'S GOT ONE, AND DAD HAAAATES BUTTHOLES.
ANDY, IF YOU'RE NOT GONNA HELP ME CLEAN THIS MESS, JUST GO TO BED ALREADY.
I'VE GOT ENOUGH TO DEAL WITH WITHOUT--
AAAGH!!!
EEEEE!!!

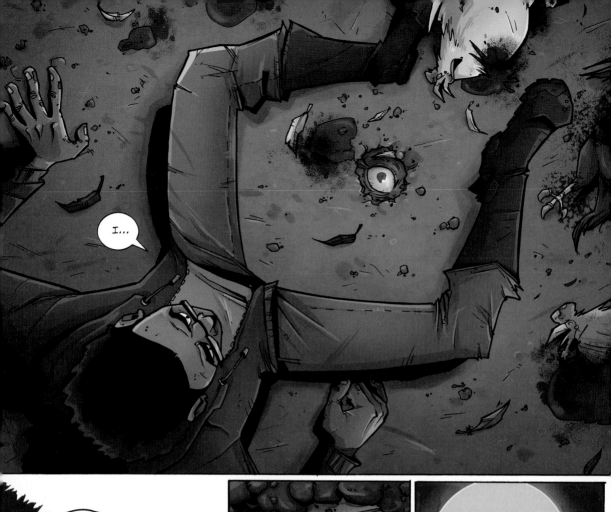

I....

WHAT IS THAT?

IT...IT'S A PERSON.

IT'S...

...DAD?

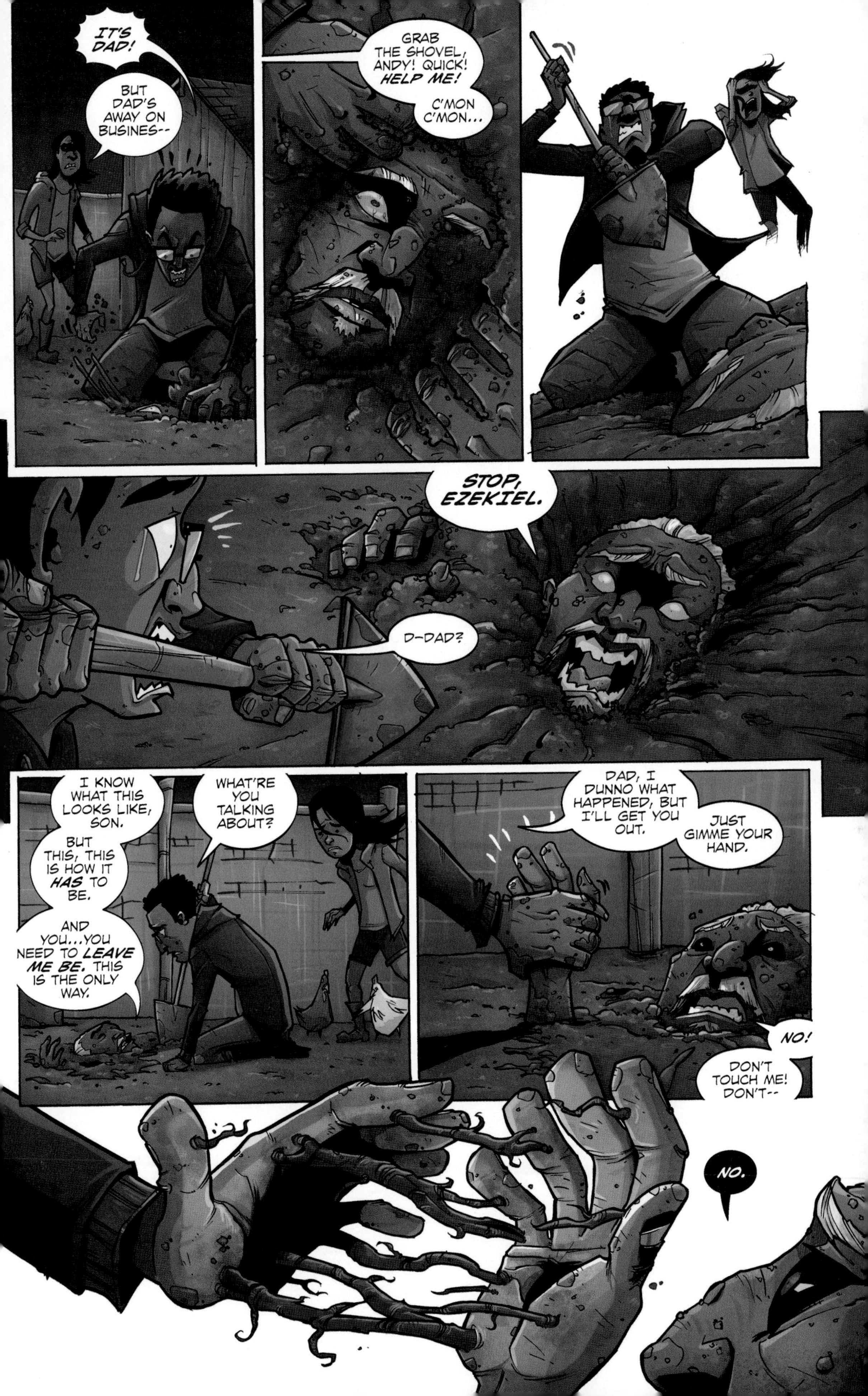
IT'S DAD!
BUT DAD'S AWAY ON BUSINES--
GRAB THE SHOVEL, ANDY! QUICK! HELP ME!
C'MON C'MON...
STOP, EZEKIEL.
D-DAD?
I KNOW WHAT THIS LOOKS LIKE, SON.
BUT THIS, THIS IS HOW IT HAS TO BE.
AND YOU...YOU NEED TO LEAVE ME BE. THIS IS THE ONLY WAY.
WHAT'RE YOU TALKING ABOUT?
DAD, I DUNNO WHAT HAPPENED, BUT I'LL GET YOU OUT.
JUST GIMME YOUR HAND.
NO!
DON'T TOUCH ME! DON'T--
NO.

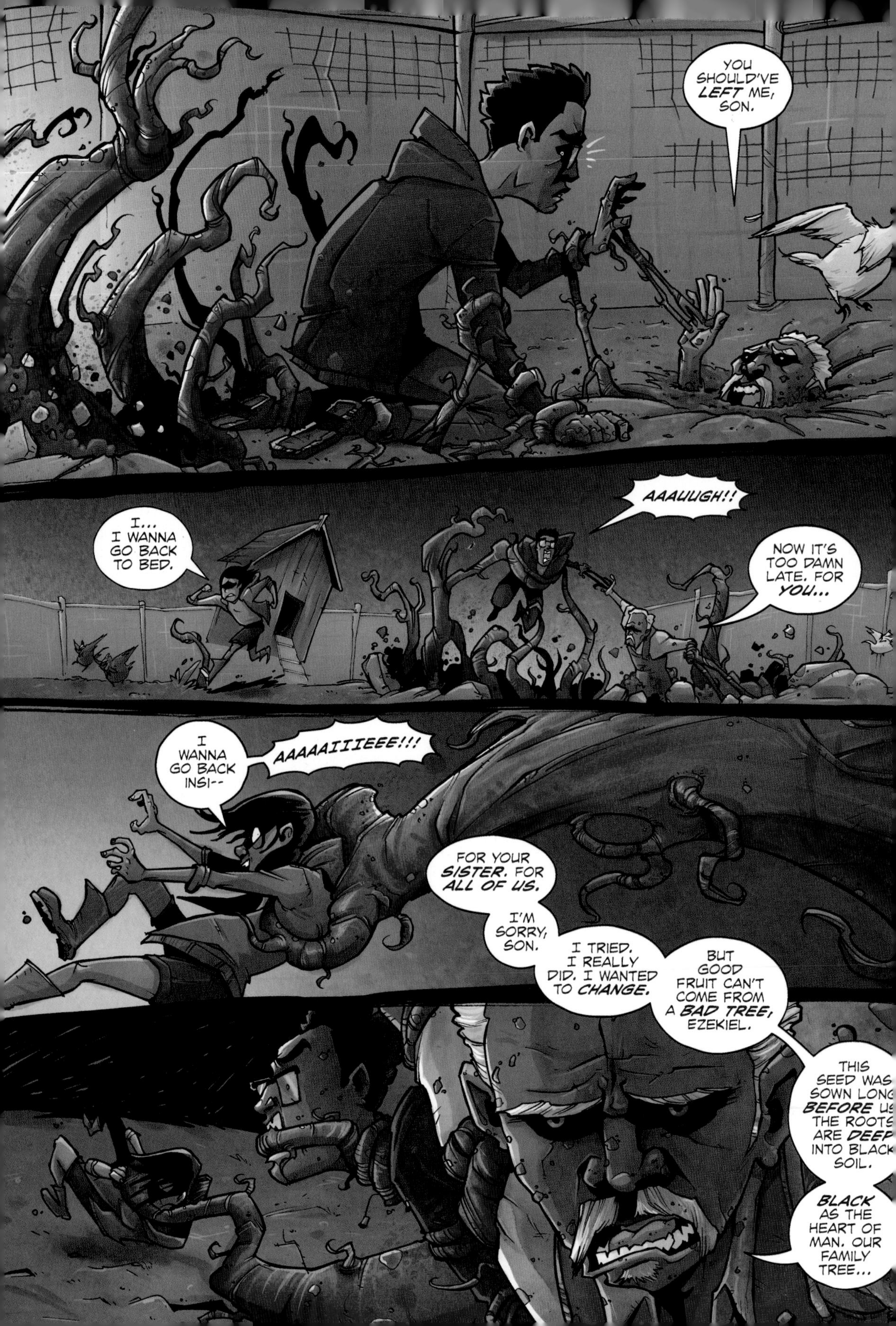
YOU SHOULD'VE LEFT ME, SON.
I... I WANNA GO BACK TO BED.
AAAUUGH!!
NOW IT'S TOO DAMN LATE. FOR YOU...
I WANNA GO BACK INSI--
AAAAAIIIEEE!!!
FOR YOUR SISTER. FOR ALL OF US.
I'M SORRY, SON.
I TRIED. I REALLY DID. I WANTED TO CHANGE.
BUT GOOD FRUIT CAN'T COME FROM A BAD TREE, EZEKIEL.
THIS SEED WAS SOWN LONG BEFORE US. THE ROOTS ARE DEEP INTO BLACK SOIL.
BLACK AS THE HEART OF MAN. OUR FAMILY TREE...

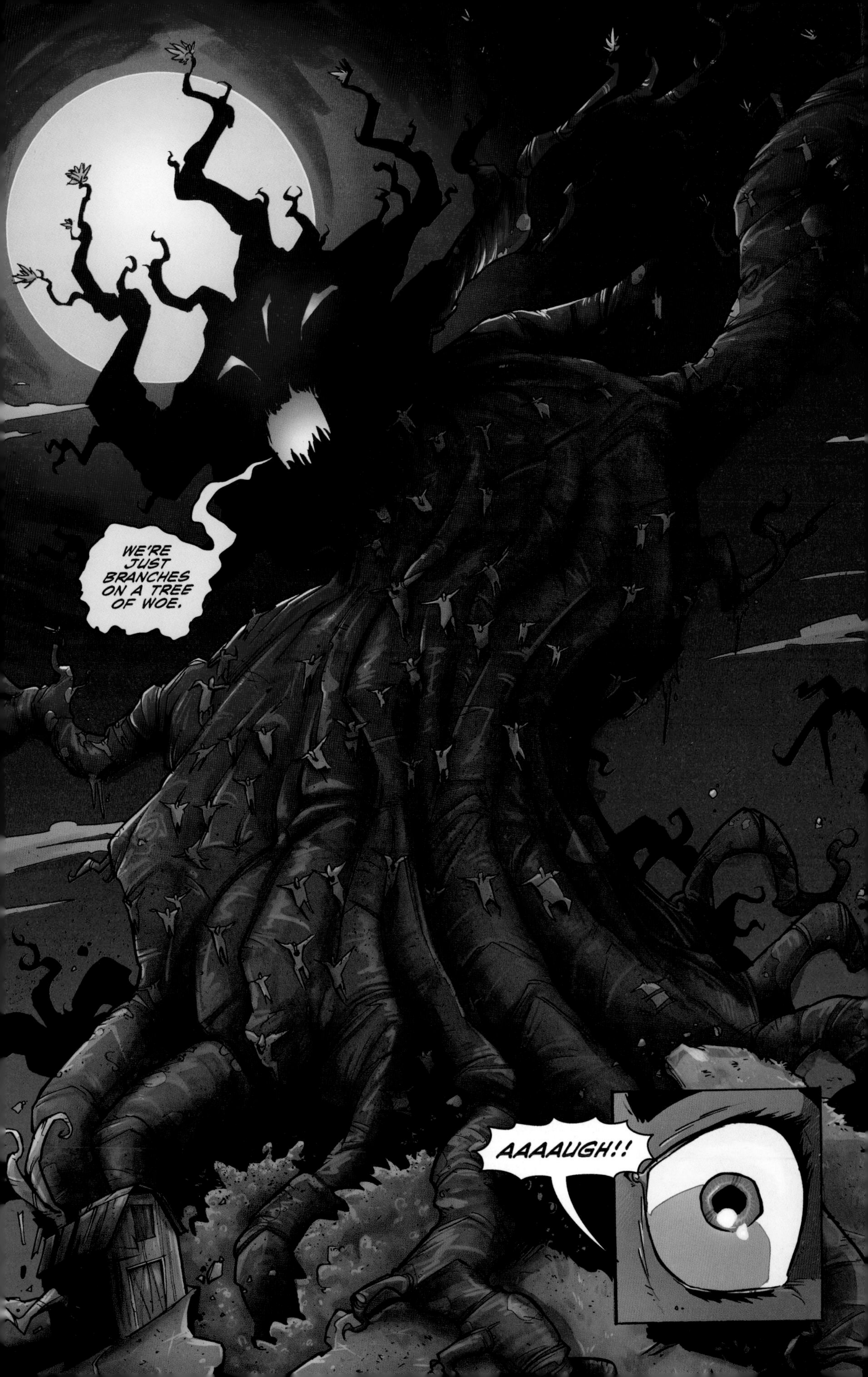
WE'RE JUST BRANCHES ON A TREE OF WOE.
AAAAUGH!!

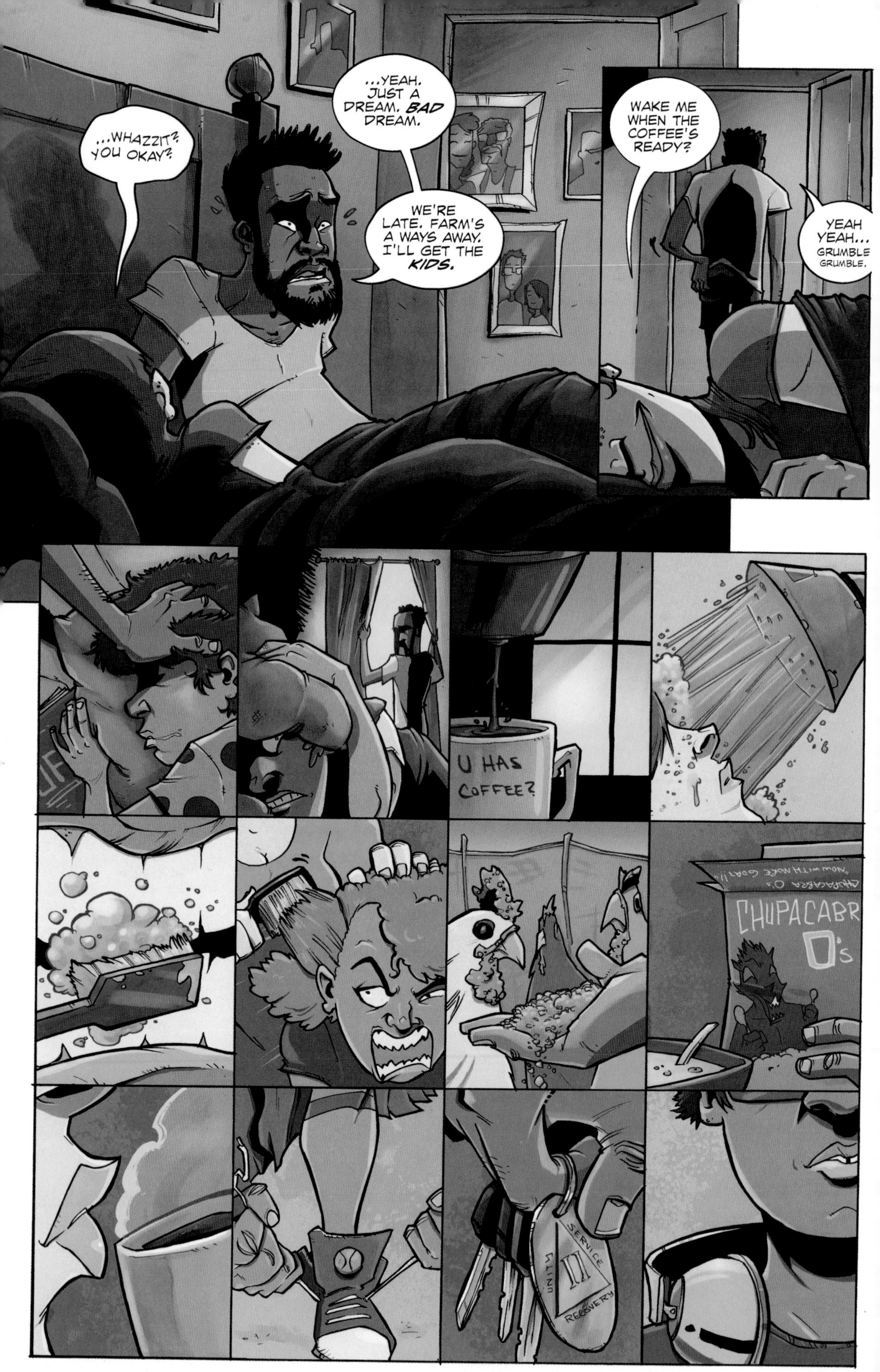

...WHAZZIT? YOU OKAY?
...YEAH. JUST A DREAM. *BAD* DREAM.
WE'RE LATE. FARM'S A WAYS AWAY. I'LL GET THE *KIDS.*
WAKE ME WHEN THE COFFEE'S READY?
YEAH YEAH... GRUMBLE GRUMBLE.
U HAS COFFEE?
CHUPACABR
O's
SERVICE
RECOVERY

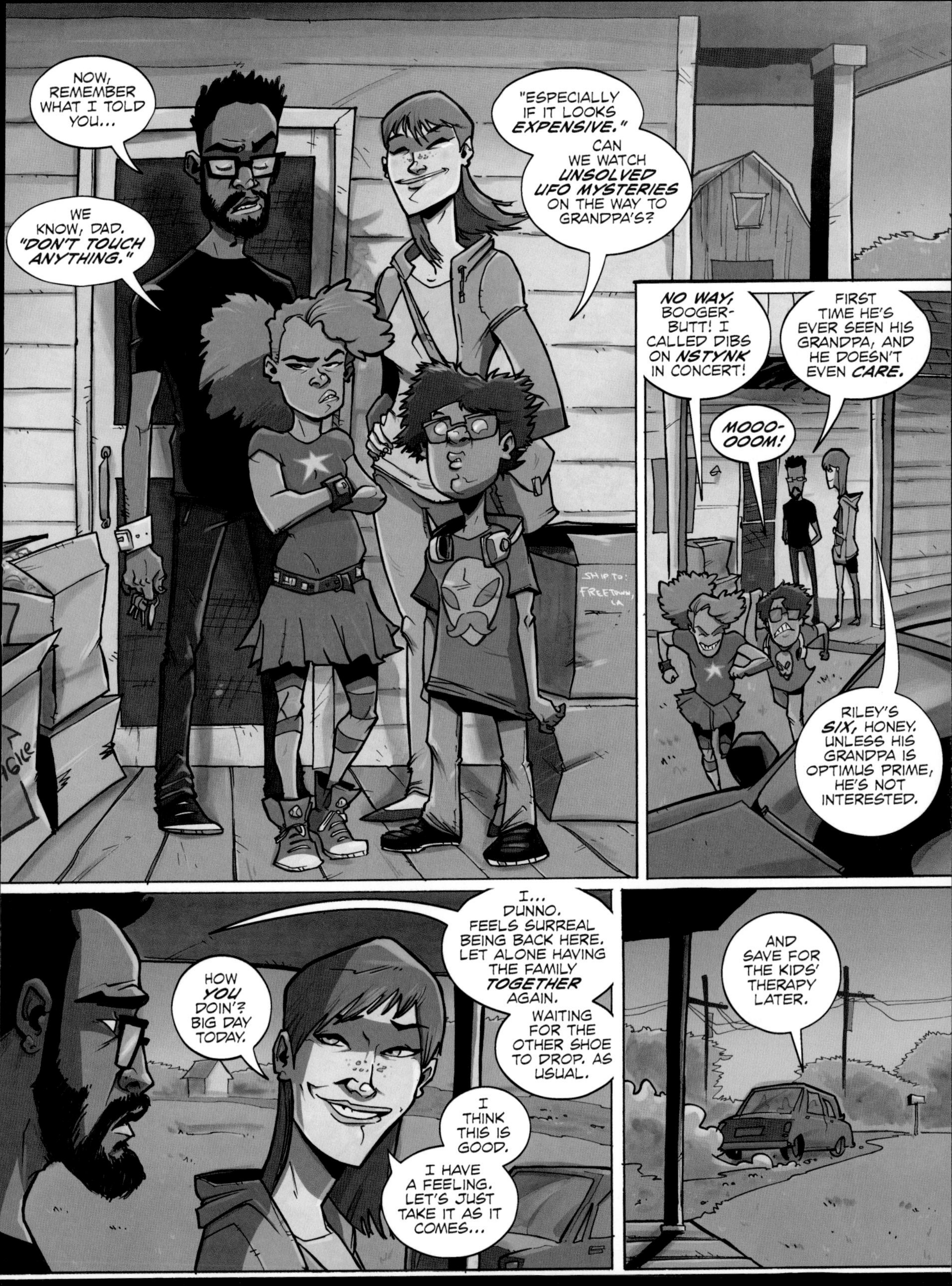
NOW, REMEMBER WHAT I TOLD YOU...
WE KNOW, DAD. "DON'T TOUCH ANYTHING."
"ESPECIALLY IF IT LOOKS EXPENSIVE." CAN WE WATCH UNSOLVED UFO MYSTERIES ON THE WAY TO GRANDPA'S?
SHIP TO: FREETOWN, LA
NO WAY, BOOGER-BUTT! I CALLED DIBS ON NSTYNK IN CONCERT!
FIRST TIME HE'S EVER SEEN HIS GRANDPA, AND HE DOESN'T EVEN CARE.
MOOO-OOOM!
RILEY'S SIX, HONEY. UNLESS HIS GRANDPA IS OPTIMUS PRIME, HE'S NOT INTERESTED.
HOW YOU DOIN'? BIG DAY TODAY.
I... DUNNO. FEELS SURREAL BEING BACK HERE. LET ALONE HAVING THE FAMILY TOGETHER AGAIN.
WAITING FOR THE OTHER SHOE TO DROP. AS USUAL.
I THINK THIS IS GOOD.
I HAVE A FEELING. LET'S JUST TAKE IT AS IT COMES...
AND SAVE FOR THE KIDS' THERAPY LATER.

CHAPTER 1: You Can Go Home Again...But Why?

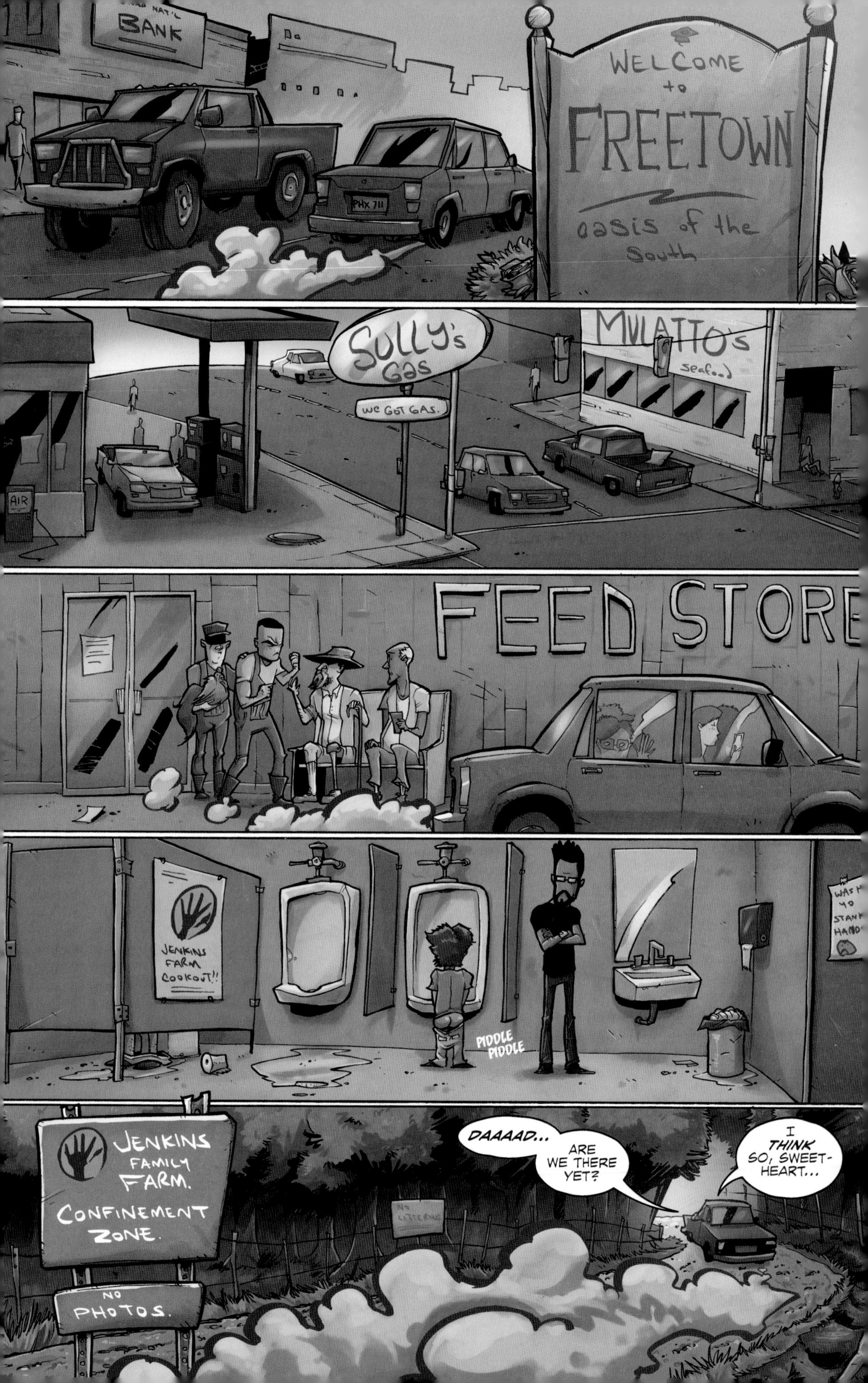
BANK
WELCOME to FREETOWN
oasis of the South
PHX 711
SULLY's Gas
we GOT GAS.
MULATTO's seafood
AIR
FEED STORE
JENKINS FARM COOKOUT!!
PIDDLE PIDDLE
JENKINS FAMILY FARM.
CONFINEMENT ZONE.
NO PHOTOS.
DAAAAD...
ARE WE THERE YET?
I *THINK* SO, SWEET-HEART...

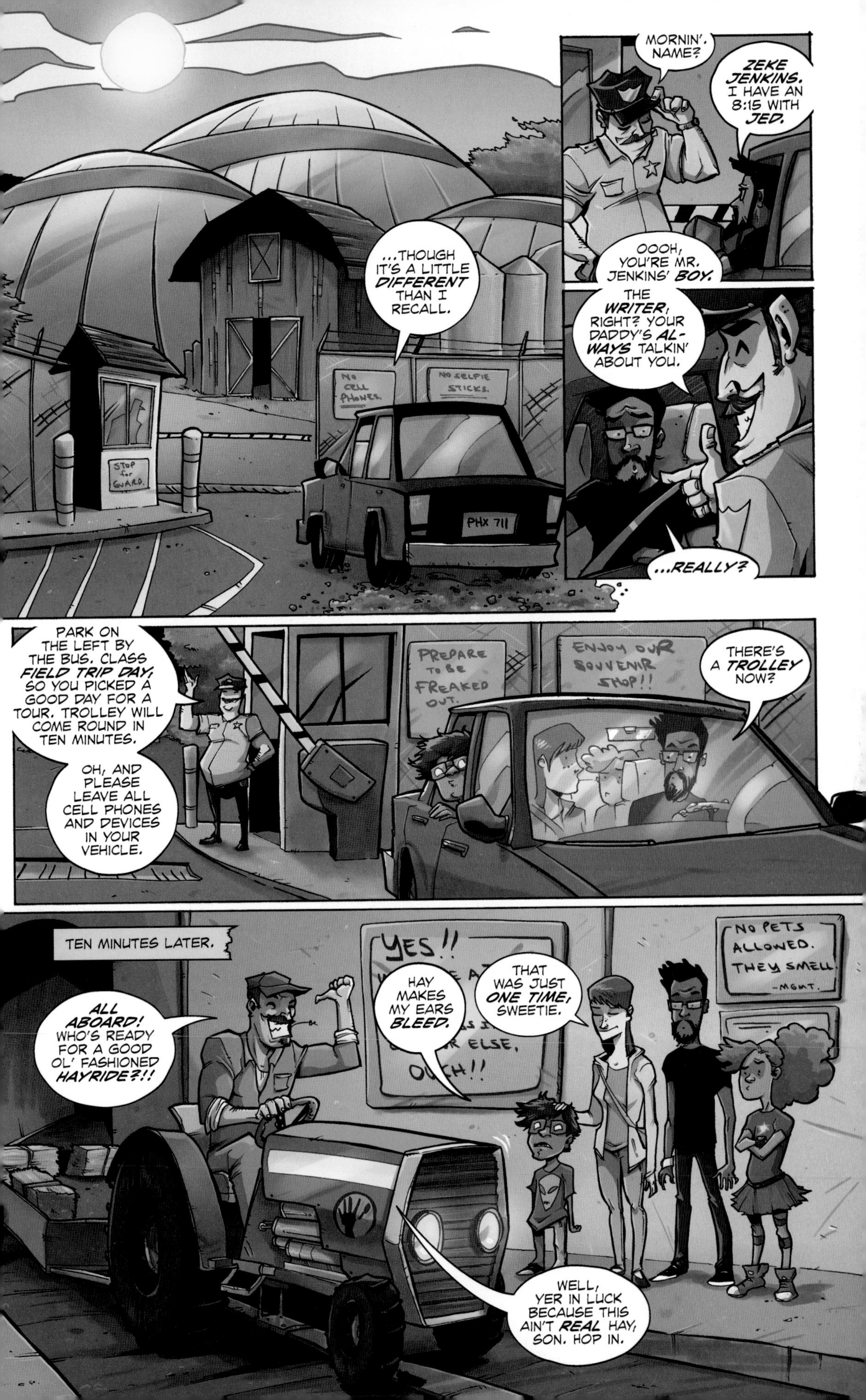
MORNIN'. NAME?
ZEKE JENKINS. I HAVE AN 8:15 WITH JED.
OOOH, YOU'RE MR. JENKINS' BOY.
...THOUGH IT'S A LITTLE DIFFERENT THAN I RECALL.
NO CELL PHONES.
NO SELFIE STICKS.
STOP for GUARD.
PHX 711
THE WRITER, RIGHT? YOUR DADDY'S AL-WAYS TALKIN' ABOUT YOU.
...REALLY?
PARK ON THE LEFT BY THE BUS. CLASS FIELD TRIP DAY, SO YOU PICKED A GOOD DAY FOR A TOUR. TROLLEY WILL COME ROUND IN TEN MINUTES.
OH, AND PLEASE LEAVE ALL CELL PHONES AND DEVICES IN YOUR VEHICLE.
PREPARE TO BE FREAKED OUT.
ENJOY OUR SOUVENIR SHOP!!
THERE'S A TROLLEY NOW?
TEN MINUTES LATER.
YES!!
NO PETS ALLOWED. THEY SMELL. -MGMT.
ALL ABOARD! WHO'S READY FOR A GOOD OL' FASHIONED HAYRIDE?!!
HAY MAKES MY EARS BLEED.
THAT WAS JUST ONE TIME, SWEETIE.
WELL, YER IN LUCK BECAUSE THIS AIN'T REAL HAY, SON. HOP IN.

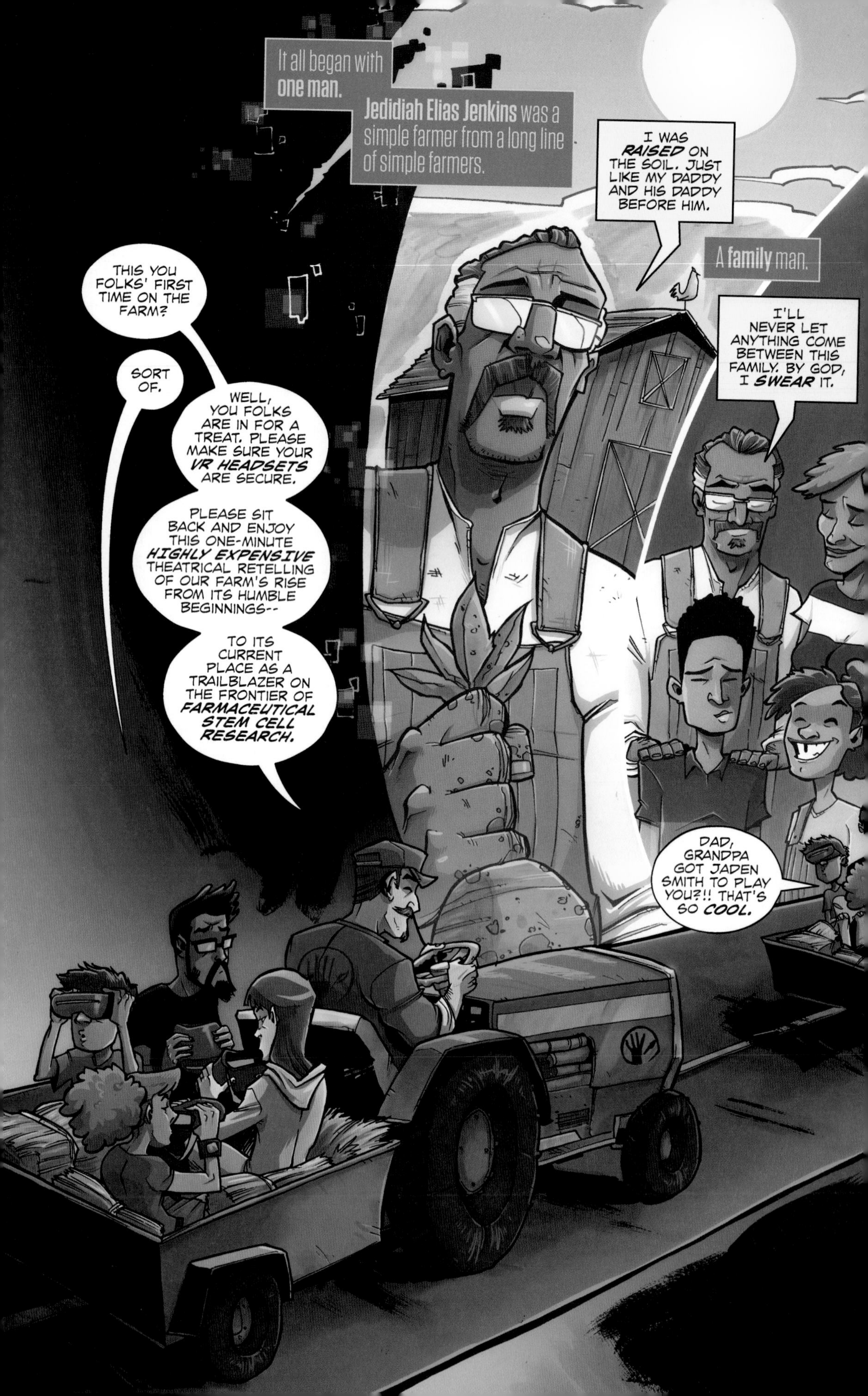

It all began with one man.
Jedidiah Elias Jenkins was a simple farmer from a long line of simple farmers.
I WAS RAISED ON THE SOIL. JUST LIKE MY DADDY AND HIS DADDY BEFORE HIM.
A family man.
I'LL NEVER LET ANYTHING COME BETWEEN THIS FAMILY. BY GOD, I SWEAR IT.
THIS YOU FOLKS' FIRST TIME ON THE FARM?
SORT OF.
WELL, YOU FOLKS ARE IN FOR A TREAT. PLEASE MAKE SURE YOUR VR HEADSETS ARE SECURE.
PLEASE SIT BACK AND ENJOY THIS ONE-MINUTE HIGHLY EXPENSIVE THEATRICAL RETELLING OF OUR FARM'S RISE FROM ITS HUMBLE BEGINNINGS--
TO ITS CURRENT PLACE AS A TRAILBLAZER ON THE FRONTIER OF FARMACEUTICAL STEM CELL RESEARCH.
DAD, GRANDPA GOT JADEN SMITH TO PLAY YOU?!! THAT'S SO COOL.

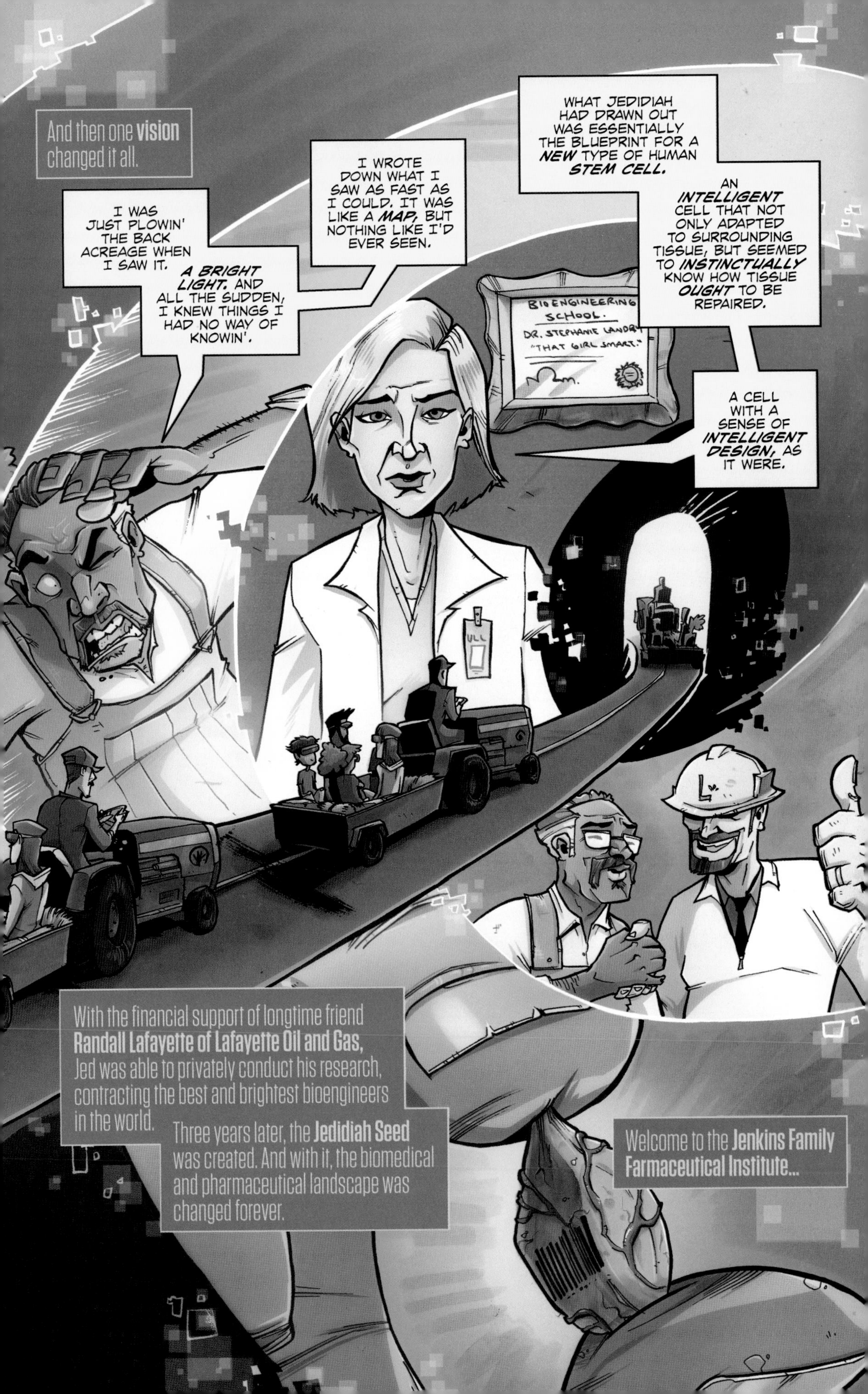

And then one **vision** changed it all.
I WAS JUST PLOWIN' THE BACK ACREAGE WHEN I SAW IT.
A BRIGHT LIGHT. AND ALL THE SUDDEN, I KNEW THINGS I HAD NO WAY OF KNOWIN'.
I WROTE DOWN WHAT I SAW AS FAST AS I COULD. IT WAS LIKE A MAP, BUT NOTHING LIKE I'D EVER SEEN.
WHAT JEDIDIAH HAD DRAWN OUT WAS ESSENTIALLY THE BLUEPRINT FOR A NEW TYPE OF HUMAN STEM CELL.
AN INTELLIGENT CELL THAT NOT ONLY ADAPTED TO SURROUNDING TISSUE, BUT SEEMED TO INSTINCTUALLY KNOW HOW TISSUE OUGHT TO BE REPAIRED.
A CELL WITH A SENSE OF INTELLIGENT DESIGN, AS IT WERE.
BIOENGINEERING SCHOOL.
DR. STEPHANIE LANDRY
"THAT GIRL SMART."
With the financial support of longtime friend **Randall Lafayette of Lafayette Oil and Gas,** Jed was able to privately conduct his research, contracting the best and brightest bioengineers in the world.
Three years later, the **Jedidiah Seed** was created. And with it, the biomedical and pharmaceutical landscape was changed forever.
Welcome to the **Jenkins Family Farmaceutical Institute...**

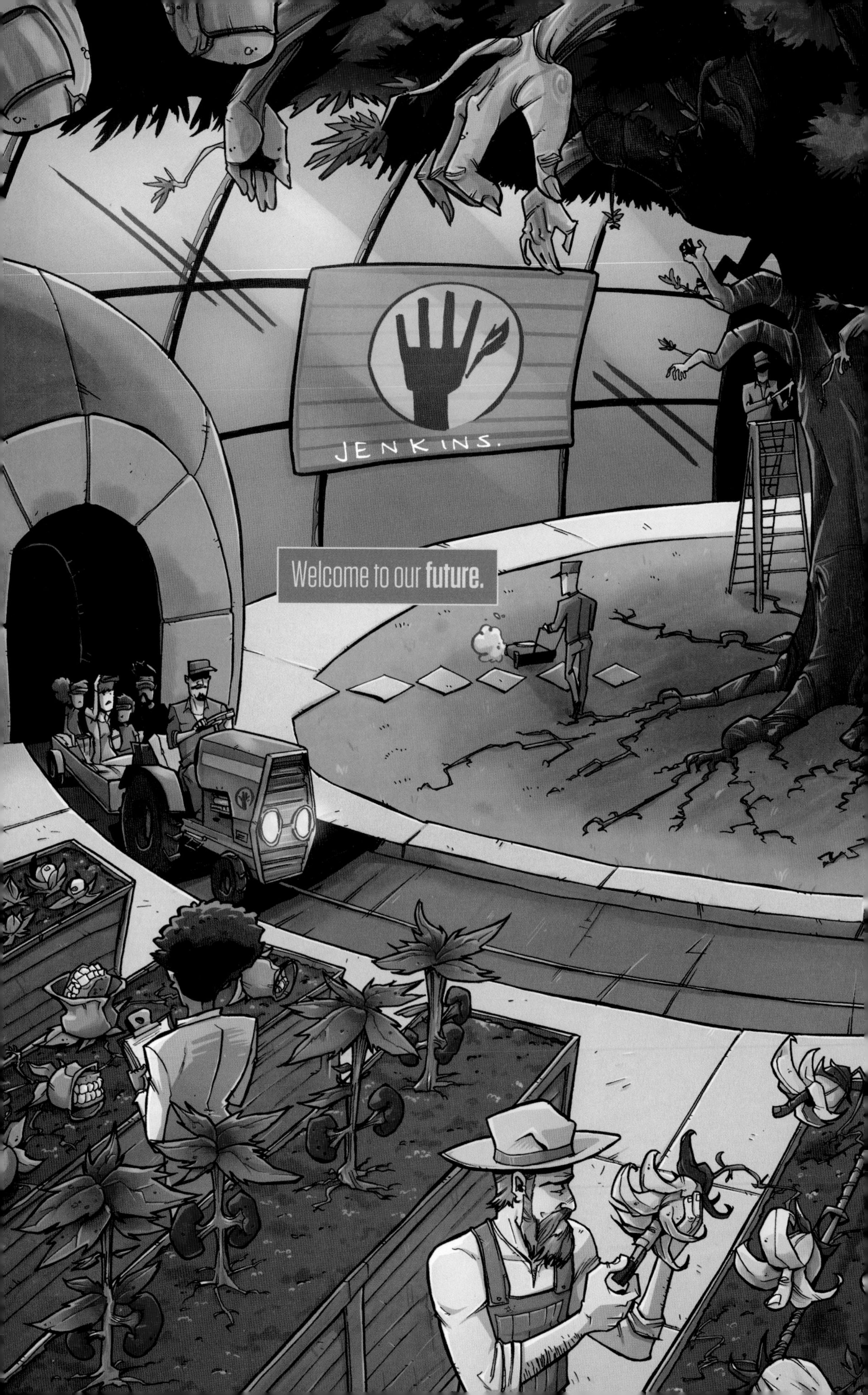
JENKINS.
Welcome to our future.

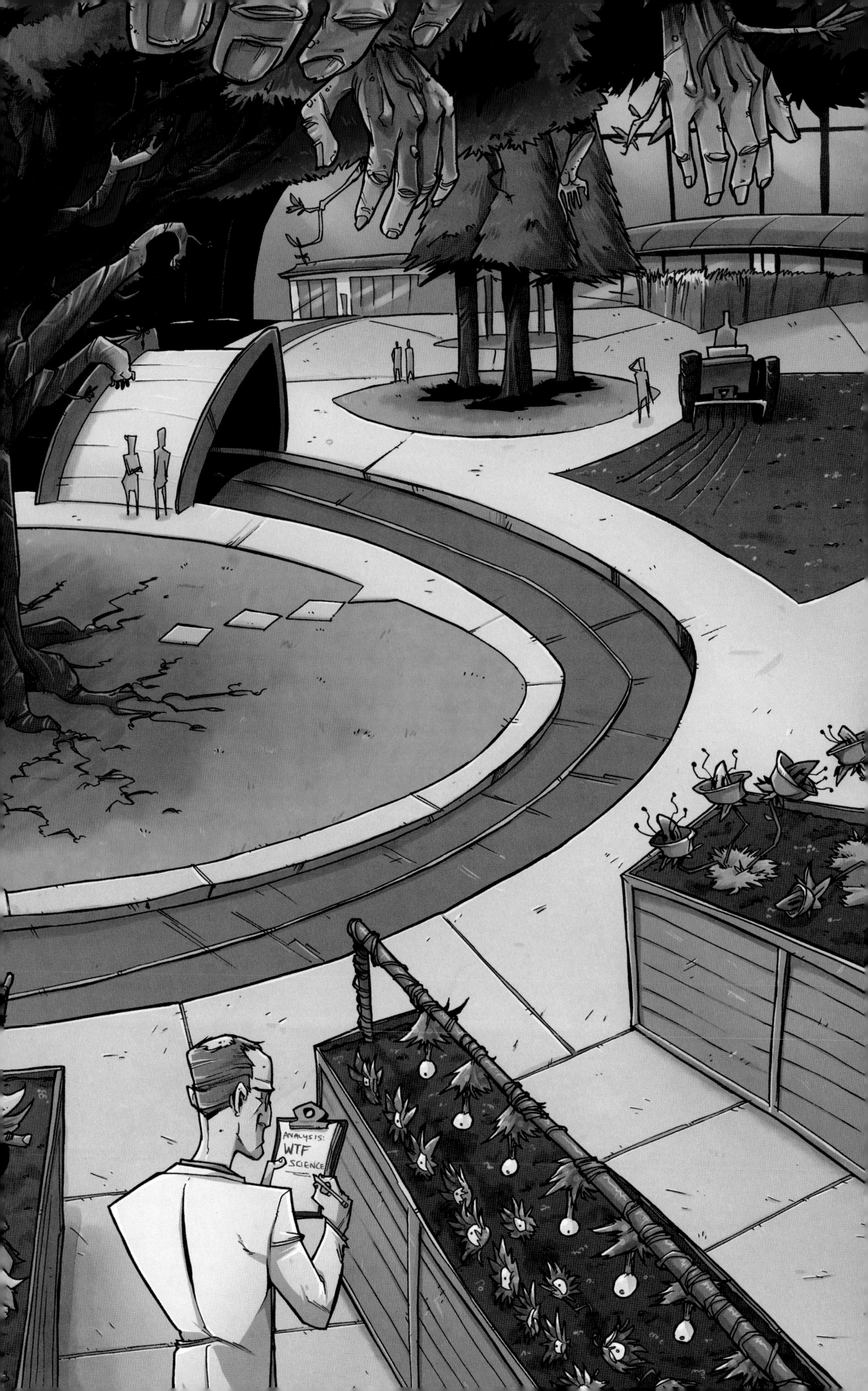
ANALYSIS:
WTF
SCIENCE

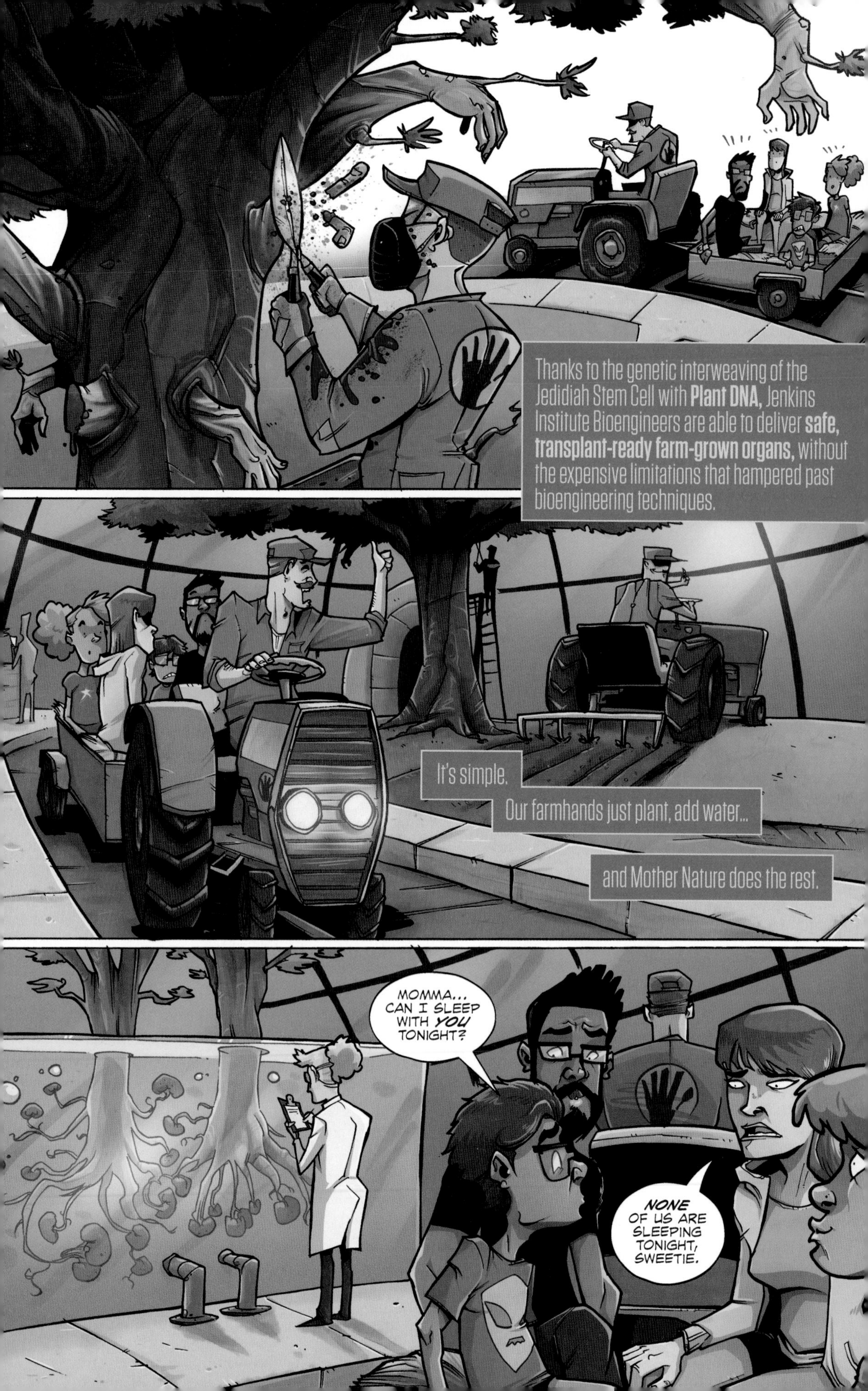
Thanks to the genetic interweaving of the Jedidiah Stem Cell with Plant DNA, Jenkins Institute Bioengineers are able to deliver safe, transplant-ready farm-grown organs, without the expensive limitations that hampered past bioengineering techniques.
It's simple.
Our farmhands just plant, add water...
and Mother Nature does the rest.
MOMMA... CAN I SLEEP WITH YOU TONIGHT?
NONE OF US ARE SLEEPING TONIGHT, SWEETIE.

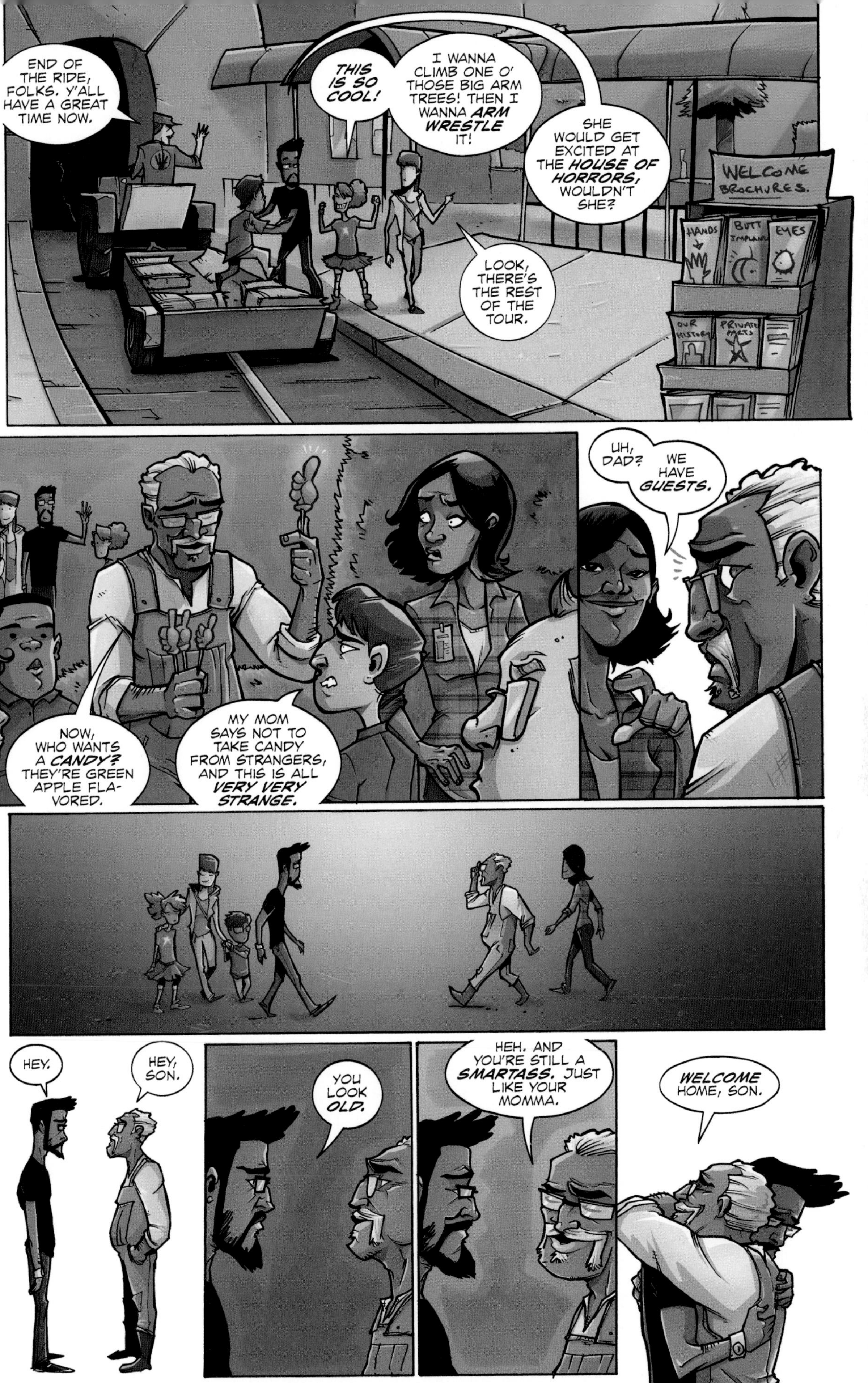
END OF THE RIDE, FOLKS. Y'ALL HAVE A GREAT TIME NOW.
THIS IS SO COOL!
I WANNA CLIMB ONE O' THOSE BIG ARM TREES! THEN I WANNA ARM WRESTLE IT!
SHE WOULD GET EXCITED AT THE HOUSE OF HORRORS, WOULDN'T SHE?
LOOK, THERE'S THE REST OF THE TOUR.
WELCOME BROCHURES.
HANDS
BUTT IMPLANTS
EYES
OUR HISTORY
PRIVATE PARTS
NOW, WHO WANTS A CANDY? THEY'RE GREEN APPLE FLAVORED.
MY MOM SAYS NOT TO TAKE CANDY FROM STRANGERS, AND THIS IS ALL VERY VERY STRANGE.
UH, DAD?
WE HAVE GUESTS.
HEY.
HEY, SON.
YOU LOOK OLD.
HEH. AND YOU'RE STILL A SMARTASS. JUST LIKE YOUR MOMMA.
WELCOME HOME, SON.

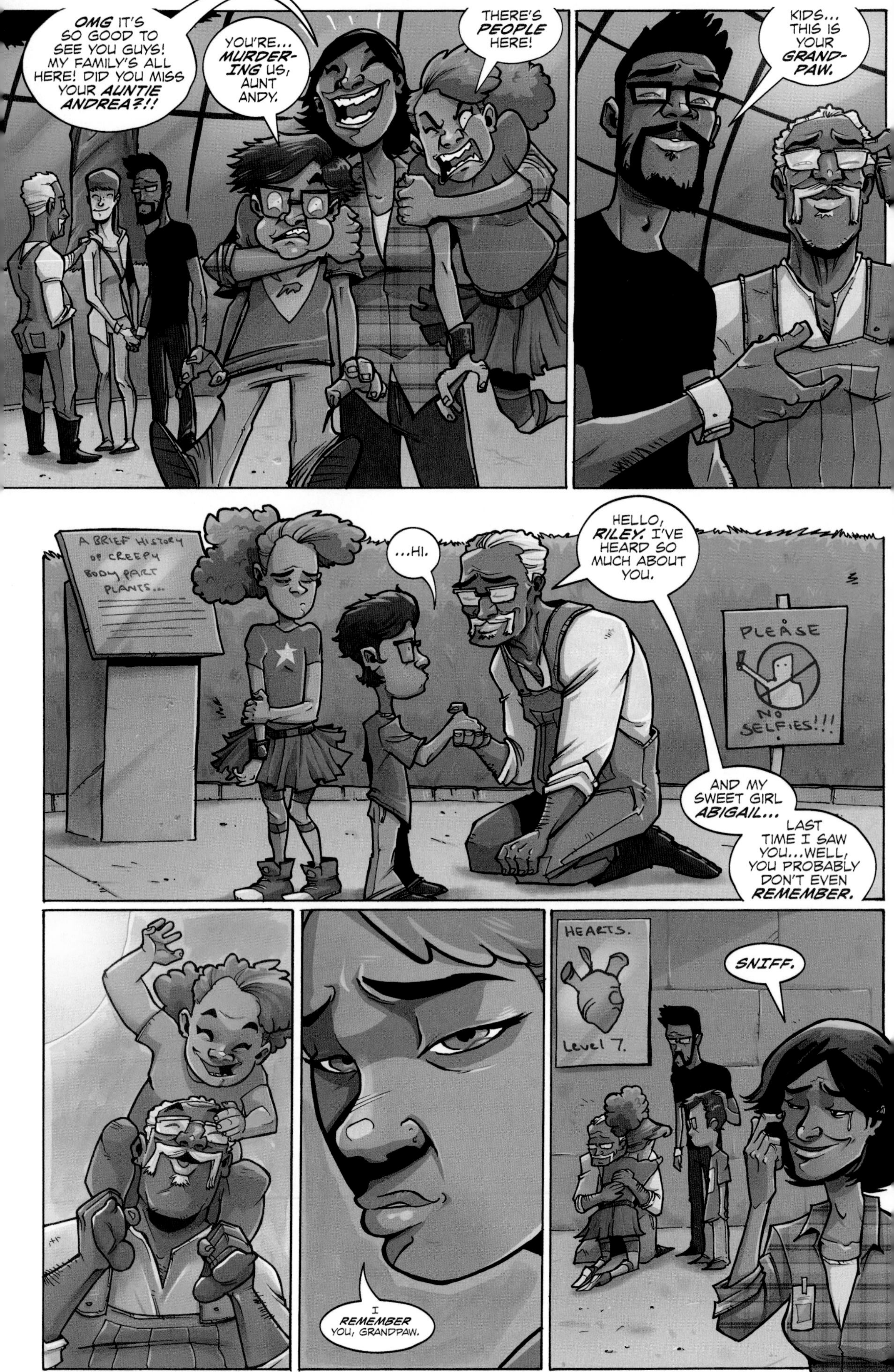
OMG IT'S SO GOOD TO SEE YOU GUYS! MY FAMILY'S ALL HERE! DID YOU MISS YOUR AUNTIE ANDREA?!!
YOU'RE... MURDERING US, AUNT ANDY.
THERE'S PEOPLE HERE!
KIDS... THIS IS YOUR GRANDPAW.
A BRIEF HISTORY OF CREEPY BODY PART PLANTS...
...HI.
HELLO, RILEY. I'VE HEARD SO MUCH ABOUT YOU.
PLEASE NO SELFIES!!!
AND MY SWEET GIRL ABIGAIL...
LAST TIME I SAW YOU...WELL, YOU PROBABLY DON'T EVEN REMEMBER.
I REMEMBER YOU, GRANDPAW.
HEARTS. Level 7.
SNIFF.

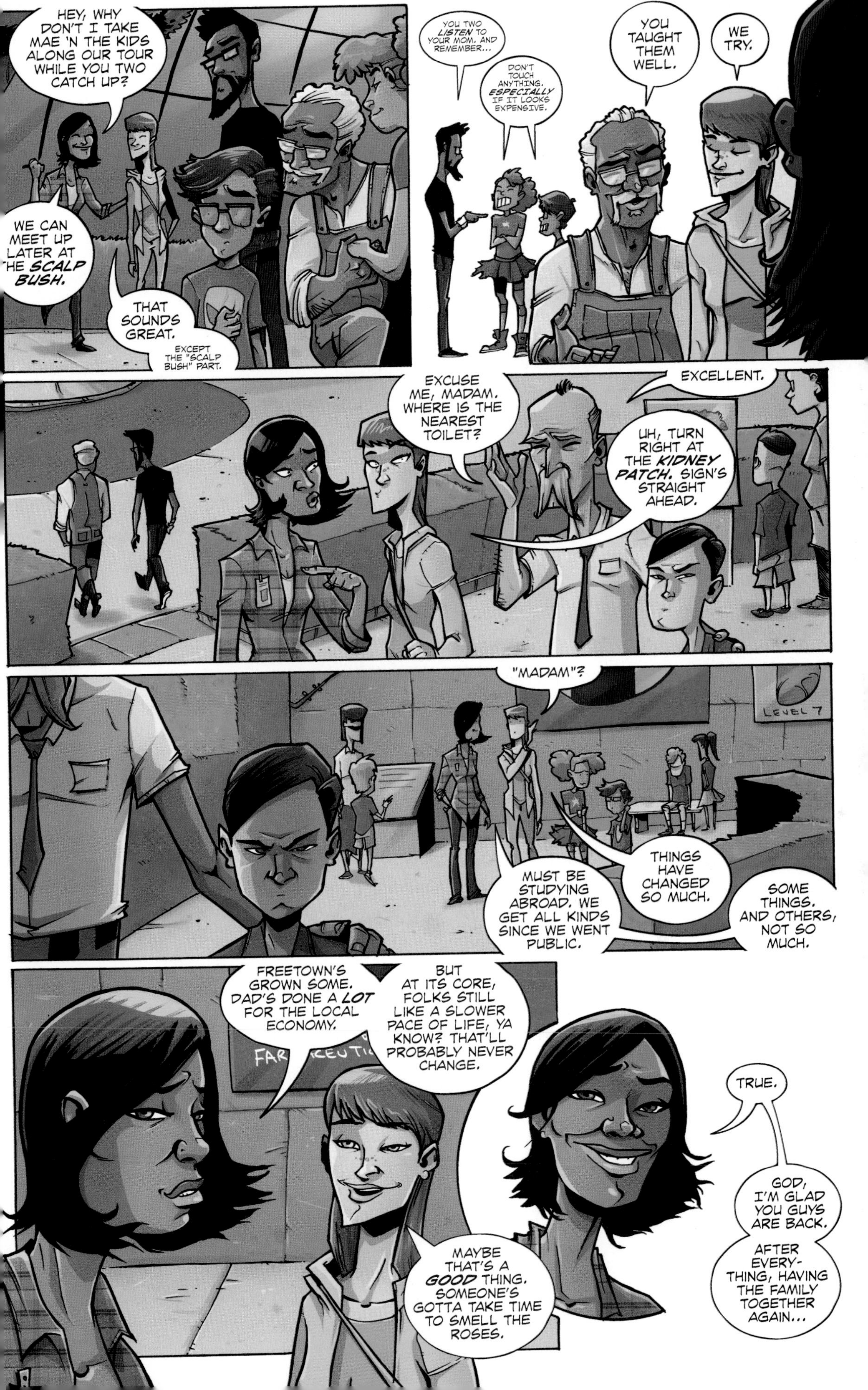
HEY, WHY DON'T I TAKE MAE 'N THE KIDS ALONG OUR TOUR WHILE YOU TWO CATCH UP?
WE CAN MEET UP LATER AT THE SCALP BUSH.
THAT SOUNDS GREAT.
EXCEPT THE "SCALP BUSH" PART.
YOU TWO LISTEN TO YOUR MOM. AND REMEMBER...
DON'T TOUCH ANYTHING. ESPECIALLY IF IT LOOKS EXPENSIVE.
YOU TAUGHT THEM WELL.
WE TRY.
EXCUSE ME, MADAM. WHERE IS THE NEAREST TOILET?
EXCELLENT.
UH, TURN RIGHT AT THE KIDNEY PATCH. SIGN'S STRAIGHT AHEAD.
"MADAM"?
LEVEL 7
MUST BE STUDYING ABROAD. WE GET ALL KINDS SINCE WE WENT PUBLIC.
THINGS HAVE CHANGED SO MUCH.
SOME THINGS. AND OTHERS, NOT SO MUCH.
FREETOWN'S GROWN SOME. DAD'S DONE A LOT FOR THE LOCAL ECONOMY.
BUT AT ITS CORE, FOLKS STILL LIKE A SLOWER PACE OF LIFE, YA KNOW? THAT'LL PROBABLY NEVER CHANGE.
MAYBE THAT'S A GOOD THING. SOMEONE'S GOTTA TAKE TIME TO SMELL THE ROSES.
TRUE.
GOD, I'M GLAD YOU GUYS ARE BACK.
AFTER EVERY-THING, HAVING THE FAMILY TOGETHER AGAIN...

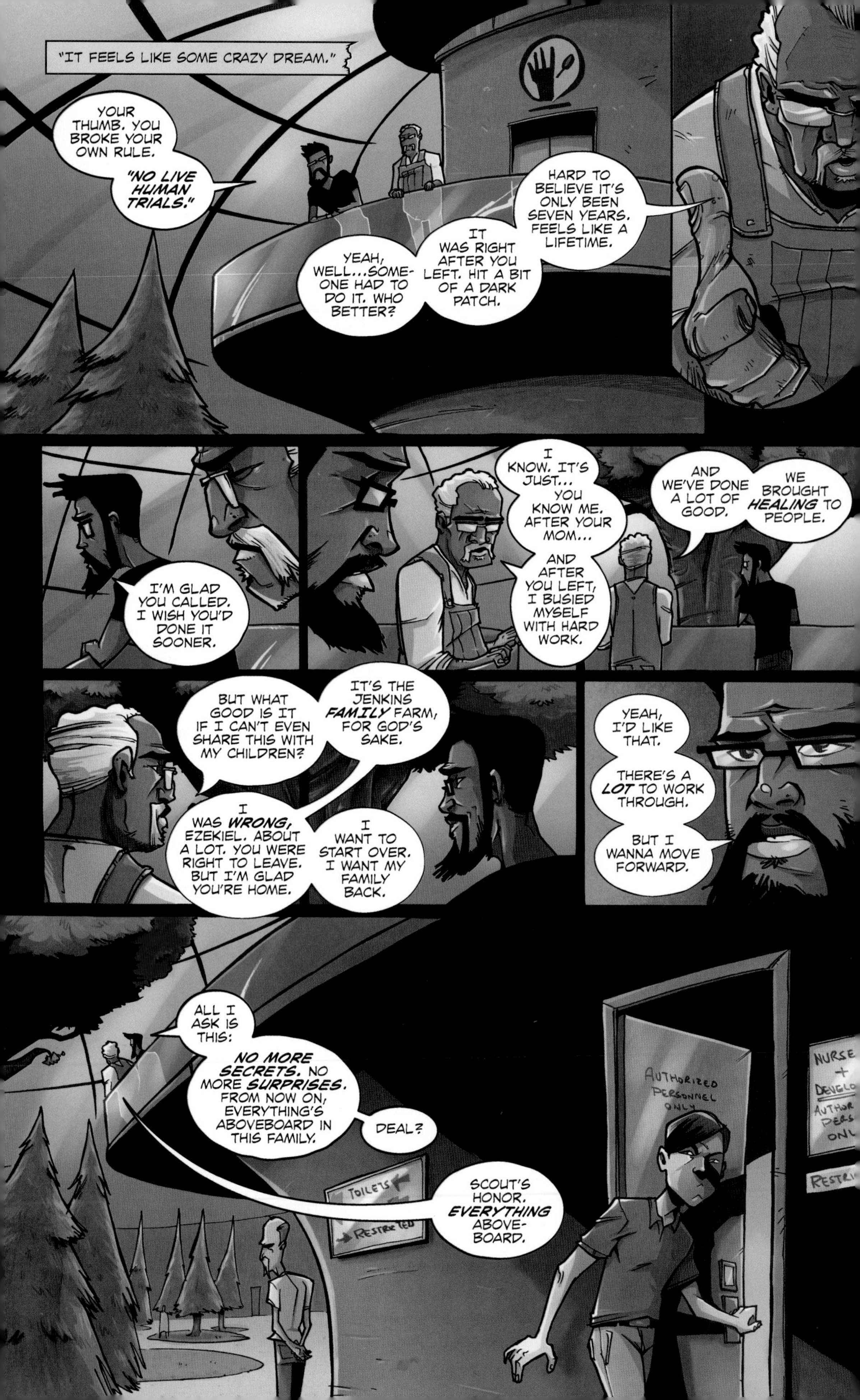
"IT FEELS LIKE SOME CRAZY DREAM."
YOUR THUMB. YOU BROKE YOUR OWN RULE.
"NO LIVE HUMAN TRIALS."
YEAH, WELL...SOME-ONE HAD TO DO IT. WHO BETTER?
IT WAS RIGHT AFTER YOU LEFT. HIT A BIT OF A DARK PATCH.
HARD TO BELIEVE IT'S ONLY BEEN SEVEN YEARS. FEELS LIKE A LIFETIME.
I'M GLAD YOU CALLED. I WISH YOU'D DONE IT SOONER.
I KNOW. IT'S JUST...
YOU KNOW ME. AFTER YOUR MOM...
AND AFTER YOU LEFT, I BUSIED MYSELF WITH HARD WORK.
AND WE'VE DONE A LOT OF GOOD.
WE BROUGHT HEALING TO PEOPLE.
BUT WHAT GOOD IS IT IF I CAN'T EVEN SHARE THIS WITH MY CHILDREN?
IT'S THE JENKINS FAMILY FARM, FOR GOD'S SAKE.
I WAS WRONG, EZEKIEL. ABOUT A LOT. YOU WERE RIGHT TO LEAVE. BUT I'M GLAD YOU'RE HOME.
I WANT TO START OVER. I WANT MY FAMILY BACK.
YEAH, I'D LIKE THAT.
THERE'S A LOT TO WORK THROUGH.
BUT I WANNA MOVE FORWARD.
ALL I ASK IS THIS:
NO MORE SECRETS. NO MORE SURPRISES. FROM NOW ON, EVERYTHING'S ABOVEBOARD IN THIS FAMILY.
DEAL?
SCOUT'S HONOR. EVERYTHING ABOVE-BOARD.
AUTHORIZED PERSONNEL ONLY
TOILETS
RESTRICTED

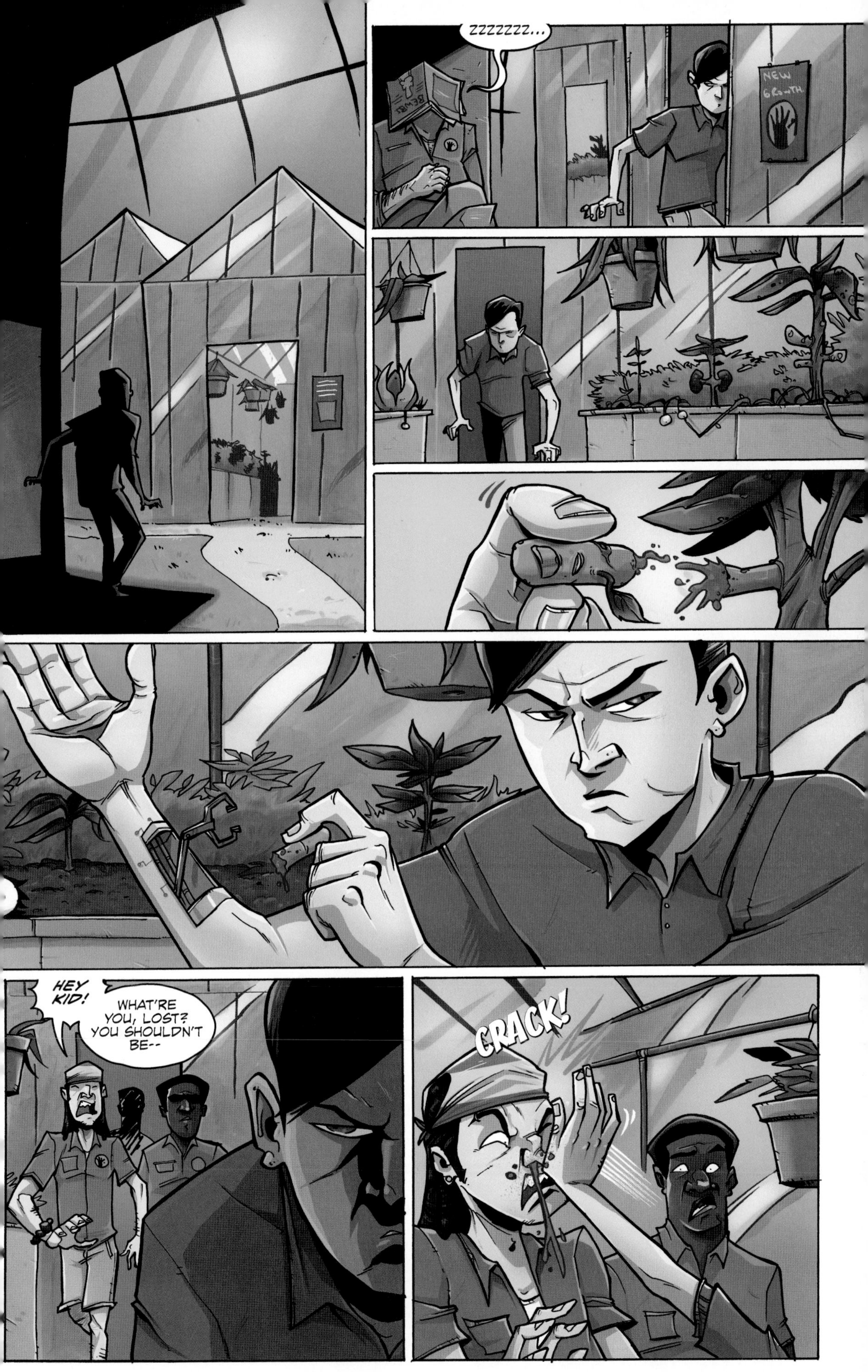
ZZZZZZZ...
NEW GROWTH
HEY KID!
WHAT'RE YOU, LOST? YOU SHOULDN'T BE--
CRACK!

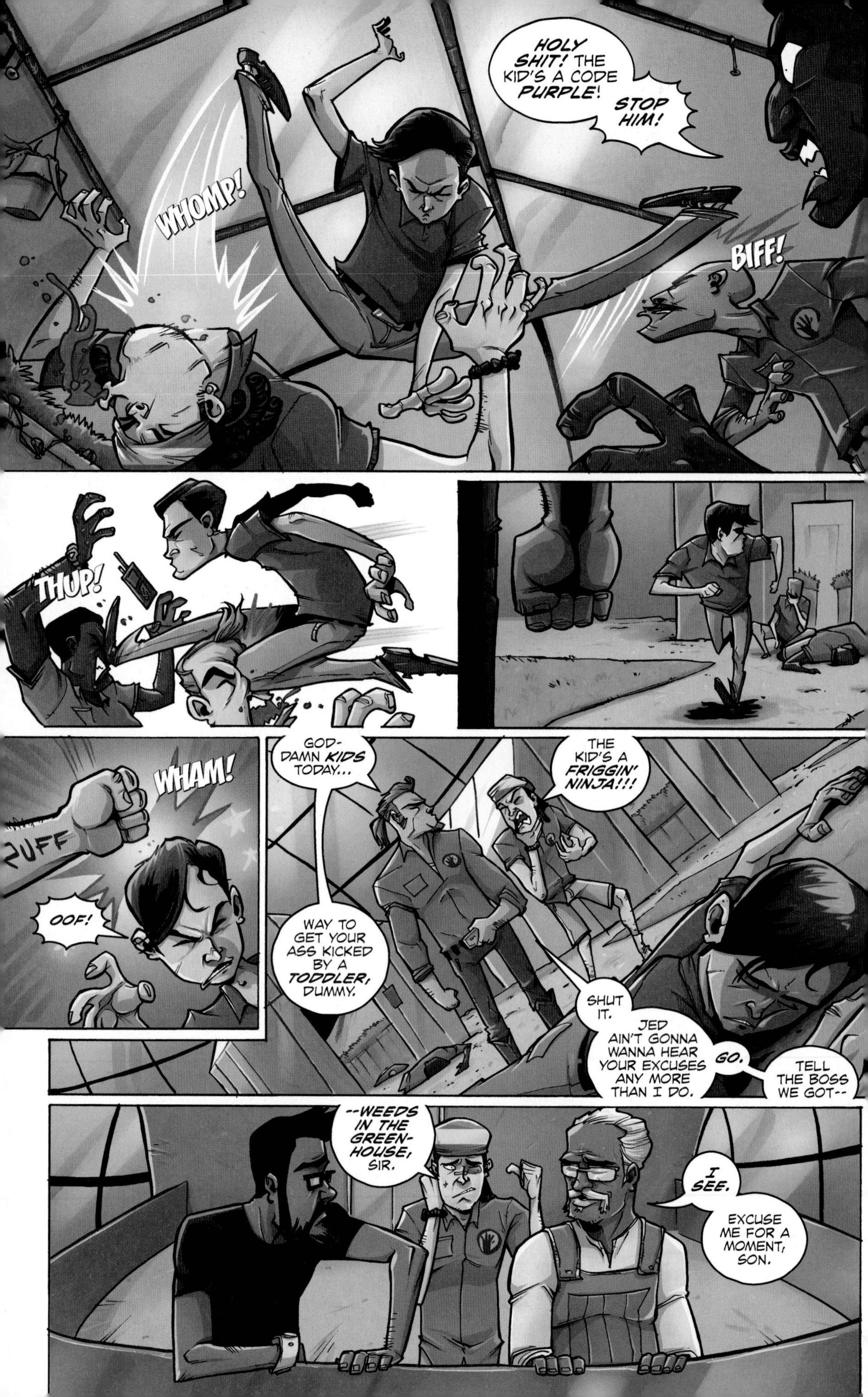
HOLY SHIT! THE KID'S A CODE PURPLE!
STOP HIM!
WHOMP!
BIFF!
THUP!
WHAM!
ZUFF
OOF!
GOD-DAMN KIDS TODAY...
WAY TO GET YOUR ASS KICKED BY A TODDLER, DUMMY.
THE KID'S A FRIGGIN' NINJA!!!
SHUT IT.
JED AIN'T GONNA WANNA HEAR YOUR EXCUSES ANY MORE THAN I DO.
GO.
TELL THE BOSS WE GOT--
--WEEDS IN THE GREEN-HOUSE, SIR.
I SEE.
EXCUSE ME FOR A MOMENT, SON.

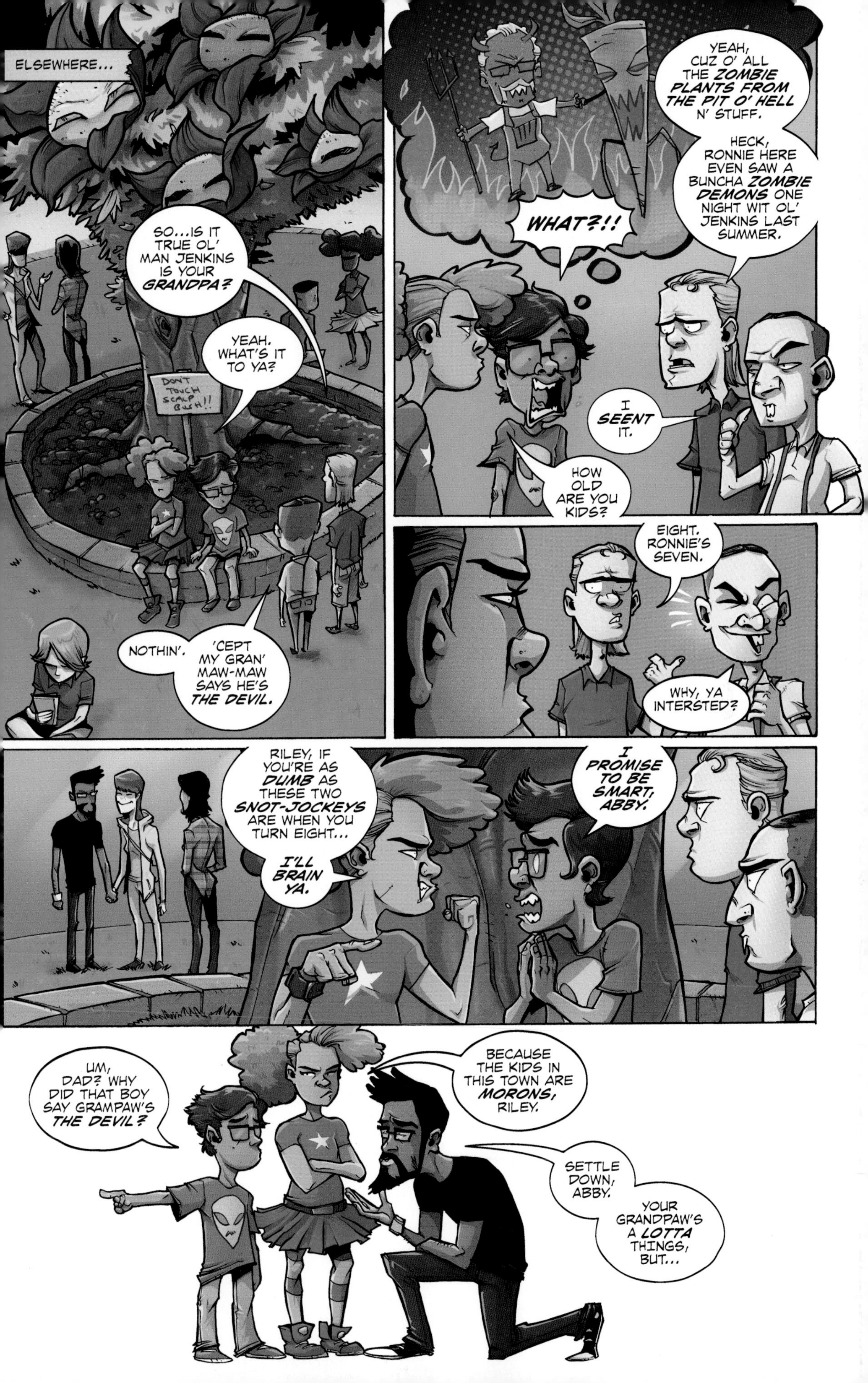

ELSEWHERE...
SO...IS IT TRUE OL' MAN JENKINS IS YOUR GRANDPA?
YEAH. WHAT'S IT TO YA?
DON'T TOUCH SCALP BUSH!!
NOTHIN'.
'CEPT MY GRAN' MAW-MAW SAYS HE'S THE DEVIL.
YEAH, CUZ O' ALL THE ZOMBIE PLANTS FROM THE PIT O' HELL N' STUFF.
HECK, RONNIE HERE EVEN SAW A BUNCHA ZOMBIE DEMONS ONE NIGHT WIT OL' JENKINS LAST SUMMER.
WHAT?!!
I SEENT IT.
HOW OLD ARE YOU KIDS?
EIGHT. RONNIE'S SEVEN.
WHY, YA INTERSTED?
RILEY, IF YOU'RE AS DUMB AS THESE TWO SNOT-JOCKEYS ARE WHEN YOU TURN EIGHT...
I'LL BRAIN YA.
I PROMISE TO BE SMART, ABBY.
UM, DAD? WHY DID THAT BOY SAY GRAMPAW'S THE DEVIL?
BECAUSE THE KIDS IN THIS TOWN ARE MORONS, RILEY.
SETTLE DOWN, ABBY.
YOUR GRANDPAW'S A LOTTA THINGS, BUT...

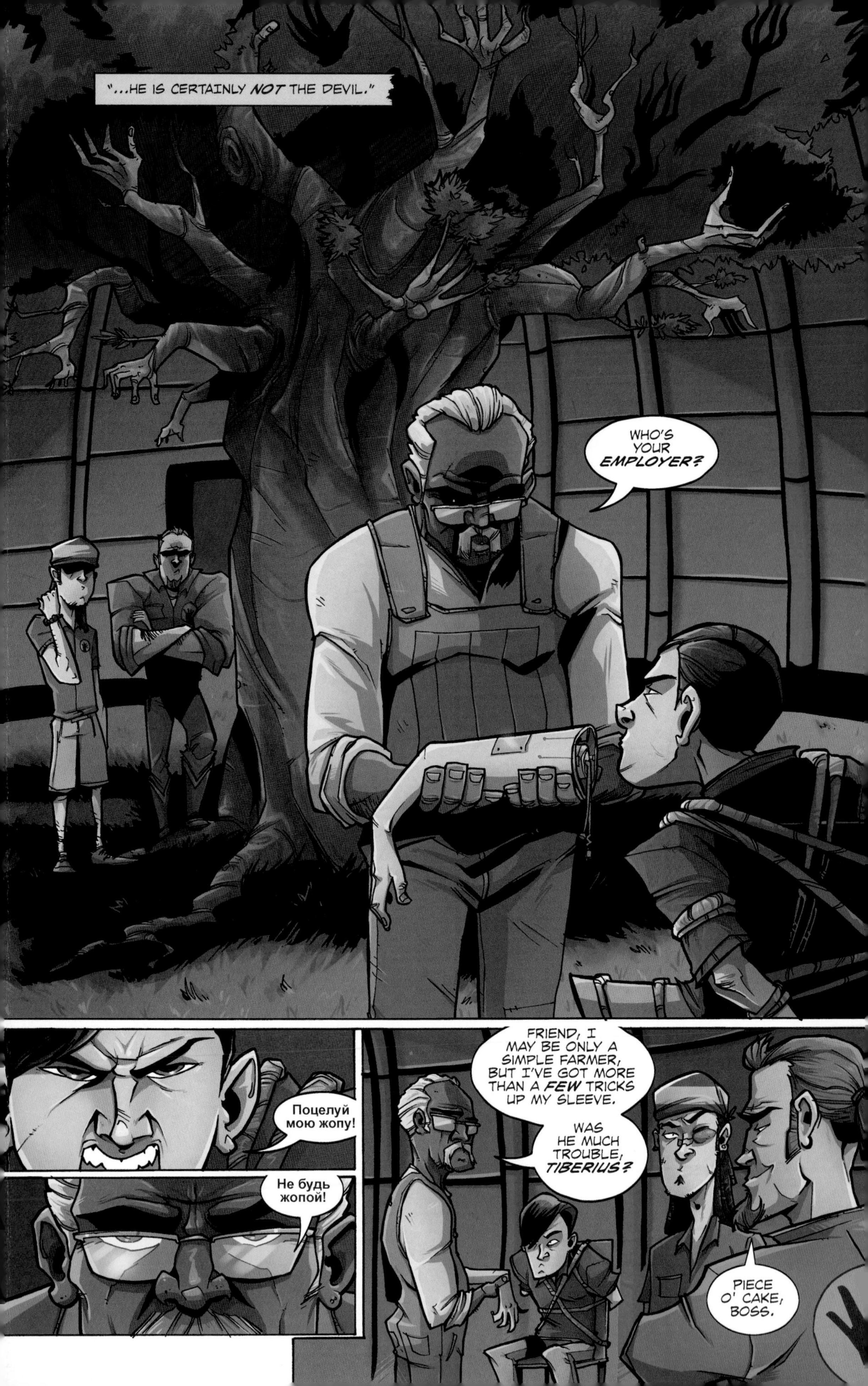
"...HE IS CERTAINLY *NOT* THE DEVIL."
WHO'S YOUR *EMPLOYER?*
Поцелуй мою жопу!
Не будь жопой!
FRIEND, I MAY BE ONLY A SIMPLE FARMER, BUT I'VE GOT MORE THAN A *FEW* TRICKS UP MY SLEEVE.
WAS HE MUCH TROUBLE, *TIBERIUS?*
PIECE O' CAKE, BOSS.

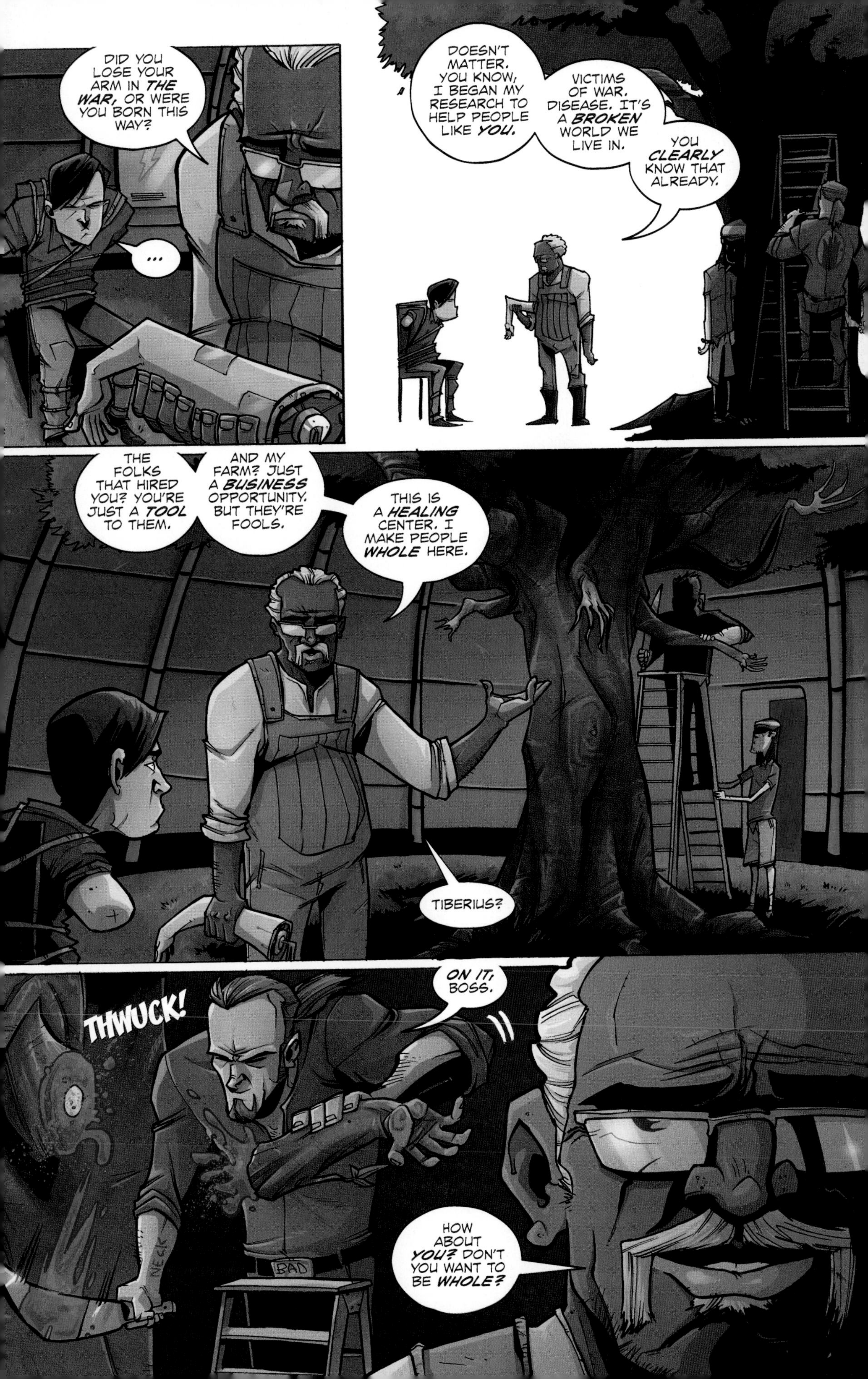
DID YOU LOSE YOUR ARM IN THE WAR, OR WERE YOU BORN THIS WAY?
...
DOESN'T MATTER. YOU KNOW, I BEGAN MY RESEARCH TO HELP PEOPLE LIKE YOU.
VICTIMS OF WAR. DISEASE. IT'S A BROKEN WORLD WE LIVE IN.
YOU CLEARLY KNOW THAT ALREADY.
THE FOLKS THAT HIRED YOU? YOU'RE JUST A TOOL TO THEM.
AND MY FARM? JUST A BUSINESS OPPORTUNITY. BUT THEY'RE FOOLS.
THIS IS A HEALING CENTER. I MAKE PEOPLE WHOLE HERE.
TIBERIUS?
THWUCK!
ON IT, BOSS.
BAD
HOW ABOUT YOU? DON'T YOU WANT TO BE WHOLE?

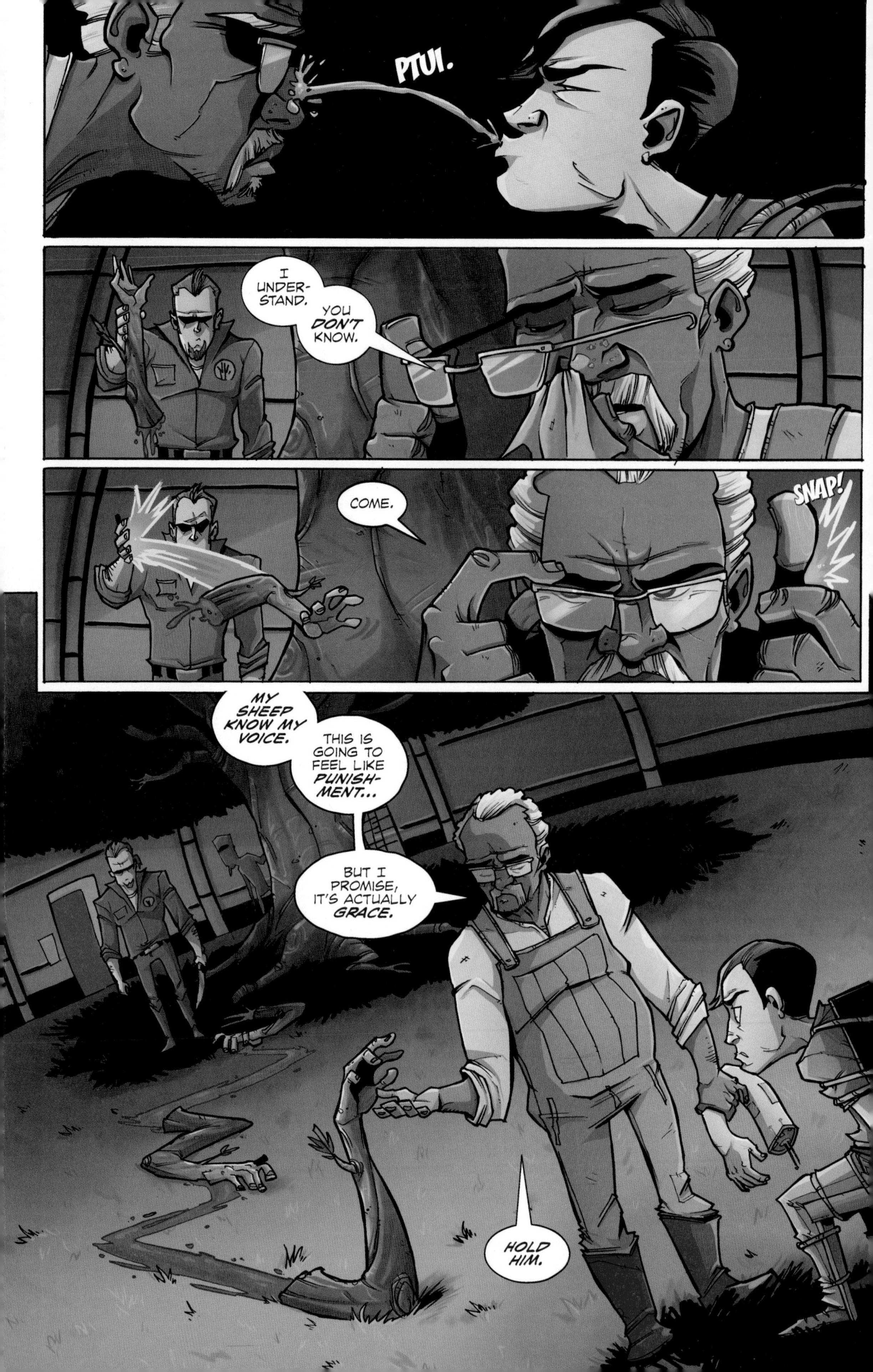
PTUI.
I UNDERSTAND.
YOU DON'T KNOW.
COME.
SNAP!
MY SHEEP KNOW MY VOICE.
THIS IS GOING TO FEEL LIKE PUNISHMENT...
BUT I PROMISE, IT'S ACTUALLY GRACE.
HOLD HIM.

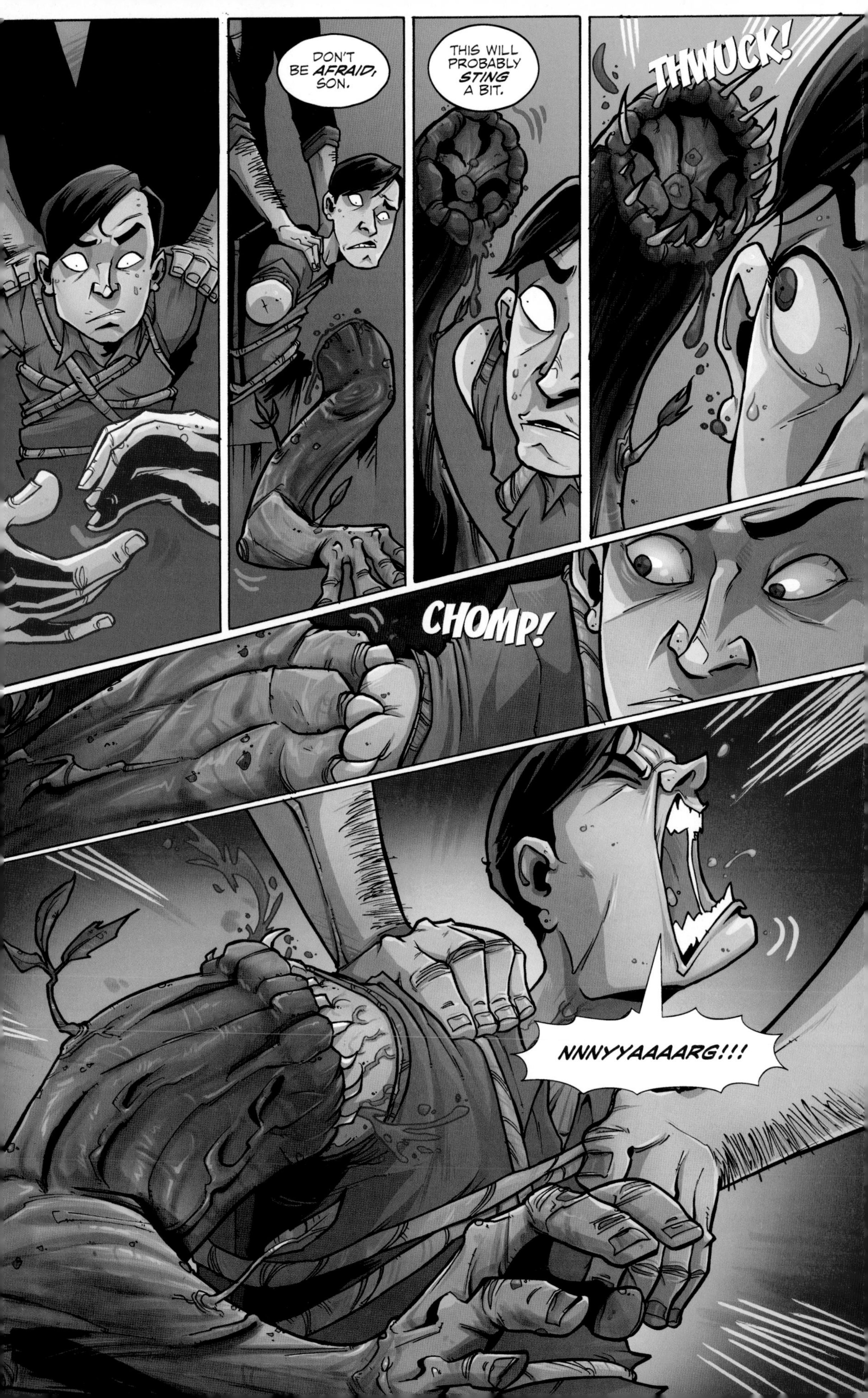
DON'T BE AFRAID, SON.
THIS WILL PROBABLY STING A BIT.
THWUCK!
CHOMP!
NNNYYAAAARG!!!

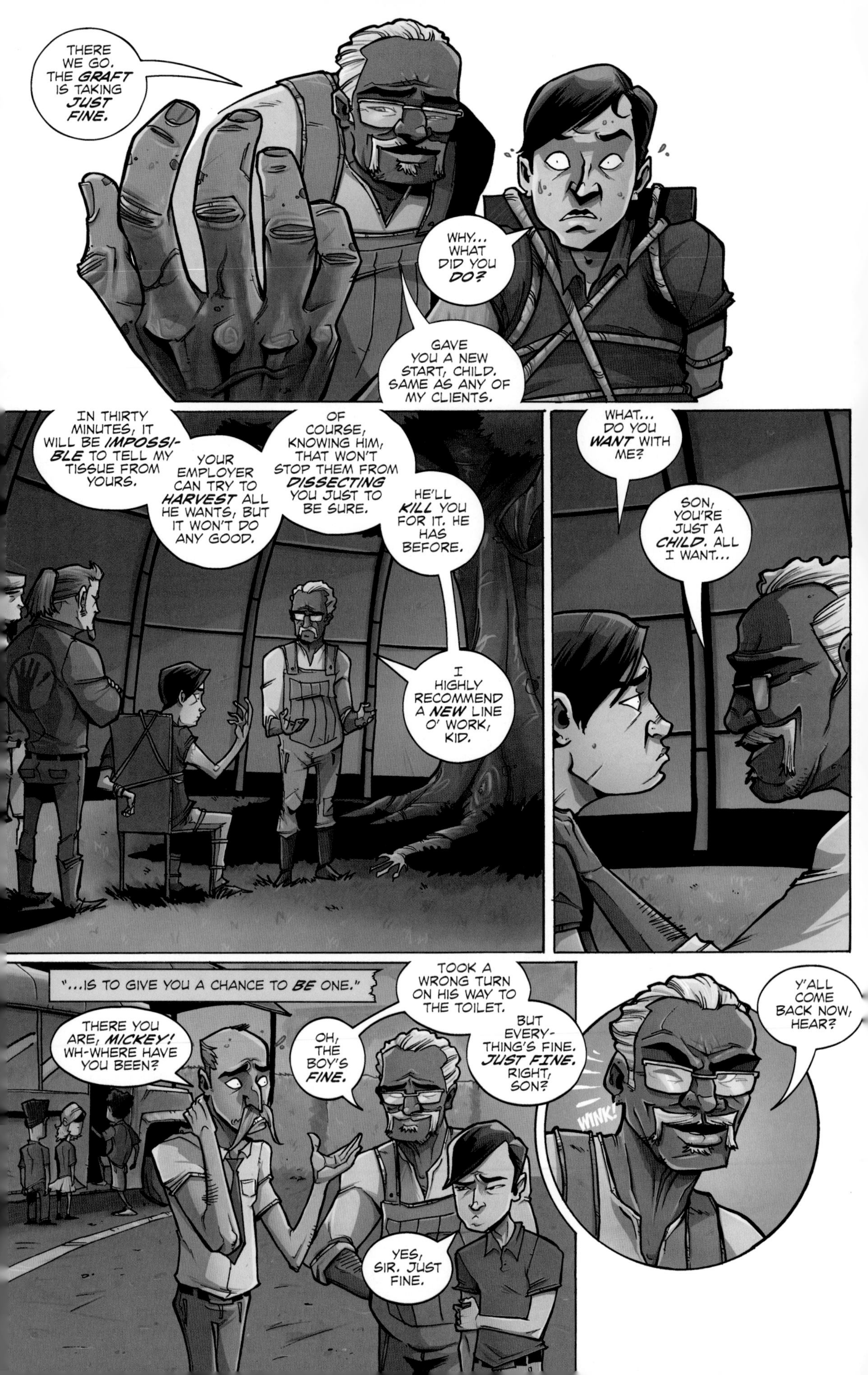
THERE WE GO. THE GRAFT IS TAKING JUST FINE.
WHY... WHAT DID YOU DO?
GAVE YOU A NEW START, CHILD. SAME AS ANY OF MY CLIENTS.
IN THIRTY MINUTES, IT WILL BE IMPOSSIBLE TO TELL MY TISSUE FROM YOURS.
YOUR EMPLOYER CAN TRY TO HARVEST ALL HE WANTS, BUT IT WON'T DO ANY GOOD.
OF COURSE, KNOWING HIM, THAT WON'T STOP THEM FROM DISSECTING YOU JUST TO BE SURE.
HE'LL KILL YOU FOR IT. HE HAS BEFORE.
I HIGHLY RECOMMEND A NEW LINE O' WORK, KID.
WHAT... DO YOU WANT WITH ME?
SON, YOU'RE JUST A CHILD. ALL I WANT...
"...IS TO GIVE YOU A CHANCE TO BE ONE."
THERE YOU ARE, MICKEY! WH-WHERE HAVE YOU BEEN?
OH, THE BOY'S FINE.
TOOK A WRONG TURN ON HIS WAY TO THE TOILET.
BUT EVERYTHING'S FINE. JUST FINE. RIGHT, SON?
YES, SIR. JUST FINE.
WINK!
Y'ALL COME BACK NOW, HEAR?

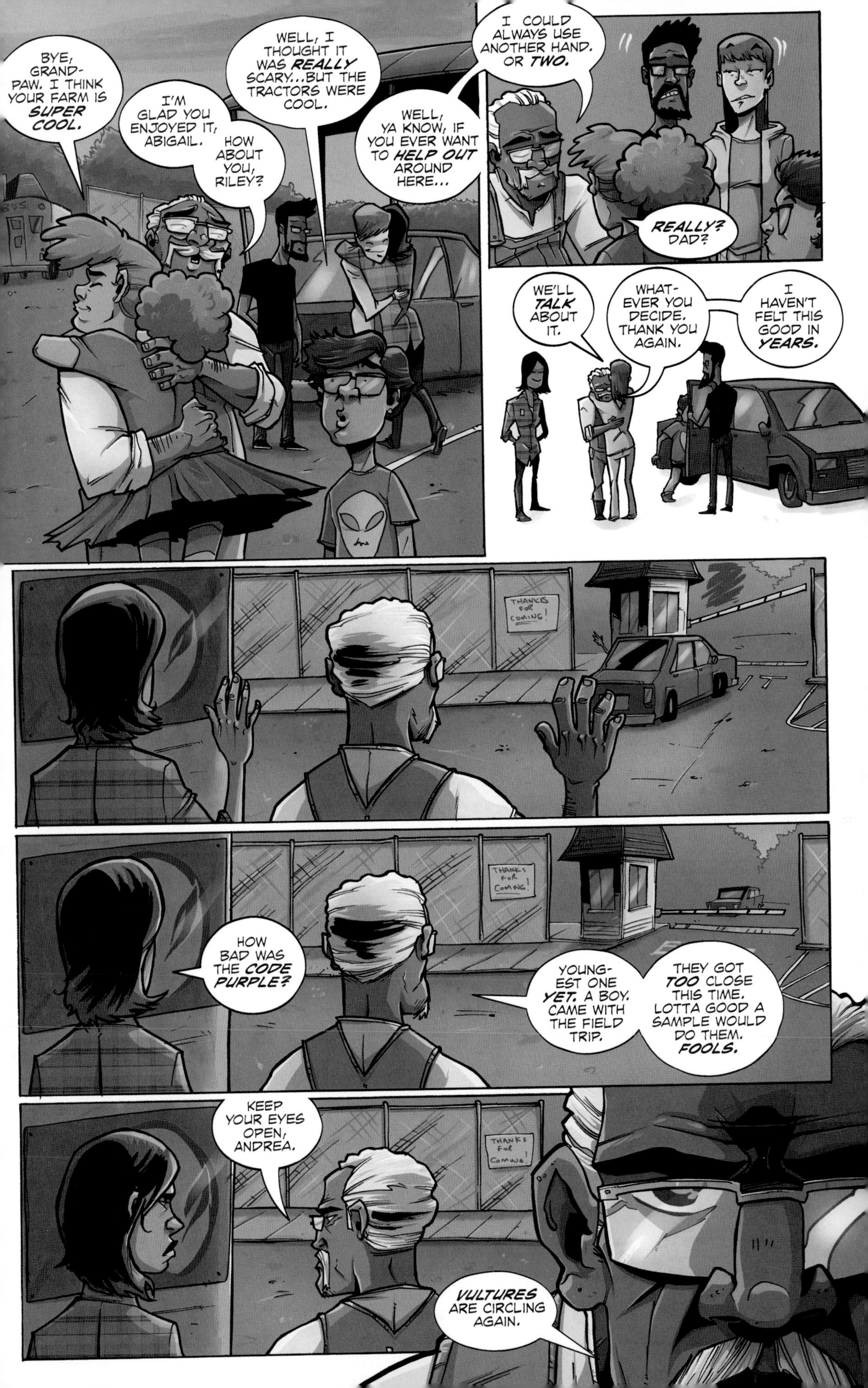
BYE, GRAND-PAW. I THINK YOUR FARM IS SUPER COOL.
I'M GLAD YOU ENJOYED IT, ABIGAIL.
HOW ABOUT YOU, RILEY?
WELL, I THOUGHT IT WAS REALLY SCARY...BUT THE TRACTORS WERE COOL.
WELL, YA KNOW, IF YOU EVER WANT TO HELP OUT AROUND HERE...
I COULD ALWAYS USE ANOTHER HAND. OR TWO.
REALLY? DAD?
WE'LL TALK ABOUT IT.
WHAT-EVER YOU DECIDE. THANK YOU AGAIN.
I HAVEN'T FELT THIS GOOD IN YEARS.
THANKS FOR COMING!
HOW BAD WAS THE CODE PURPLE?
YOUNG-EST ONE YET. A BOY. CAME WITH THE FIELD TRIP.
THEY GOT TOO CLOSE THIS TIME. LOTTA GOOD A SAMPLE WOULD DO THEM. FOOLS.
KEEP YOUR EYES OPEN, ANDREA.
VULTURES ARE CIRCLING AGAIN.

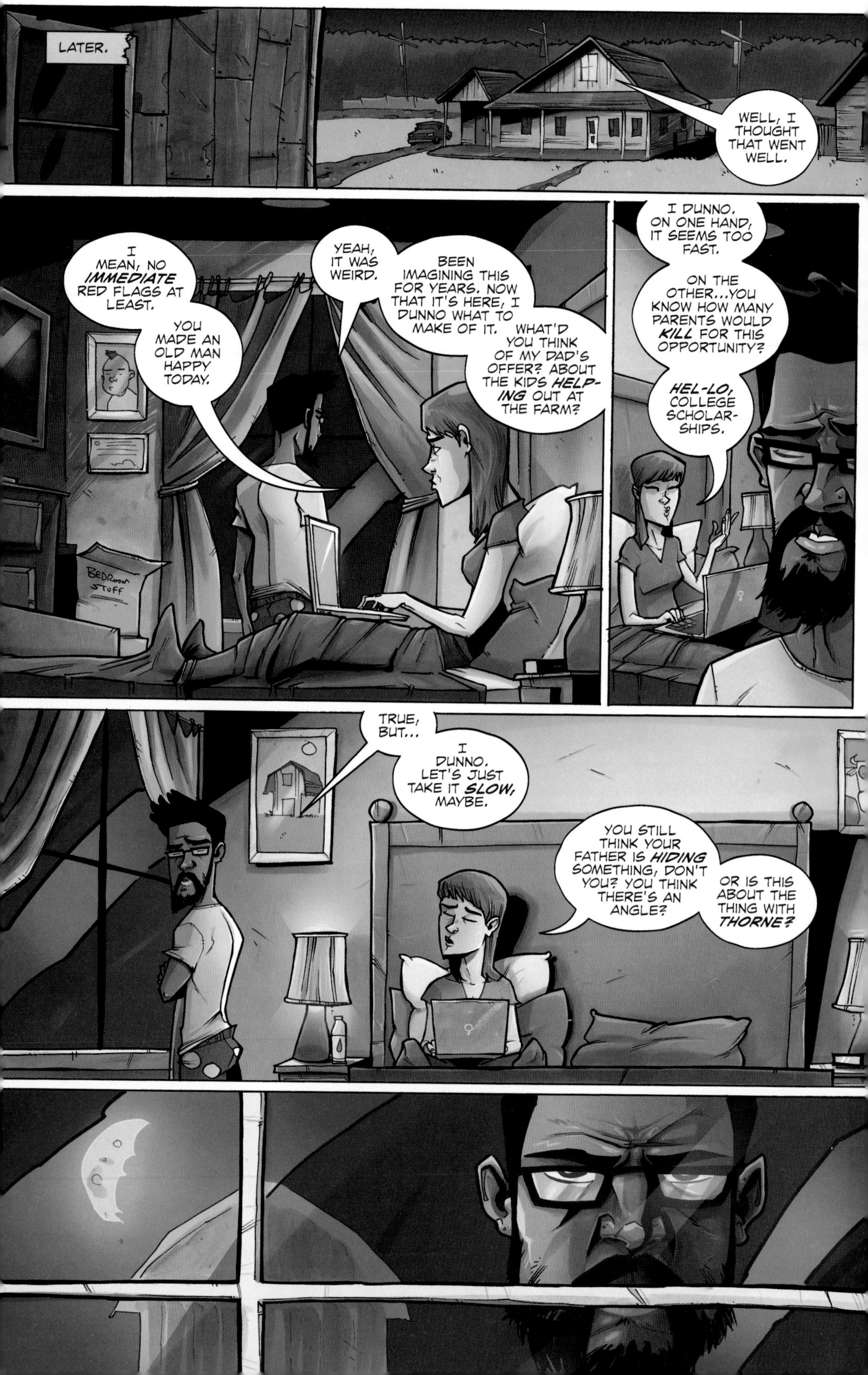
LATER.
WELL, I THOUGHT THAT WENT WELL.
I MEAN, NO IMMEDIATE RED FLAGS AT LEAST.
YOU MADE AN OLD MAN HAPPY TODAY.
YEAH, IT WAS WEIRD.
BEEN IMAGINING THIS FOR YEARS. NOW THAT IT'S HERE, I DUNNO WHAT TO MAKE OF IT.
WHAT'D YOU THINK OF MY DAD'S OFFER? ABOUT THE KIDS HELPING OUT AT THE FARM?
BEDROOM STUFF
I DUNNO. ON ONE HAND, IT SEEMS TOO FAST.
ON THE OTHER...YOU KNOW HOW MANY PARENTS WOULD KILL FOR THIS OPPORTUNITY?
HEL-LO, COLLEGE SCHOLARSHIPS.
TRUE, BUT...
I DUNNO. LET'S JUST TAKE IT SLOW, MAYBE.
YOU STILL THINK YOUR FATHER IS HIDING SOMETHING, DON'T YOU? YOU THINK THERE'S AN ANGLE?
OR IS THIS ABOUT THE THING WITH THORNE?

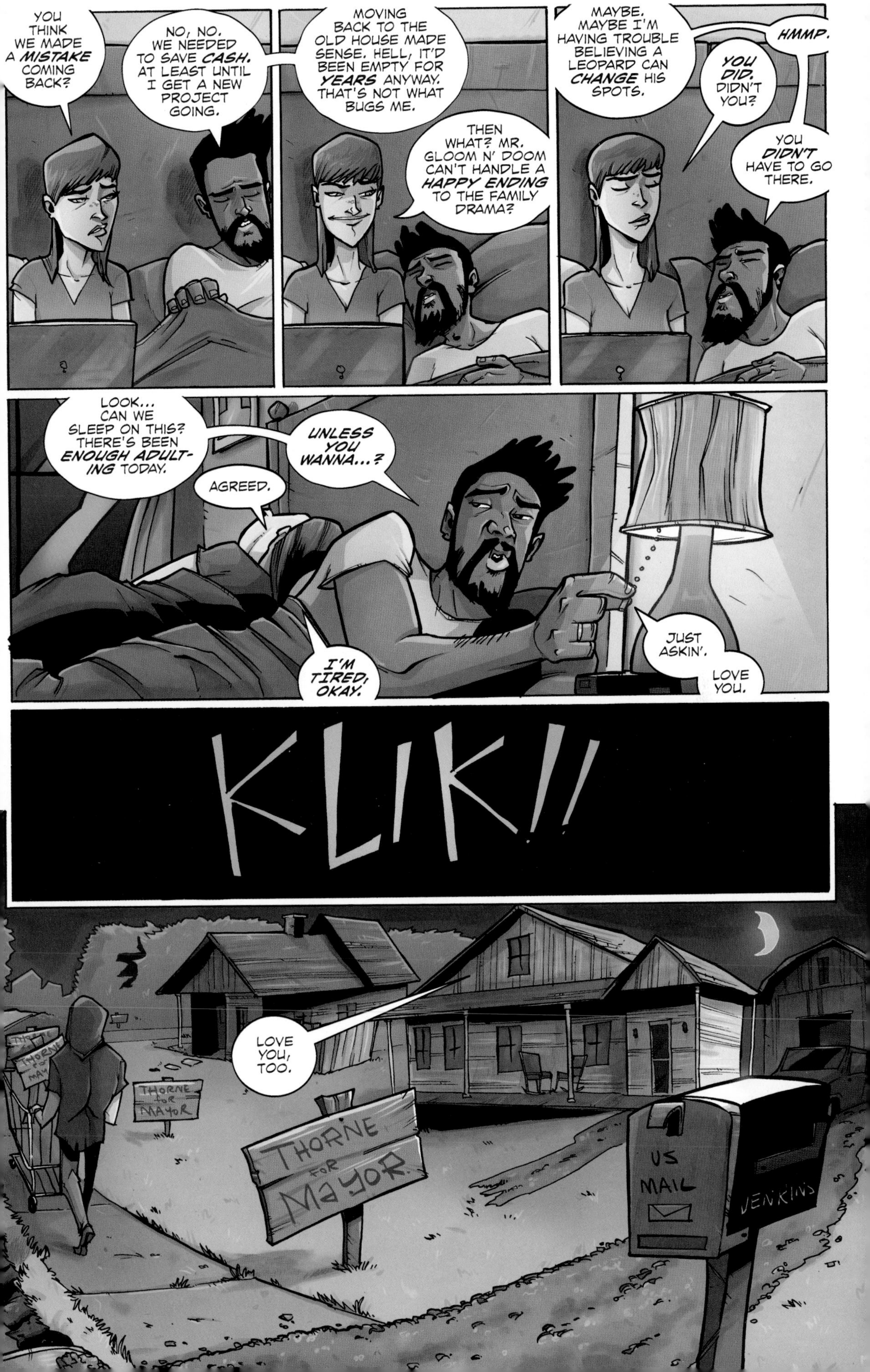
YOU THINK WE MADE A MISTAKE COMING BACK?
NO, NO. WE NEEDED TO SAVE CASH. AT LEAST UNTIL I GET A NEW PROJECT GOING.
MOVING BACK TO THE OLD HOUSE MADE SENSE. HELL, IT'D BEEN EMPTY FOR YEARS ANYWAY. THAT'S NOT WHAT BUGS ME.
THEN WHAT? MR. GLOOM N' DOOM CAN'T HANDLE A HAPPY ENDING TO THE FAMILY DRAMA?
MAYBE. MAYBE I'M HAVING TROUBLE BELIEVING A LEOPARD CAN CHANGE HIS SPOTS.
HMMP.
YOU DID. DIDN'T YOU?
YOU DIDN'T HAVE TO GO THERE.
LOOK... CAN WE SLEEP ON THIS? THERE'S BEEN ENOUGH ADULTING TODAY.
UNLESS YOU WANNA...?
AGREED.
I'M TIRED, OKAY.
JUST ASKIN'.
LOVE YOU.
KLIK!!
LOVE YOU, TOO.
THORNE FOR MAYOR
THORNE FOR MAYOR
THORNE FOR MAYOR
US MAIL
JENKINS

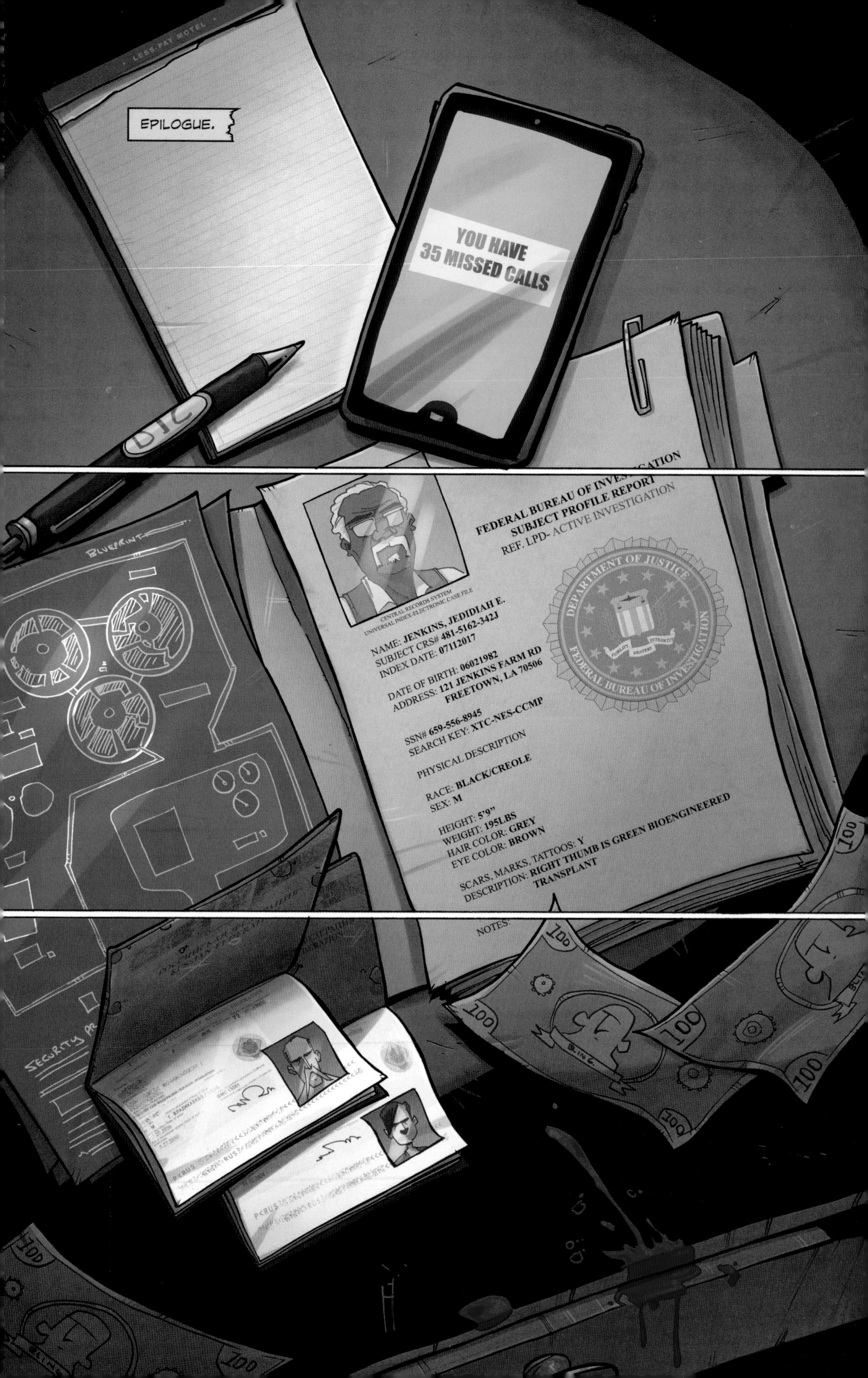

LESS-PAY MOTEL
EPILOGUE.
YOU HAVE 35 MISSED CALLS
FEDERAL BUREAU OF INVESTIGATION
SUBJECT PROFILE REPORT
REF. LPD- ACTIVE INVESTIGATION
CENTRAL RECORDS SYSTEM
UNIVERSAL INDEX-ELECTRONIC CASE FILE
NAME: JENKINS, JEDIDIAH E.
SUBJECT CRS# 481-5162-342J
INDEX DATE: 07112017
DATE OF BIRTH: 06021982
ADDRESS: 121 JENKINS FARM RD FREETOWN, LA 70506
SSN# 659-556-8945
SEARCH KEY: XTC-NES-CCMP
PHYSICAL DESCRIPTION
RACE: BLACK/CREOLE
SEX: M
HEIGHT: 5'9"
WEIGHT: 195LBS
HAIR COLOR: GREY
EYE COLOR: BROWN
SCARS, MARKS, TATTOOS: Y
DESCRIPTION: RIGHT THUMB IS GREEN BIOENGINEERED TRANSPLANT
NOTES:
DEPARTMENT OF JUSTICE
FEDERAL BUREAU OF INVESTIGATION
FIDELITY BRAVERY INTEGRITY
BLUEPRINT
SECURITY
100
BLING.

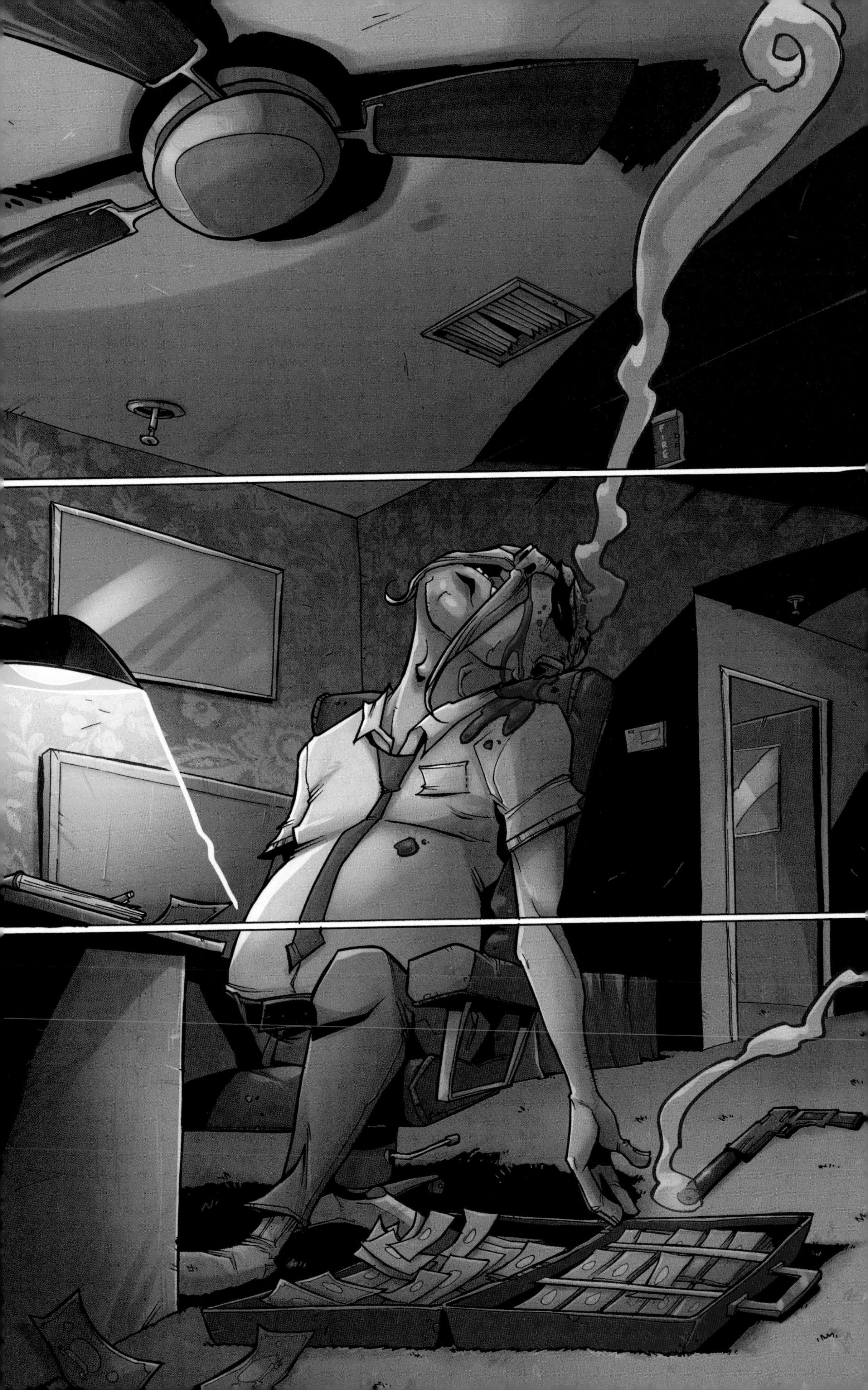
FIRE

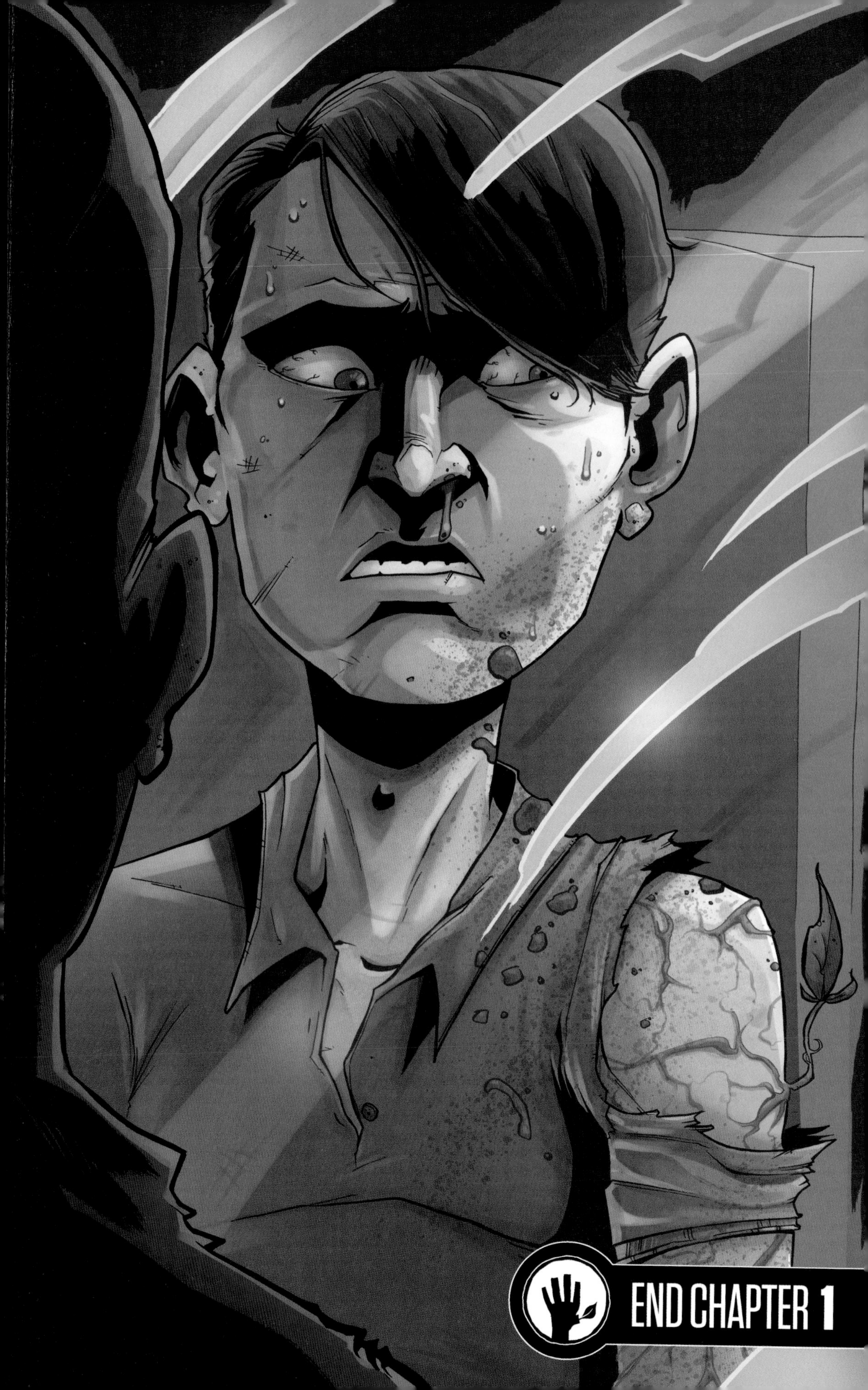
END CHAPTER 1

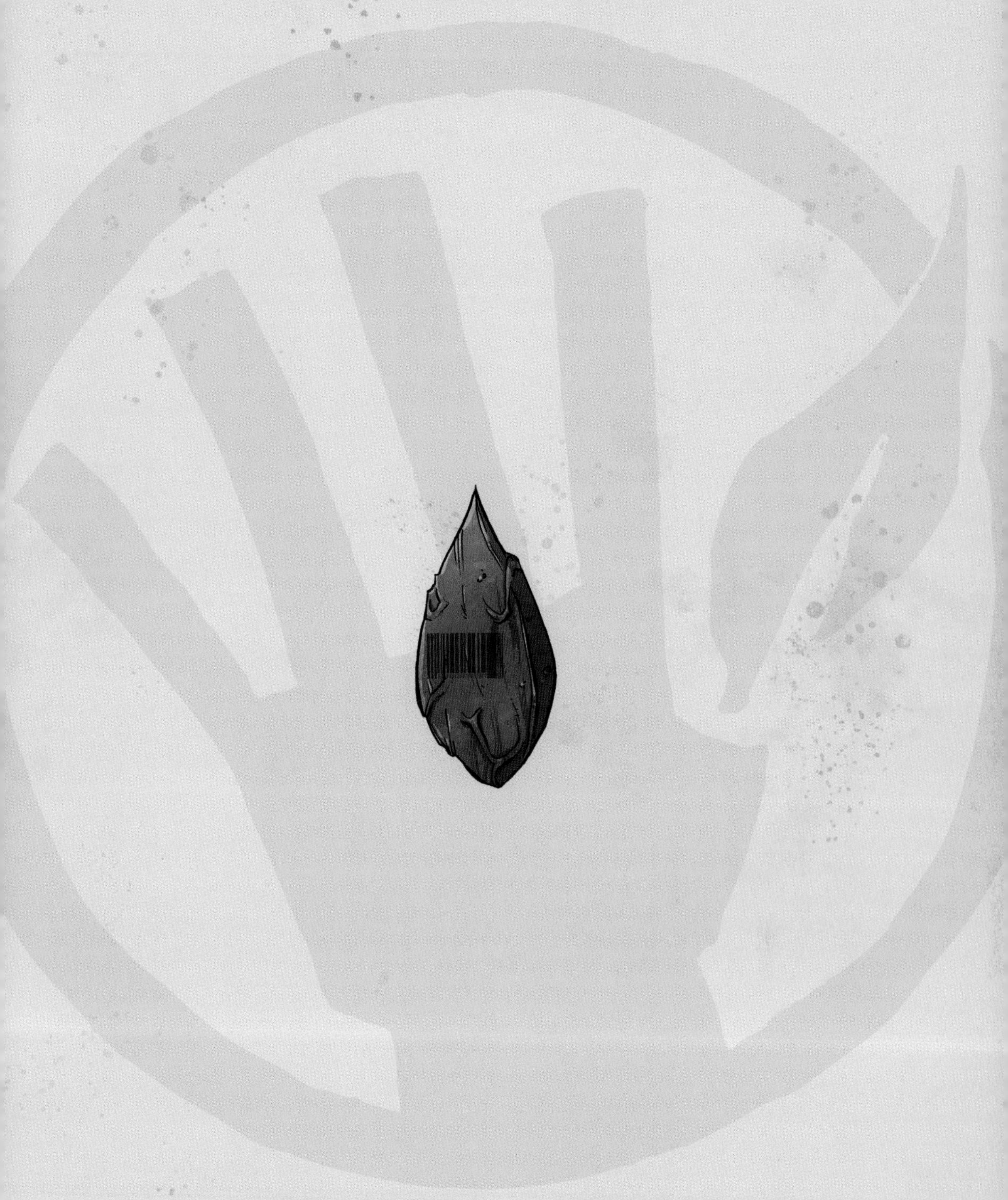

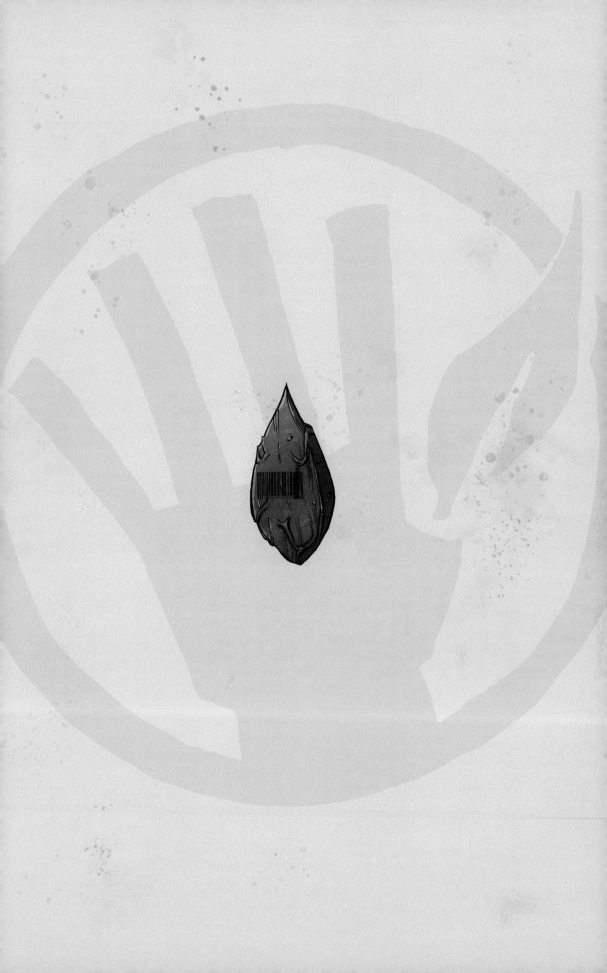

CHAPTER 2

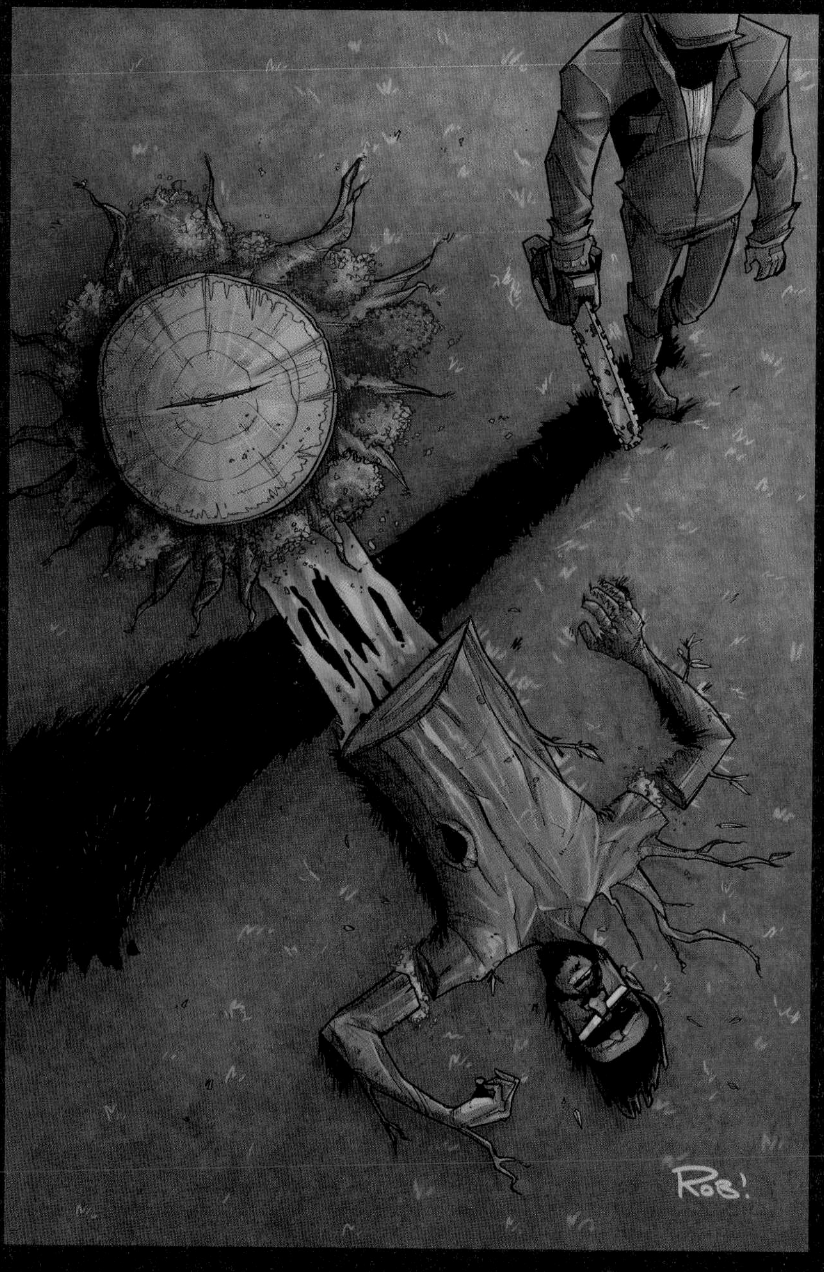

ROB!

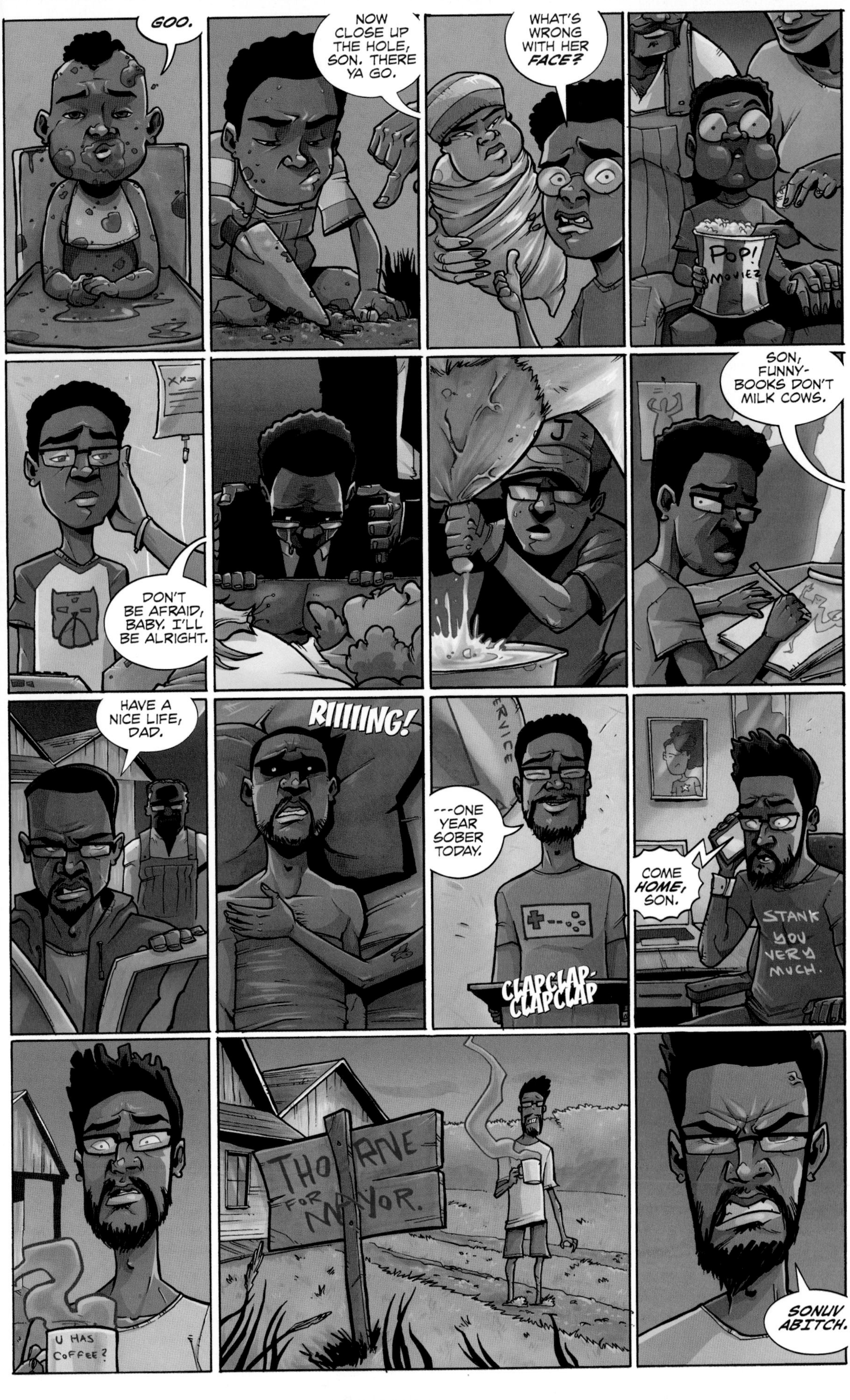
GOO.
NOW CLOSE UP THE HOLE, SON. THERE YA GO.
WHAT'S WRONG WITH HER FACE?
POP! MOVIEZ
DON'T BE AFRAID, BABY. I'LL BE ALRIGHT.
J
SON, FUNNY-BOOKS DON'T MILK COWS.
HAVE A NICE LIFE, DAD.
RIIIIING!
---ONE YEAR SOBER TODAY.
CLAPCLAP-CLAPCLAP
COME HOME, SON.
STANK YOU VERY MUCH.
U HAS COFFEE?
THORNE FOR MAYOR.
SONUV ABITCH.

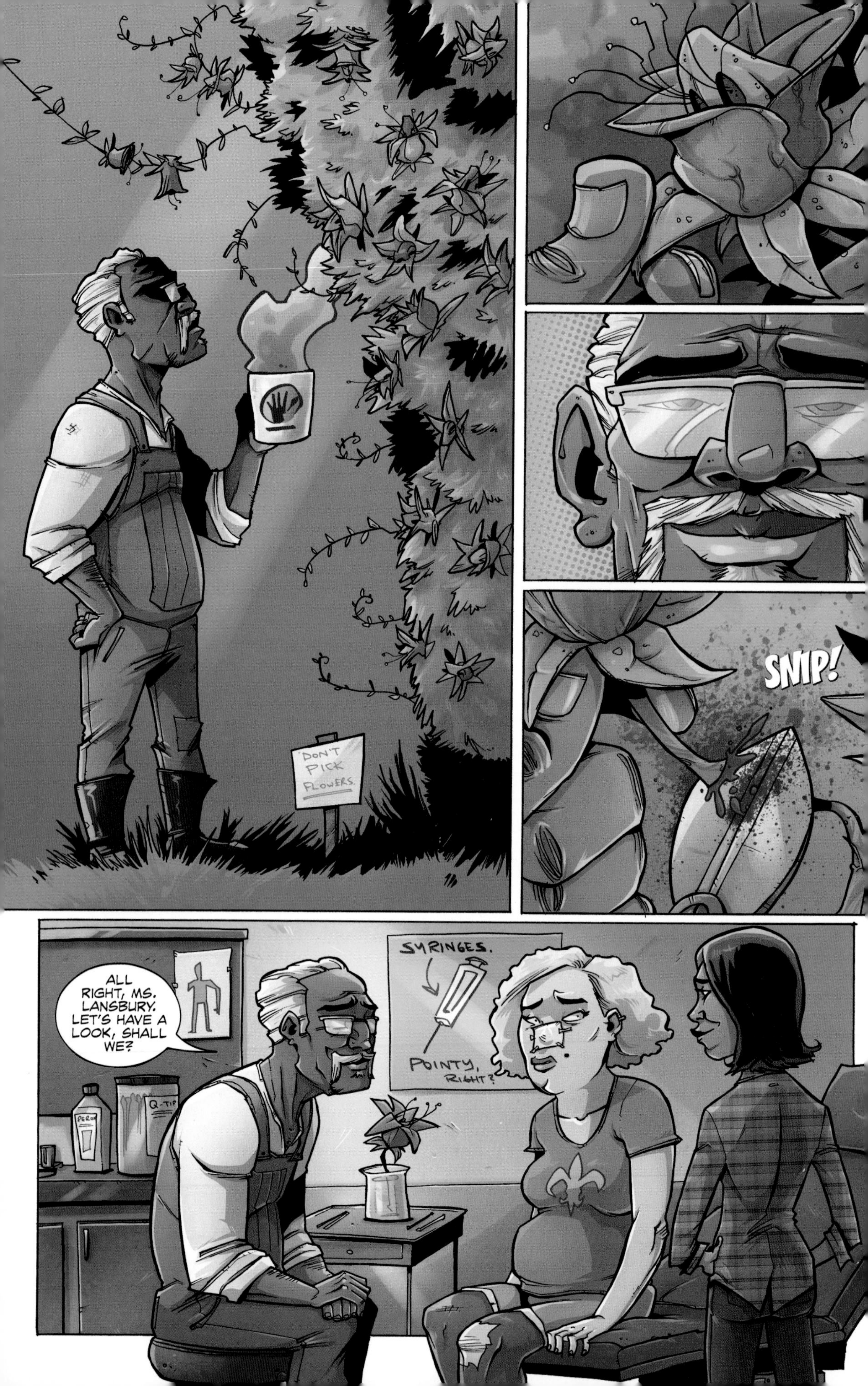
DON'T PICK FLOWERS.
SNIP!
SYRINGES.
POINTY, RIGHT?
Q-TIP
ALL RIGHT, MS. LANSBURY. LET'S HAVE A LOOK, SHALL WE?

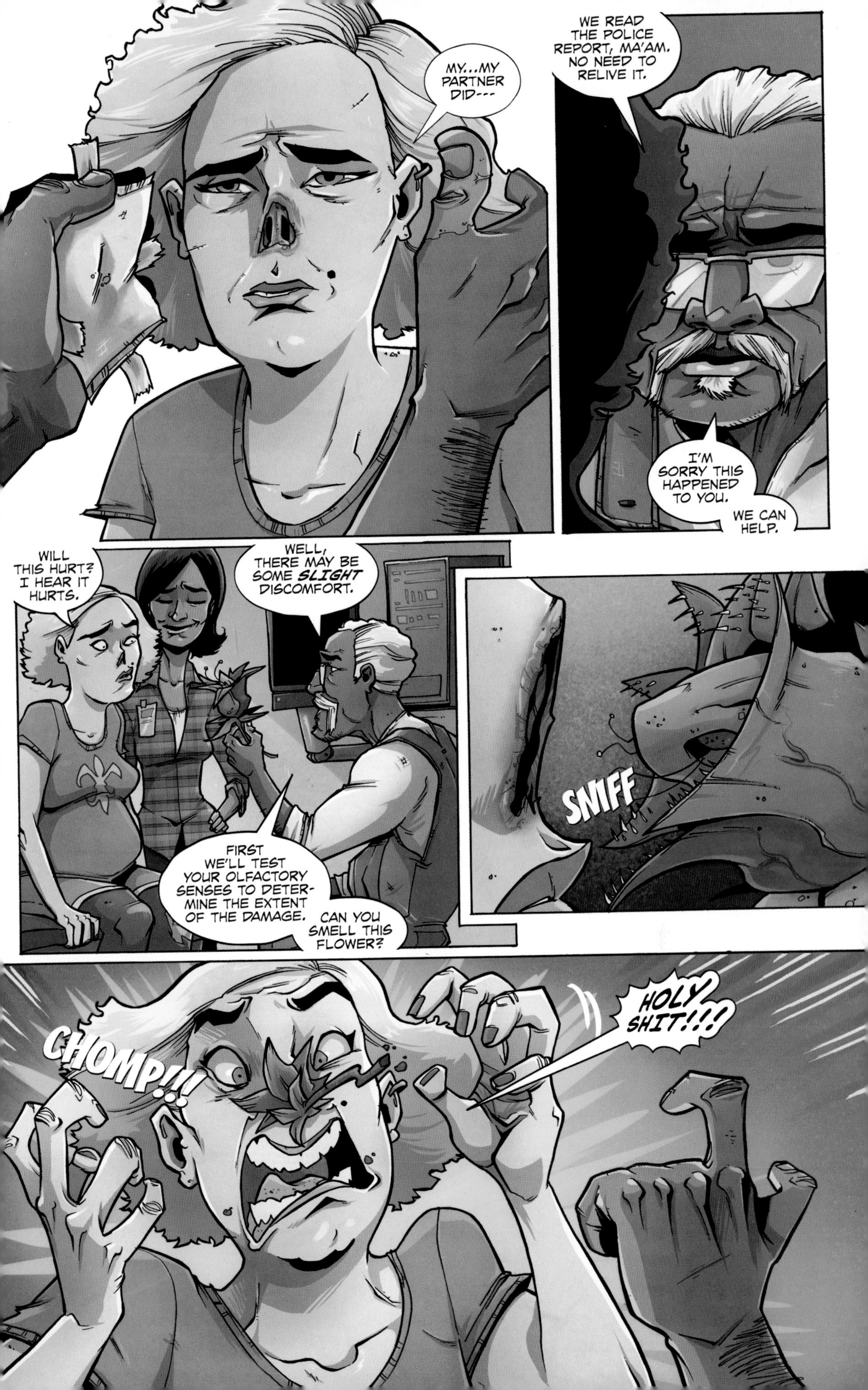
MY...MY PARTNER DID---
WE READ THE POLICE REPORT, MA'AM. NO NEED TO RELIVE IT.
I'M SORRY THIS HAPPENED TO YOU.
WE CAN HELP.
WILL THIS HURT? I HEAR IT HURTS.
WELL, THERE MAY BE SOME SLIGHT DISCOMFORT.
FIRST WE'LL TEST YOUR OLFACTORY SENSES TO DETERMINE THE EXTENT OF THE DAMAGE.
CAN YOU SMELL THIS FLOWER?
SNIFF
CHOMP!!!
HOLY SHIT!!!

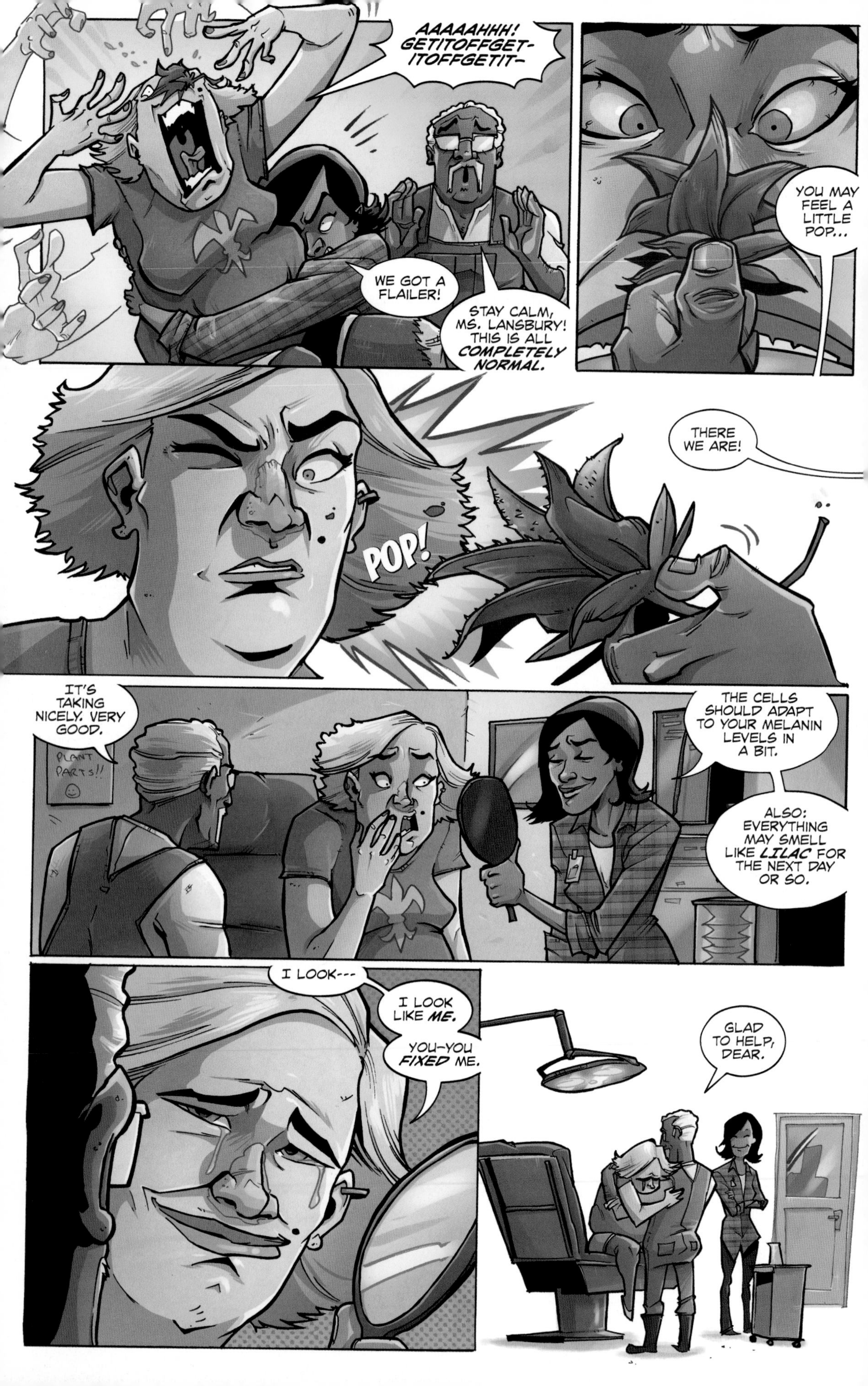
AAAAAHHH! GETITOFFGET-ITOFFGETIT–
WE GOT A FLAILER!
STAY CALM, MS. LANSBURY! THIS IS ALL COMPLETELY NORMAL.
YOU MAY FEEL A LITTLE POP...
POP!
THERE WE ARE!
IT'S TAKING NICELY. VERY GOOD.
PLANT PARTS!!
THE CELLS SHOULD ADAPT TO YOUR MELANIN LEVELS IN A BIT.
ALSO: EVERYTHING MAY SMELL LIKE LILAC FOR THE NEXT DAY OR SO.
I LOOK---
I LOOK LIKE ME.
YOU–YOU FIXED ME.
GLAD TO HELP, DEAR.

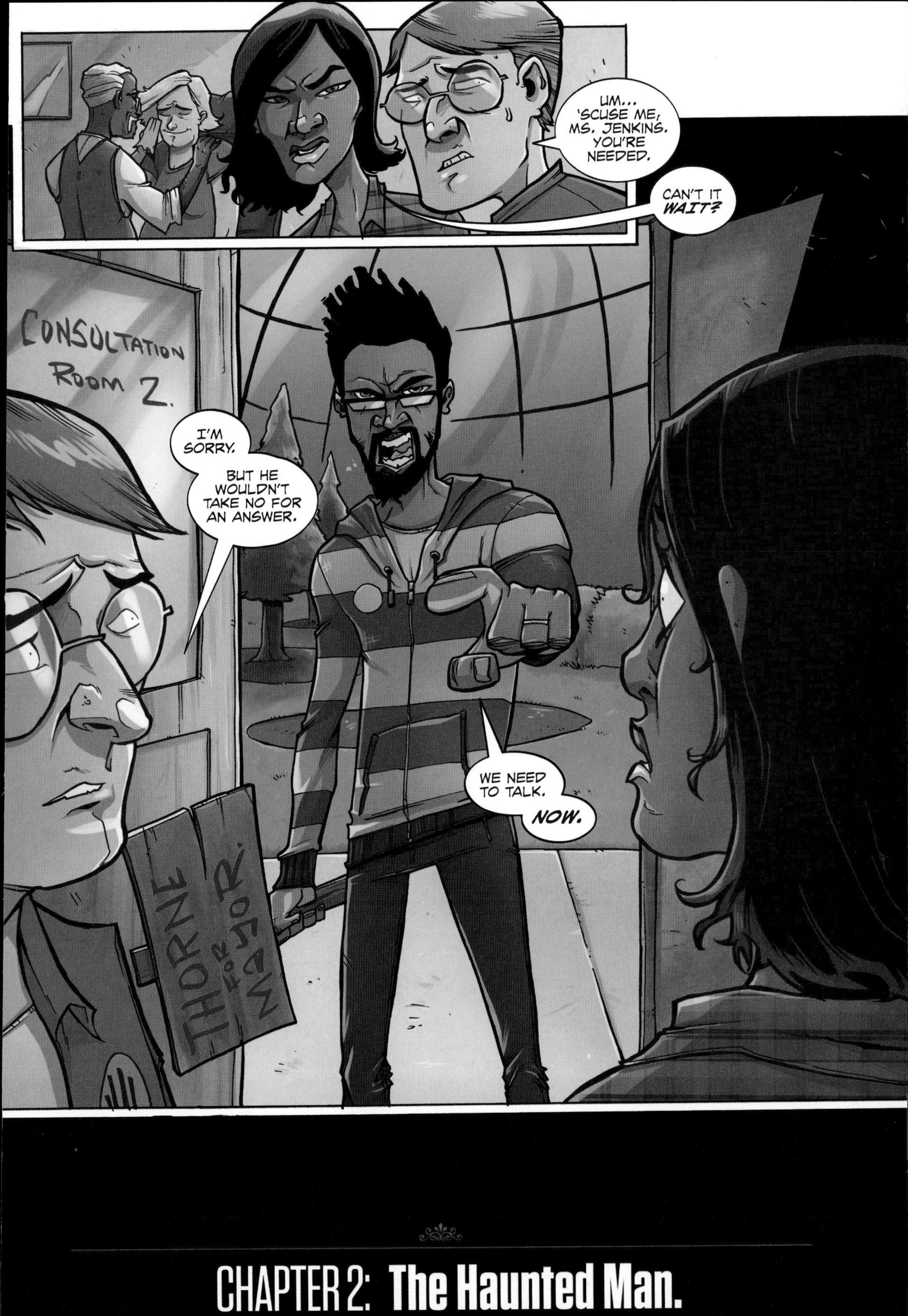
UM... 'SCUSE ME, MS. JENKINS. YOU'RE NEEDED.
CAN'T IT *WAIT?*
CONSULTATION ROOM 2.
I'M SORRY.
BUT HE WOULDN'T TAKE NO FOR AN ANSWER.
WE NEED TO TALK.
NOW.
THORNE FOR MAJOR

CHAPTER 2: The Haunted Man.

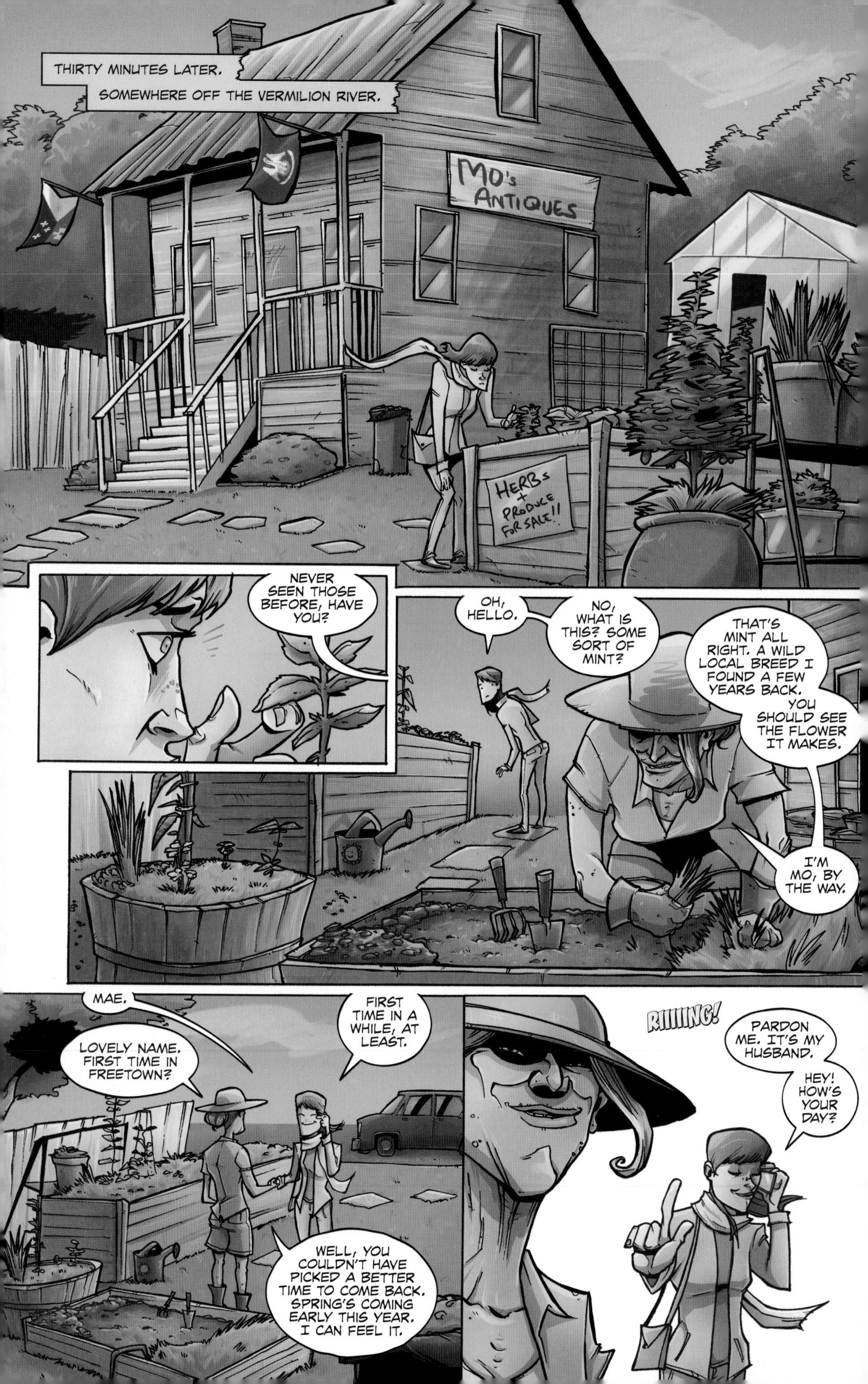
THIRTY MINUTES LATER.
SOMEWHERE OFF THE VERMILION RIVER.
MO'S ANTIQUES
HERBS + PRODUCE FOR SALE!!
NEVER SEEN THOSE BEFORE, HAVE YOU?
OH, HELLO.
NO, WHAT IS THIS? SOME SORT OF MINT?
THAT'S MINT ALL RIGHT. A WILD LOCAL BREED I FOUND A FEW YEARS BACK.
YOU SHOULD SEE THE FLOWER IT MAKES.
I'M MO, BY THE WAY.
MAE.
LOVELY NAME. FIRST TIME IN FREETOWN?
FIRST TIME IN A WHILE, AT LEAST.
WELL, YOU COULDN'T HAVE PICKED A BETTER TIME TO COME BACK. SPRING'S COMING EARLY THIS YEAR. I CAN FEEL IT.
RIIIIING!
PARDON ME. IT'S MY HUSBAND.
HEY! HOW'S YOUR DAY?

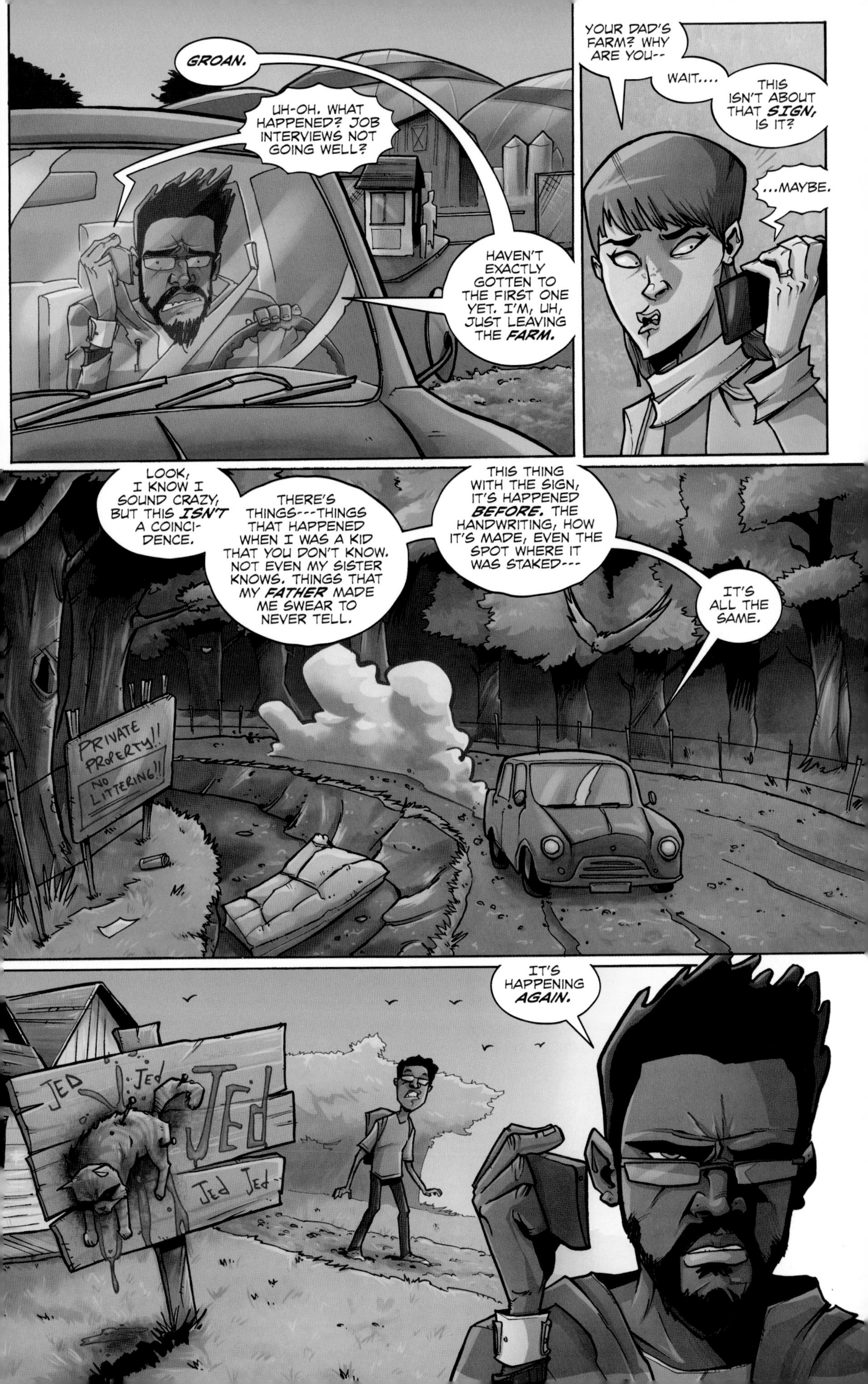
GROAN.
UH-OH. WHAT HAPPENED? JOB INTERVIEWS NOT GOING WELL?
HAVEN'T EXACTLY GOTTEN TO THE FIRST ONE YET. I'M, UH, JUST LEAVING THE FARM.
YOUR DAD'S FARM? WHY ARE YOU--
WAIT....
THIS ISN'T ABOUT THAT SIGN, IS IT?
...MAYBE.
LOOK, I KNOW I SOUND CRAZY, BUT THIS ISN'T A COINCIDENCE.
THERE'S THINGS---THINGS THAT HAPPENED WHEN I WAS A KID THAT YOU DON'T KNOW. NOT EVEN MY SISTER KNOWS. THINGS THAT MY FATHER MADE ME SWEAR TO NEVER TELL.
THIS THING WITH THE SIGN, IT'S HAPPENED BEFORE. THE HANDWRITING, HOW IT'S MADE, EVEN THE SPOT WHERE IT WAS STAKED---
IT'S ALL THE SAME.
PRIVATE PROPERTY!!
NO LITTERING!!
IT'S HAPPENING AGAIN.
JED
JED
JED
JED JED

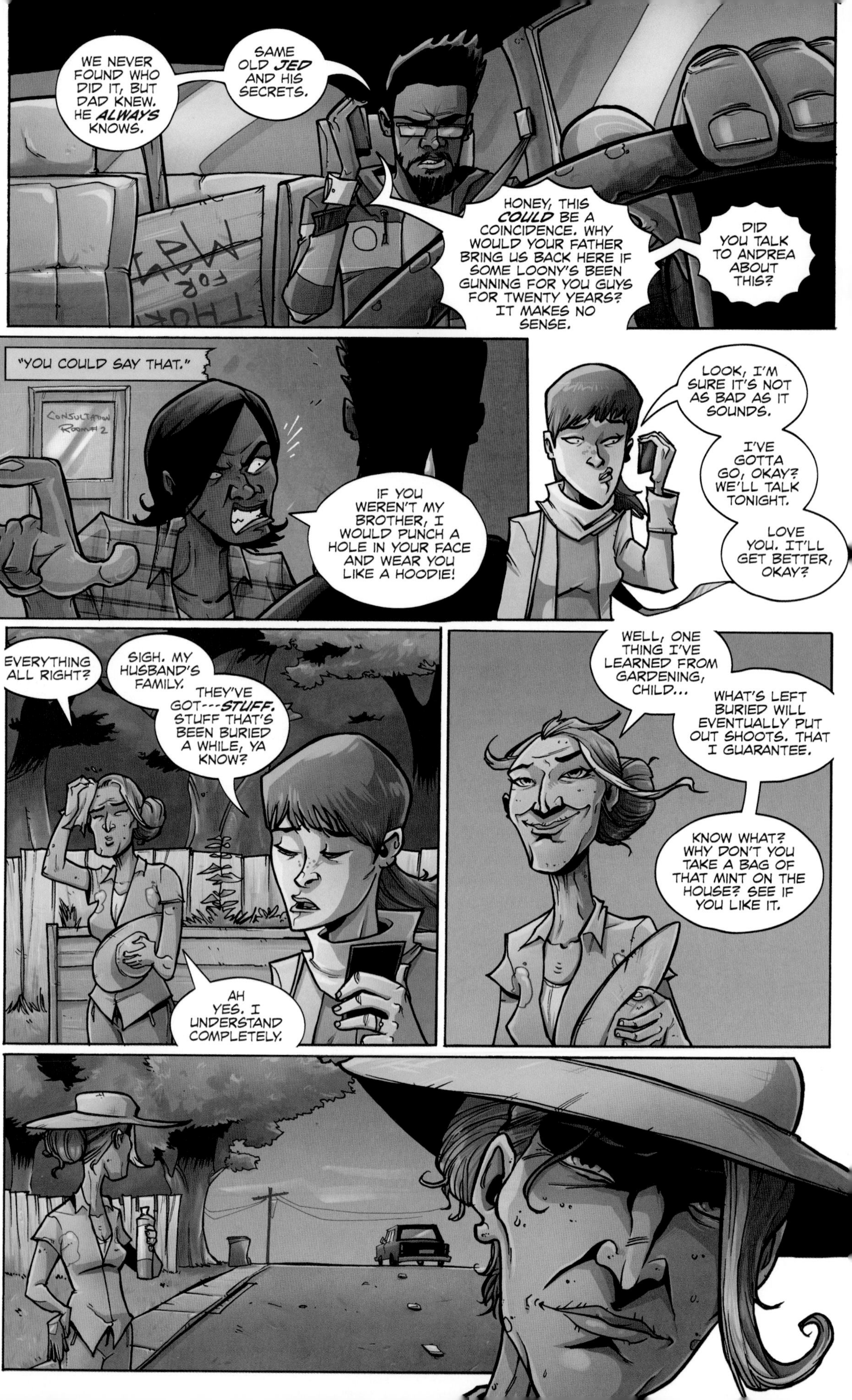
WE NEVER FOUND WHO DID IT, BUT DAD KNEW. HE ALWAYS KNOWS.
SAME OLD JED AND HIS SECRETS.
HONEY, THIS COULD BE A COINCIDENCE. WHY WOULD YOUR FATHER BRING US BACK HERE IF SOME LOONY'S BEEN GUNNING FOR YOU GUYS FOR TWENTY YEARS? IT MAKES NO SENSE.
DID YOU TALK TO ANDREA ABOUT THIS?
"YOU COULD SAY THAT."
CONSULTATION ROOM #2
IF YOU WEREN'T MY BROTHER, I WOULD PUNCH A HOLE IN YOUR FACE AND WEAR YOU LIKE A HOODIE!
LOOK, I'M SURE IT'S NOT AS BAD AS IT SOUNDS.
I'VE GOTTA GO, OKAY? WE'LL TALK TONIGHT.
LOVE YOU. IT'LL GET BETTER, OKAY?
EVERYTHING ALL RIGHT?
SIGH. MY HUSBAND'S FAMILY.
THEY'VE GOT---STUFF. STUFF THAT'S BEEN BURIED A WHILE, YA KNOW?
AH YES. I UNDERSTAND COMPLETELY.
WELL, ONE THING I'VE LEARNED FROM GARDENING, CHILD...
WHAT'S LEFT BURIED WILL EVENTUALLY PUT OUT SHOOTS. THAT I GUARANTEE.
KNOW WHAT? WHY DON'T YOU TAKE A BAG OF THAT MINT ON THE HOUSE? SEE IF YOU LIKE IT.

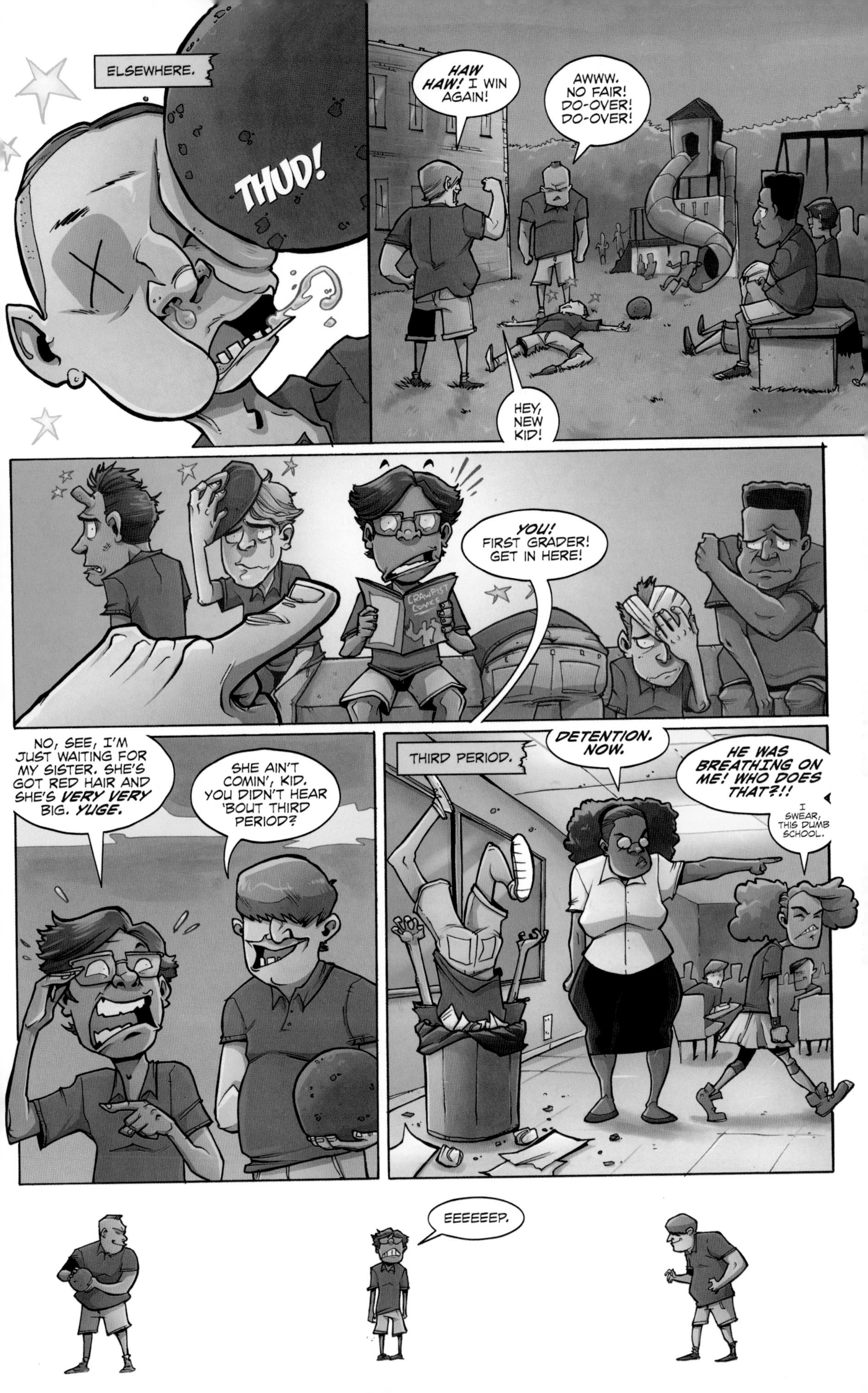
ELSEWHERE.
THUD!
HAW HAW! I WIN AGAIN!
AWWW. NO FAIR! DO-OVER! DO-OVER!
HEY, NEW KID!
YOU! FIRST GRADER! GET IN HERE!
CRAWFIST COMICS
NO, SEE, I'M JUST WAITING FOR MY SISTER. SHE'S GOT RED HAIR AND SHE'S VERY VERY BIG. YUGE.
SHE AIN'T COMIN', KID. YOU DIDN'T HEAR 'BOUT THIRD PERIOD?
THIRD PERIOD.
DETENTION. NOW.
HE WAS BREATHING ON ME! WHO DOES THAT?!!
I SWEAR, THIS DUMB SCHOOL.
EEEEEEP.

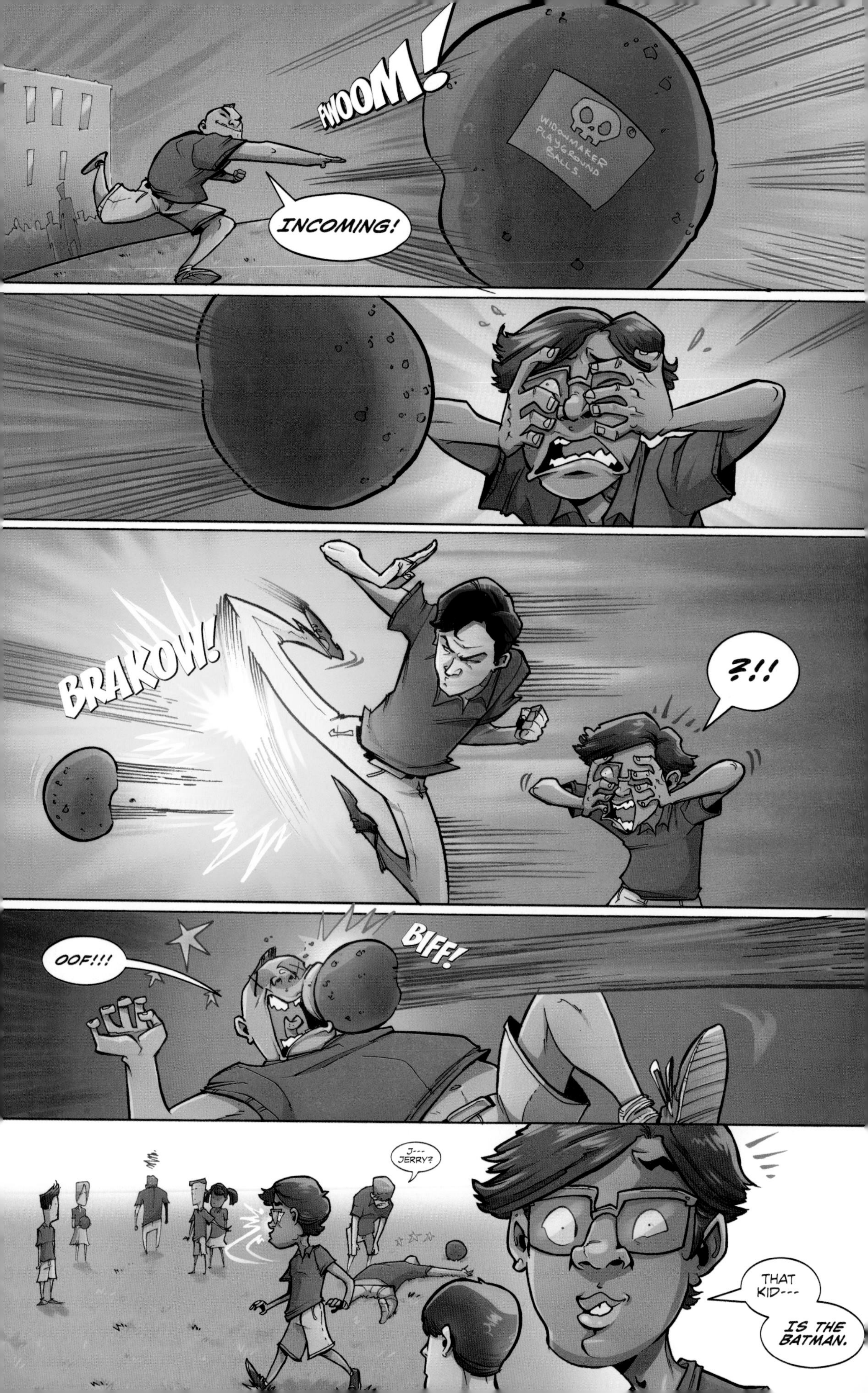
FWOOM!
WIDOWMAKER PLAYGROUND BALLS
INCOMING!
BRAKOW!
?!!
OOF!!!
BIFF!
J--- JERRY?
THAT KID---
IS THE BATMAN.

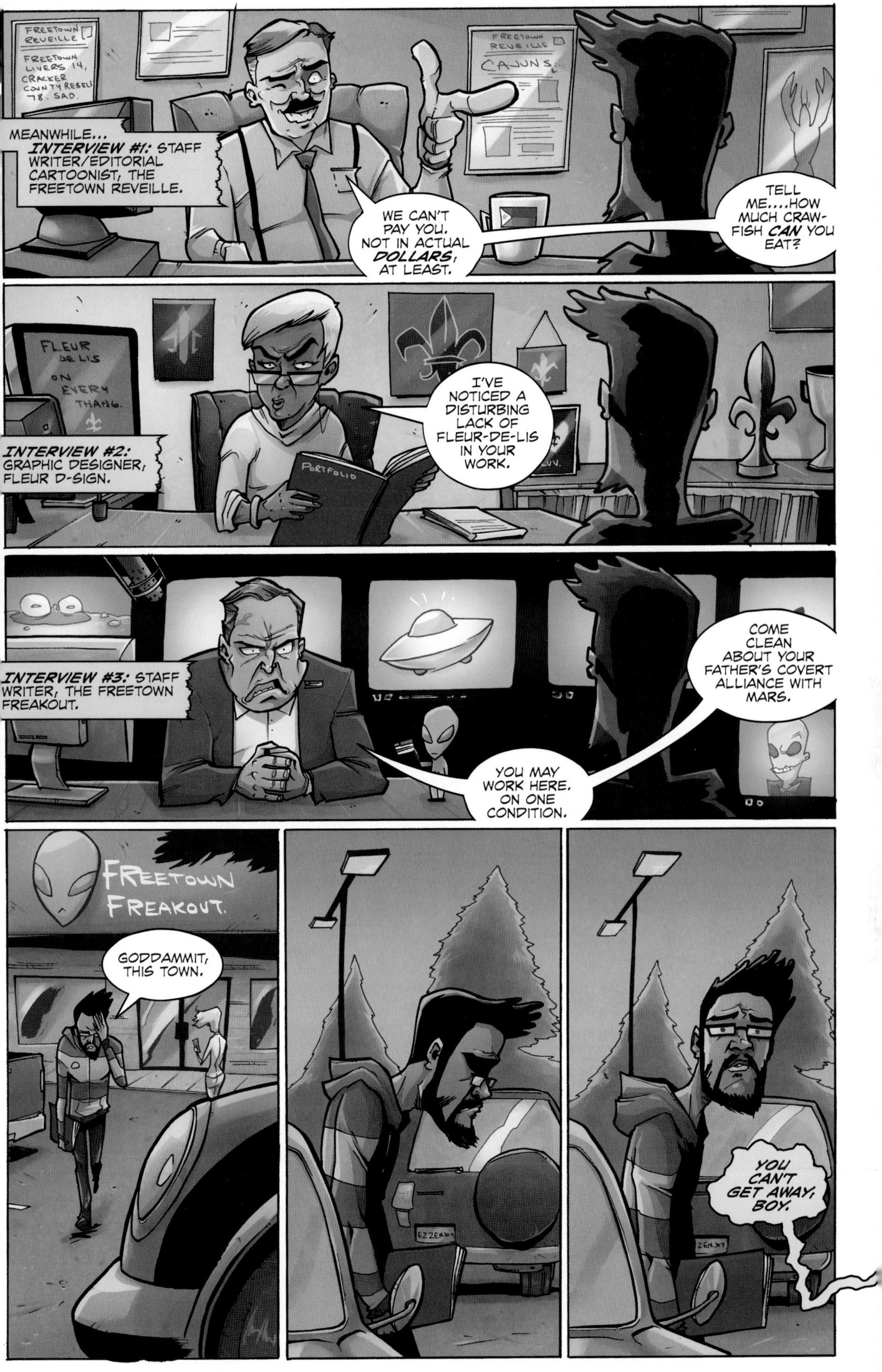
FREETOWN REVEILLE
FREETOWN LIVERS 14, CRACKER COUNTY REBELS 78. SAD.
FREETOWN REVEILLE
CAJUNS...
MEANWHILE... INTERVIEW #1: STAFF WRITER/EDITORIAL CARTOONIST, THE FREETOWN REVEILLE.
WE CAN'T PAY YOU. NOT IN ACTUAL DOLLARS, AT LEAST.
TELL ME....HOW MUCH CRAW-FISH CAN YOU EAT?
FLEUR DE LIS ON EVERY THANG.
INTERVIEW #2: GRAPHIC DESIGNER, FLEUR D-SIGN.
PORTFOLIO
I'VE NOTICED A DISTURBING LACK OF FLEUR-DE-LIS IN YOUR WORK.
INTERVIEW #3: STAFF WRITER, THE FREETOWN FREAKOUT.
YOU MAY WORK HERE. ON ONE CONDITION.
COME CLEAN ABOUT YOUR FATHER'S COVERT ALLIANCE WITH MARS.
FREETOWN FREAKOUT.
GODDAMMIT, THIS TOWN.
EZZENJOY
YOU CAN'T GET AWAY, BOY.

MOONSHINE'S
XXX
LIQUOR
+ SPIRITS
40 OZ!
IT IS ONLY A MATTER OF TIME.
MY OTHER CAR CAN ONLY BE BIGGER.
SERVICE
II
UNITY
RECOVERY
MOONSHINE'S
XXX
LIQUOR
+ SPIRITS
SONUVABITC

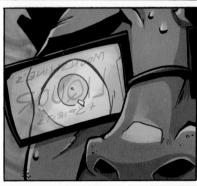

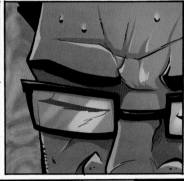

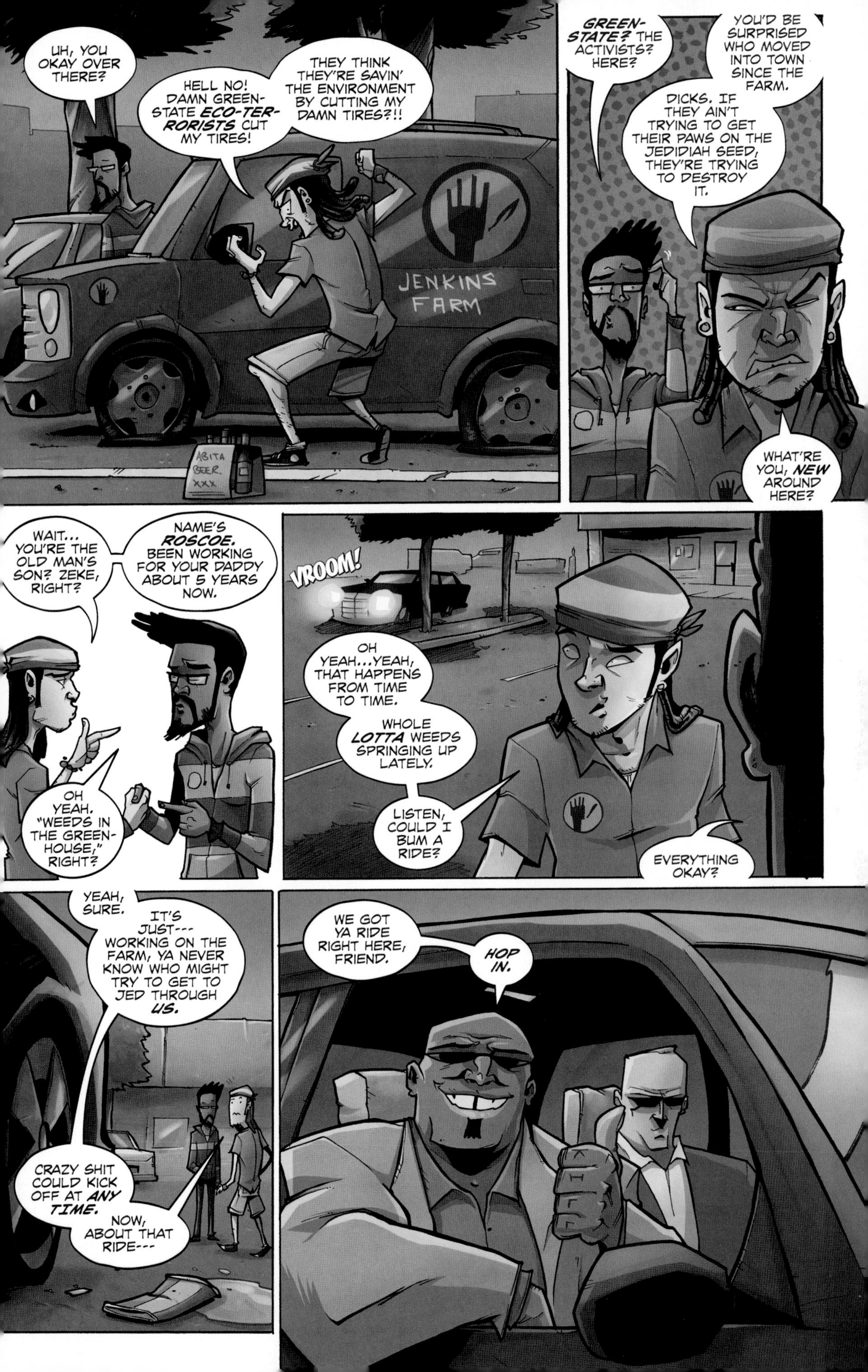
UH, YOU OKAY OVER THERE?
HELL NO! DAMN GREEN-STATE ECO-TER-RORISTS CUT MY TIRES!
THEY THINK THEY'RE SAVIN' THE ENVIRONMENT BY CUTTING MY DAMN TIRES?!!
JENKINS FARM
ABITA BEER XXX
GREEN-STATE? THE ACTIVISTS? HERE?
YOU'D BE SURPRISED WHO MOVED INTO TOWN SINCE THE FARM.
DICKS. IF THEY AIN'T TRYING TO GET THEIR PAWS ON THE JEDIDIAH SEED, THEY'RE TRYING TO DESTROY IT.
WHAT'RE YOU, NEW AROUND HERE?
WAIT... YOU'RE THE OLD MAN'S SON? ZEKE, RIGHT?
NAME'S ROSCOE. BEEN WORKING FOR YOUR DADDY ABOUT 5 YEARS NOW.
OH YEAH. "WEEDS IN THE GREEN-HOUSE," RIGHT?
VROOM!
OH YEAH...YEAH, THAT HAPPENS FROM TIME TO TIME.
WHOLE LOTTA WEEDS SPRINGING UP LATELY.
LISTEN, COULD I BUM A RIDE?
EVERYTHING OKAY?
YEAH, SURE.
IT'S JUST--- WORKING ON THE FARM, YA NEVER KNOW WHO MIGHT TRY TO GET TO JED THROUGH US.
CRAZY SHIT COULD KICK OFF AT ANY TIME.
NOW, ABOUT THAT RIDE---
WE GOT YA RIDE RIGHT HERE, FRIEND.
HOP IN.

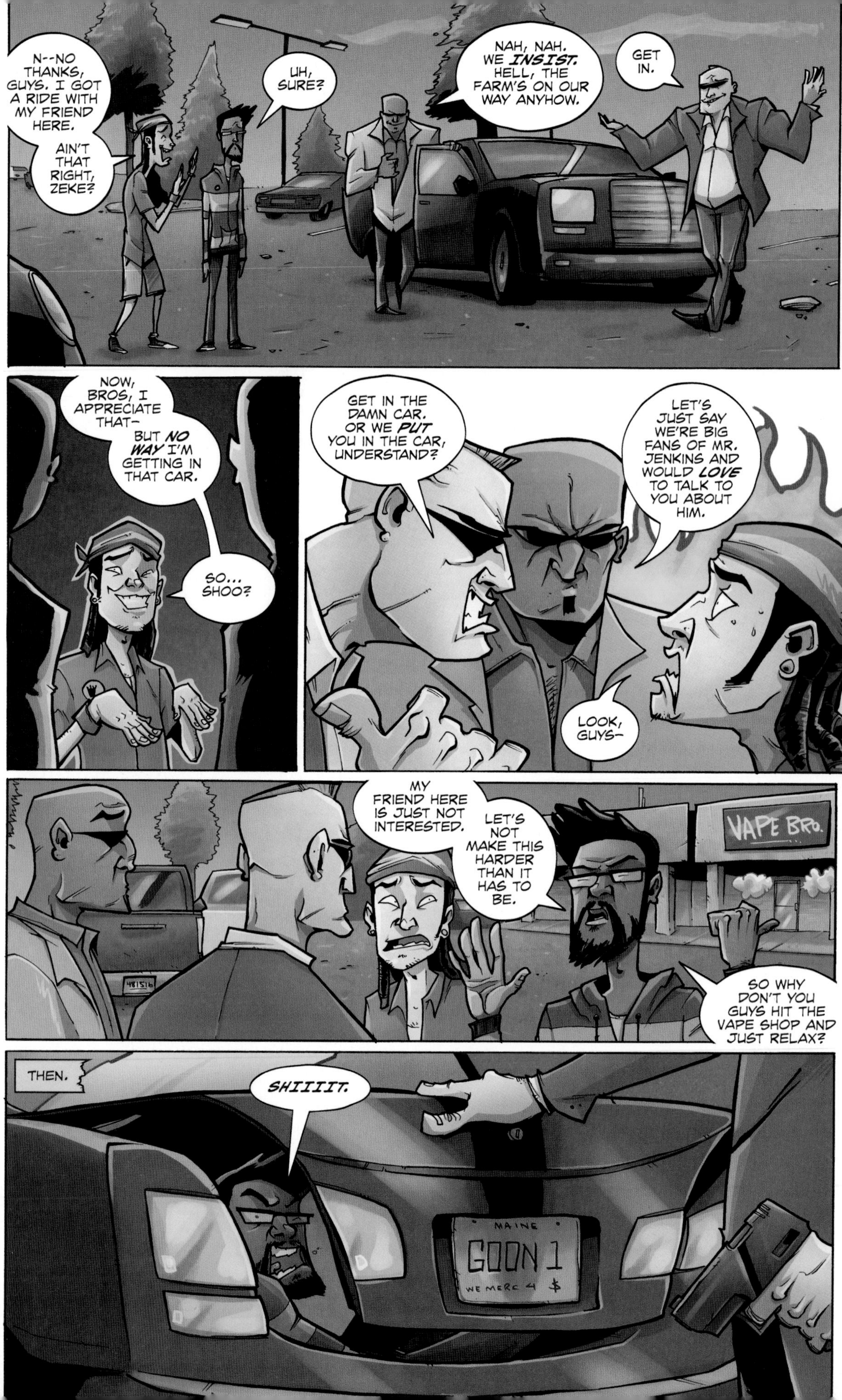

N--NO THANKS, GUYS. I GOT A RIDE WITH MY FRIEND HERE.
AIN'T THAT RIGHT, ZEKE?
UH, SURE?
NAH, NAH. WE INSIST. HELL, THE FARM'S ON OUR WAY ANYHOW.
GET IN.
NOW, BROS, I APPRECIATE THAT-
BUT NO WAY I'M GETTING IN THAT CAR.
SO... SHOO?
GET IN THE DAMN CAR. OR WE PUT YOU IN THE CAR, UNDERSTAND?
LET'S JUST SAY WE'RE BIG FANS OF MR. JENKINS AND WOULD LOVE TO TALK TO YOU ABOUT HIM.
LOOK, GUYS-
MY FRIEND HERE IS JUST NOT INTERESTED.
LET'S NOT MAKE THIS HARDER THAN IT HAS TO BE.
VAPE BRO.
481516
SO WHY DON'T YOU GUYS HIT THE VAPE SHOP AND JUST RELAX?
THEN.
SHIIIIT.
MAINE
GOON 1
WE MERC 4 $

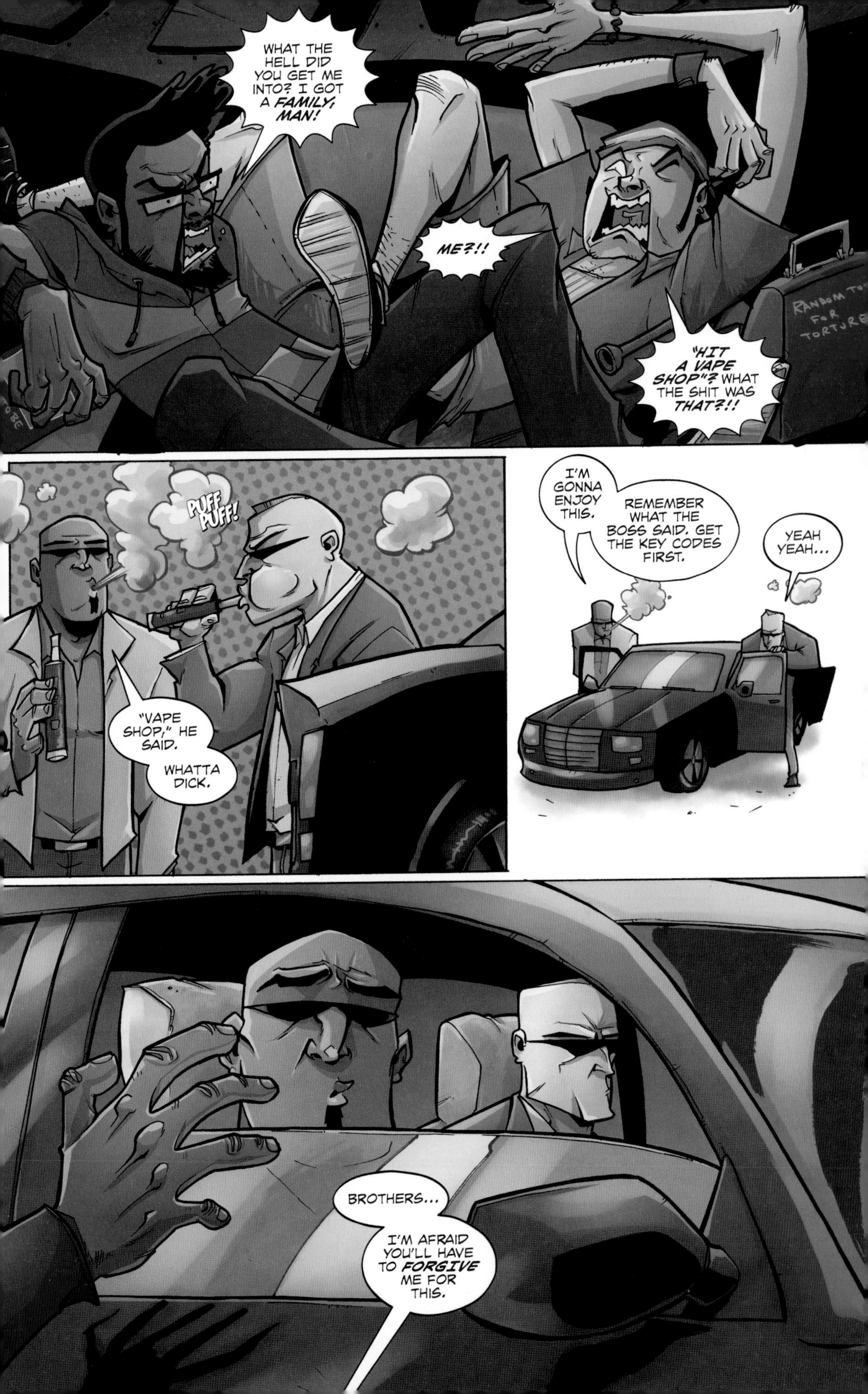
WHAT THE HELL DID YOU GET ME INTO? I GOT A *FAMILY*, *MAN!*
ME?!!
"HIT A VAPE SHOP"? WHAT THE SHIT WAS *THAT?!!*
RANDOM TOOLS FOR TORTURE
PUFF PUFF!
"VAPE SHOP," HE SAID.
WHATTA DICK.
I'M GONNA ENJOY THIS.
REMEMBER WHAT THE BOSS SAID. GET THE KEY CODES FIRST.
YEAH YEAH...
BROTHERS...
I'M AFRAID YOU'LL HAVE TO *FORGIVE* ME FOR THIS.

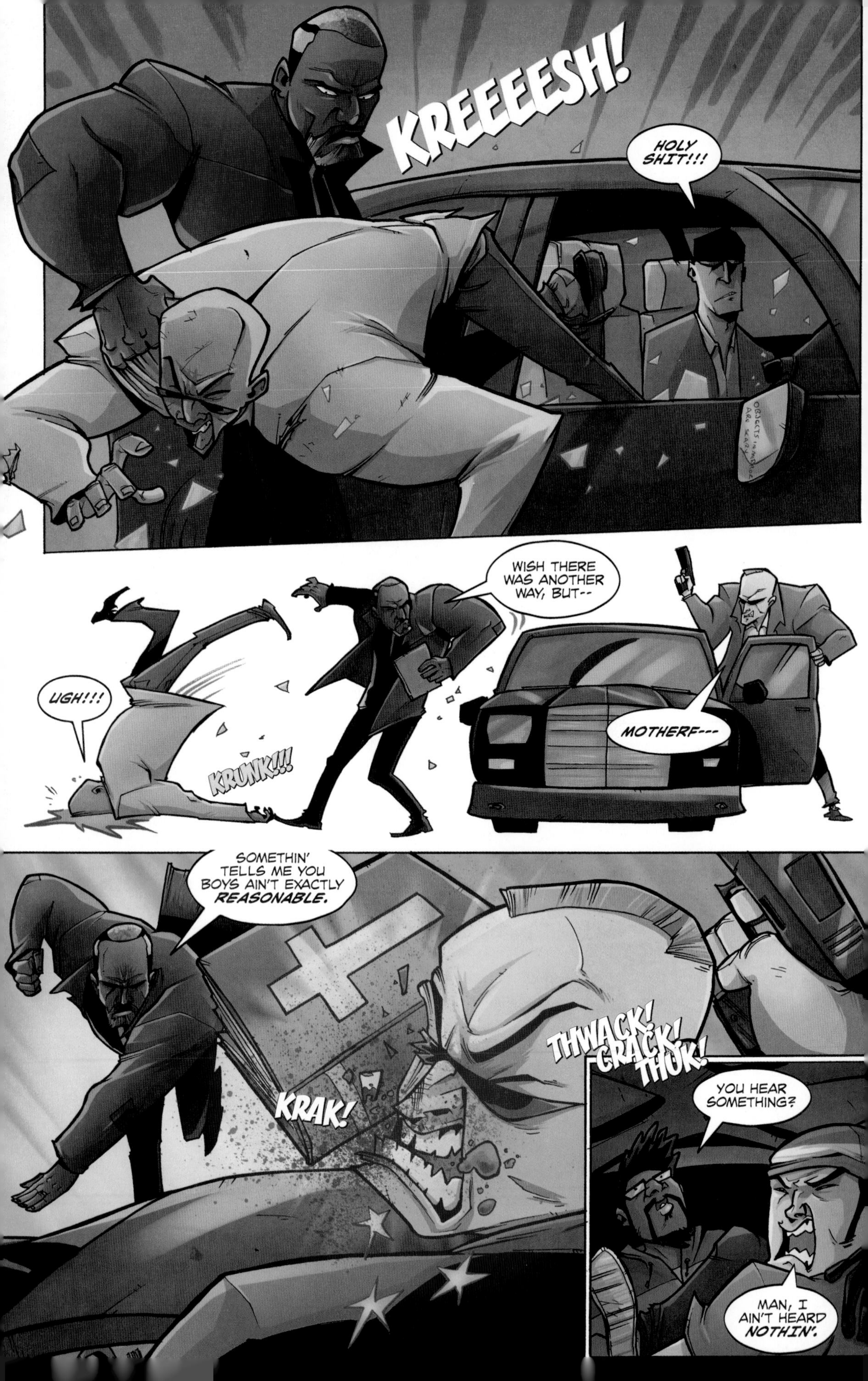
KREEEEESH!
HOLY SHIT!!!
UGH!!!
KRUNK!!!
WISH THERE WAS ANOTHER WAY, BUT--
MOTHERF---
SOMETHIN' TELLS ME YOU BOYS AIN'T EXACTLY *REASONABLE.*
KRAK!
THWACK! CRACK! THUK!
YOU HEAR SOMETHING?
MAN, I AIN'T HEARD *NOTHIN'.*

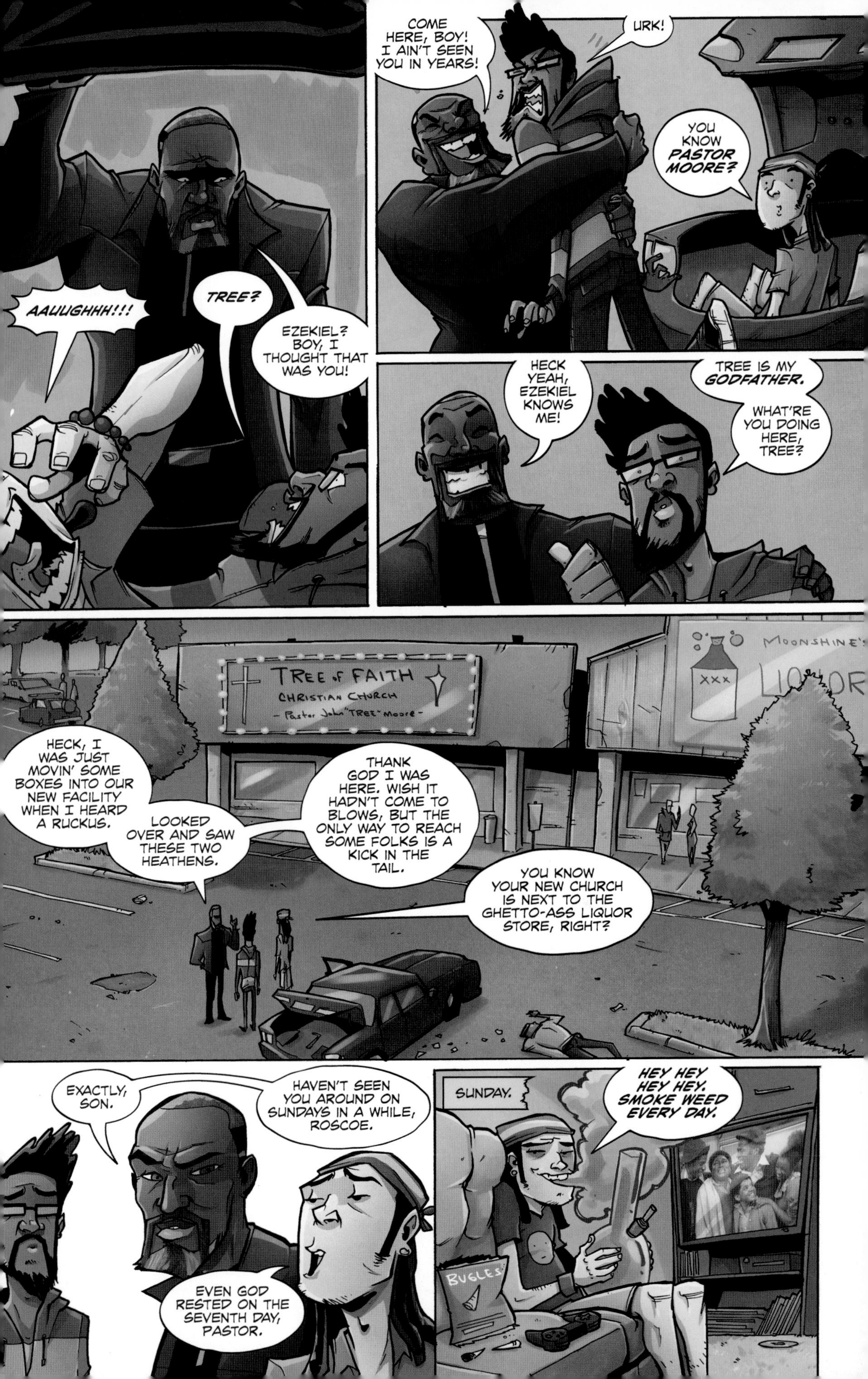
AAUUGHHH!!!
TREE?
EZEKIEL? BOY, I THOUGHT THAT WAS YOU!
COME HERE, BOY! I AIN'T SEEN YOU IN YEARS!
URK!
YOU KNOW PASTOR MOORE?
HECK YEAH, EZEKIEL KNOWS ME!
TREE IS MY GODFATHER.
WHAT'RE YOU DOING HERE, TREE?
TREE of FAITH
CHRISTIAN CHURCH
- Pastor John "TREE" Moore -
MOONSHINE'S
XXX
HECK, I WAS JUST MOVIN' SOME BOXES INTO OUR NEW FACILITY WHEN I HEARD A RUCKUS.
LOOKED OVER AND SAW THESE TWO HEATHENS.
THANK GOD I WAS HERE. WISH IT HADN'T COME TO BLOWS, BUT THE ONLY WAY TO REACH SOME FOLKS IS A KICK IN THE TAIL.
YOU KNOW YOUR NEW CHURCH IS NEXT TO THE GHETTO-ASS LIQUOR STORE, RIGHT?
EXACTLY, SON.
HAVEN'T SEEN YOU AROUND ON SUNDAYS IN A WHILE, ROSCOE.
EVEN GOD RESTED ON THE SEVENTH DAY, PASTOR.
SUNDAY.
HEY HEY HEY HEY. SMOKE WEED EVERY DAY.
BUGLES

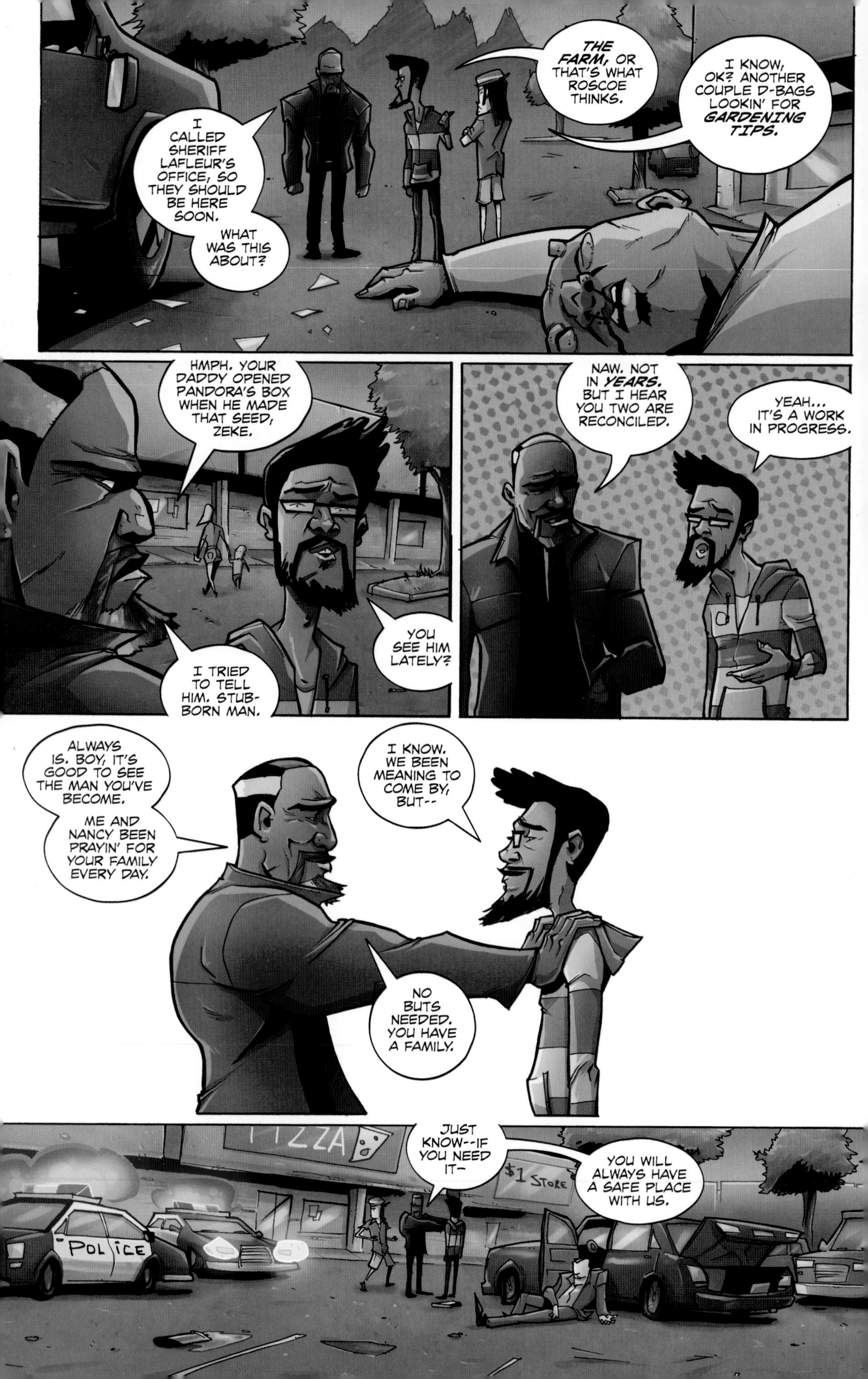
I CALLED SHERIFF LAFLEUR'S OFFICE, SO THEY SHOULD BE HERE SOON.
WHAT WAS THIS ABOUT?
THE FARM, OR THAT'S WHAT ROSCOE THINKS.
I KNOW, OK? ANOTHER COUPLE D-BAGS LOOKIN' FOR GARDENING TIPS.
HMPH. YOUR DADDY OPENED PANDORA'S BOX WHEN HE MADE THAT SEED, ZEKE.
I TRIED TO TELL HIM. STUB-BORN MAN.
YOU SEE HIM LATELY?
NAW. NOT IN YEARS. BUT I HEAR YOU TWO ARE RECONCILED.
YEAH... IT'S A WORK IN PROGRESS.
ALWAYS IS. BOY, IT'S GOOD TO SEE THE MAN YOU'VE BECOME.
ME AND NANCY BEEN PRAYIN' FOR YOUR FAMILY EVERY DAY.
I KNOW. WE BEEN MEANING TO COME BY, BUT--
NO BUTS NEEDED. YOU HAVE A FAMILY.
JUST KNOW--IF YOU NEED IT-
YOU WILL ALWAYS HAVE A SAFE PLACE WITH US.
PIZZA
$1 STORE
POLICE

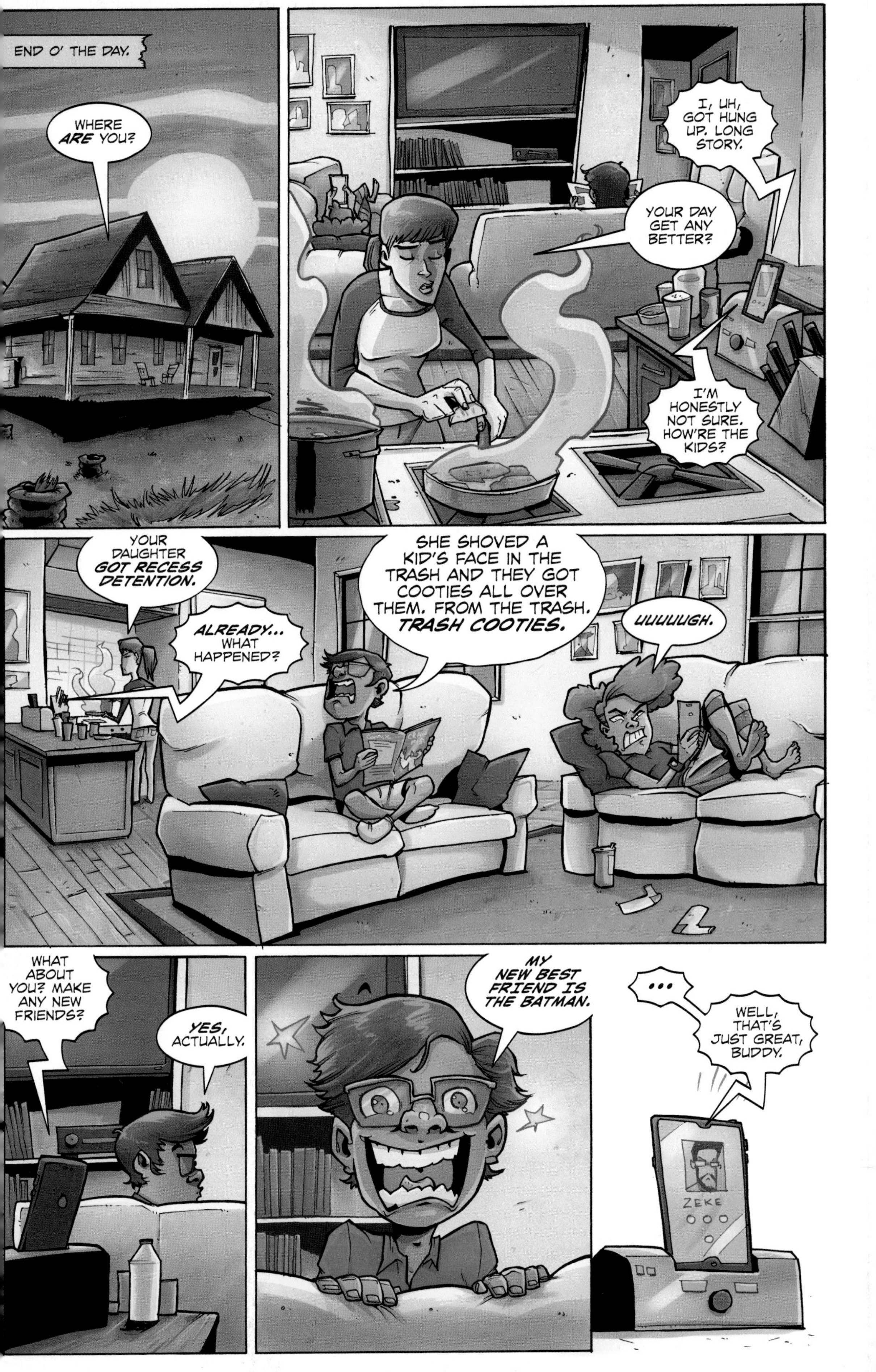
END O' THE DAY.
WHERE *ARE* YOU?
I, UH, GOT HUNG UP. LONG STORY.
YOUR DAY GET ANY BETTER?
I'M HONESTLY NOT SURE. HOW'RE THE KIDS?
YOUR DAUGHTER *GOT RECESS DETENTION.*
ALREADY... WHAT HAPPENED?
SHE SHOVED A KID'S FACE IN THE TRASH AND THEY GOT COOTIES ALL OVER THEM. FROM THE TRASH. *TRASH COOTIES.*
UUUUUGH.
WHAT ABOUT YOU? MAKE ANY NEW FRIENDS?
YES, ACTUALLY.
MY NEW BEST FRIEND IS THE BATMAN.
...
WELL, THAT'S JUST GREAT, BUDDY.
ZEKE

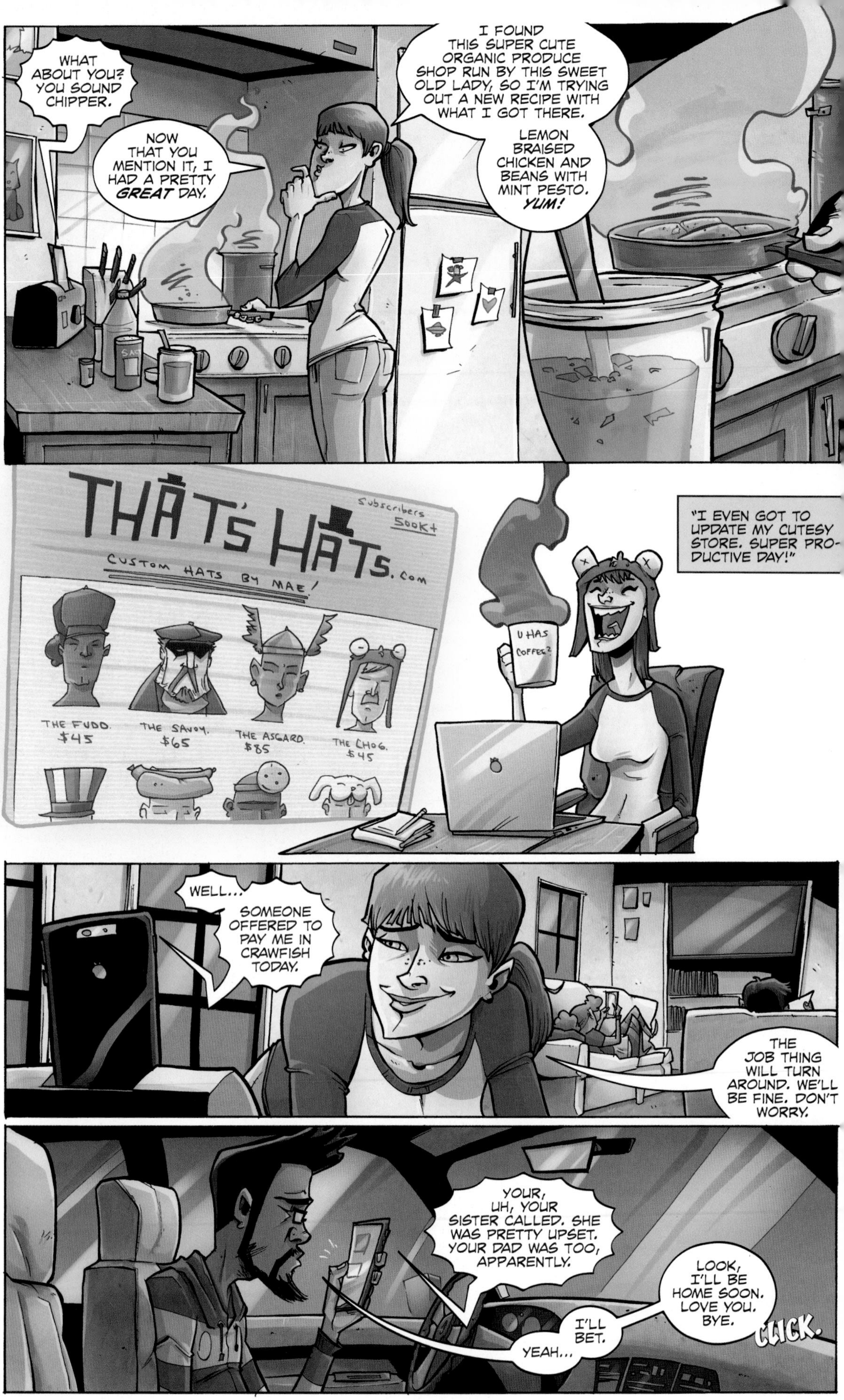
WHAT ABOUT YOU? YOU SOUND CHIPPER.
NOW THAT YOU MENTION IT, I HAD A PRETTY GREAT DAY.
I FOUND THIS SUPER CUTE ORGANIC PRODUCE SHOP RUN BY THIS SWEET OLD LADY, SO I'M TRYING OUT A NEW RECIPE WITH WHAT I GOT THERE.
LEMON BRAISED CHICKEN AND BEANS WITH MINT PESTO. YUM!
THAT'S HATS
Subscribers 500K+
CUSTOM HATS BY MAE! .com
THE FUDO $45
THE SAVOY $65
THE ASGARD $85
THE CHOG $45
U HAS COFFEE?
"I EVEN GOT TO UPDATE MY CUTESY STORE. SUPER PRODUCTIVE DAY!"
WELL...
SOMEONE OFFERED TO PAY ME IN CRAWFISH TODAY.
THE JOB THING WILL TURN AROUND. WE'LL BE FINE. DON'T WORRY.
YOUR, UH, YOUR SISTER CALLED. SHE WAS PRETTY UPSET. YOUR DAD WAS TOO, APPARENTLY.
YEAH...
I'LL BET.
LOOK, I'LL BE HOME SOON. LOVE YOU. BYE.
CLICK.

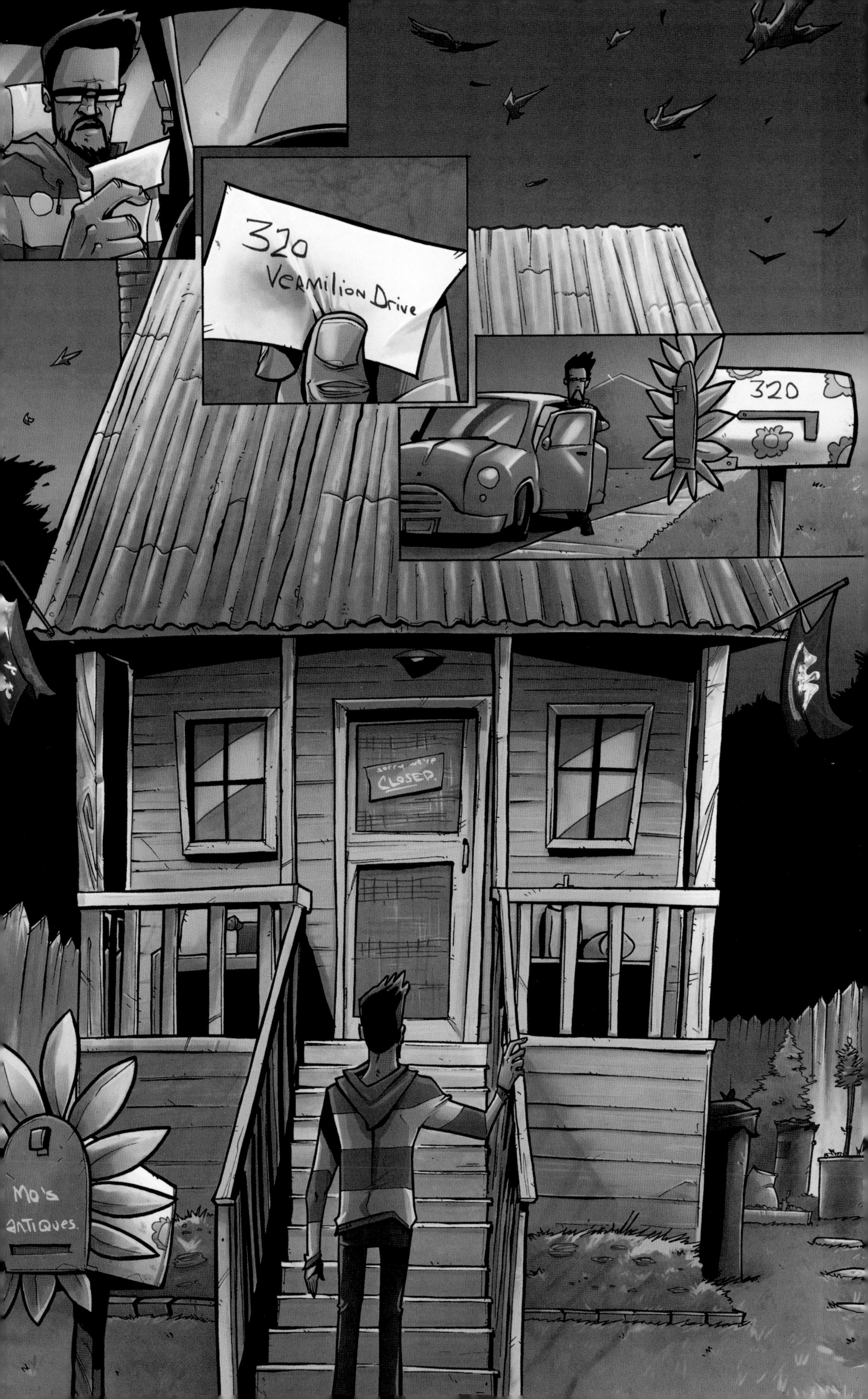

320
Vermilion Drive
320
sorry we're
CLOSED.
Mo's
antiques.

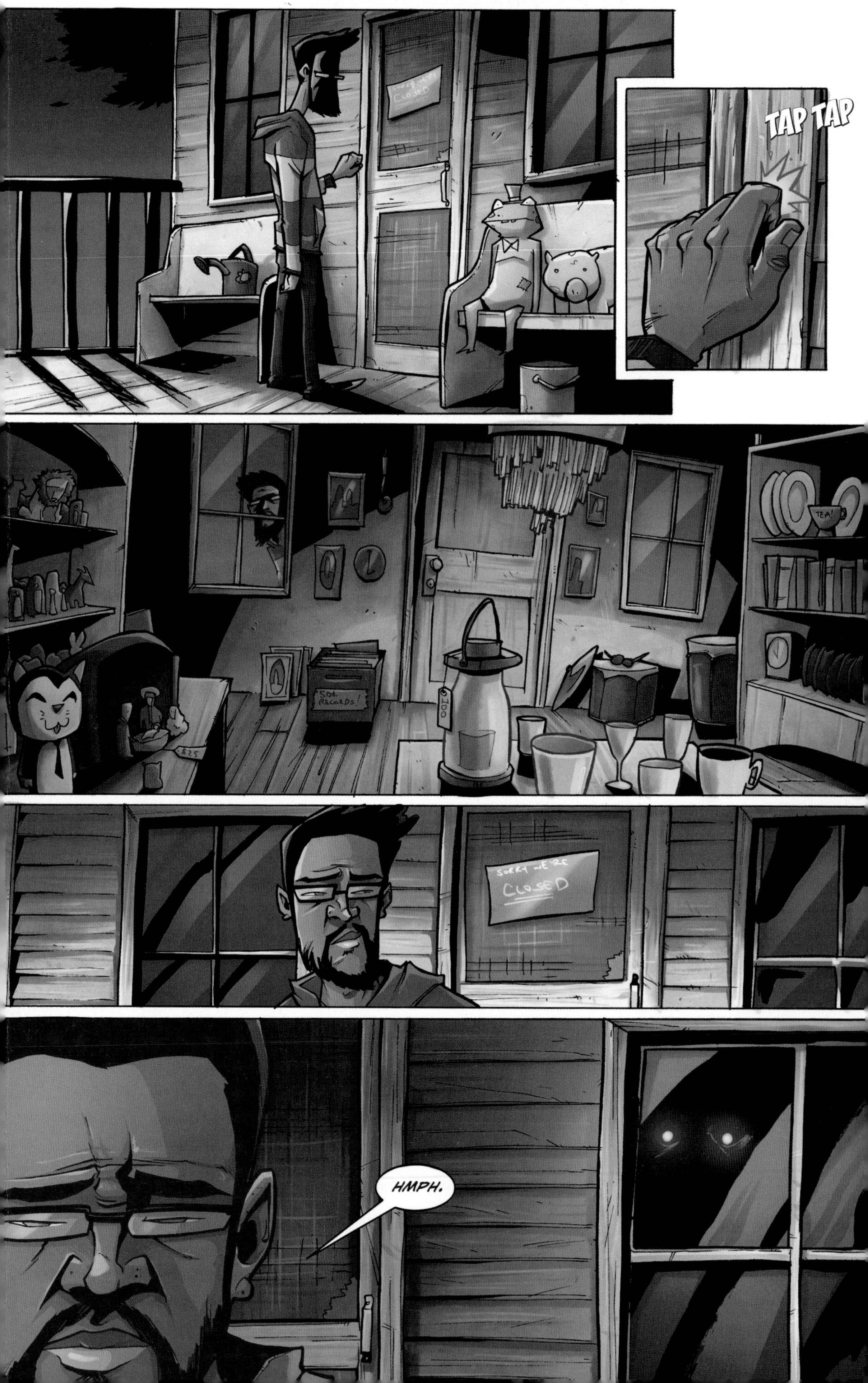
TAP TAP
SORRY WE'RE CLOSED
HMPH.

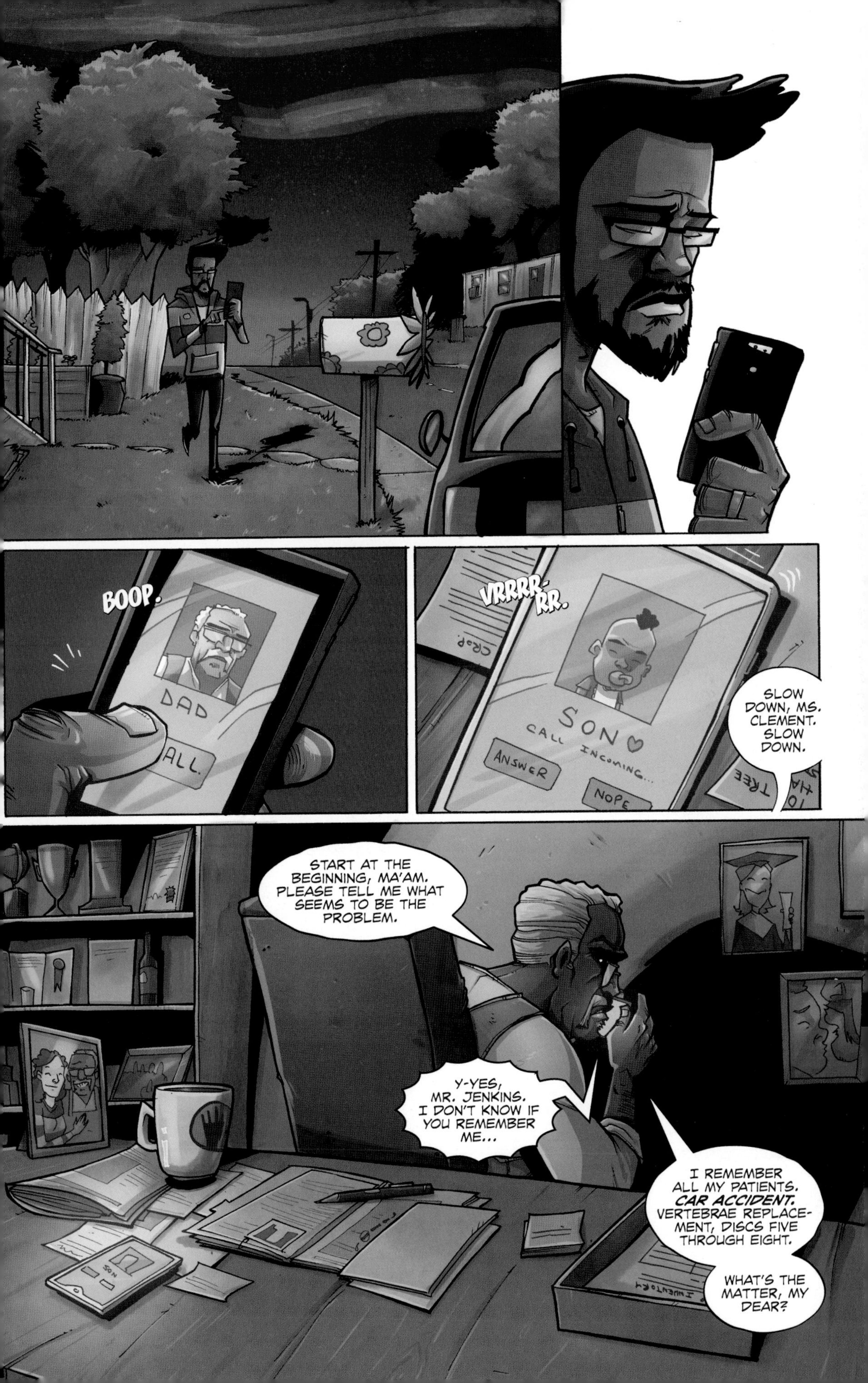
BOOP.
DAD
ALL.
VRRRR-RR.
CROP.
SON
CALL INCOMING...
ANSWER
NOPE
SLOW DOWN, MS. CLEMENT. SLOW DOWN.
START AT THE BEGINNING, MA'AM. PLEASE TELL ME WHAT SEEMS TO BE THE PROBLEM.
Y-YES, MR. JENKINS. I DON'T KNOW IF YOU REMEMBER ME...
I REMEMBER ALL MY PATIENTS. ***CAR ACCIDENT.*** VERTEBRAE REPLACEMENT, DISCS FIVE THROUGH EIGHT.
WHAT'S THE MATTER, MY DEAR?

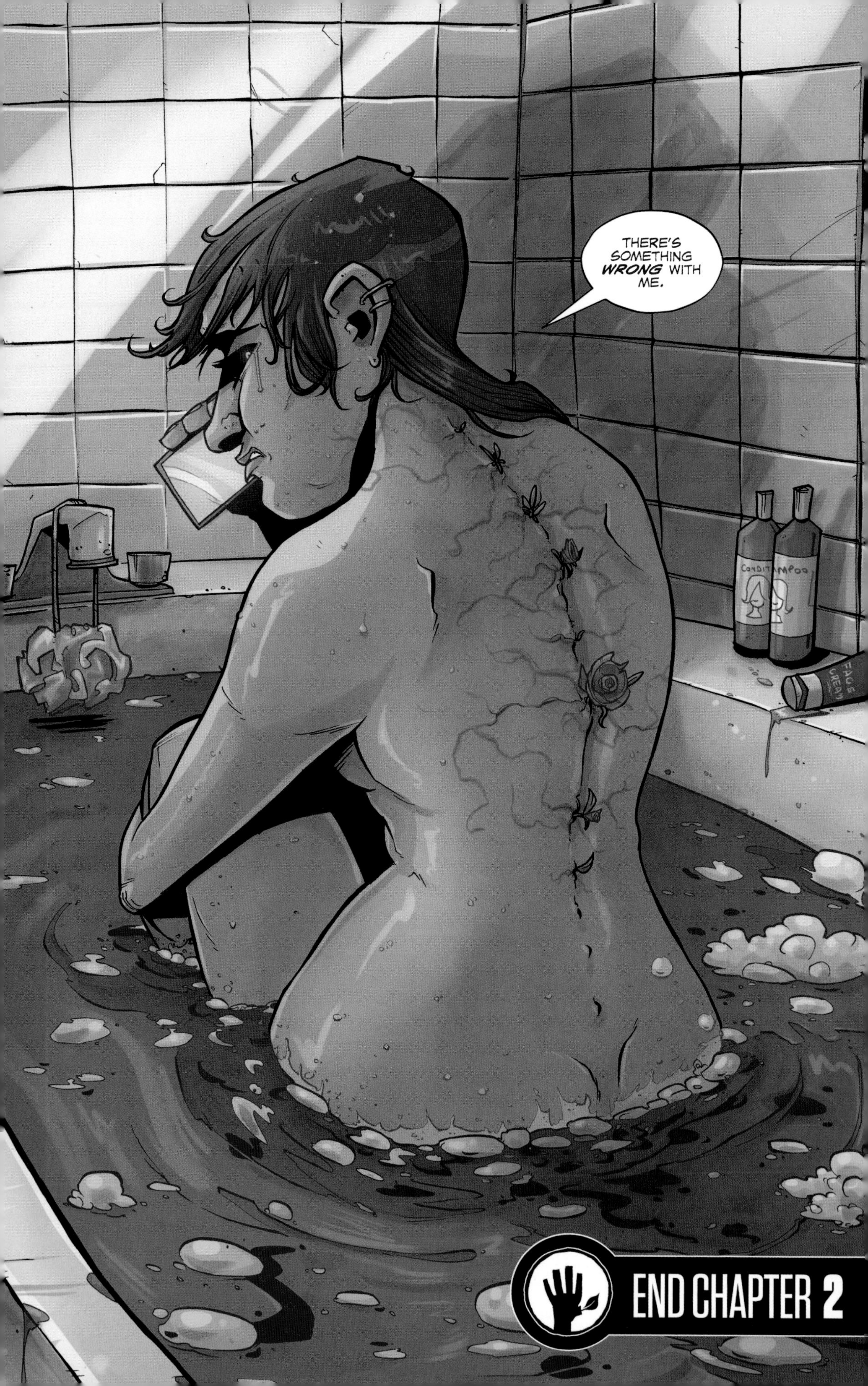
THERE'S SOMETHING **WRONG** WITH ME.
END CHAPTER 2

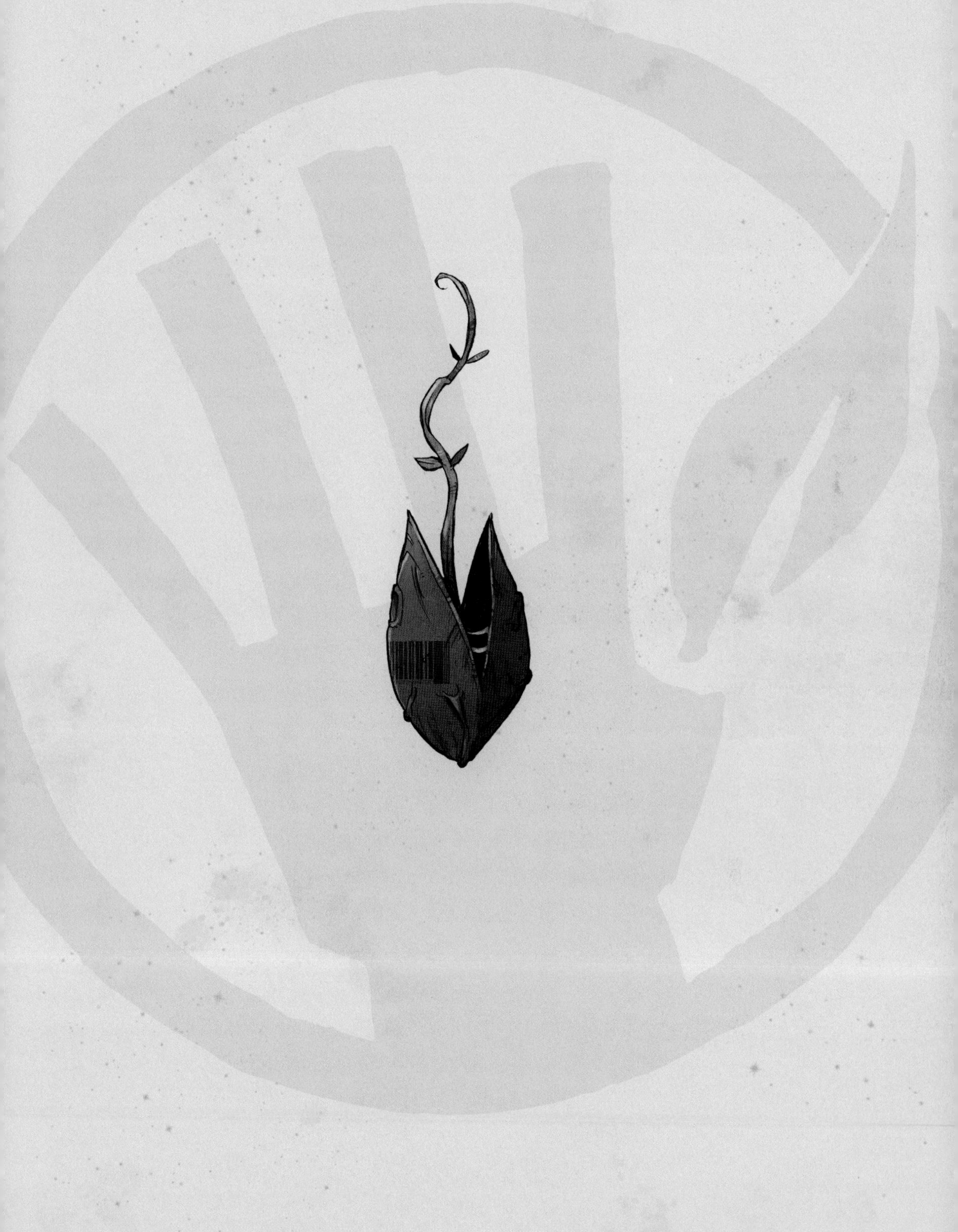

CHAPTER 3

ROB!

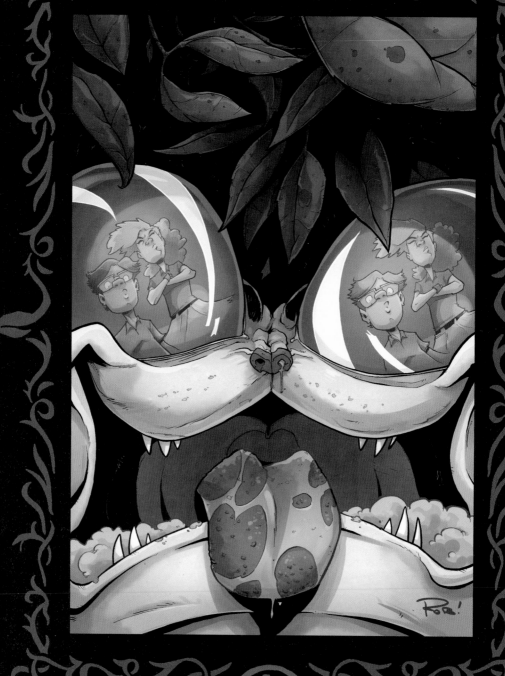

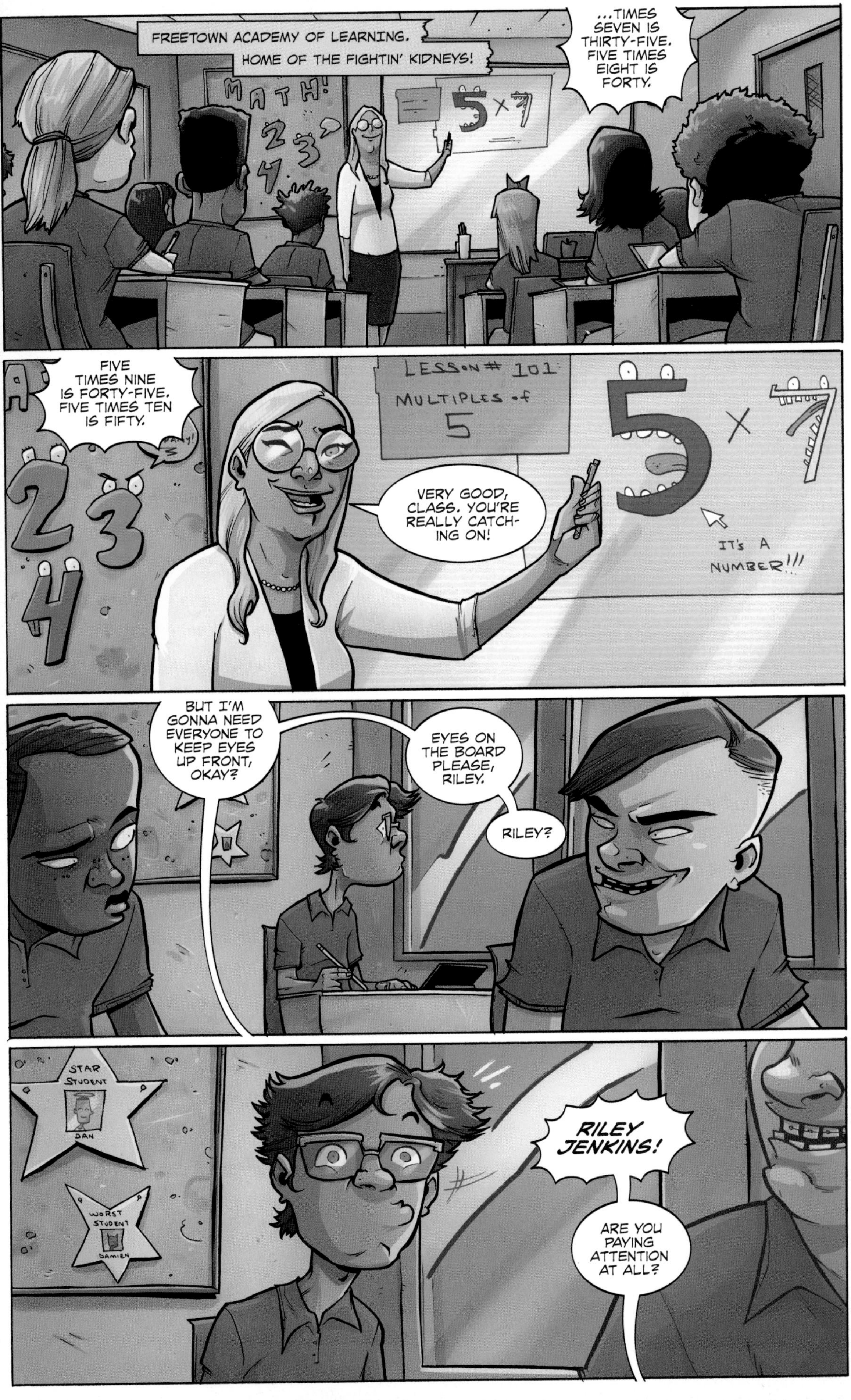

FREETOWN ACADEMY OF LEARNING.
HOME OF THE FIGHTIN' KIDNEYS!
...TIMES SEVEN IS THIRTY-FIVE. FIVE TIMES EIGHT IS FORTY.
MATH!
FIVE TIMES NINE IS FORTY-FIVE. FIVE TIMES TEN IS FIFTY.
LESSON # 101: MULTIPLES of 5
VERY GOOD, CLASS. YOU'RE REALLY CATCHING ON!
IT'S A NUMBER!!!
BUT I'M GONNA NEED EVERYONE TO KEEP EYES UP FRONT, OKAY?
EYES ON THE BOARD PLEASE, RILEY.
RILEY?
STAR STUDENT
DAN
WORST STUDENT
DAMIEN
RILEY JENKINS!
ARE YOU PAYING ATTENTION AT ALL?

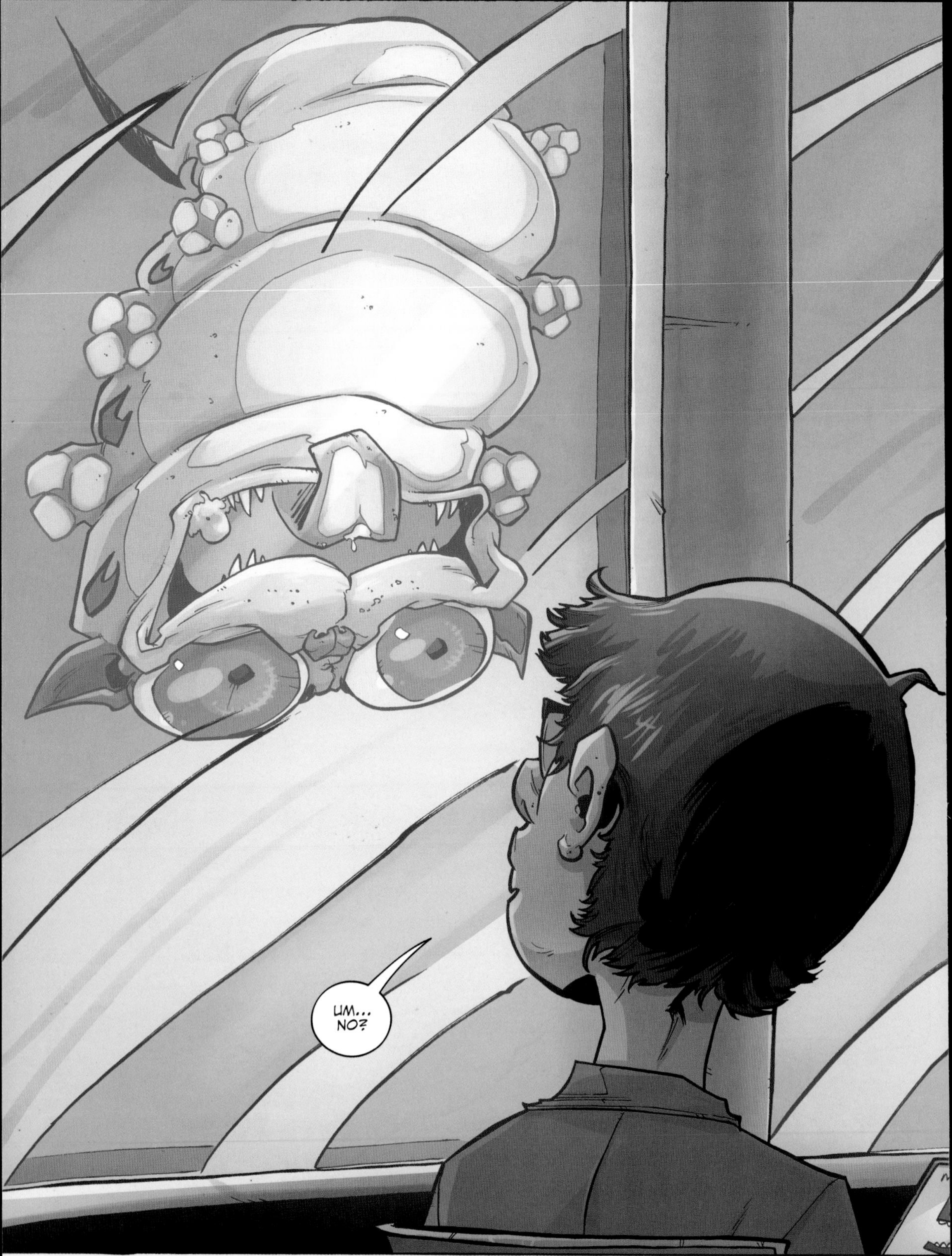
UM... NO?

CHAPTER 3: **PET SINS.**

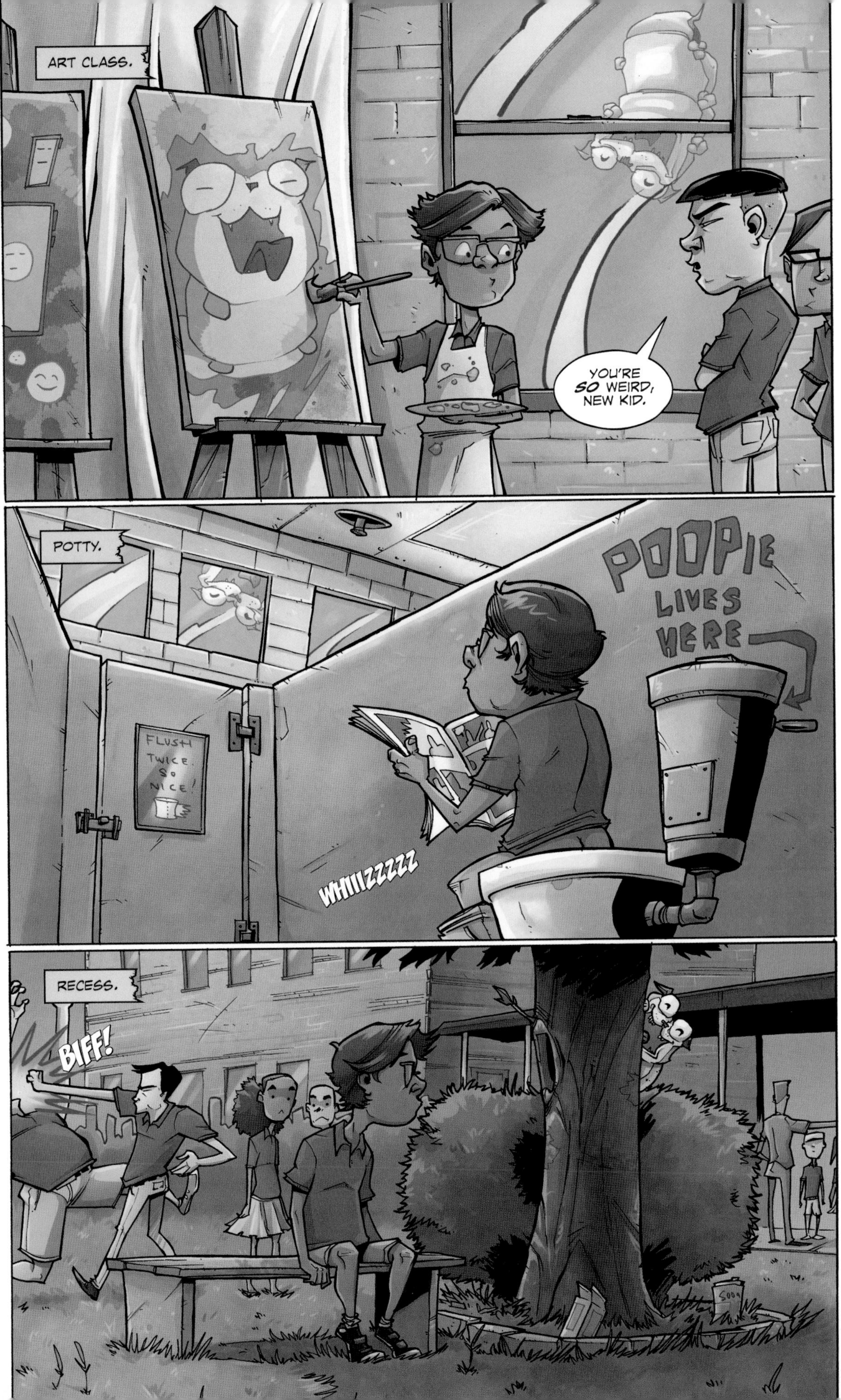
ART CLASS.
YOU'RE SO WEIRD, NEW KID.
POTTY.
POOPIE LIVES HERE
FLUSH TWICE. SO NICE!
WHIIIZZZZZ
RECESS.
BIFF!

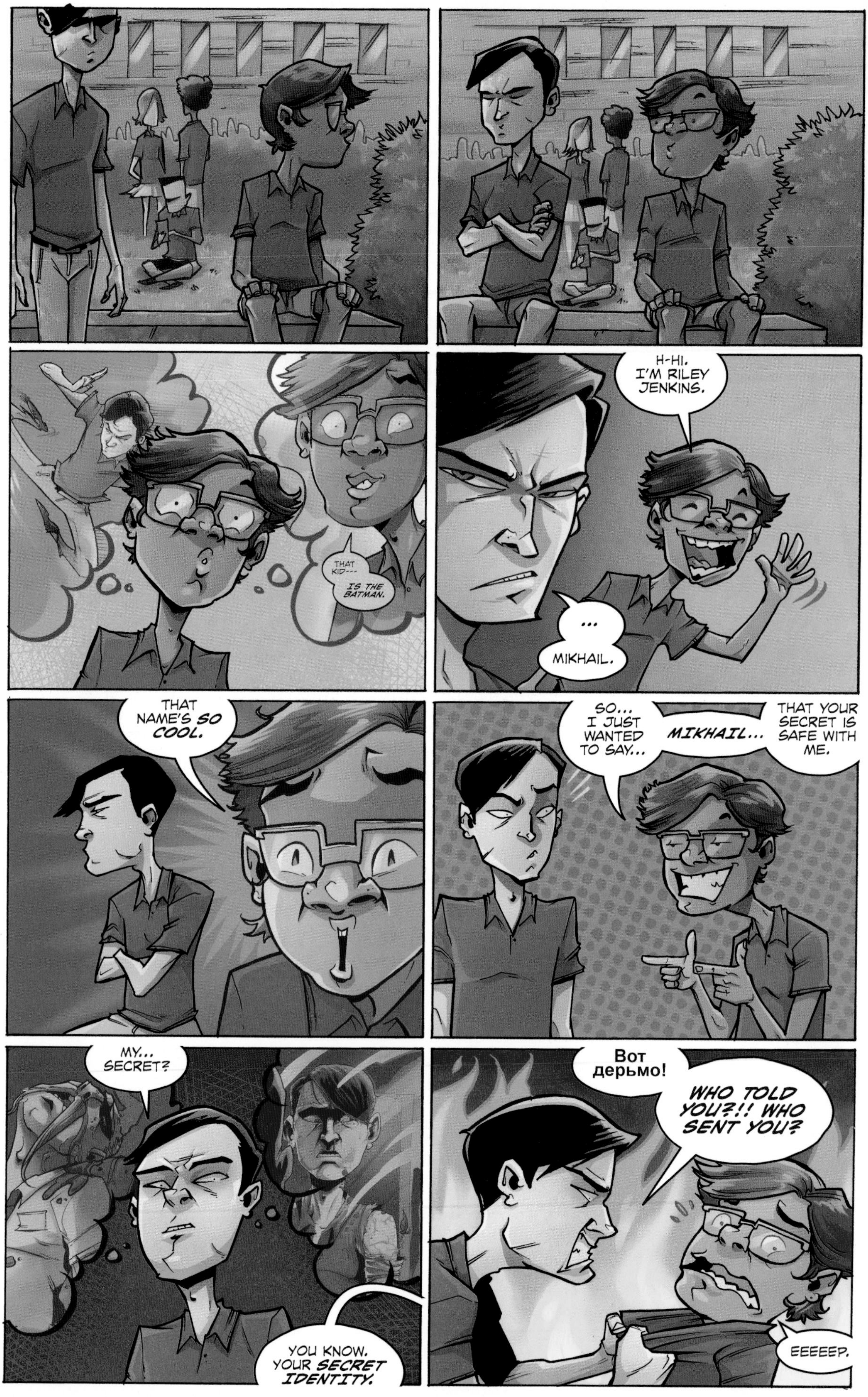
THAT KID--- IS THE BATMAN.
H-HI. I'M RILEY JENKINS.
...
MIKHAIL.
THAT NAME'S *SO COOL.*
SO... I JUST WANTED TO SAY...
MIKHAIL...
THAT YOUR SECRET IS SAFE WITH ME.
MY... SECRET?
YOU KNOW. YOUR *SECRET IDENTITY.*
Вот дерьмо!
WHO TOLD YOU?!! WHO SENT YOU?
EEEEEP.

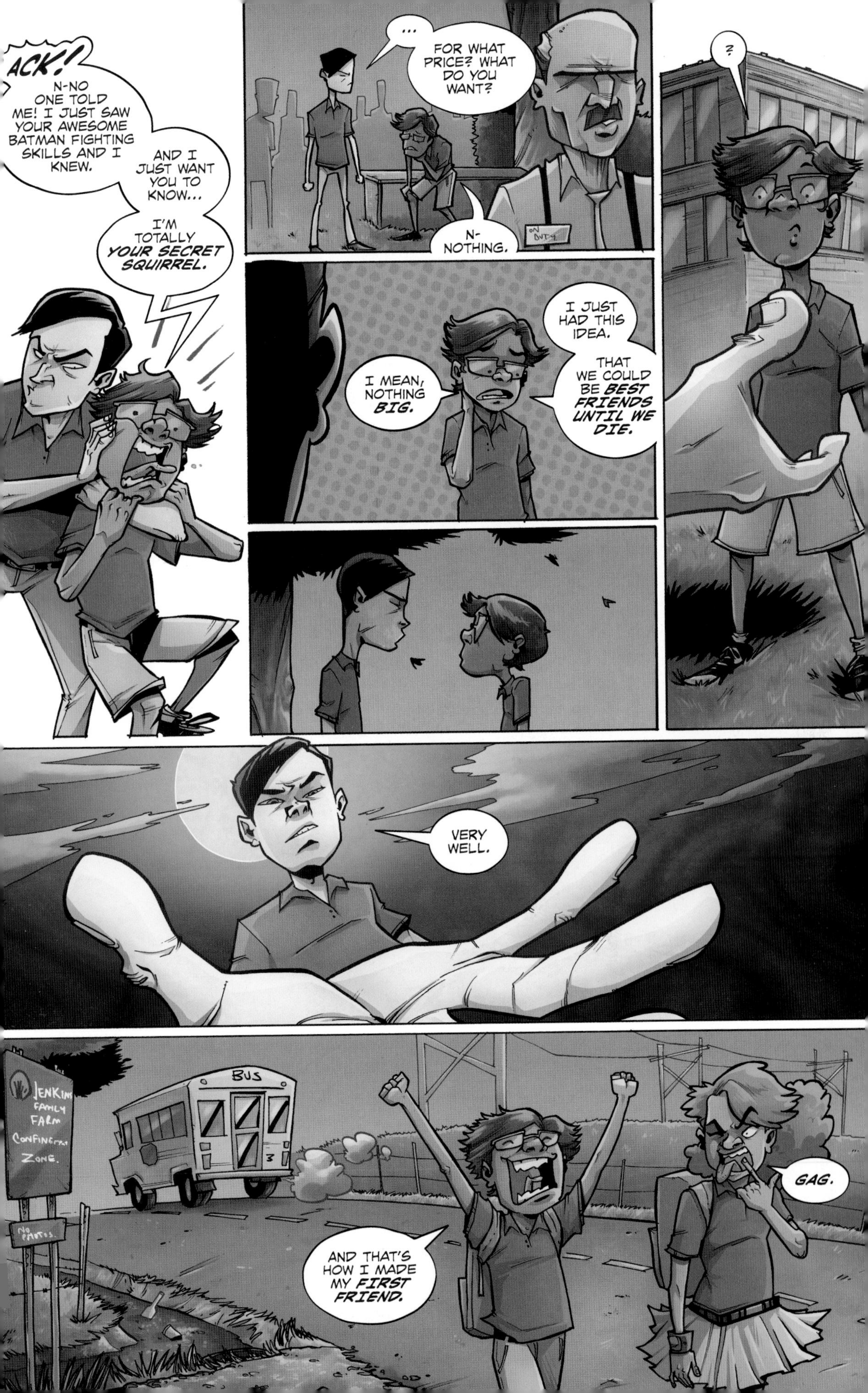
ACK!
N-NO ONE TOLD ME! I JUST SAW YOUR AWESOME BATMAN FIGHTING SKILLS AND I KNEW.
AND I JUST WANT YOU TO KNOW...
I'M TOTALLY *YOUR SECRET SQUIRREL.*
...
FOR WHAT PRICE? WHAT DO YOU WANT?
ON DUTY
N- NOTHING.
I MEAN, NOTHING *BIG.*
I JUST HAD THIS IDEA.
THAT WE COULD BE *BEST FRIENDS UNTIL WE DIE.*
?
VERY WELL.
JENKINS FAMILY FARM CONFINEMENT ZONE.
NO PHOTOS.
BUS
3
AND THAT'S HOW I MADE MY *FIRST FRIEND.*
GAG.

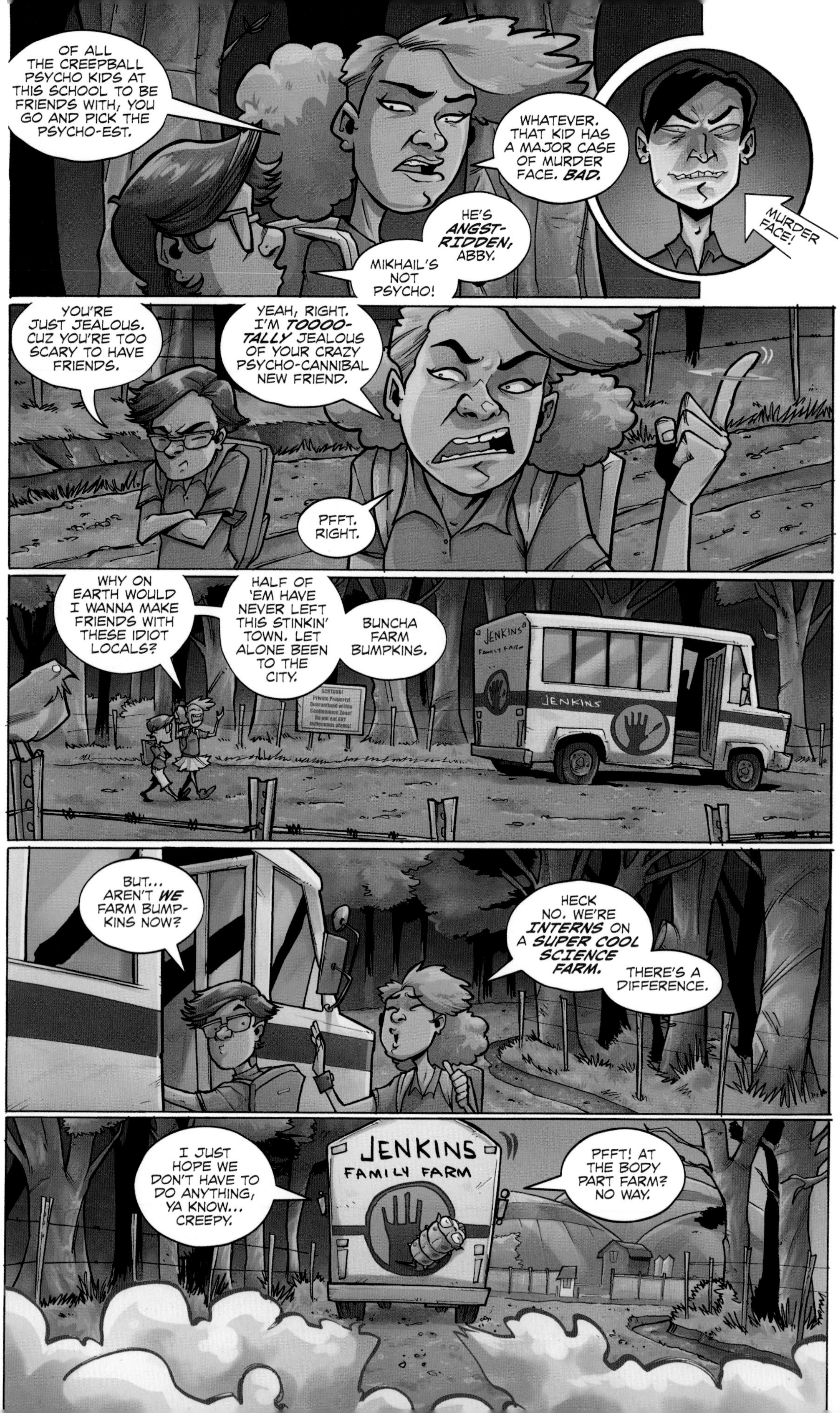
OF ALL THE CREEPBALL PSYCHO KIDS AT THIS SCHOOL TO BE FRIENDS WITH, YOU GO AND PICK THE PSYCHO-EST.
WHATEVER. THAT KID HAS A MAJOR CASE OF MURDER FACE. BAD.
MURDER FACE!
HE'S ANGST-RIDDEN, ABBY.
MIKHAIL'S NOT PSYCHO!
YOU'RE JUST JEALOUS. CUZ YOU'RE TOO SCARY TO HAVE FRIENDS.
YEAH, RIGHT. I'M TOOOO-TALLY JEALOUS OF YOUR CRAZY PSYCHO-CANNIBAL NEW FRIEND.
PFFT. RIGHT.
WHY ON EARTH WOULD I WANNA MAKE FRIENDS WITH THESE IDIOT LOCALS?
HALF OF 'EM HAVE NEVER LEFT THIS STINKIN' TOWN. LET ALONE BEEN TO THE CITY.
BUNCHA FARM BUMPKINS.
ACHTUNG! Private Property! Quarantined within Confinement Zone! Do not eat ANY indigenous plants!
JENKINS FAMILY FARM
JENKINS
BUT... AREN'T WE FARM BUMP-KINS NOW?
HECK NO. WE'RE INTERNS ON A SUPER COOL SCIENCE FARM.
THERE'S A DIFFERENCE.
I JUST HOPE WE DON'T HAVE TO DO ANYTHING, YA KNOW... CREEPY.
JENKINS FAMILY FARM
PFFT! AT THE BODY PART FARM? NO WAY.

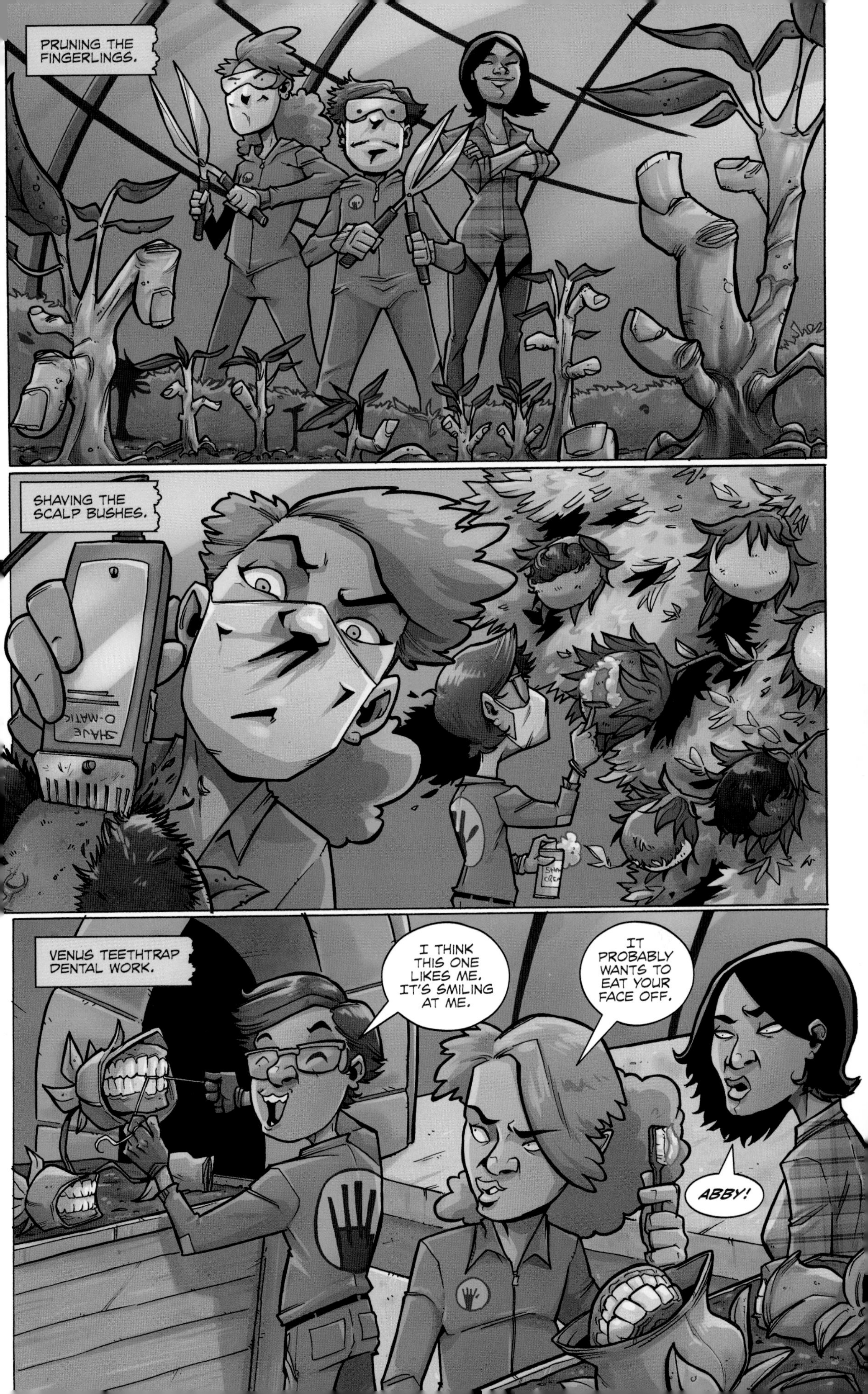
PRUNING THE FINGERLINGS.
SHAVING THE SCALP BUSHES.
SHAVE O-MATIC
VENUS TEETHTRAP DENTAL WORK.
I THINK THIS ONE LIKES ME. IT'S SMILING AT ME.
IT PROBABLY WANTS TO EAT YOUR FACE OFF.
ABBY!

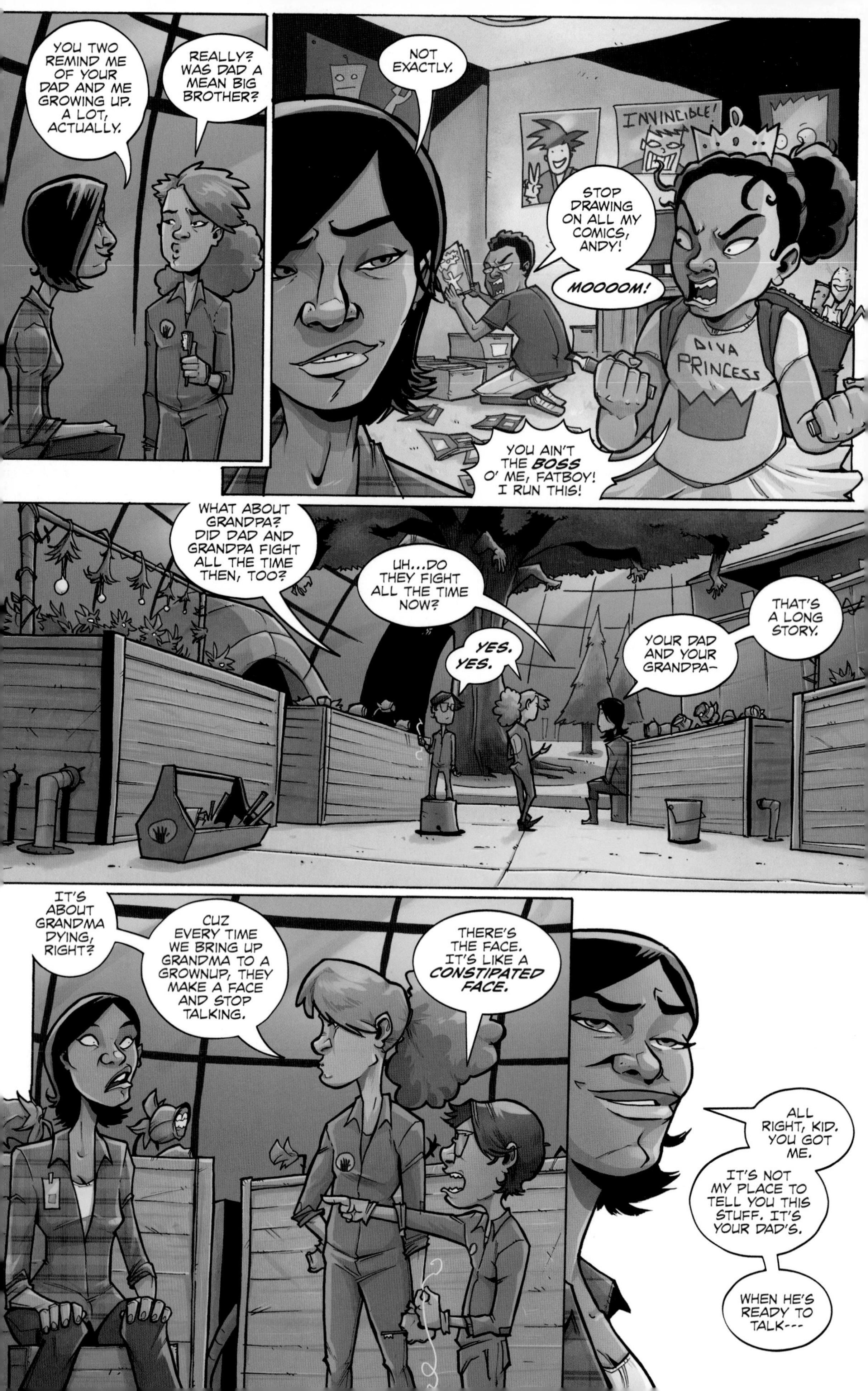
YOU TWO REMIND ME OF YOUR DAD AND ME GROWING UP. A LOT, ACTUALLY.
REALLY? WAS DAD A MEAN BIG BROTHER?
NOT EXACTLY.
INVINCIBLE!
STOP DRAWING ON ALL MY COMICS, ANDY!
MOOOOM!
DIVA PRINCESS
YOU AIN'T THE BOSS O' ME, FATBOY! I RUN THIS!
WHAT ABOUT GRANDPA? DID DAD AND GRANDPA FIGHT ALL THE TIME THEN, TOO?
UH...DO THEY FIGHT ALL THE TIME NOW?
YES. YES.
YOUR DAD AND YOUR GRANDPA–
THAT'S A LONG STORY.
IT'S ABOUT GRANDMA DYING, RIGHT?
CUZ EVERY TIME WE BRING UP GRANDMA TO A GROWNUP, THEY MAKE A FACE AND STOP TALKING.
THERE'S THE FACE. IT'S LIKE A CONSTIPATED FACE.
ALL RIGHT, KID. YOU GOT ME.
IT'S NOT MY PLACE TO TELL YOU THIS STUFF. IT'S YOUR DAD'S.
WHEN HE'S READY TO TALK---

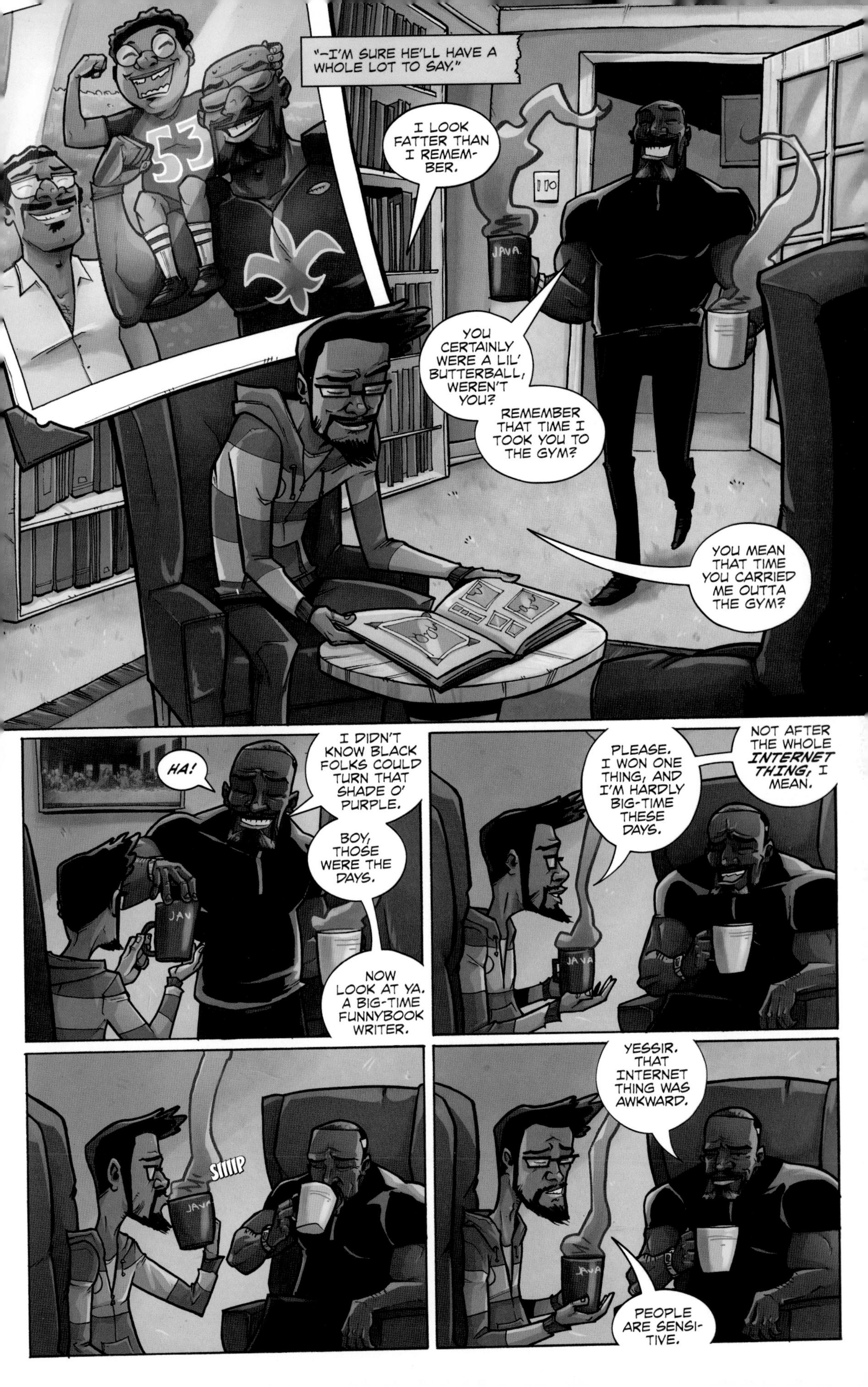
"–I'M SURE HE'LL HAVE A WHOLE LOT TO SAY."
I LOOK FATTER THAN I REMEMBER.
YOU CERTAINLY WERE A LIL' BUTTERBALL, WEREN'T YOU?
REMEMBER THAT TIME I TOOK YOU TO THE GYM?
YOU MEAN THAT TIME YOU CARRIED ME OUTTA THE GYM?
JAVA.
HA!
I DIDN'T KNOW BLACK FOLKS COULD TURN THAT SHADE O' PURPLE.
BOY, THOSE WERE THE DAYS.
NOW LOOK AT YA. A BIG-TIME FUNNYBOOK WRITER.
PLEASE. I WON ONE THING, AND I'M HARDLY BIG-TIME THESE DAYS.
NOT AFTER THE WHOLE *INTERNET THING,* I MEAN.
SIIIIP
YESSIR. THAT INTERNET THING WAS AWKWARD.
PEOPLE ARE SENSITIVE.

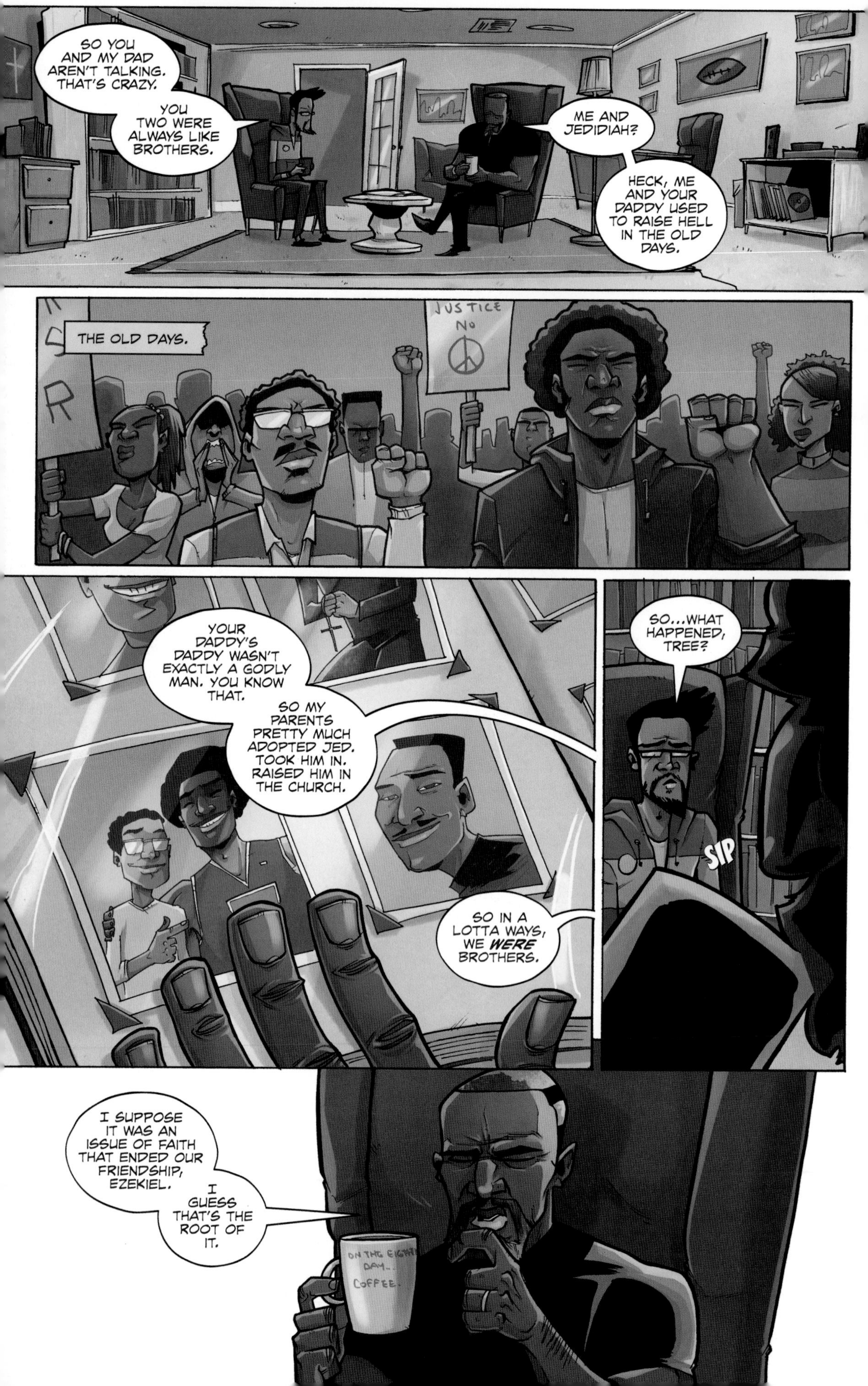
SO YOU AND MY DAD AREN'T TALKING. THAT'S CRAZY.
YOU TWO WERE ALWAYS LIKE BROTHERS.
ME AND JEDIDIAH?
HECK, ME AND YOUR DADDY USED TO RAISE HELL IN THE OLD DAYS.
THE OLD DAYS.
JUSTICE NO
YOUR DADDY'S DADDY WASN'T EXACTLY A GODLY MAN. YOU KNOW THAT.
SO MY PARENTS PRETTY MUCH ADOPTED JED. TOOK HIM IN. RAISED HIM IN THE CHURCH.
SO IN A LOTTA WAYS, WE ***WERE*** BROTHERS.
SO...WHAT HAPPENED, TREE?
SIP
I SUPPOSE IT WAS AN ISSUE OF FAITH THAT ENDED OUR FRIENDSHIP, EZEKIEL.
I GUESS THAT'S THE ROOT OF IT.
ON THE EIGHTH DAY.. COFFEE.

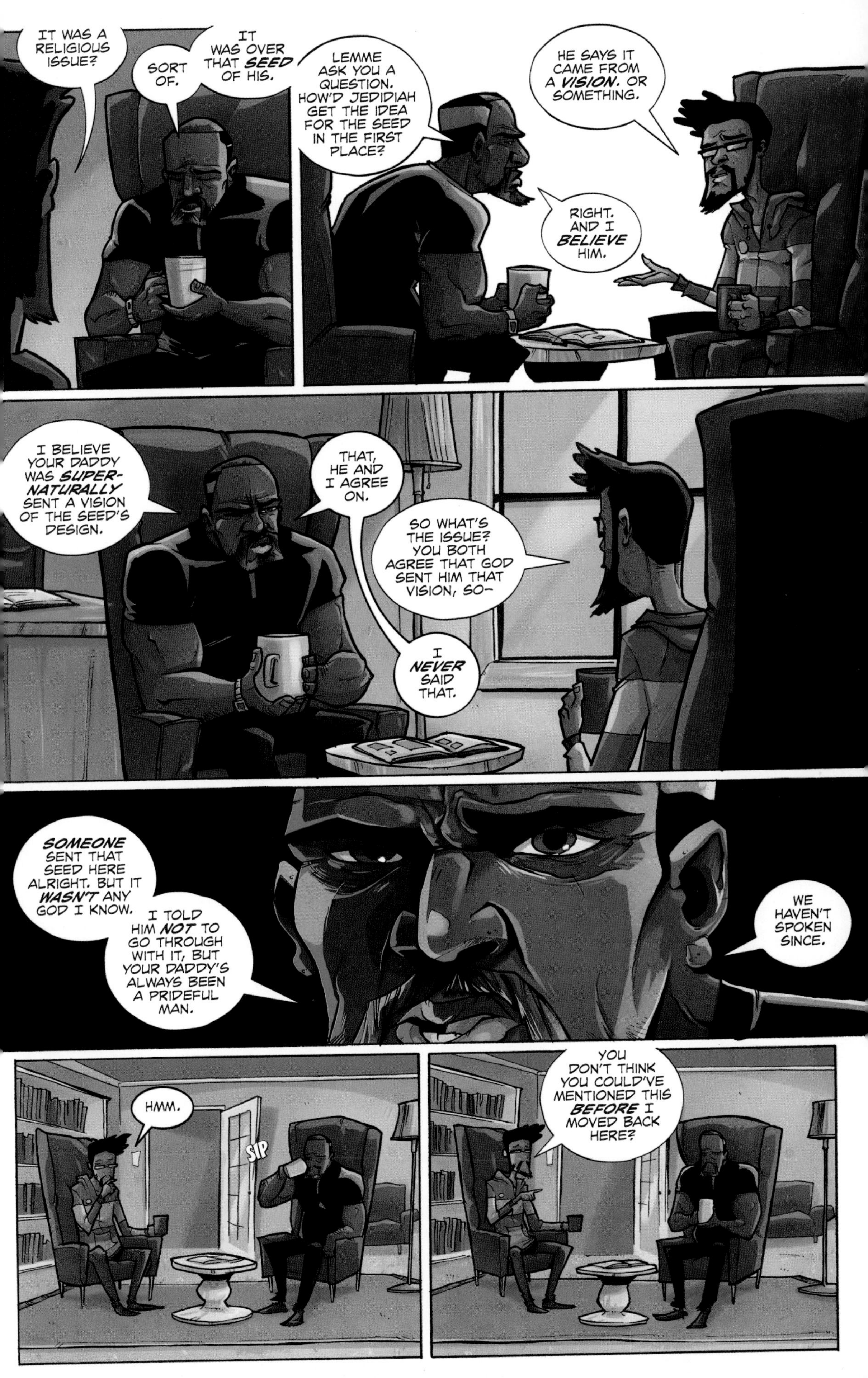
IT WAS A RELIGIOUS ISSUE?
SORT OF.
IT WAS OVER THAT SEED OF HIS.
LEMME ASK YOU A QUESTION. HOW'D JEDIDIAH GET THE IDEA FOR THE SEED IN THE FIRST PLACE?
HE SAYS IT CAME FROM A VISION. OR SOMETHING.
RIGHT. AND I BELIEVE HIM.
I BELIEVE YOUR DADDY WAS SUPER-NATURALLY SENT A VISION OF THE SEED'S DESIGN.
THAT, HE AND I AGREE ON.
SO WHAT'S THE ISSUE? YOU BOTH AGREE THAT GOD SENT HIM THAT VISION, SO–
I NEVER SAID THAT.
SOMEONE SENT THAT SEED HERE ALRIGHT. BUT IT WASN'T ANY GOD I KNOW.
I TOLD HIM NOT TO GO THROUGH WITH IT, BUT YOUR DADDY'S ALWAYS BEEN A PRIDEFUL MAN.
WE HAVEN'T SPOKEN SINCE.
HMM.
SIP
YOU DON'T THINK YOU COULD'VE MENTIONED THIS BEFORE I MOVED BACK HERE?

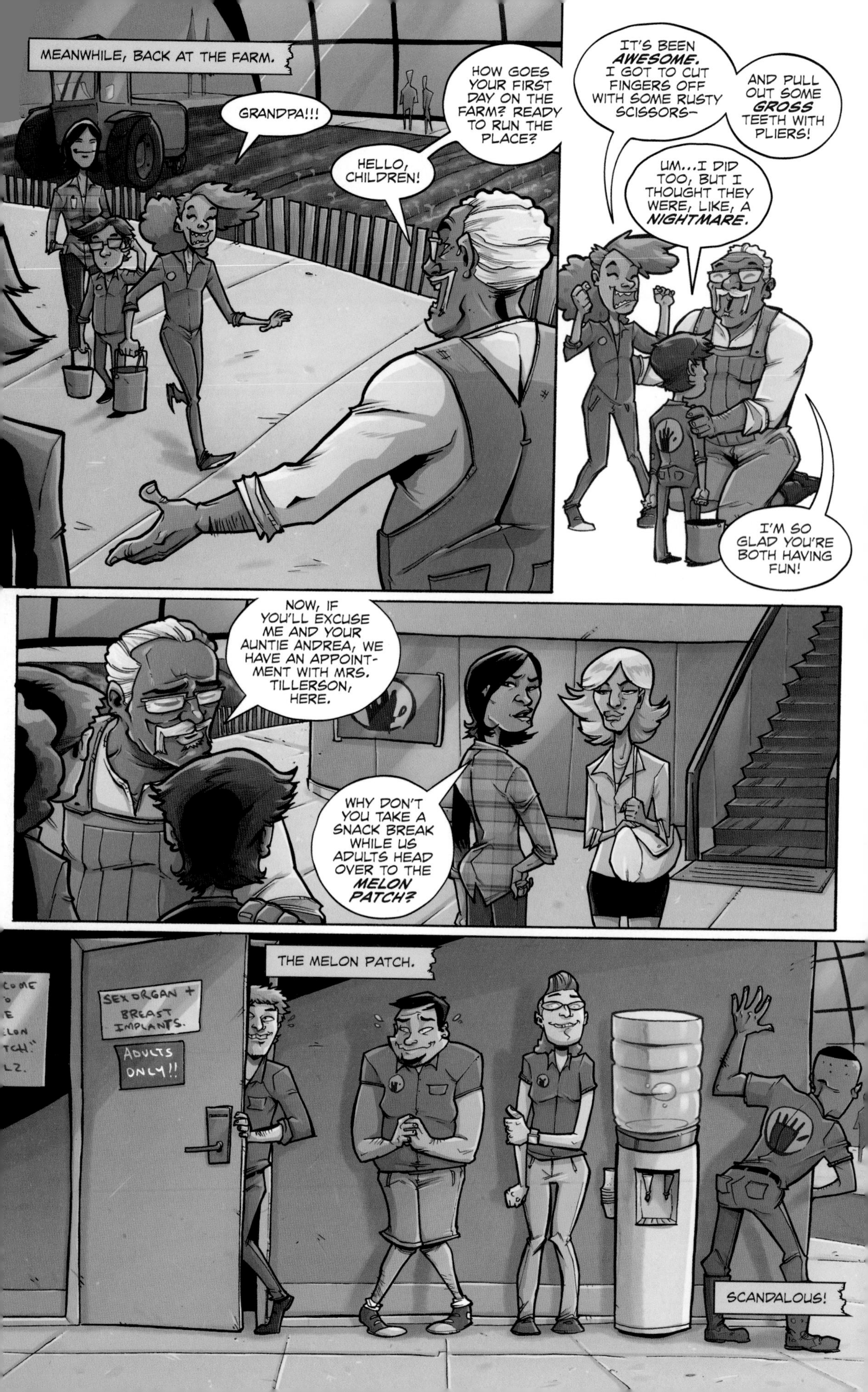
MEANWHILE, BACK AT THE FARM.
GRANDPA!!!
HELLO, CHILDREN!
HOW GOES YOUR FIRST DAY ON THE FARM? READY TO RUN THE PLACE?
IT'S BEEN AWESOME. I GOT TO CUT FINGERS OFF WITH SOME RUSTY SCISSORS—
AND PULL OUT SOME GROSS TEETH WITH PLIERS!
UM...I DID TOO, BUT I THOUGHT THEY WERE, LIKE, A NIGHTMARE.
I'M SO GLAD YOU'RE BOTH HAVING FUN!
NOW, IF YOU'LL EXCUSE ME AND YOUR AUNTIE ANDREA, WE HAVE AN APPOINTMENT WITH MRS. TILLERSON, HERE.
WHY DON'T YOU TAKE A SNACK BREAK WHILE US ADULTS HEAD OVER TO THE MELON PATCH?
THE MELON PATCH.
SEX ORGAN + BREAST IMPLANTS.
ADULTS ONLY!!
SCANDALOUS!

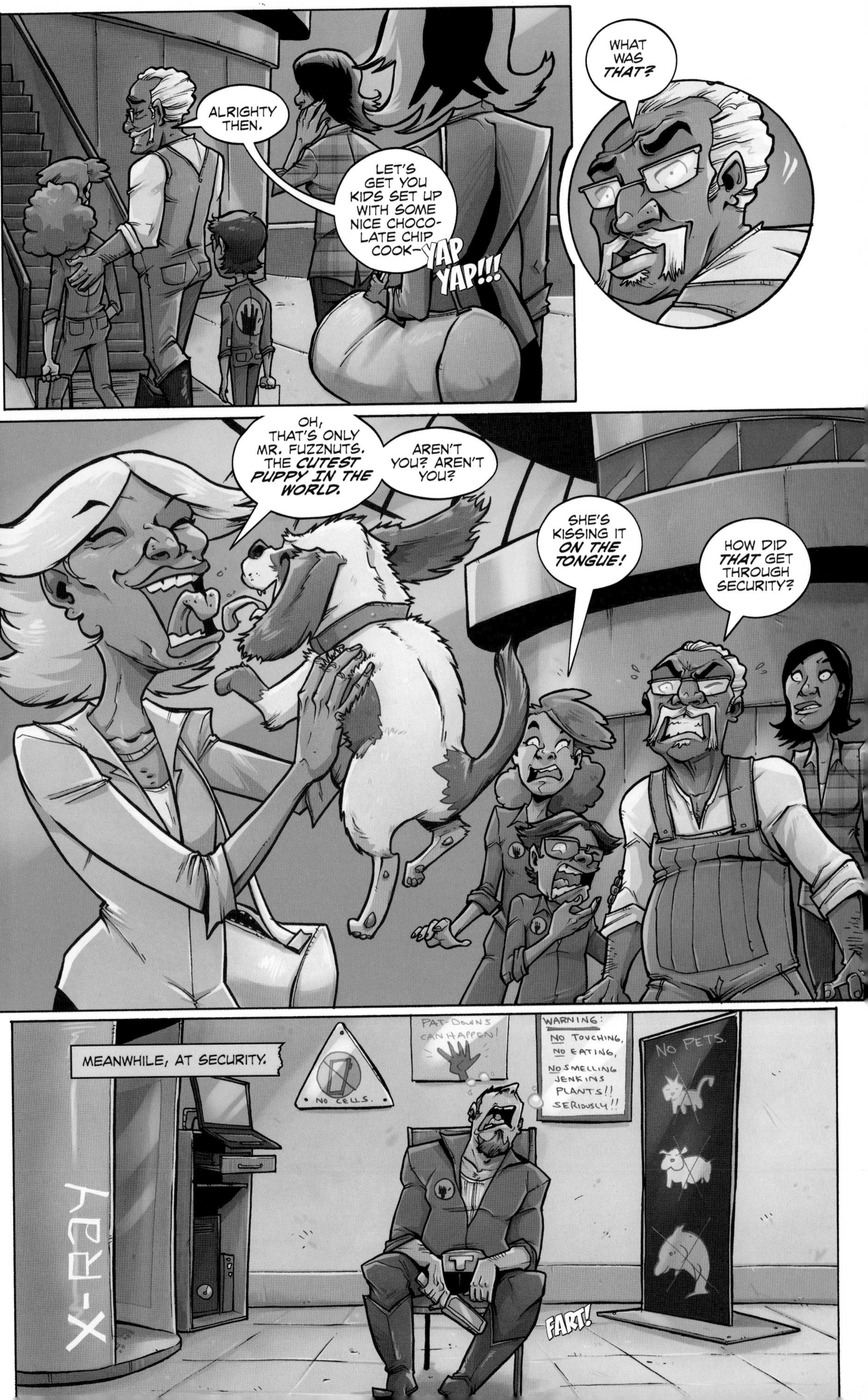
ALRIGHTY THEN.
LET'S GET YOU KIDS SET UP WITH SOME NICE CHOCO-LATE CHIP COOK–
YAP YAP!!!
WHAT WAS *THAT?*
OH, THAT'S ONLY MR. FUZZNUTS. THE *CUTEST PUPPY IN THE WORLD.*
AREN'T YOU? AREN'T YOU?
SHE'S KISSING IT *ON THE TONGUE!*
HOW DID *THAT* GET THROUGH SECURITY?
MEANWHILE, AT SECURITY.
NO CELLS.
PAT-DOWNS CAN HAPPEN!
WARNING: NO TOUCHING, NO EATING, NO SMELLING JENKINS PLANTS!! SERIOUSLY!!
NO PETS.
X-RAY
FART!

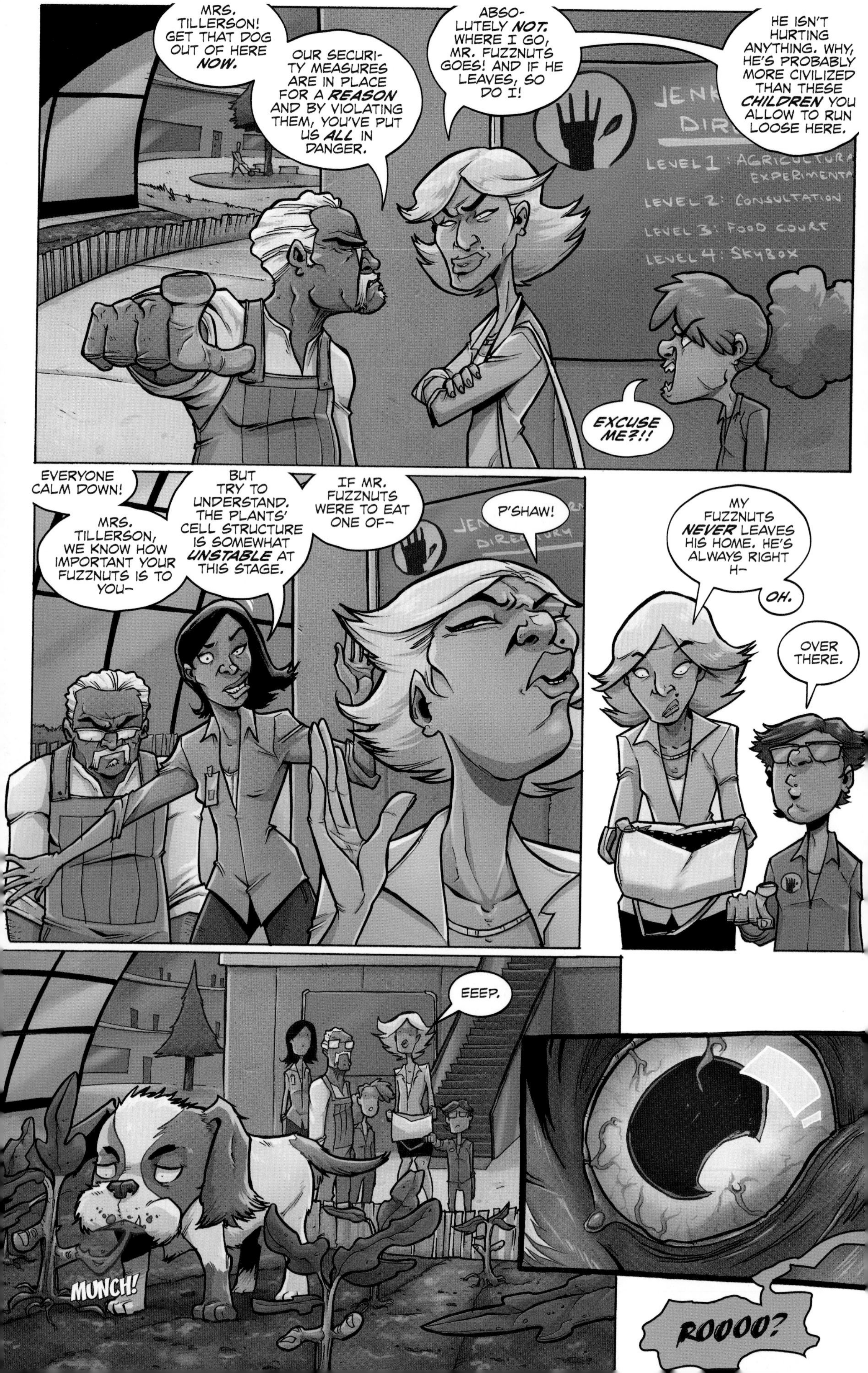
MRS. TILLERSON! GET THAT DOG OUT OF HERE NOW.
OUR SECURITY MEASURES ARE IN PLACE FOR A REASON AND BY VIOLATING THEM, YOU'VE PUT US ALL IN DANGER.
ABSOLUTELY NOT. WHERE I GO, MR. FUZZNUTS GOES! AND IF HE LEAVES, SO DO I!
HE ISN'T HURTING ANYTHING. WHY, HE'S PROBABLY MORE CIVILIZED THAN THESE CHILDREN YOU ALLOW TO RUN LOOSE HERE.
LEVEL 1: AGRICULTURA EXPERIMENTA
LEVEL 2: CONSULTATION
LEVEL 3: FOOD COURT
LEVEL 4: SKYBOX
EXCUSE ME?!!
EVERYONE CALM DOWN!
MRS. TILLERSON, WE KNOW HOW IMPORTANT YOUR FUZZNUTS IS TO YOU-
BUT TRY TO UNDERSTAND. THE PLANTS' CELL STRUCTURE IS SOMEWHAT UNSTABLE AT THIS STAGE.
IF MR. FUZZNUTS WERE TO EAT ONE OF-
P'SHAW!
MY FUZZNUTS NEVER LEAVES HIS HOME. HE'S ALWAYS RIGHT H-
OH.
OVER THERE.
EEEP.
MUNCH!
ROOOO?

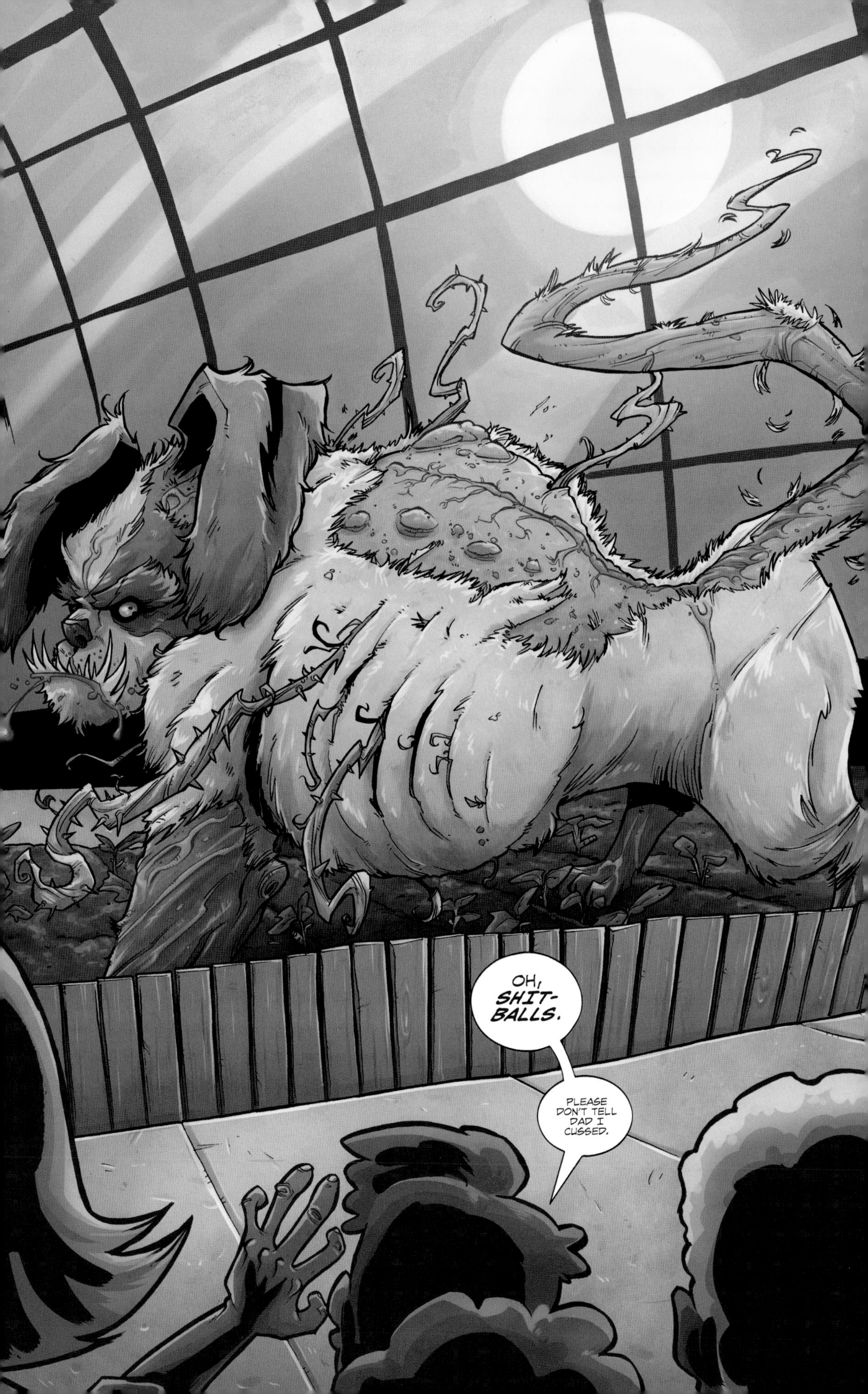
OH, SHIT-BALLS.
PLEASE DON'T TELL DAD I CUSSED.

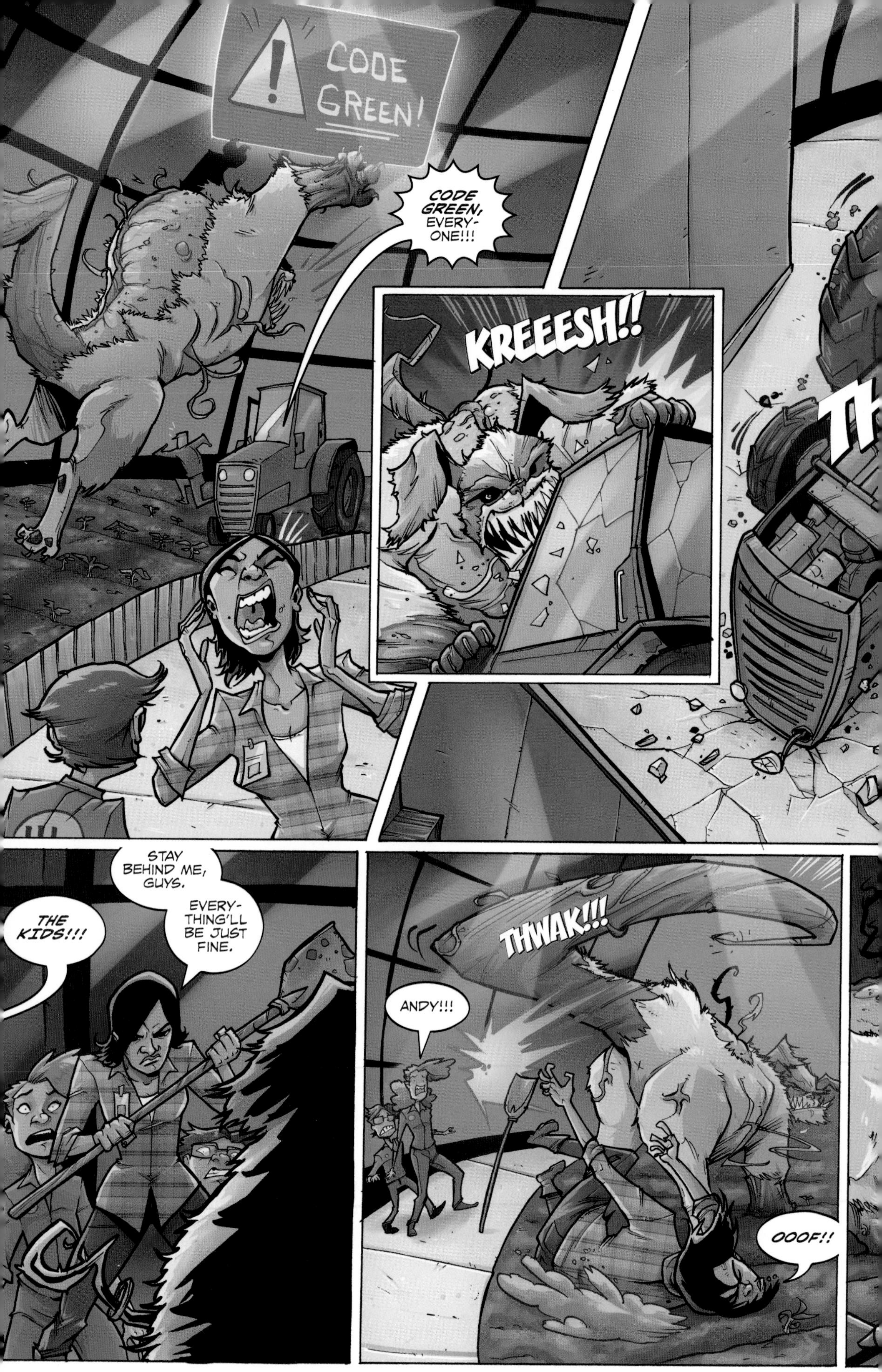
CODE GREEN!
CODE GREEN, EVERY-ONE!!!
KREEESH!!
STAY BEHIND ME, GUYS.
EVERY-THING'LL BE JUST FINE.
THE KIDS!!!
THWAK!!!
ANDY!!!
OOOF!!

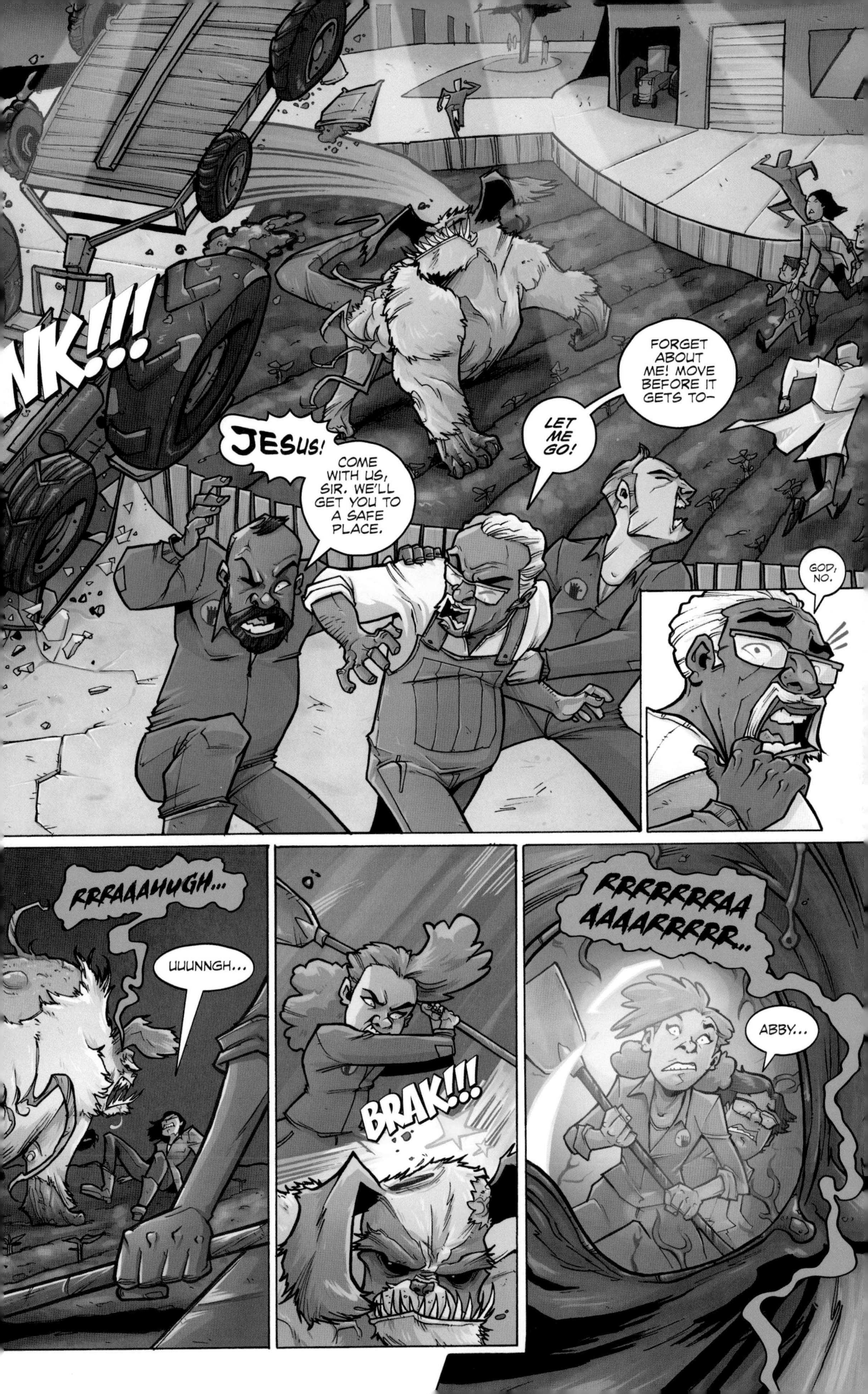
NK!!!
JESUS!
COME WITH US, SIR. WE'LL GET YOU TO A SAFE PLACE.
LET ME GO!
FORGET ABOUT ME! MOVE BEFORE IT GETS TO–
GOD, NO.
RRRAAAHUGH...
UUUNNGH...
BRAK!!!
RRRRRRRAA AAAARRRRR...
ABBY...

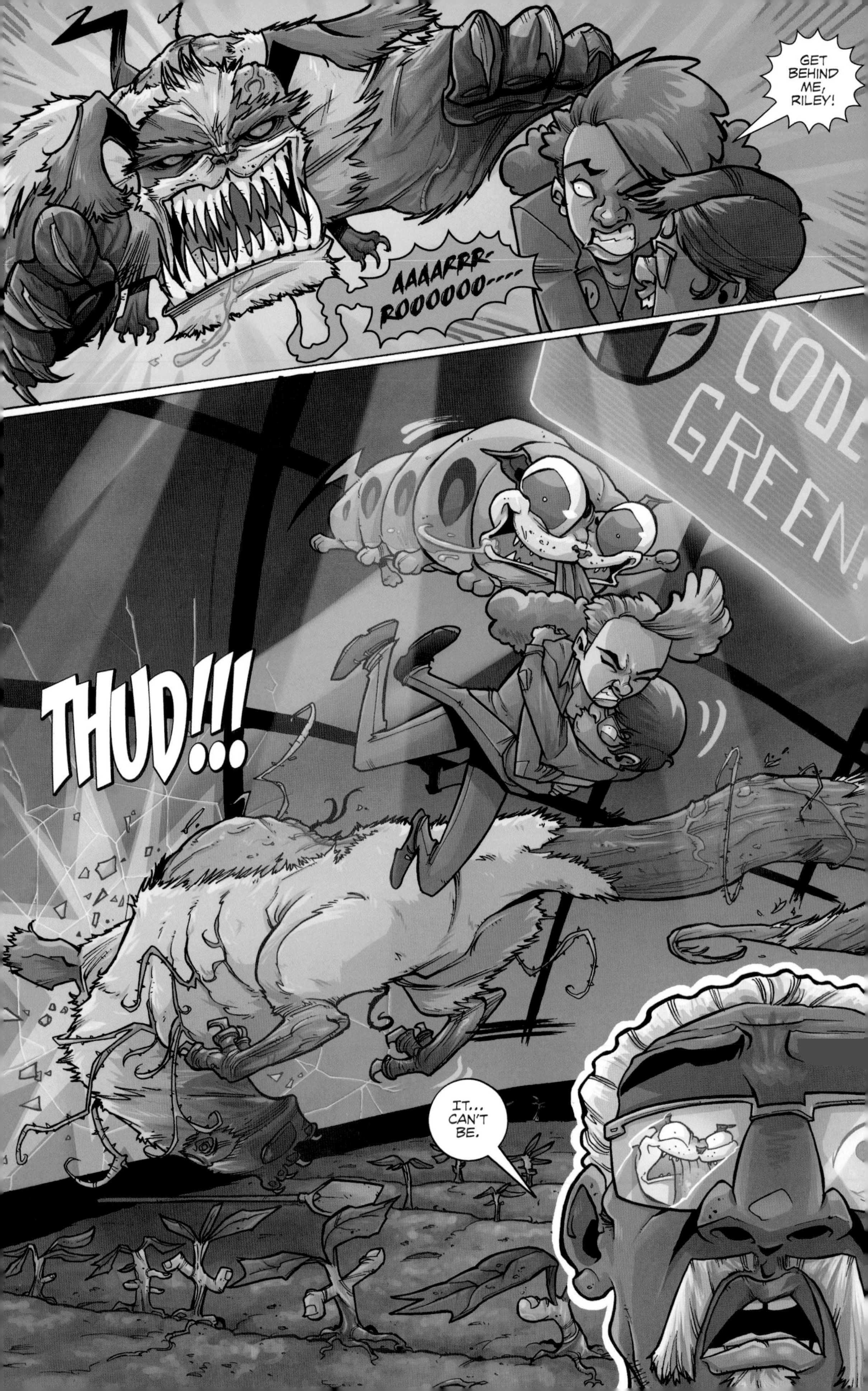
AAAARRR-ROOOOOO----
GET BEHIND ME, RILEY!
CODE GREEN
THUD!!!
IT... CAN'T BE.

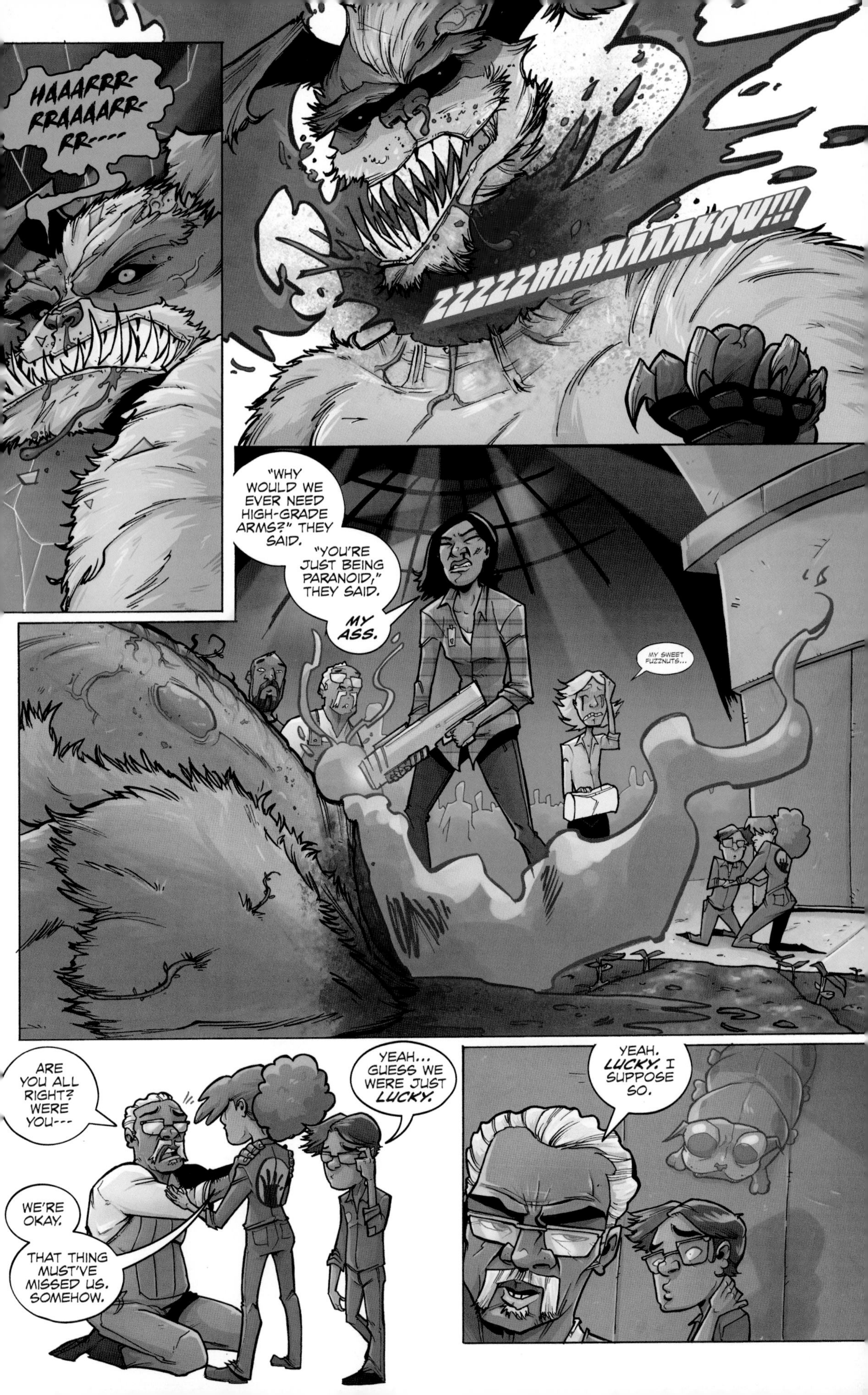
HAAARRR-RRAAAARR-RR----
ZZZZZRRRAAAAAKOW!!!
"WHY WOULD WE EVER NEED HIGH-GRADE ARMS?" THEY SAID.
"YOU'RE JUST BEING PARANOID," THEY SAID.
MY ASS.
MY SWEET FUZZNUTS...
ARE YOU ALL RIGHT? WERE YOU---
YEAH... GUESS WE WERE JUST LUCKY.
WE'RE OKAY.
THAT THING MUST'VE MISSED US. SOMEHOW.
YEAH. LUCKY. I SUPPOSE SO.

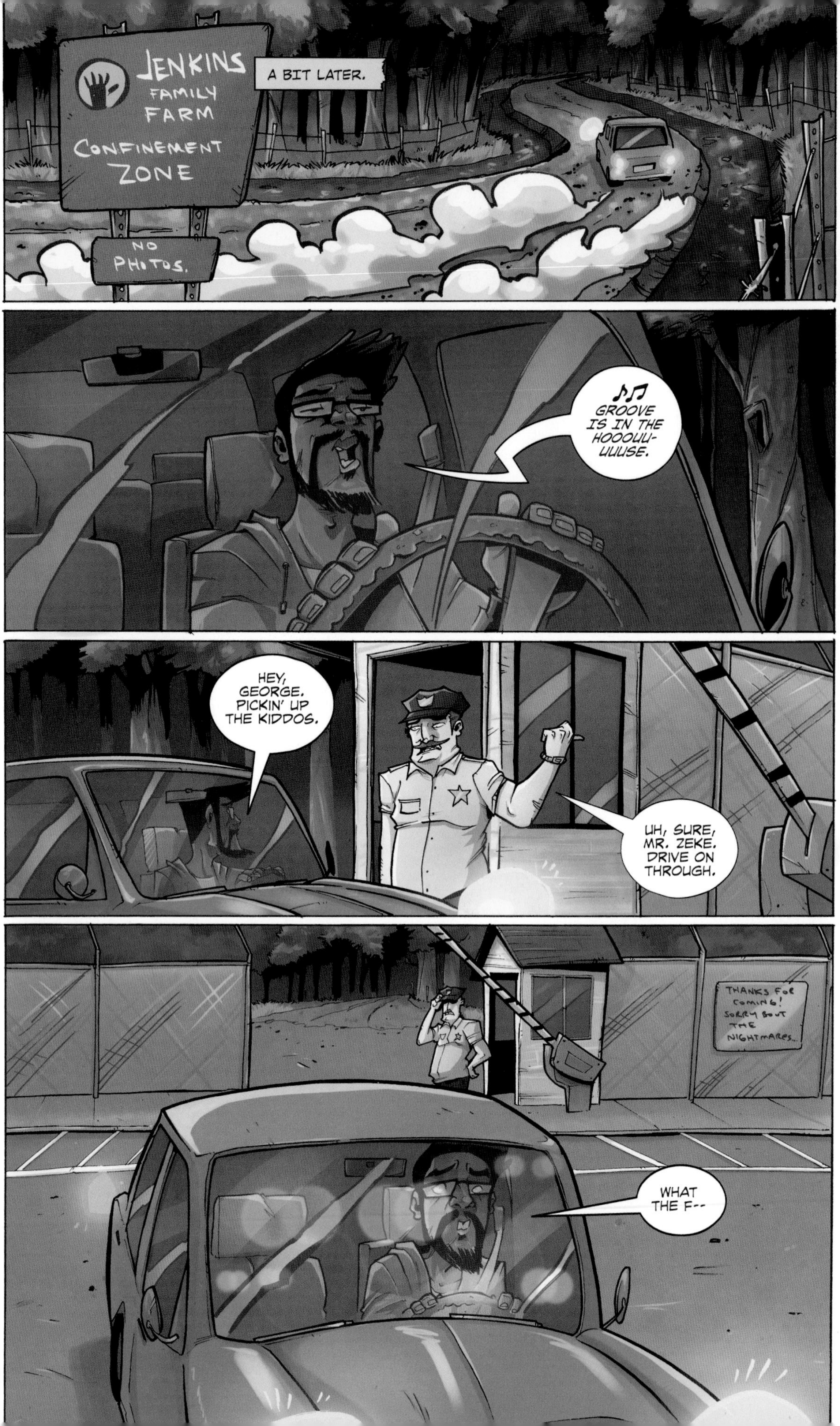
JENKINS FAMILY FARM CONFINEMENT ZONE
NO PHOTOS.
A BIT LATER.
♪♫ GROOVE IS IN THE HOOOUU-UUUSE.
HEY, GEORGE. PICKIN' UP THE KIDDOS.
UH, SURE, MR. ZEKE. DRIVE ON THROUGH.
THANKS FOR COMING! SORRY BOUT THE NIGHTMARES...
WHAT THE F--

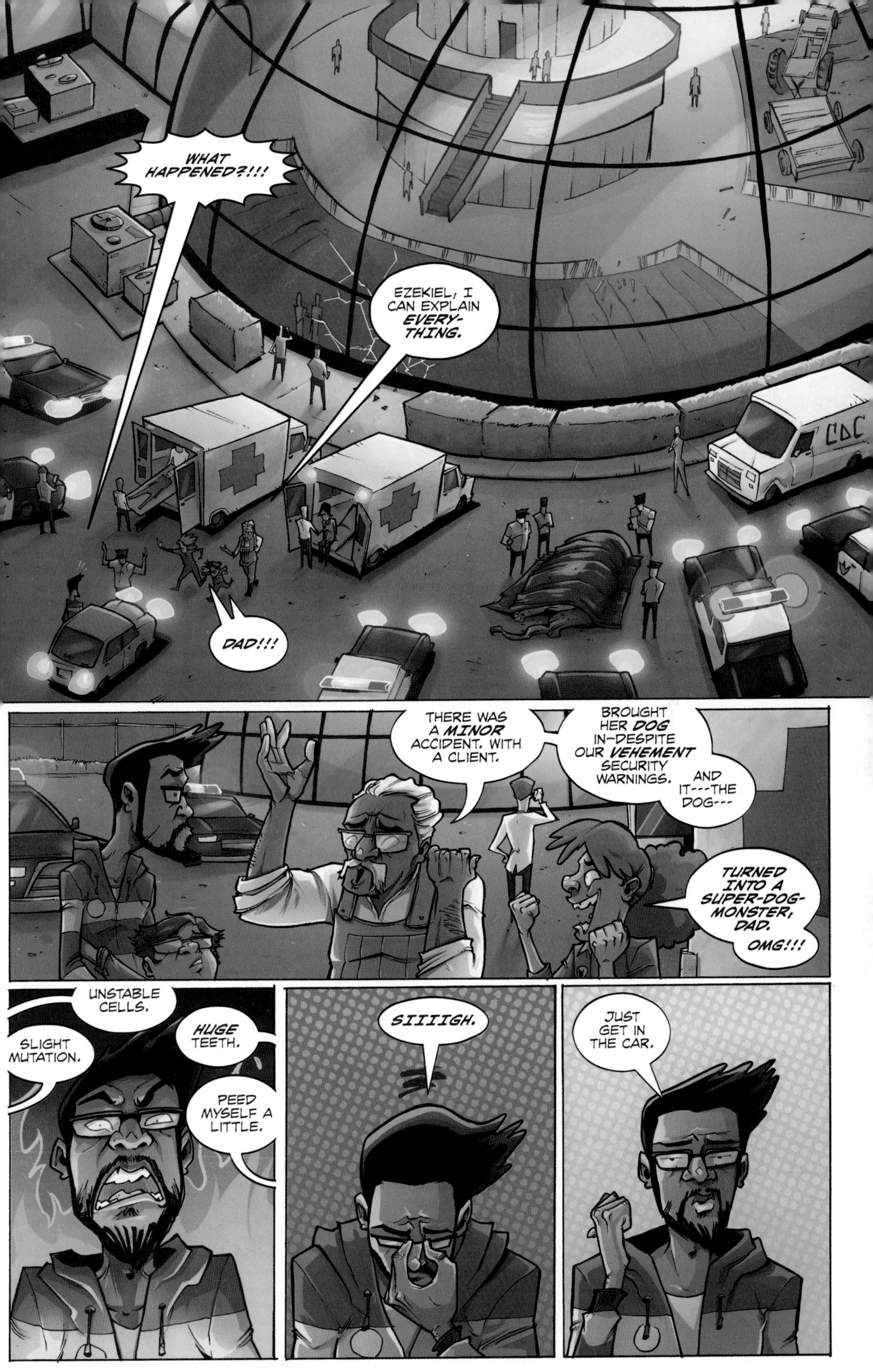
WHAT HAPPENED?!!!
EZEKIEL, I CAN EXPLAIN EVERY-THING.
DAD!!!
CDC
THERE WAS A MINOR ACCIDENT. WITH A CLIENT.
BROUGHT HER DOG IN-DESPITE OUR VEHEMENT SECURITY WARNINGS.
AND IT---THE DOG---
TURNED INTO A SUPER-DOG-MONSTER, DAD.
OMG!!!
UNSTABLE CELLS.
SLIGHT MUTATION.
HUGE TEETH.
PEED MYSELF A LITTLE.
SIIIIGH.
JUST GET IN THE CAR.

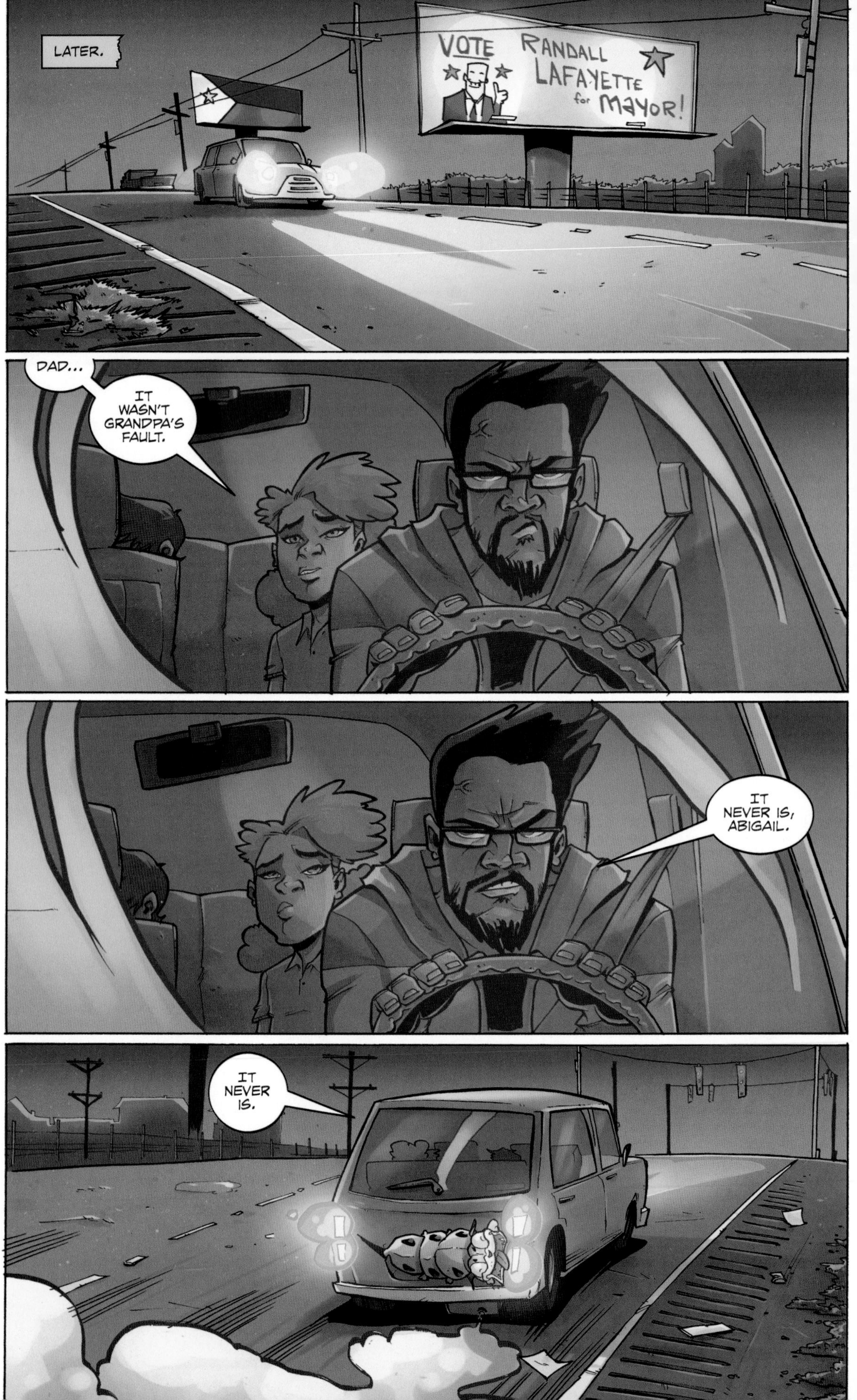
LATER.
VOTE RANDALL LAFAYETTE for MAYOR!
DAD...
IT WASN'T GRANDPA'S FAULT.
IT NEVER IS, ABIGAIL.
IT NEVER IS.

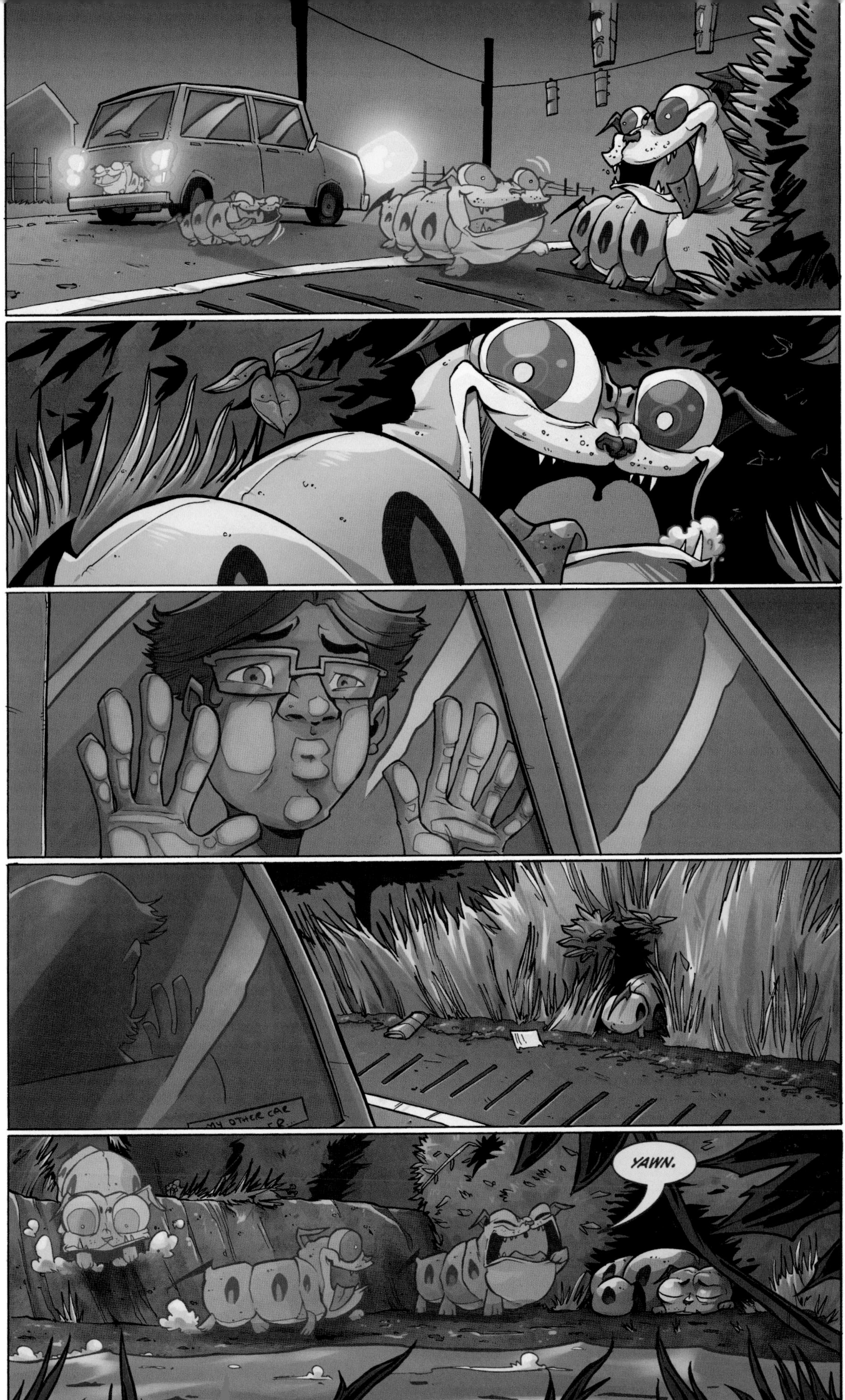
MY OTHER CAR
YAWN.

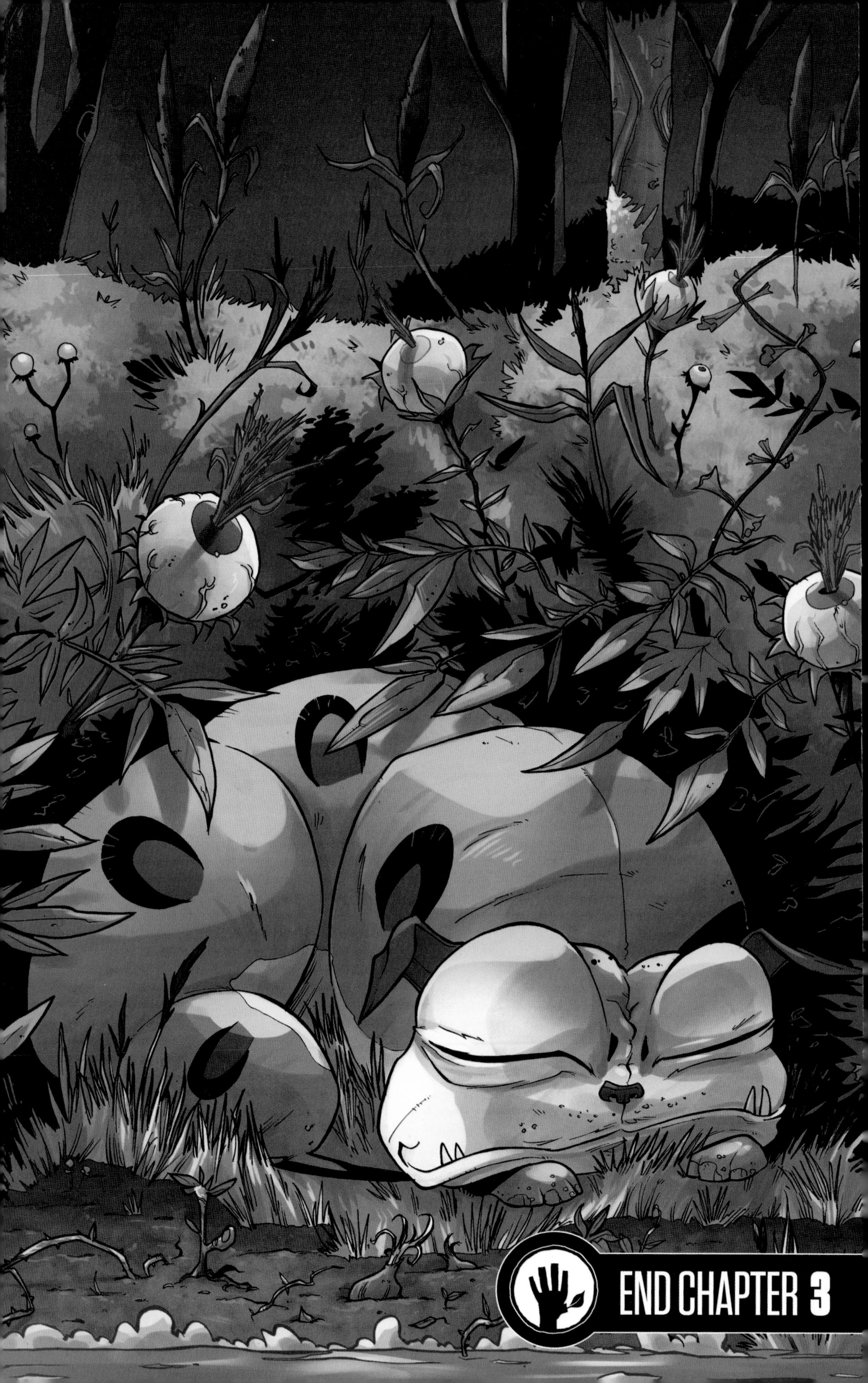
END CHAPTER 3

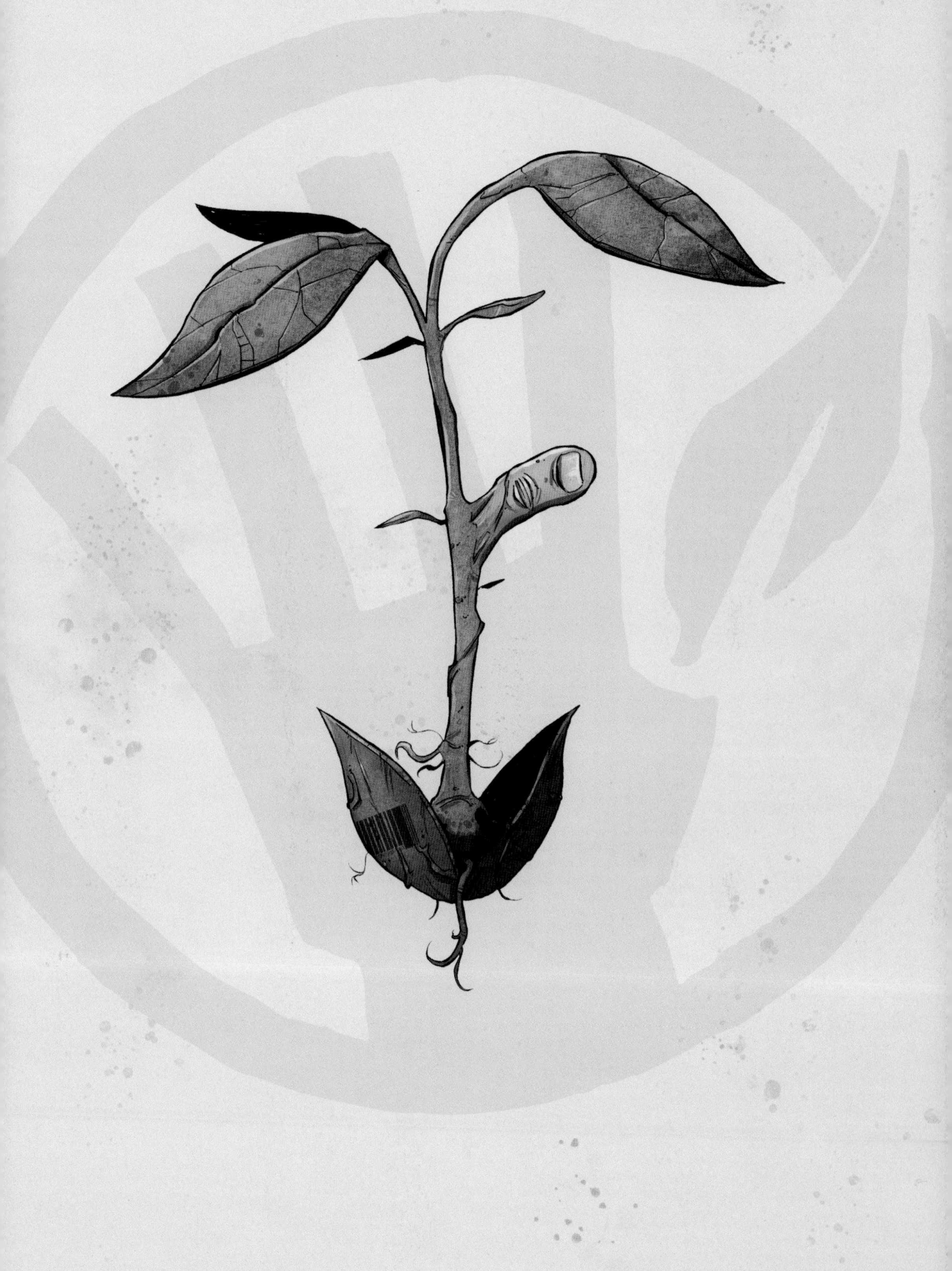

CHAPTER 4

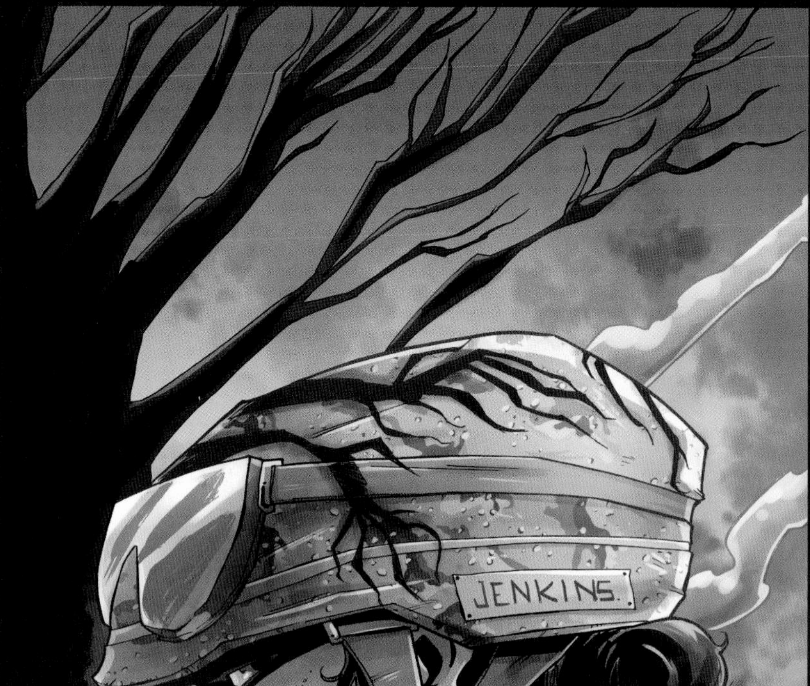

JENKINS.

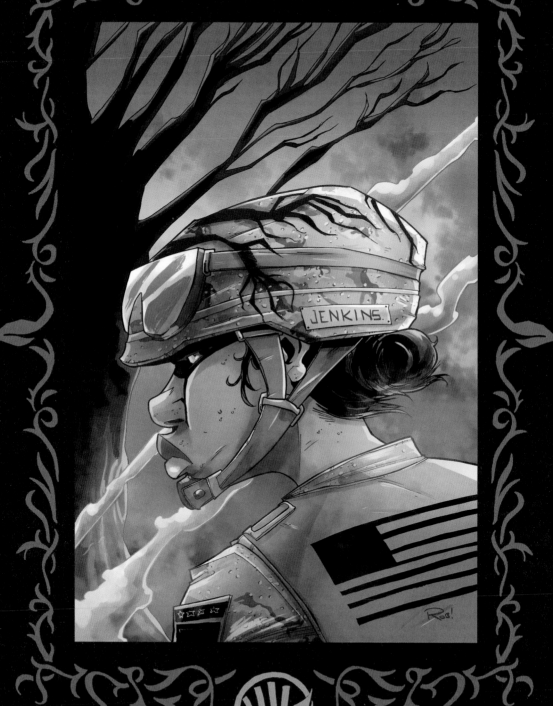

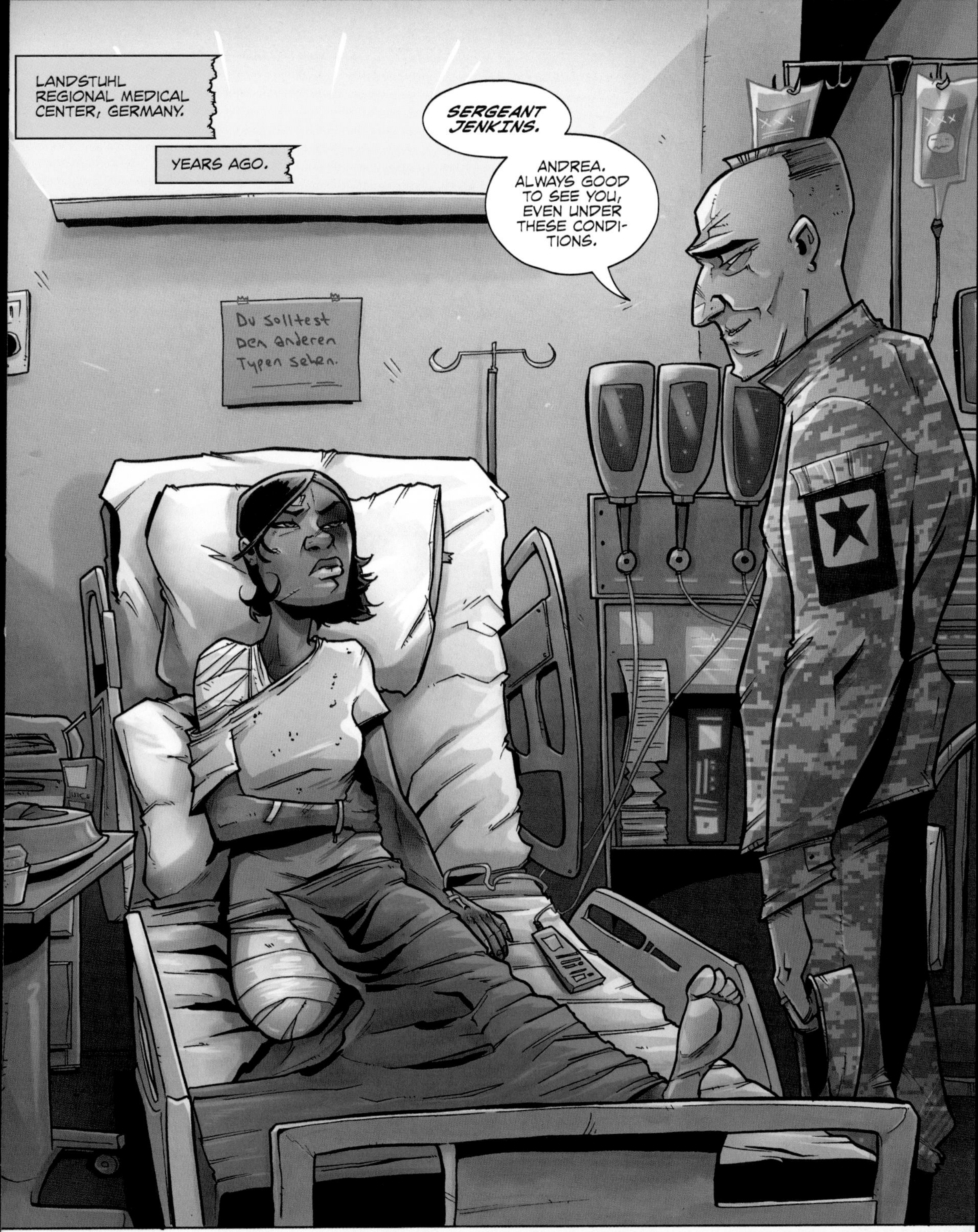
LANDSTUHL REGIONAL MEDICAL CENTER, GERMANY.
YEARS AGO.
SERGEANT JENKINS.
ANDREA. ALWAYS GOOD TO SEE YOU, EVEN UNDER THESE CONDI-TIONS.
Du solltest Den anderen Typen sehen.

CHAPTER 4: **Between Worlds.**

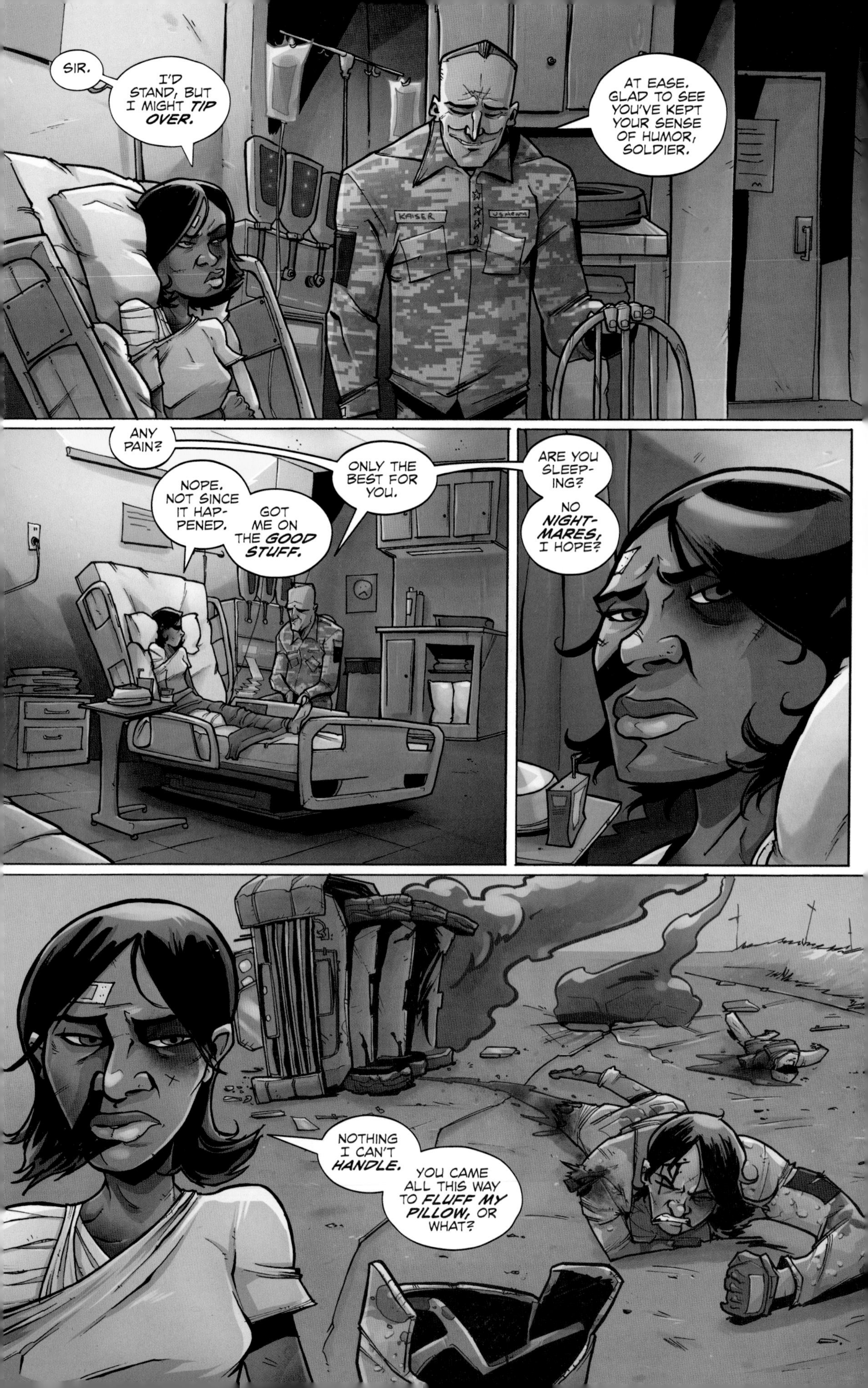

SIR.
I'D STAND, BUT I MIGHT TIP OVER.
AT EASE. GLAD TO SEE YOU'VE KEPT YOUR SENSE OF HUMOR, SOLDIER.
KAISER
U.S. ARMY
ANY PAIN?
NOPE. NOT SINCE IT HAP-PENED.
GOT ME ON THE GOOD STUFF.
ONLY THE BEST FOR YOU.
ARE YOU SLEEP-ING?
NO NIGHT-MARES, I HOPE?
NOTHING I CAN'T HANDLE.
YOU CAME ALL THIS WAY TO FLUFF MY PILLOW, OR WHAT?

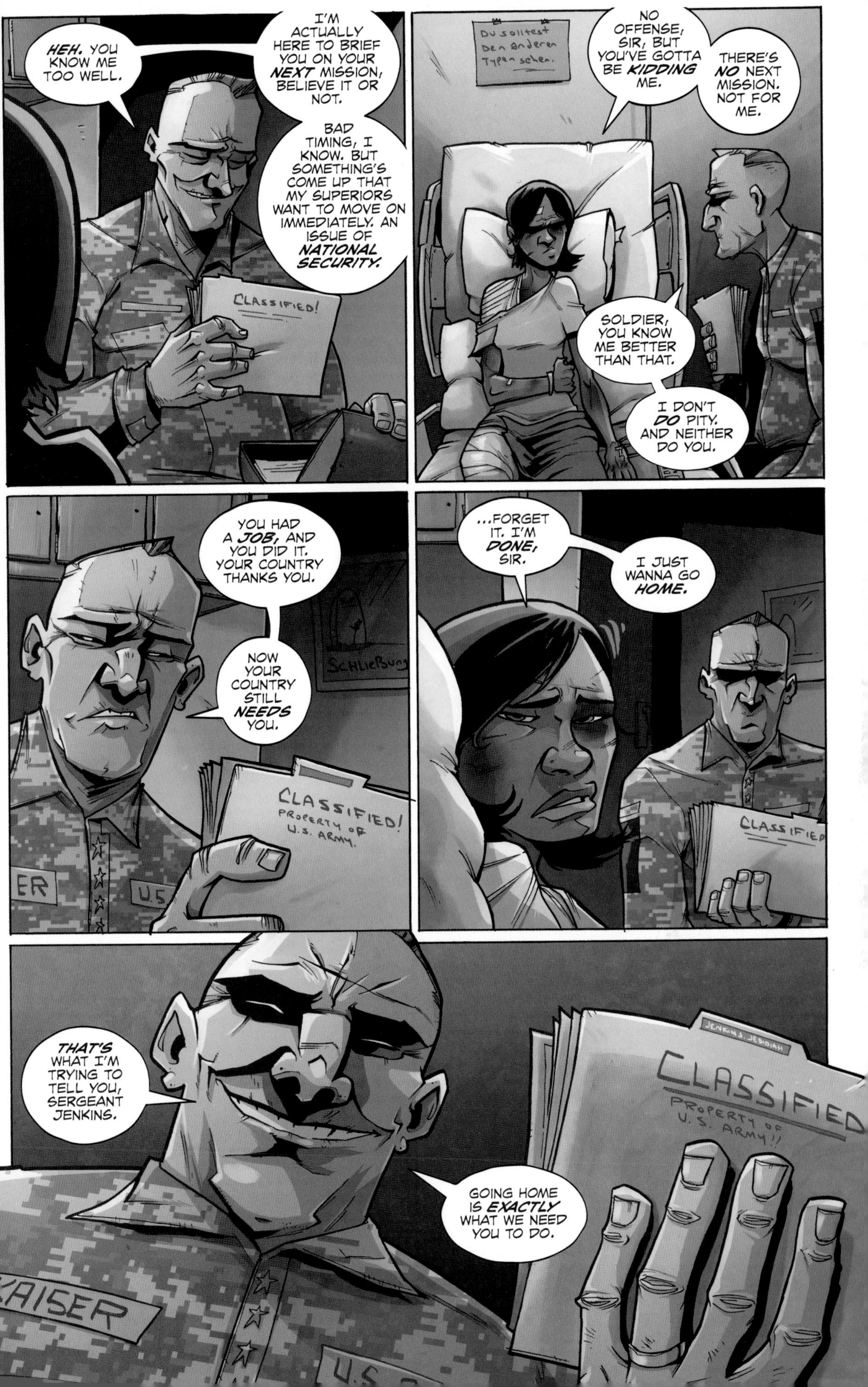

HEH. YOU KNOW ME TOO WELL.
I'M ACTUALLY HERE TO BRIEF YOU ON YOUR NEXT MISSION, BELIEVE IT OR NOT.
BAD TIMING, I KNOW. BUT SOMETHING'S COME UP THAT MY SUPERIORS WANT TO MOVE ON IMMEDIATELY. AN ISSUE OF NATIONAL SECURITY.
CLASSIFIED!
Du solltest Den anderen Typen sehen.
NO OFFENSE, SIR, BUT YOU'VE GOTTA BE KIDDING ME.
THERE'S NO NEXT MISSION. NOT FOR ME.
SOLDIER, YOU KNOW ME BETTER THAN THAT.
I DON'T DO PITY. AND NEITHER DO YOU.
YOU HAD A JOB, AND YOU DID IT. YOUR COUNTRY THANKS YOU.
NOW YOUR COUNTRY STILL NEEDS YOU.
SCHLIEBUNG
CLASSIFIED! PROPERTY OF U.S. ARMY.
...FORGET IT. I'M DONE, SIR.
I JUST WANNA GO HOME.
CLASSIFIED
THAT'S WHAT I'M TRYING TO TELL YOU, SERGEANT JENKINS.
JENKINS, JEDIDIAH
CLASSIFIED PROPERTY OF U.S. ARMY!!
GOING HOME IS EXACTLY WHAT WE NEED YOU TO DO.
KAISER

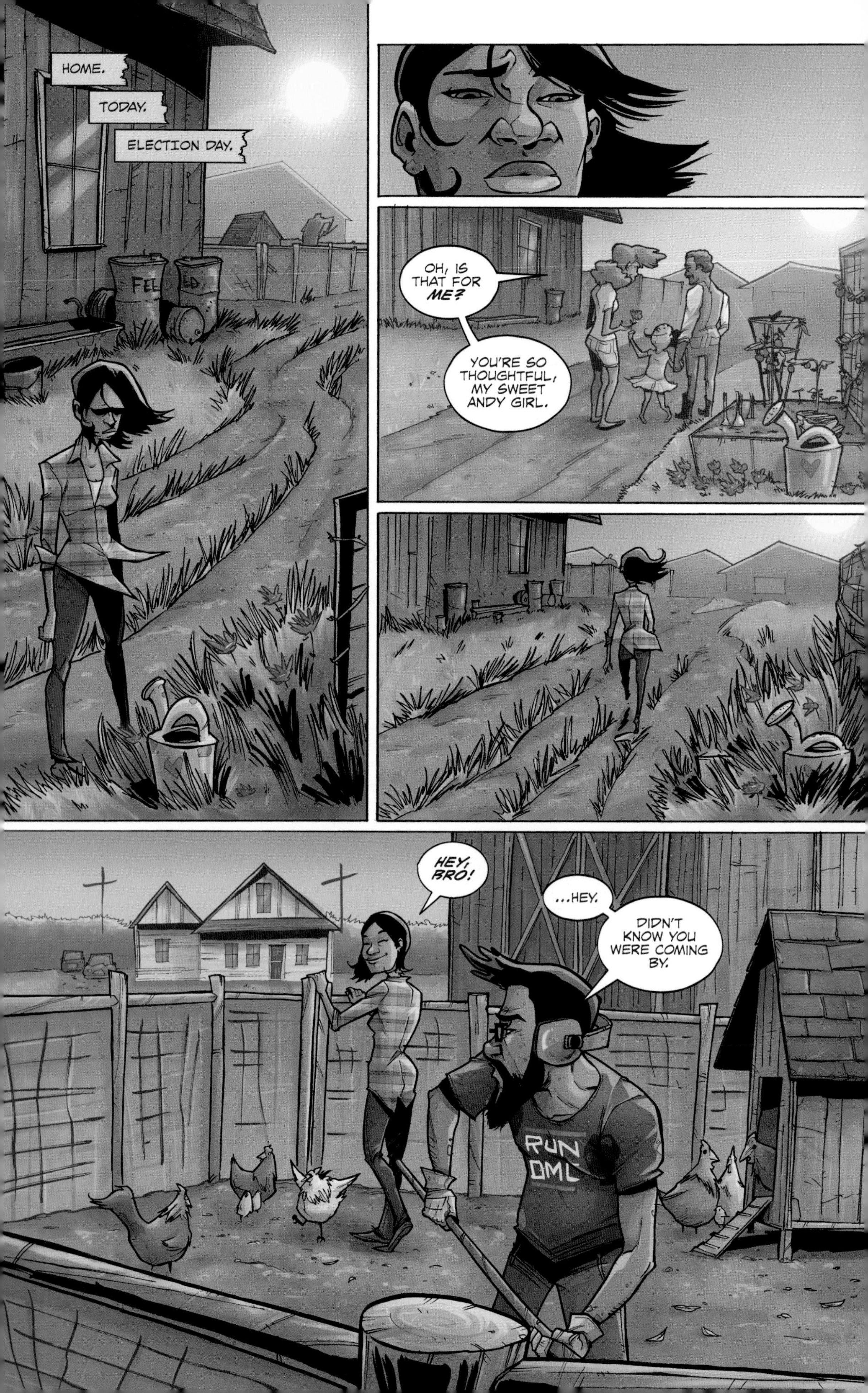
HOME.
TODAY.
ELECTION DAY.
OH, IS THAT FOR ME?
YOU'RE SO THOUGHTFUL, MY SWEET ANDY GIRL.
HEY, BRO!
...HEY.
DIDN'T KNOW YOU WERE COMING BY.
RUN DML

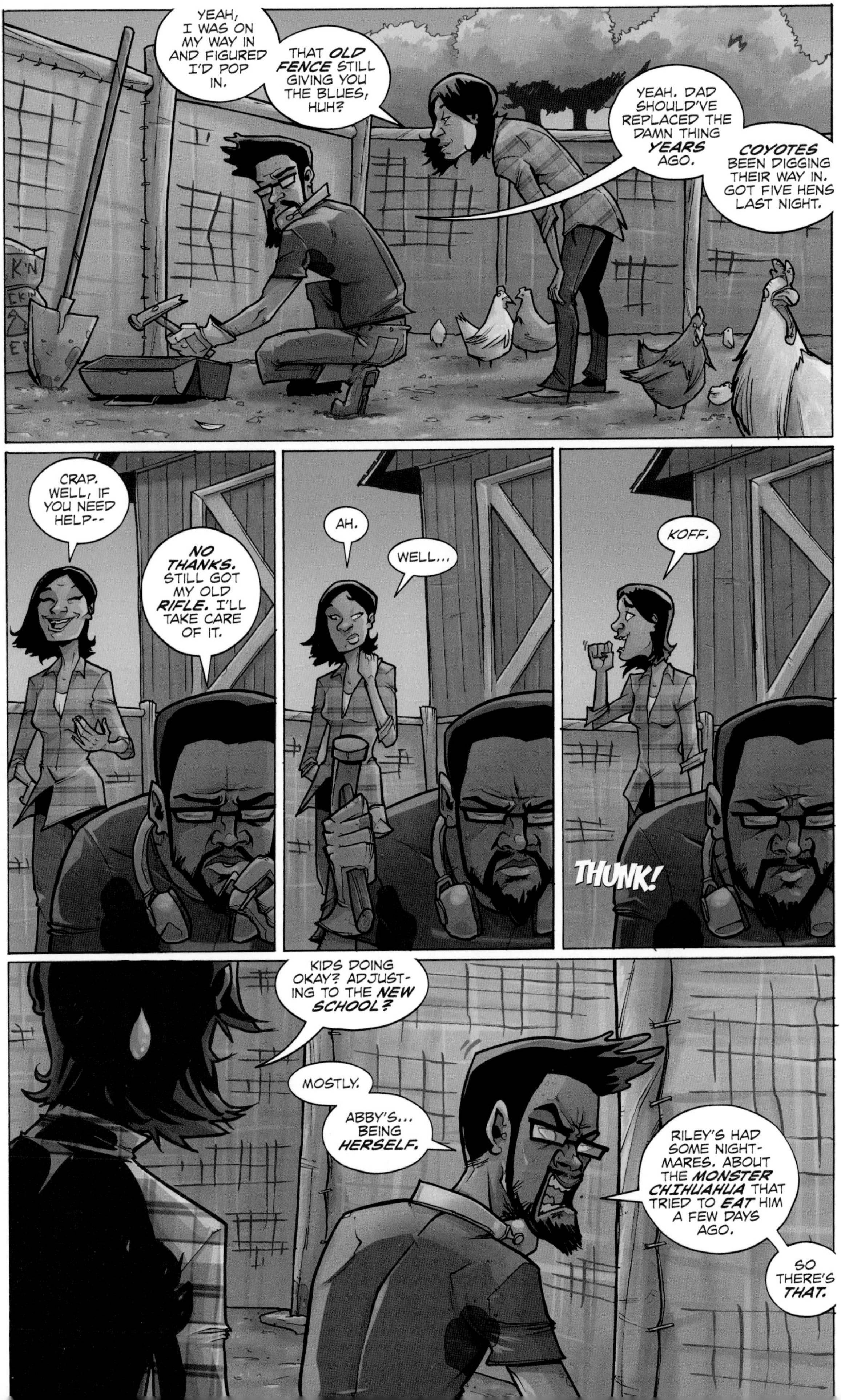
YEAH, I WAS ON MY WAY IN AND FIGURED I'D POP IN.
THAT OLD FENCE STILL GIVING YOU THE BLUES, HUH?
YEAH. DAD SHOULD'VE REPLACED THE DAMN THING YEARS AGO.
COYOTES BEEN DIGGING THEIR WAY IN. GOT FIVE HENS LAST NIGHT.
CRAP. WELL, IF YOU NEED HELP--
NO THANKS. STILL GOT MY OLD RIFLE. I'LL TAKE CARE OF IT.
AH.
WELL...
KOFF.
THUNK!
KIDS DOING OKAY? ADJUSTING TO THE NEW SCHOOL?
MOSTLY.
ABBY'S... BEING HERSELF.
RILEY'S HAD SOME NIGHTMARES. ABOUT THE MONSTER CHIHUAHUA THAT TRIED TO EAT HIM A FEW DAYS AGO.
SO THERE'S THAT.

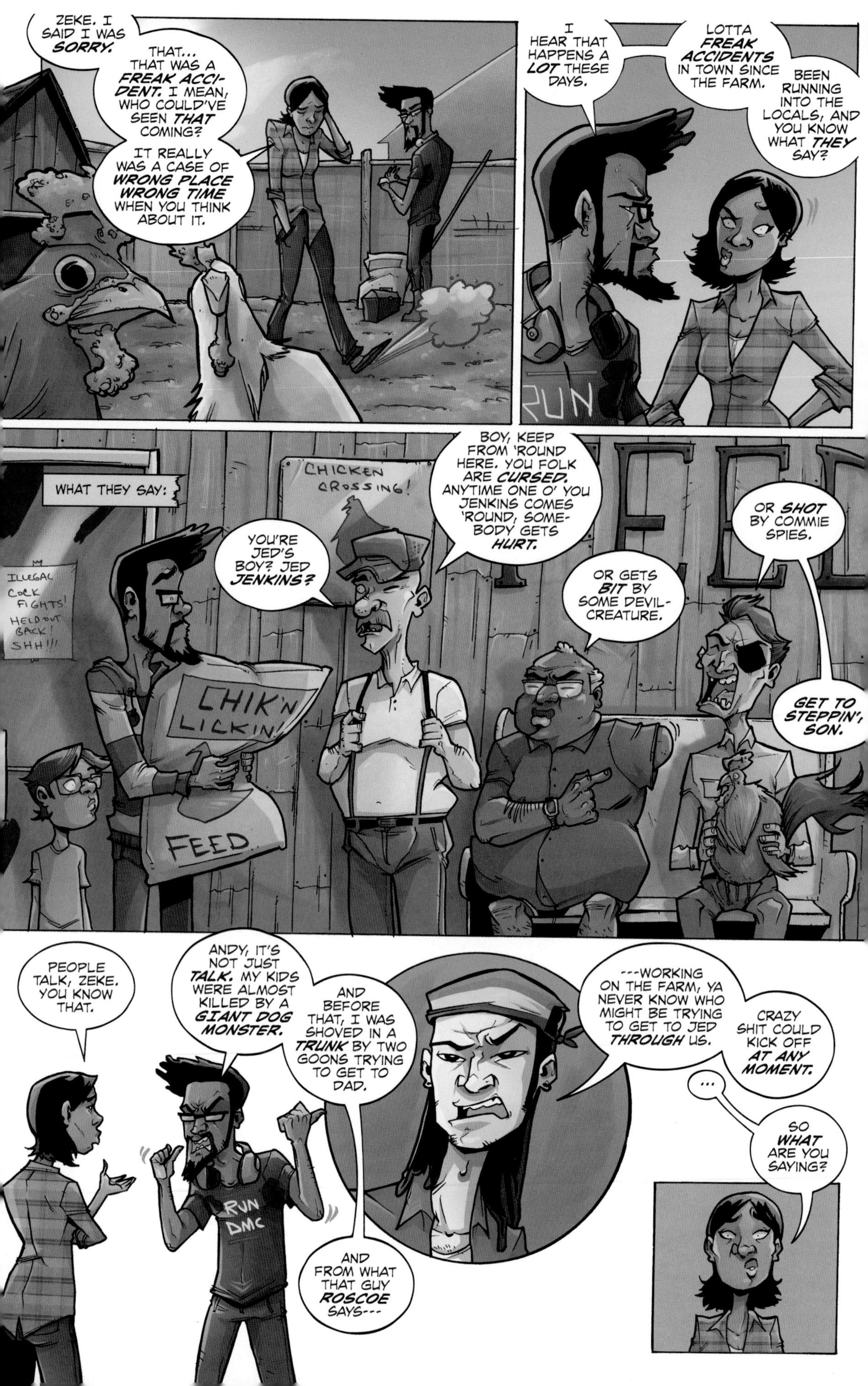
ZEKE. I SAID I WAS SORRY.
THAT... THAT WAS A FREAK ACCIDENT. I MEAN, WHO COULD'VE SEEN THAT COMING?
IT REALLY WAS A CASE OF WRONG PLACE WRONG TIME WHEN YOU THINK ABOUT IT.
I HEAR THAT HAPPENS A LOT THESE DAYS.
LOTTA FREAK ACCIDENTS IN TOWN SINCE THE FARM.
BEEN RUNNING INTO THE LOCALS, AND YOU KNOW WHAT THEY SAY?
RUN
WHAT THEY SAY:
CHICKEN CROSSING!
ILLEGAL COCK FIGHTS! HELD OUT BACK! SHH!!!
YOU'RE JED'S BOY? JED JENKINS?
BOY, KEEP FROM 'ROUND HERE. YOU FOLK ARE CURSED. ANYTIME ONE O' YOU JENKINS COMES 'ROUND, SOMEBODY GETS HURT.
OR GETS BIT BY SOME DEVIL-CREATURE.
OR SHOT BY COMMIE SPIES.
GET TO STEPPIN', SON.
CHIK'N LICKIN
FEED
PEOPLE TALK, ZEKE. YOU KNOW THAT.
ANDY, IT'S NOT JUST TALK. MY KIDS WERE ALMOST KILLED BY A GIANT DOG MONSTER.
AND BEFORE THAT, I WAS SHOVED IN A TRUNK BY TWO GOONS TRYING TO GET TO DAD.
AND FROM WHAT THAT GUY ROSCOE SAYS---
RUN DMC
---WORKING ON THE FARM, YA NEVER KNOW WHO MIGHT BE TRYING TO GET TO JED THROUGH US.
CRAZY SHIT COULD KICK OFF AT ANY MOMENT.
...
SO WHAT ARE YOU SAYING?

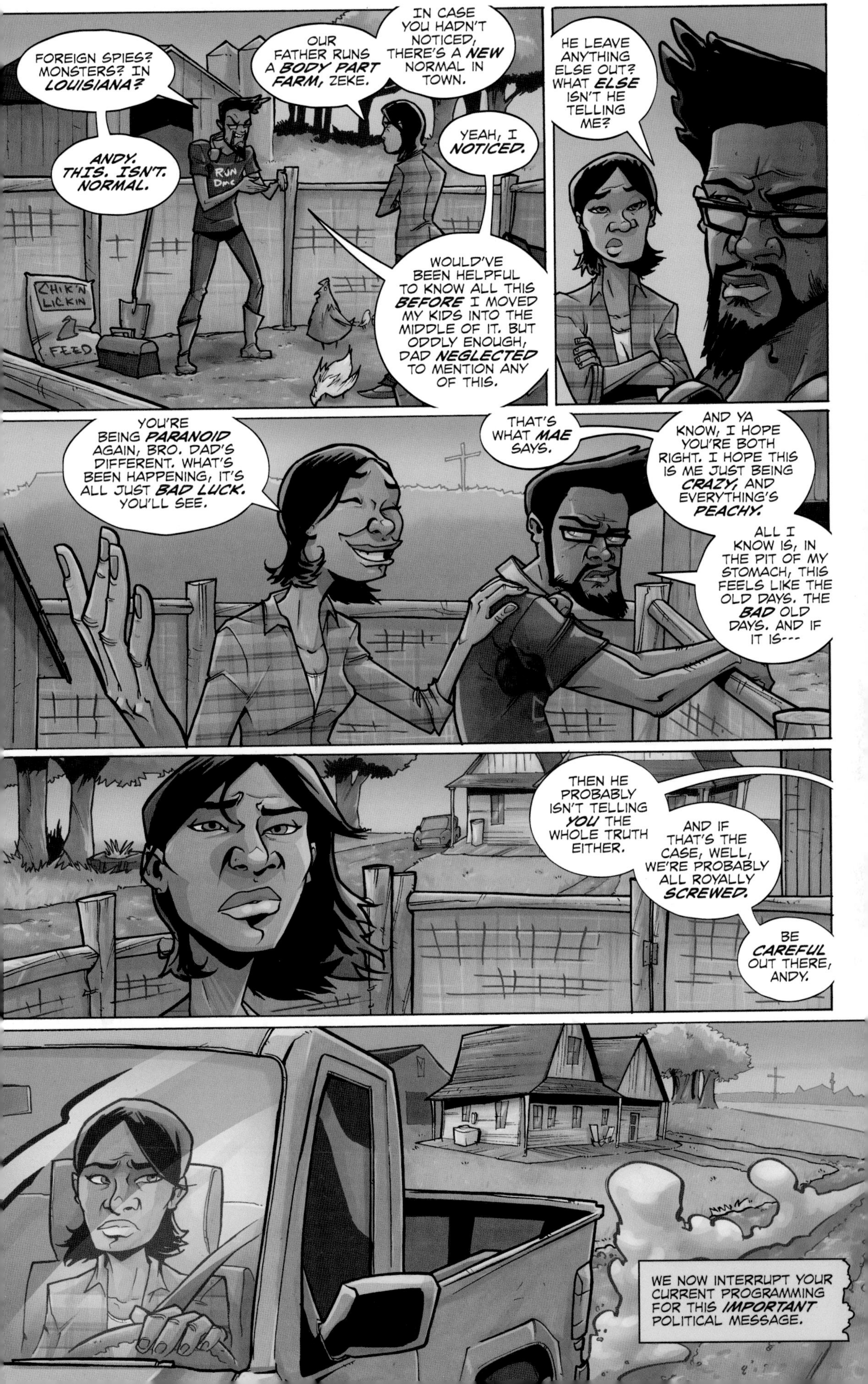
FOREIGN SPIES? MONSTERS? IN LOUISIANA?
OUR FATHER RUNS A BODY PART FARM, ZEKE.
IN CASE YOU HADN'T NOTICED, THERE'S A NEW NORMAL IN TOWN.
ANDY. THIS. ISN'T. NORMAL.
YEAH, I NOTICED.
WOULD'VE BEEN HELPFUL TO KNOW ALL THIS BEFORE I MOVED MY KIDS INTO THE MIDDLE OF IT. BUT ODDLY ENOUGH, DAD NEGLECTED TO MENTION ANY OF THIS.
CHIK'N LICKIN FEED
RUN DMC
HE LEAVE ANYTHING ELSE OUT? WHAT ELSE ISN'T HE TELLING ME?
YOU'RE BEING PARANOID AGAIN, BRO. DAD'S DIFFERENT. WHAT'S BEEN HAPPENING, IT'S ALL JUST BAD LUCK. YOU'LL SEE.
THAT'S WHAT MAE SAYS.
AND YA KNOW, I HOPE YOU'RE BOTH RIGHT. I HOPE THIS IS ME JUST BEING CRAZY, AND EVERYTHING'S PEACHY.
ALL I KNOW IS, IN THE PIT OF MY STOMACH, THIS FEELS LIKE THE OLD DAYS. THE BAD OLD DAYS. AND IF IT IS---
THEN HE PROBABLY ISN'T TELLING YOU THE WHOLE TRUTH EITHER.
AND IF THAT'S THE CASE, WELL, WE'RE PROBABLY ALL ROYALLY SCREWED.
BE CAREFUL OUT THERE, ANDY.
WE NOW INTERRUPT YOUR CURRENT PROGRAMMING FOR THIS IMPORTANT POLITICAL MESSAGE.

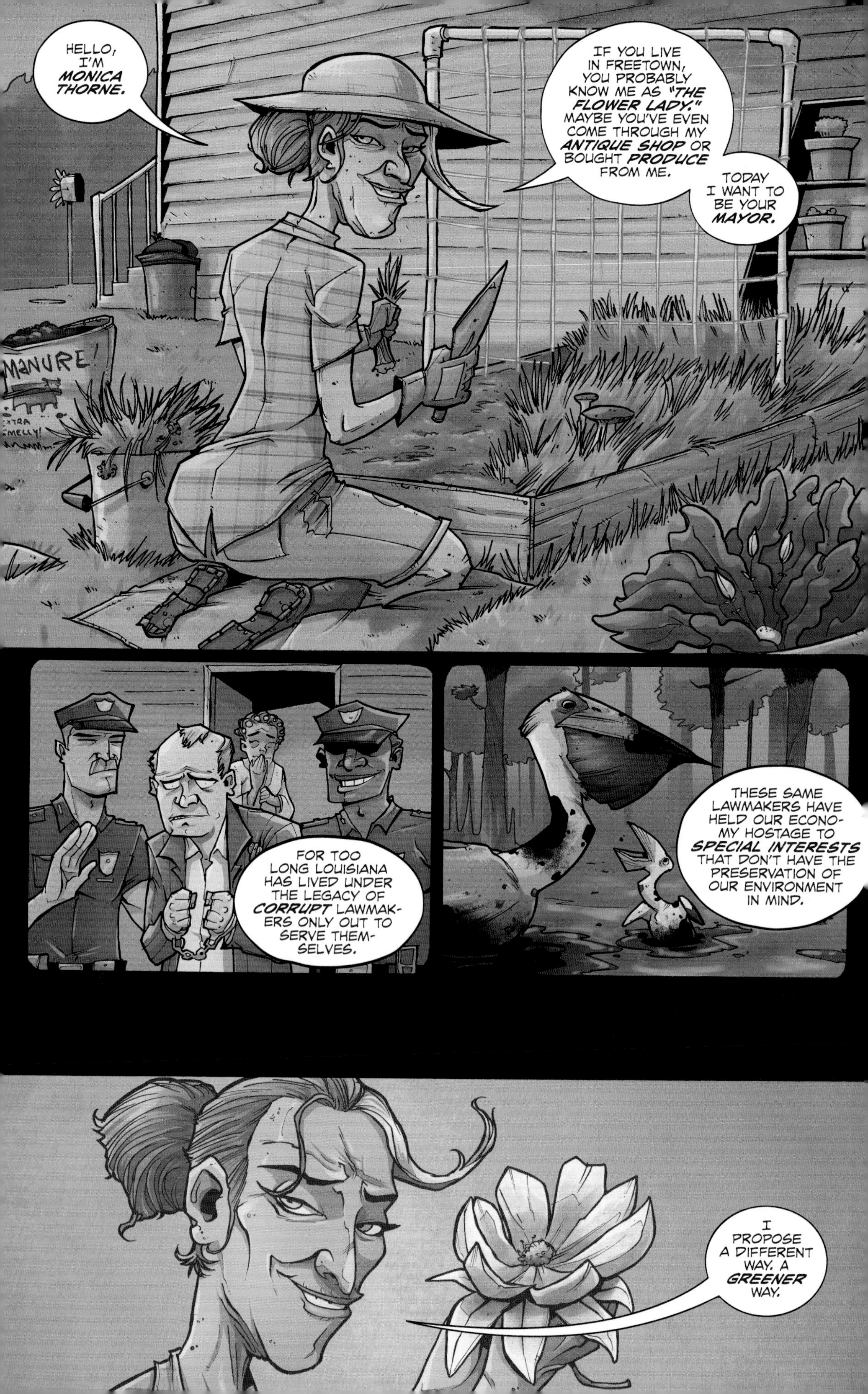
HELLO, I'M MONICA THORNE.
IF YOU LIVE IN FREETOWN, YOU PROBABLY KNOW ME AS "THE FLOWER LADY." MAYBE YOU'VE EVEN COME THROUGH MY ANTIQUE SHOP OR BOUGHT PRODUCE FROM ME.
TODAY I WANT TO BE YOUR MAYOR.
MANURE!
EXTRA SMELLY!
FOR TOO LONG LOUISIANA HAS LIVED UNDER THE LEGACY OF CORRUPT LAWMAKERS ONLY OUT TO SERVE THEMSELVES.
THESE SAME LAWMAKERS HAVE HELD OUR ECONOMY HOSTAGE TO SPECIAL INTERESTS THAT DON'T HAVE THE PRESERVATION OF OUR ENVIRONMENT IN MIND.
I PROPOSE A DIFFERENT WAY. A GREENER WAY.

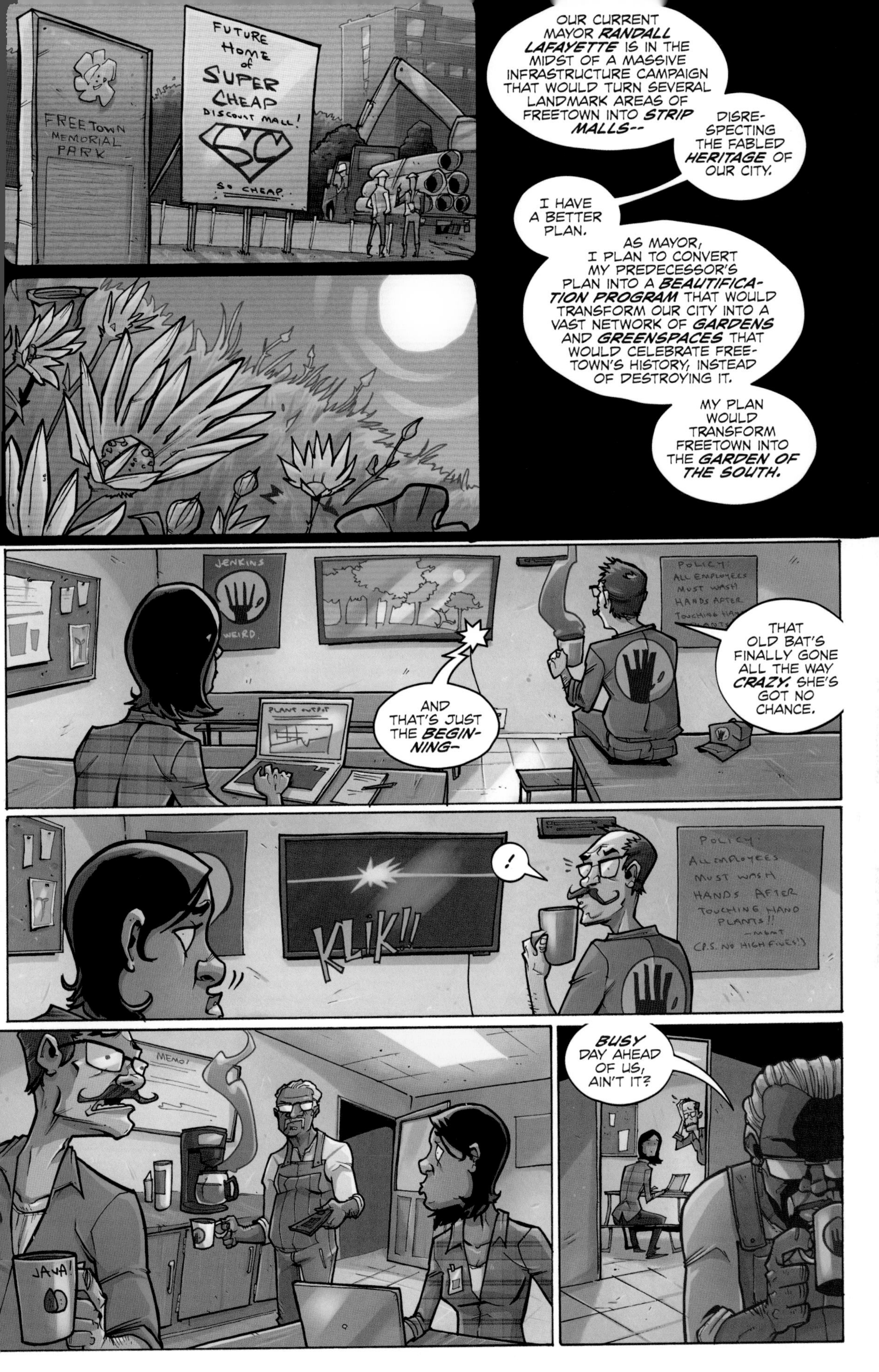
FUTURE Home of SUPER CHEAP DISCOUNT MALL!
SO CHEAP.
FREETOWN MEMORIAL PARK
OUR CURRENT MAYOR RANDALL LAFAYETTE IS IN THE MIDST OF A MASSIVE INFRASTRUCTURE CAMPAIGN THAT WOULD TURN SEVERAL LANDMARK AREAS OF FREETOWN INTO STRIP MALLS--
DISRE-SPECTING THE FABLED HERITAGE OF OUR CITY.
I HAVE A BETTER PLAN.
AS MAYOR, I PLAN TO CONVERT MY PREDECESSOR'S PLAN INTO A BEAUTIFICA-TION PROGRAM THAT WOULD TRANSFORM OUR CITY INTO A VAST NETWORK OF GARDENS AND GREENSPACES THAT WOULD CELEBRATE FREE-TOWN'S HISTORY, INSTEAD OF DESTROYING IT.
MY PLAN WOULD TRANSFORM FREETOWN INTO THE GARDEN OF THE SOUTH.
JENKINS WEIRD
PLANT OUTPUT
AND THAT'S JUST THE BEGIN-NING-
THAT OLD BAT'S FINALLY GONE ALL THE WAY CRAZY. SHE'S GOT NO CHANCE.
!
KLIK!!
POLICY: ALL EMPLOYEES MUST WASH HANDS AFTER TOUCHING HAND PLANTS!! —MGMT (P.S. NO HIGH FIVES!)
MEMO!
JAVA!
BUSY DAY AHEAD OF US, AIN'T IT?

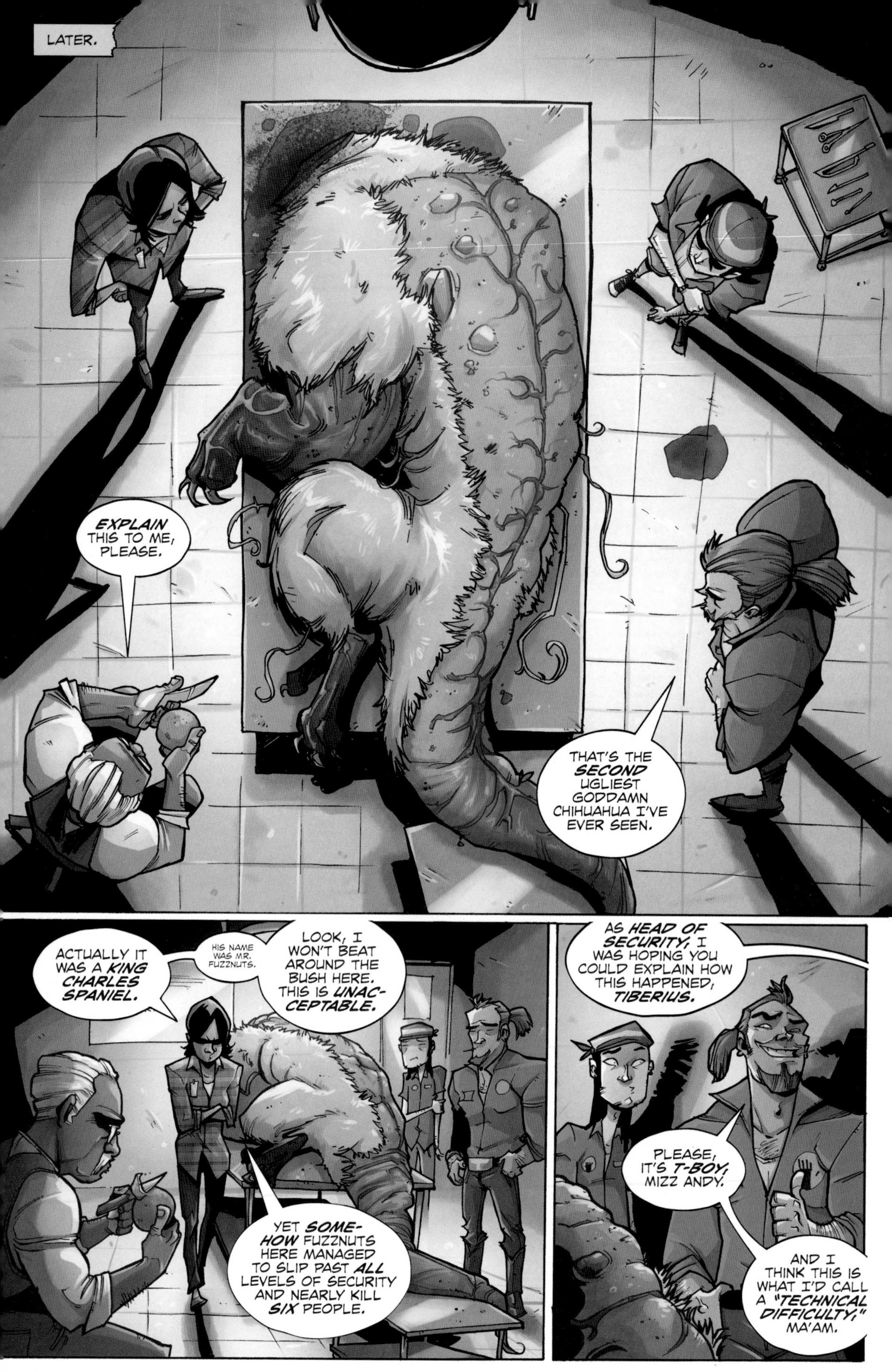
LATER.
EXPLAIN THIS TO ME, PLEASE.
THAT'S THE SECOND UGLIEST GODDAMN CHIHUAHUA I'VE EVER SEEN.
ACTUALLY IT WAS A KING CHARLES SPANIEL.
HIS NAME WAS MR. FUZZNUTS.
LOOK, I WON'T BEAT AROUND THE BUSH HERE. THIS IS UNACCEPTABLE.
YET SOMEHOW FUZZNUTS HERE MANAGED TO SLIP PAST ALL LEVELS OF SECURITY AND NEARLY KILL SIX PEOPLE.
AS HEAD OF SECURITY, I WAS HOPING YOU COULD EXPLAIN HOW THIS HAPPENED, TIBERIUS.
PLEASE, IT'S T-BOY, MIZZ ANDY.
AND I THINK THIS IS WHAT I'D CALL A "TECHNICAL DIFFICULTY," MA'AM.

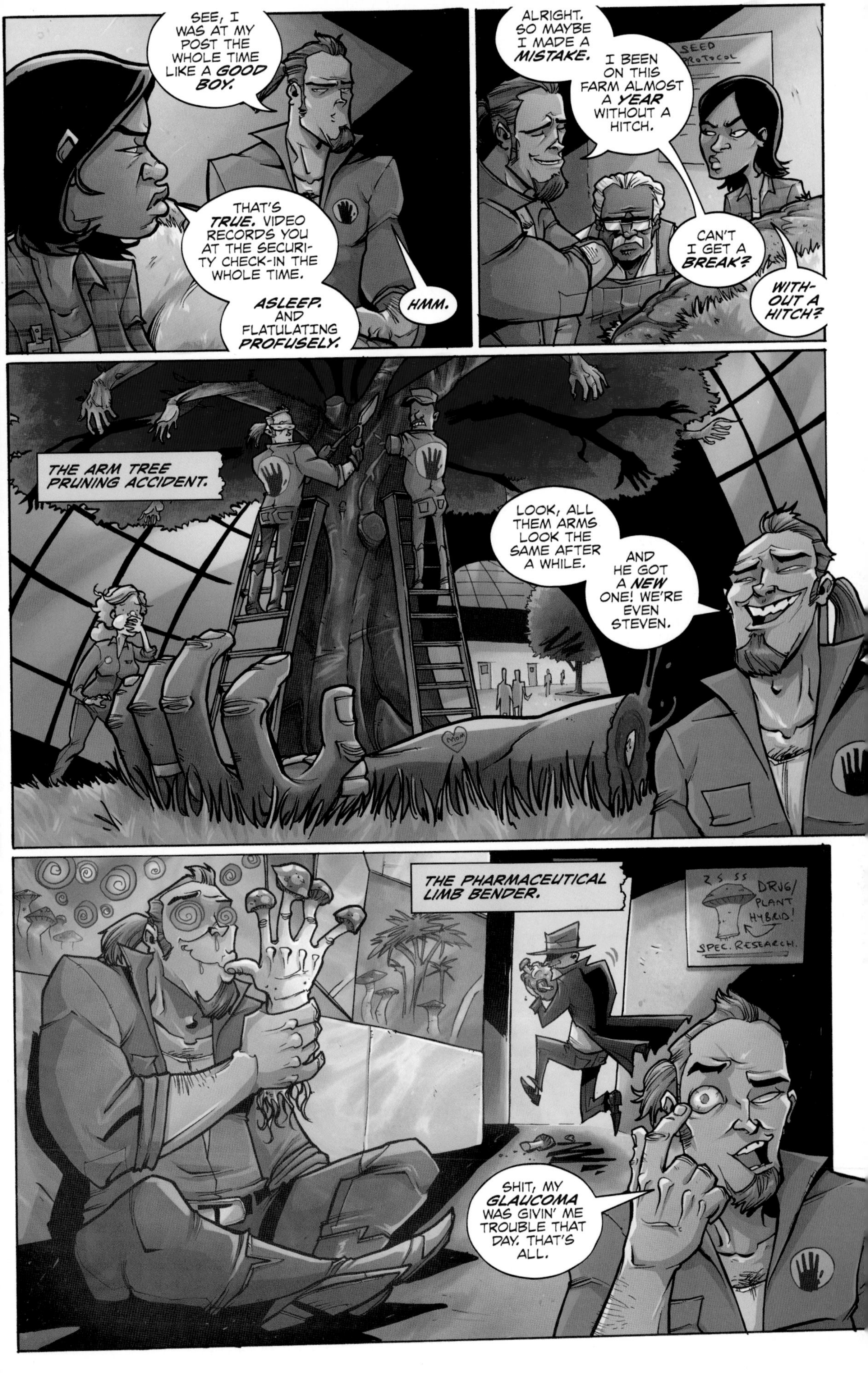
SEE, I WAS AT MY POST THE WHOLE TIME LIKE A GOOD BOY.
THAT'S TRUE. VIDEO RECORDS YOU AT THE SECURITY CHECK-IN THE WHOLE TIME.
ASLEEP. AND FLATULATING PROFUSELY.
HMM.
ALRIGHT. SO MAYBE I MADE A MISTAKE.
I BEEN ON THIS FARM ALMOST A YEAR WITHOUT A HITCH.
CAN'T I GET A BREAK?
WITH-OUT A HITCH?
SEED PROTOCOL
THE ARM TREE PRUNING ACCIDENT.
LOOK, ALL THEM ARMS LOOK THE SAME AFTER A WHILE.
AND HE GOT A NEW ONE! WE'RE EVEN STEVEN.
MOM
THE PHARMACEUTICAL LIMB BENDER.
DRUG/ PLANT HYBRID!
SPEC. RESEARCH.
SHIT, MY GLAUCOMA WAS GIVIN' ME TROUBLE THAT DAY. THAT'S ALL.

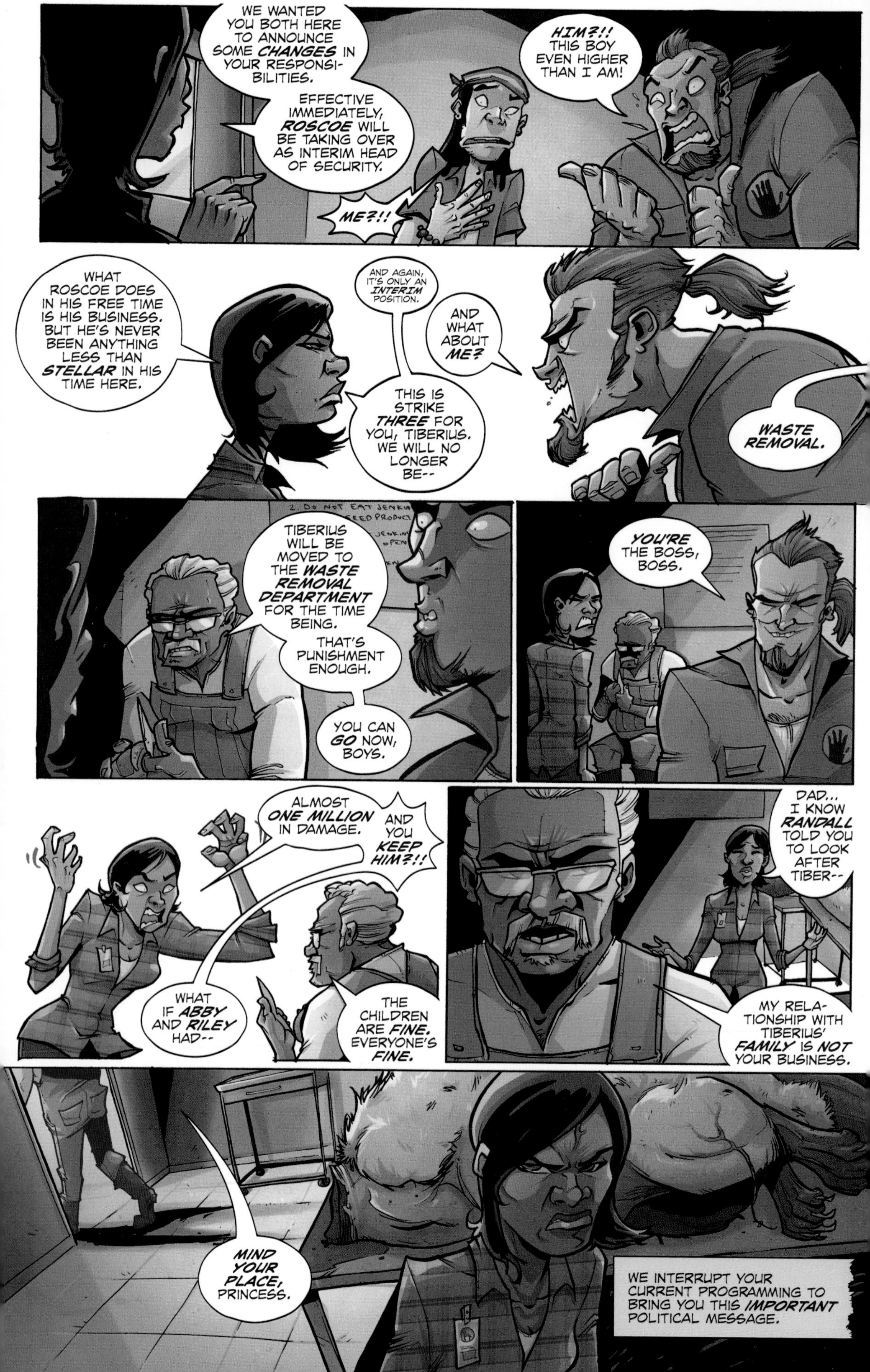
WE WANTED YOU BOTH HERE TO ANNOUNCE SOME CHANGES IN YOUR RESPONSI-BILITIES.
EFFECTIVE IMMEDIATELY, ROSCOE WILL BE TAKING OVER AS INTERIM HEAD OF SECURITY.
ME?!!
HIM?!! THIS BOY EVEN HIGHER THAN I AM!
WHAT ROSCOE DOES IN HIS FREE TIME IS HIS BUSINESS. BUT HE'S NEVER BEEN ANYTHING LESS THAN STELLAR IN HIS TIME HERE.
AND AGAIN, IT'S ONLY AN INTERIM POSITION.
AND WHAT ABOUT ME?
THIS IS STRIKE THREE FOR YOU, TIBERIUS. WE WILL NO LONGER BE--
WASTE REMOVAL.
TIBERIUS WILL BE MOVED TO THE WASTE REMOVAL DEPARTMENT FOR THE TIME BEING.
THAT'S PUNISHMENT ENOUGH.
YOU CAN GO NOW, BOYS.
YOU'RE THE BOSS, BOSS.
ALMOST ONE MILLION IN DAMAGE.
AND YOU KEEP HIM?!!
WHAT IF ABBY AND RILEY HAD--
THE CHILDREN ARE FINE. EVERYONE'S FINE.
DAD... I KNOW RANDALL TOLD YOU TO LOOK AFTER TIBER--
MY RELA-TIONSHIP WITH TIBERIUS' FAMILY IS NOT YOUR BUSINESS.
MIND YOUR PLACE, PRINCESS.
WE INTERRUPT YOUR CURRENT PROGRAMMING TO BRING YOU THIS IMPORTANT POLITICAL MESSAGE.

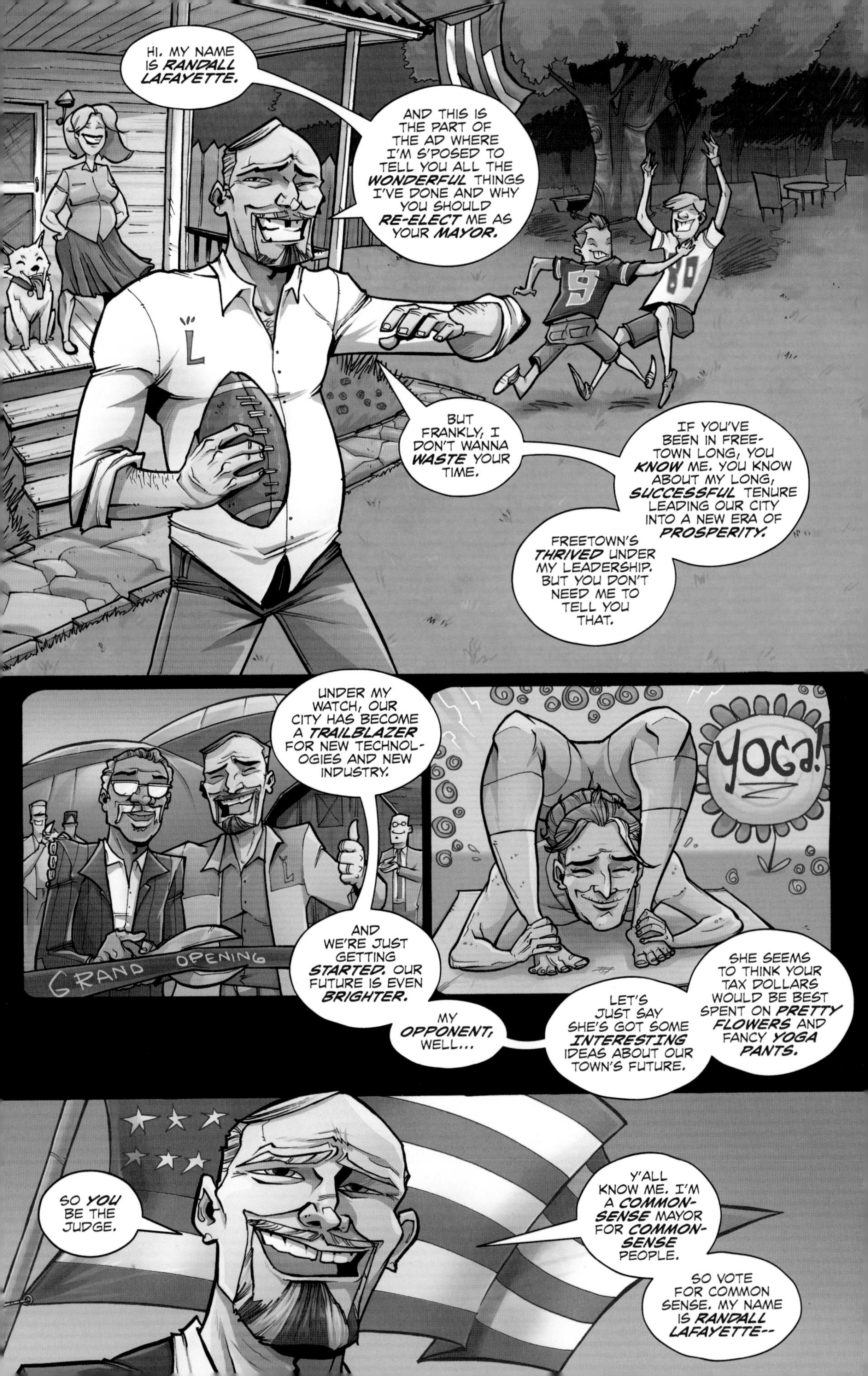
HI. MY NAME IS RANDALL LAFAYETTE.
AND THIS IS THE PART OF THE AD WHERE I'M S'POSED TO TELL YOU ALL THE WONDERFUL THINGS I'VE DONE AND WHY YOU SHOULD RE-ELECT ME AS YOUR MAYOR.
BUT FRANKLY, I DON'T WANNA WASTE YOUR TIME.
IF YOU'VE BEEN IN FREE-TOWN LONG, YOU KNOW ME. YOU KNOW ABOUT MY LONG, SUCCESSFUL TENURE LEADING OUR CITY INTO A NEW ERA OF PROSPERITY.
FREETOWN'S THRIVED UNDER MY LEADERSHIP. BUT YOU DON'T NEED ME TO TELL YOU THAT.
UNDER MY WATCH, OUR CITY HAS BECOME A TRAILBLAZER FOR NEW TECHNOLOGIES AND NEW INDUSTRY.
GRAND OPENING
YOGA!
AND WE'RE JUST GETTING STARTED. OUR FUTURE IS EVEN BRIGHTER.
MY OPPONENT, WELL...
LET'S JUST SAY SHE'S GOT SOME INTERESTING IDEAS ABOUT OUR TOWN'S FUTURE.
SHE SEEMS TO THINK YOUR TAX DOLLARS WOULD BE BEST SPENT ON PRETTY FLOWERS AND FANCY YOGA PANTS.
SO YOU BE THE JUDGE.
Y'ALL KNOW ME. I'M A COMMON-SENSE MAYOR FOR COMMON-SENSE PEOPLE.
SO VOTE FOR COMMON SENSE. MY NAME IS RANDALL LAFAYETTE--

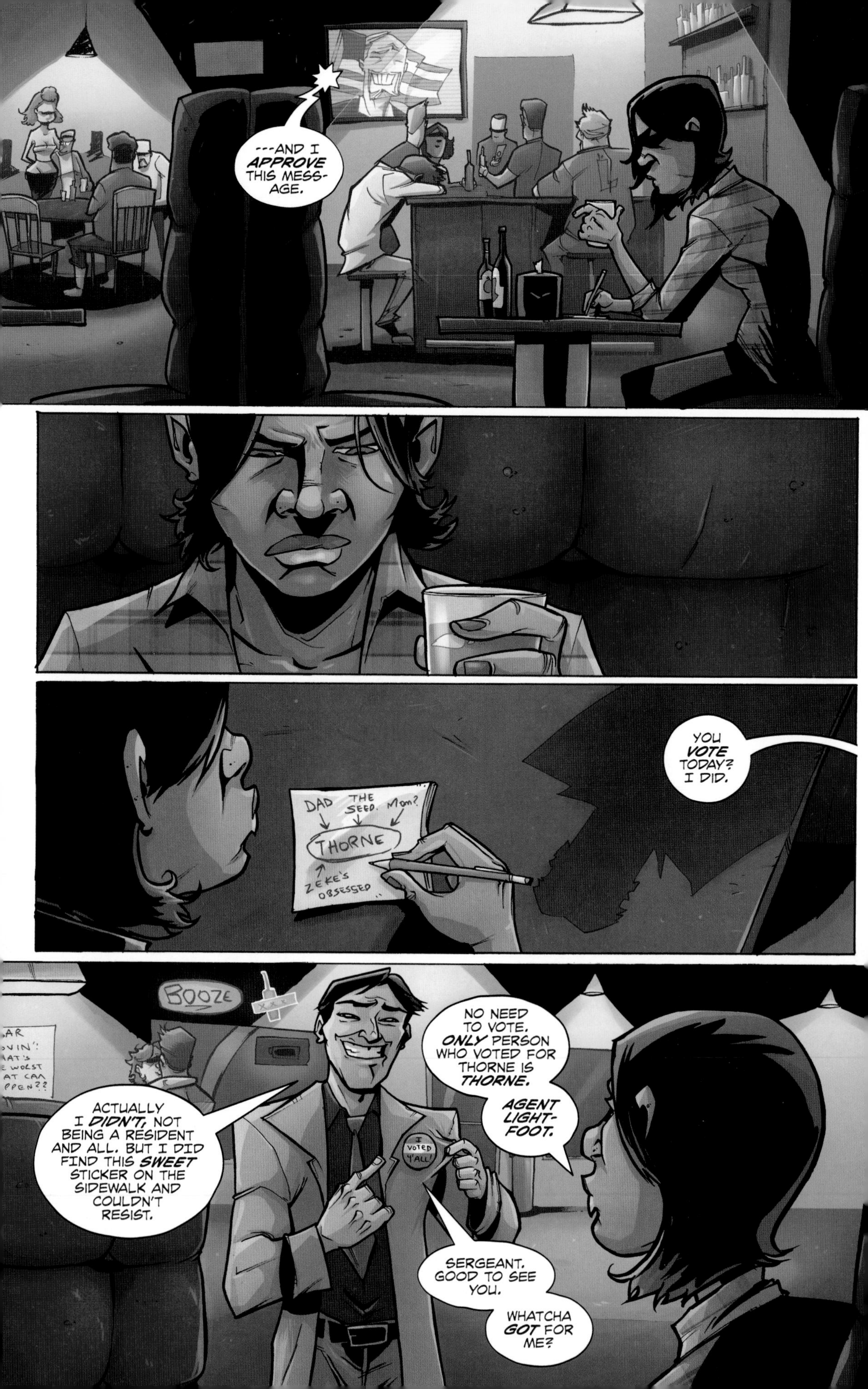

---AND I *APPROVE* THIS MESS-AGE.
YOU *VOTE* TODAY? I DID.
DAD
THE SEED.
Mom?
THORNE
ZEKE'S OBSESSED
BOOZE
ACTUALLY I *DIDN'T,* NOT BEING A RESIDENT AND ALL. BUT I DID FIND THIS *SWEET* STICKER ON THE SIDEWALK AND COULDN'T RESIST.
I VOTED Y'ALL!
NO NEED TO VOTE. *ONLY* PERSON WHO VOTED FOR THORNE IS *THORNE.*
AGENT LIGHT-FOOT.
SERGEANT. GOOD TO SEE YOU.
WHATCHA *GOT* FOR ME?

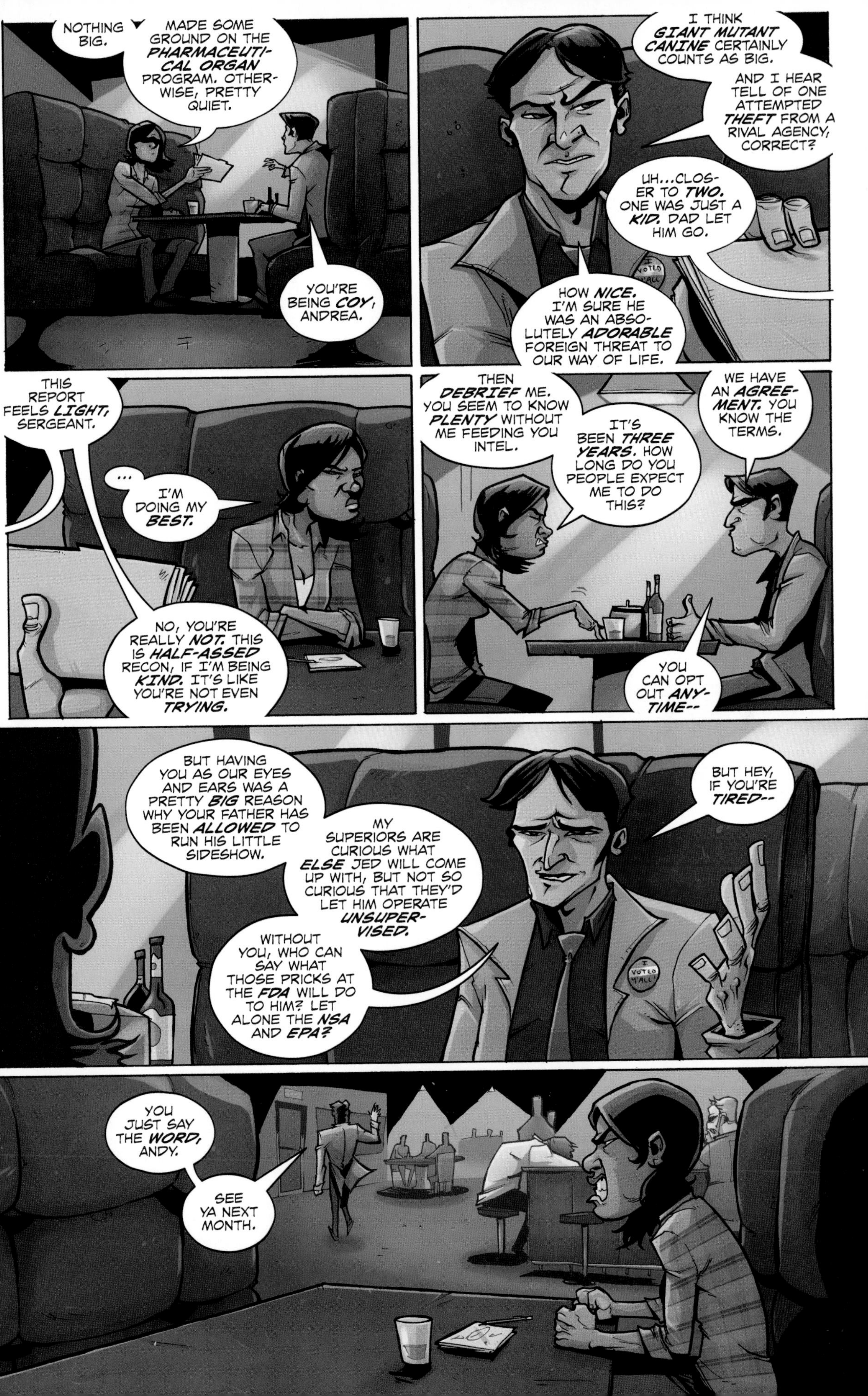
NOTHING BIG.
MADE SOME GROUND ON THE PHARMACEUTICAL ORGAN PROGRAM. OTHERWISE, PRETTY QUIET.
YOU'RE BEING COY, ANDREA.
I THINK GIANT MUTANT CANINE CERTAINLY COUNTS AS BIG.
AND I HEAR TELL OF ONE ATTEMPTED THEFT FROM A RIVAL AGENCY, CORRECT?
UH...CLOSER TO TWO. ONE WAS JUST A KID. DAD LET HIM GO.
HOW NICE. I'M SURE HE WAS AN ABSOLUTELY ADORABLE FOREIGN THREAT TO OUR WAY OF LIFE.
THIS REPORT FEELS LIGHT, SERGEANT.
...
I'M DOING MY BEST.
NO, YOU'RE REALLY NOT. THIS IS HALF-ASSED RECON, IF I'M BEING KIND. IT'S LIKE YOU'RE NOT EVEN TRYING.
THEN DEBRIEF ME. YOU SEEM TO KNOW PLENTY WITHOUT ME FEEDING YOU INTEL.
IT'S BEEN THREE YEARS. HOW LONG DO YOU PEOPLE EXPECT ME TO DO THIS?
WE HAVE AN AGREEMENT. YOU KNOW THE TERMS.
YOU CAN OPT OUT ANYTIME--
BUT HAVING YOU AS OUR EYES AND EARS WAS A PRETTY BIG REASON WHY YOUR FATHER HAS BEEN ALLOWED TO RUN HIS LITTLE SIDESHOW.
MY SUPERIORS ARE CURIOUS WHAT ELSE JED WILL COME UP WITH, BUT NOT SO CURIOUS THAT THEY'D LET HIM OPERATE UNSUPERVISED.
WITHOUT YOU, WHO CAN SAY WHAT THOSE PRICKS AT THE FDA WILL DO TO HIM? LET ALONE THE NSA AND EPA?
BUT HEY, IF YOU'RE TIRED--
I VOTED Y'ALL
YOU JUST SAY THE WORD, ANDY.
SEE YA NEXT MONTH.

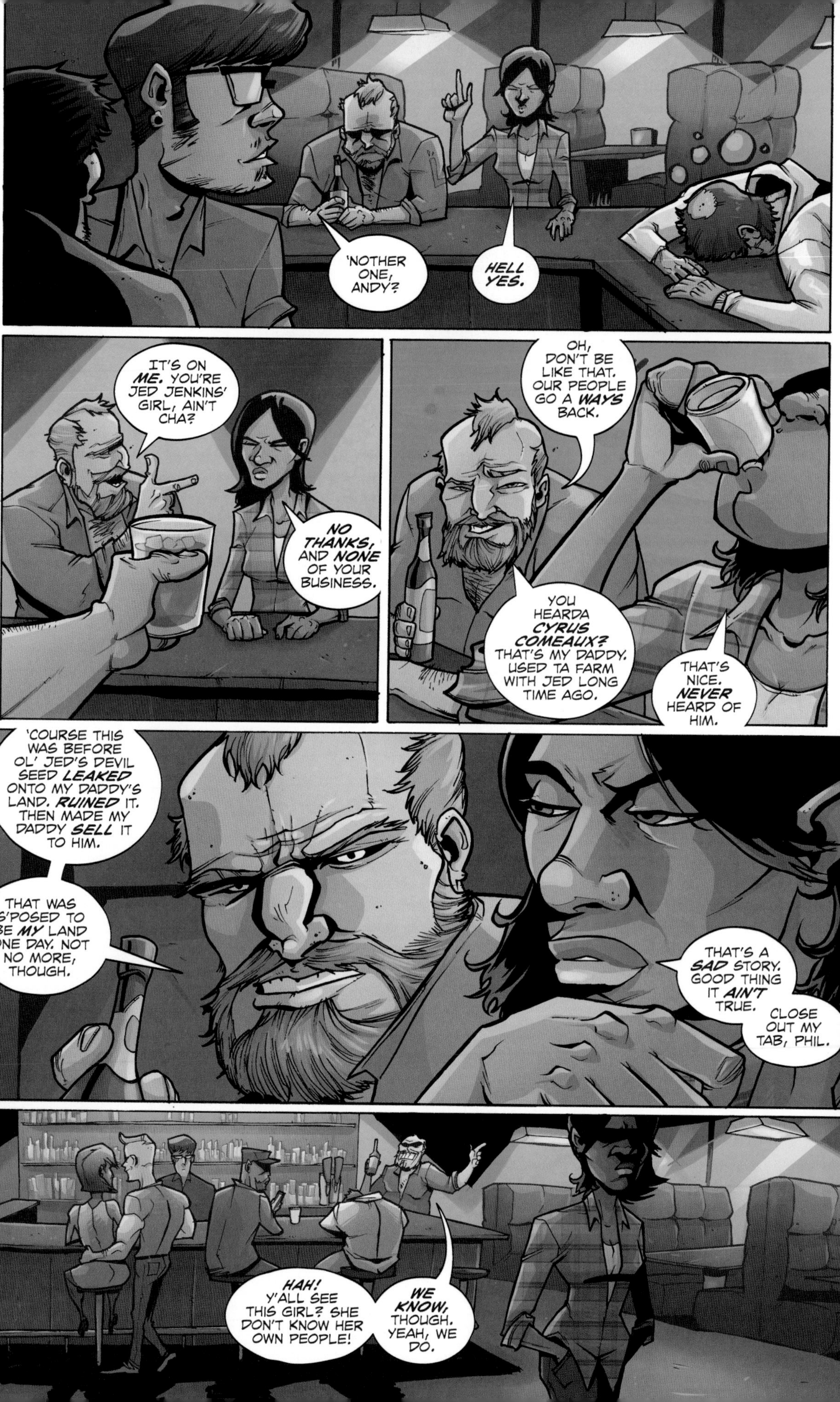
'NOTHER ONE, ANDY?
HELL YES.
IT'S ON ME. YOU'RE JED JENKINS' GIRL, AIN'T CHA?
NO THANKS, AND NONE OF YOUR BUSINESS.
OH, DON'T BE LIKE THAT. OUR PEOPLE GO A WAYS BACK.
YOU HEARDA CYRUS COMEAUX? THAT'S MY DADDY. USED TA FARM WITH JED LONG TIME AGO.
THAT'S NICE. NEVER HEARD OF HIM.
'COURSE THIS WAS BEFORE OL' JED'S DEVIL SEED LEAKED ONTO MY DADDY'S LAND. RUINED IT. THEN MADE MY DADDY SELL IT TO HIM.
THAT WAS S'POSED TO BE MY LAND ONE DAY. NOT NO MORE, THOUGH.
THAT'S A SAD STORY. GOOD THING IT AIN'T TRUE.
CLOSE OUT MY TAB, PHIL.
HAH! Y'ALL SEE THIS GIRL? SHE DON'T KNOW HER OWN PEOPLE!
WE KNOW, THOUGH. YEAH, WE DO.

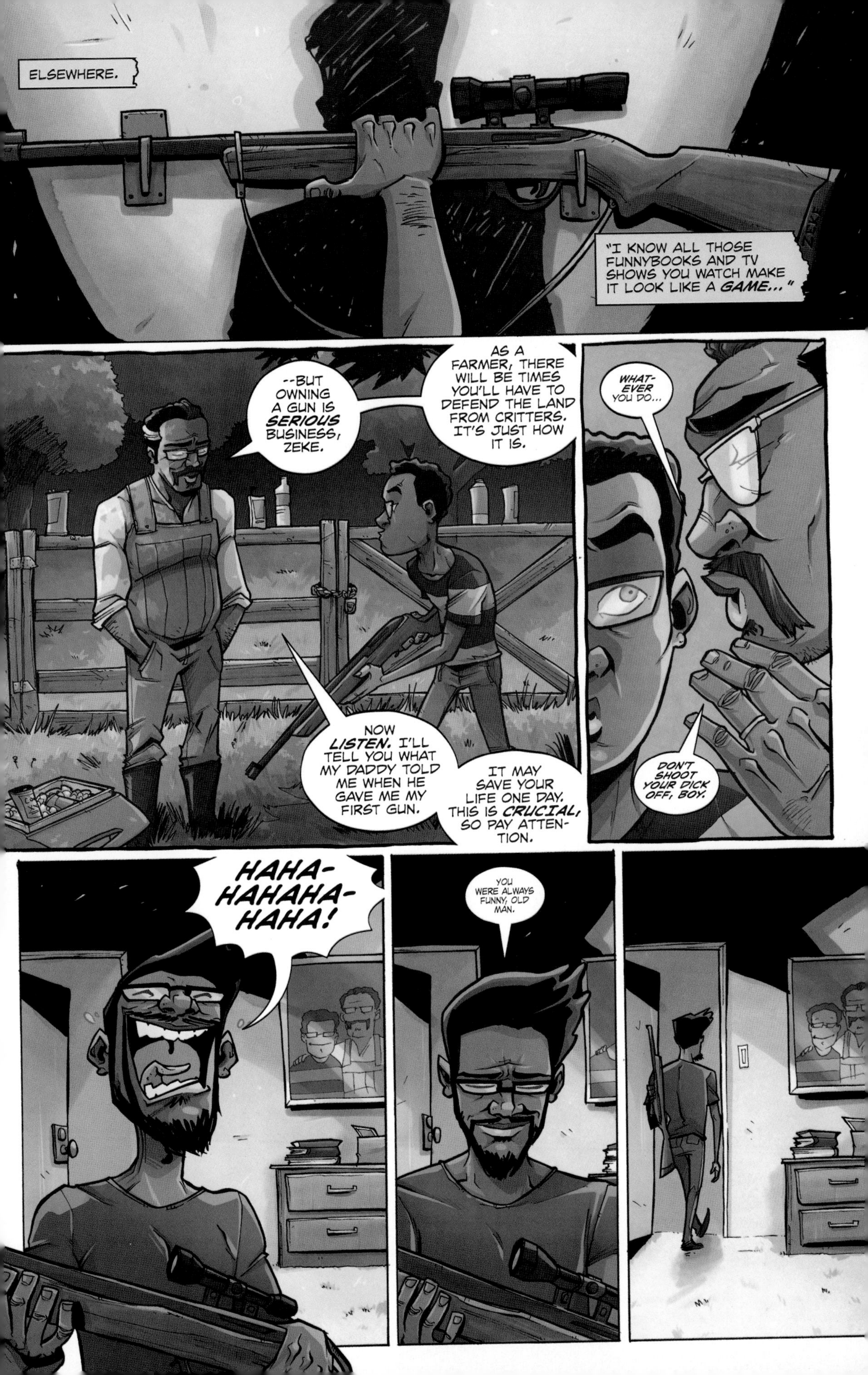
ELSEWHERE.
"I KNOW ALL THOSE FUNNYBOOKS AND TV SHOWS YOU WATCH MAKE IT LOOK LIKE A GAME..."
--BUT OWNING A GUN IS SERIOUS BUSINESS, ZEKE.
AS A FARMER, THERE WILL BE TIMES YOU'LL HAVE TO DEFEND THE LAND FROM CRITTERS. IT'S JUST HOW IT IS.
NOW LISTEN. I'LL TELL YOU WHAT MY DADDY TOLD ME WHEN HE GAVE ME MY FIRST GUN.
IT MAY SAVE YOUR LIFE ONE DAY. THIS IS CRUCIAL, SO PAY ATTEN-TION.
WHAT-EVER YOU DO...
DON'T SHOOT YOUR DICK OFF, BOY.
HAHA-HAHAHA-HAHA!
YOU WERE ALWAYS FUNNY, OLD MAN.

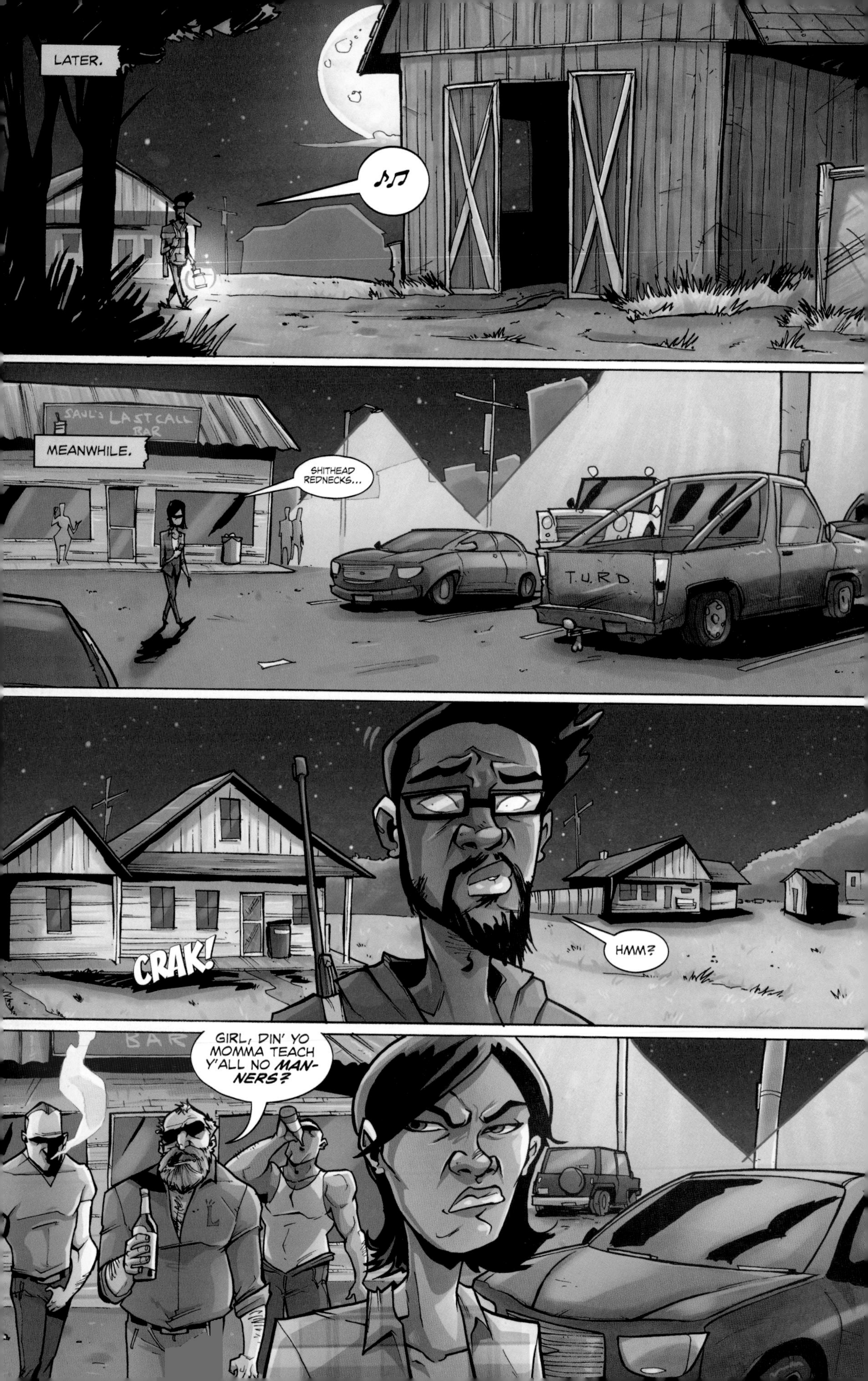
LATER.
♪♫
SAUL'S LAST CALL BAR
MEANWHILE.
SHITHEAD REDNECKS...
T.U.R.D.
CRAK!
HMM?
BAR
GIRL, DIN' YO MOMMA TEACH Y'ALL NO *MAN-NERS?*

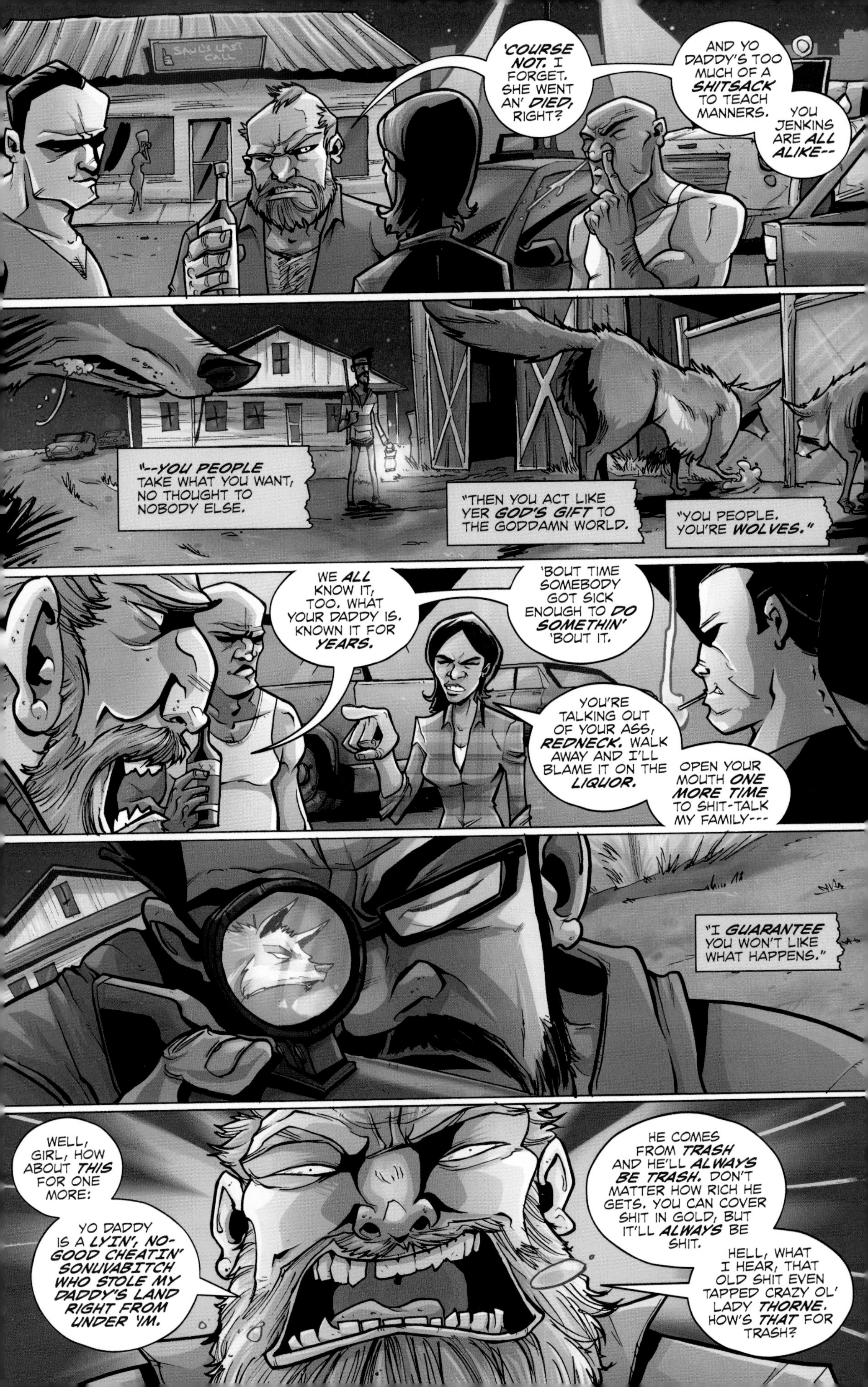
SAUL'S LAST CALL
'COURSE NOT. I FORGET. SHE WENT AN' DIED, RIGHT?
AND YO DADDY'S TOO MUCH OF A SHITSACK TO TEACH MANNERS.
YOU JENKINS ARE ALL ALIKE--
"--YOU PEOPLE TAKE WHAT YOU WANT, NO THOUGHT TO NOBODY ELSE.
"THEN YOU ACT LIKE YER GOD'S GIFT TO THE GODDAMN WORLD.
"YOU PEOPLE. YOU'RE WOLVES."
WE ALL KNOW IT, TOO. WHAT YOUR DADDY IS. KNOWN IT FOR YEARS.
'BOUT TIME SOMEBODY GOT SICK ENOUGH TO DO SOMETHIN' 'BOUT IT.
YOU'RE TALKING OUT OF YOUR ASS, REDNECK. WALK AWAY AND I'LL BLAME IT ON THE LIQUOR.
OPEN YOUR MOUTH ONE MORE TIME TO SHIT-TALK MY FAMILY---
"I GUARANTEE YOU WON'T LIKE WHAT HAPPENS."
WELL, GIRL, HOW ABOUT THIS FOR ONE MORE:
YO DADDY IS A LYIN', NO-GOOD CHEATIN' SONUVABITCH WHO STOLE MY DADDY'S LAND RIGHT FROM UNDER 'IM.
HE COMES FROM TRASH AND HE'LL ALWAYS BE TRASH. DON'T MATTER HOW RICH HE GETS. YOU CAN COVER SHIT IN GOLD, BUT IT'LL ALWAYS BE SHIT.
HELL, WHAT I HEAR, THAT OLD SHIT EVEN TAPPED CRAZY OL' LADY THORNE. HOW'S THAT FOR TRASH?

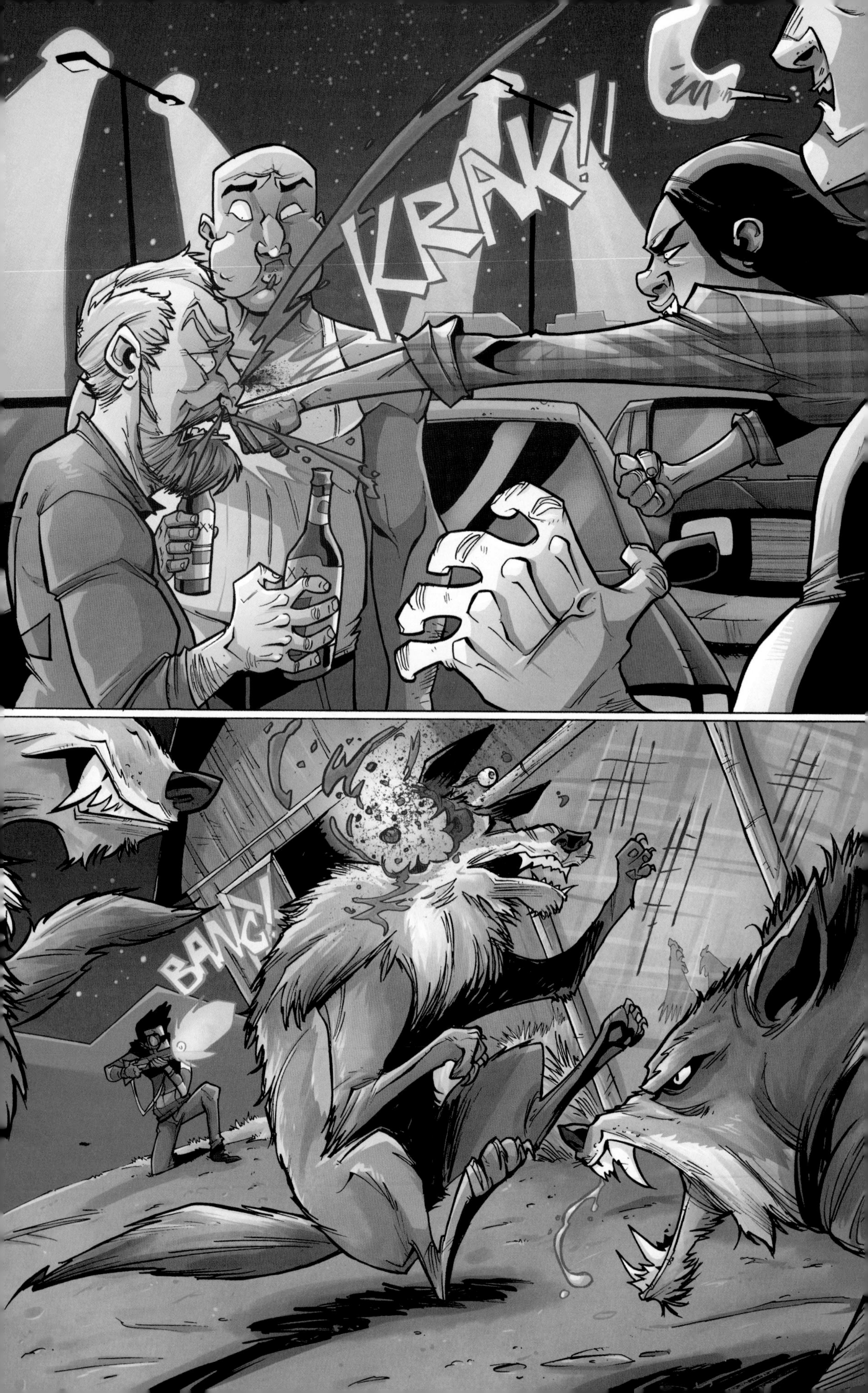
KRAK!!
BANG!

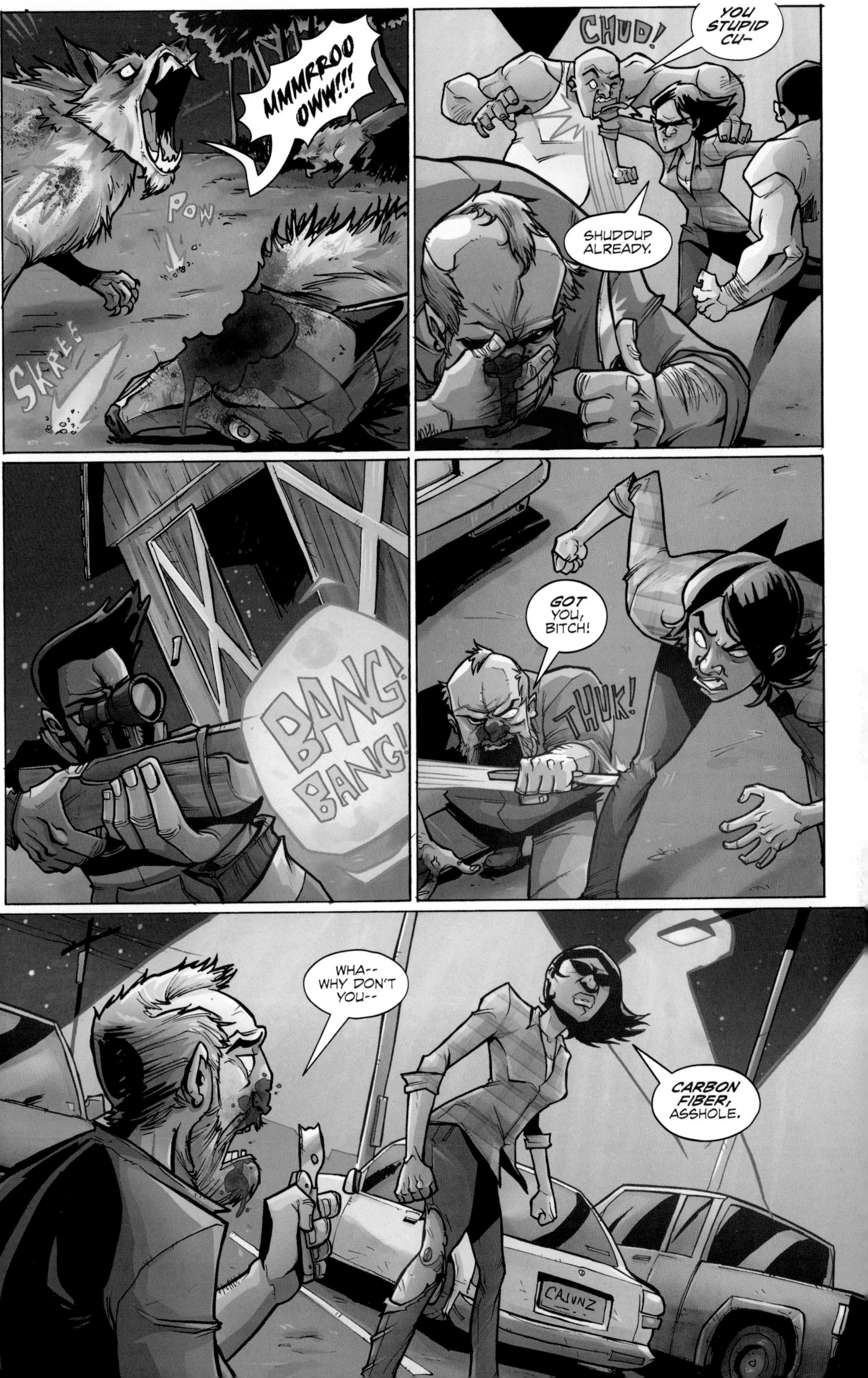
MMMRROO OWW!!!
POW
SKREE
CHUD!
YOU STUPID CU-
SHUDDUP ALREADY.
BANG! BANG!
GOT YOU, BITCH!
THUK!
WHA-- WHY DON'T YOU--
CARBON FIBER, ASSHOLE.
CAJUNZ

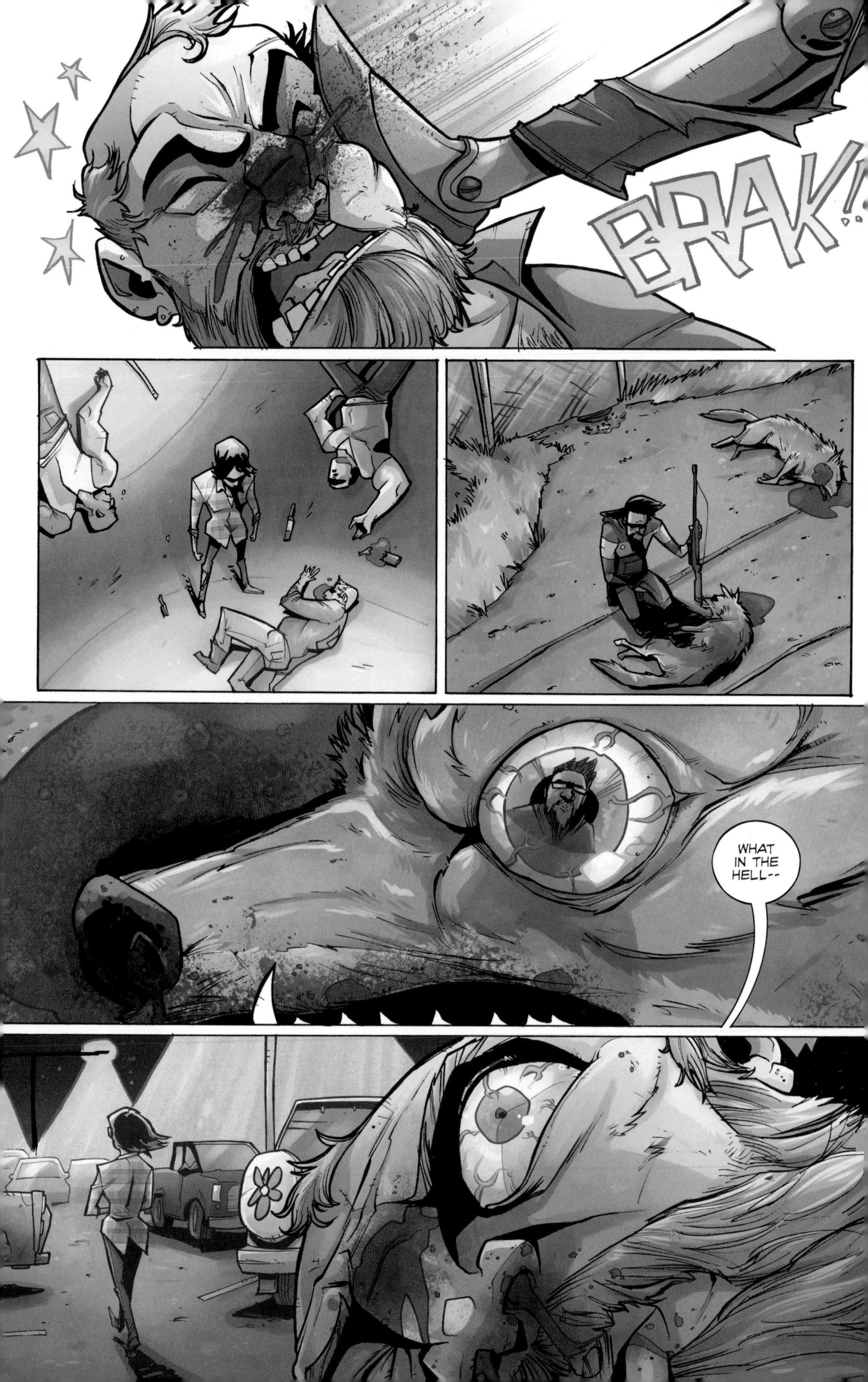
BRAK!!
WHAT IN THE HELL--

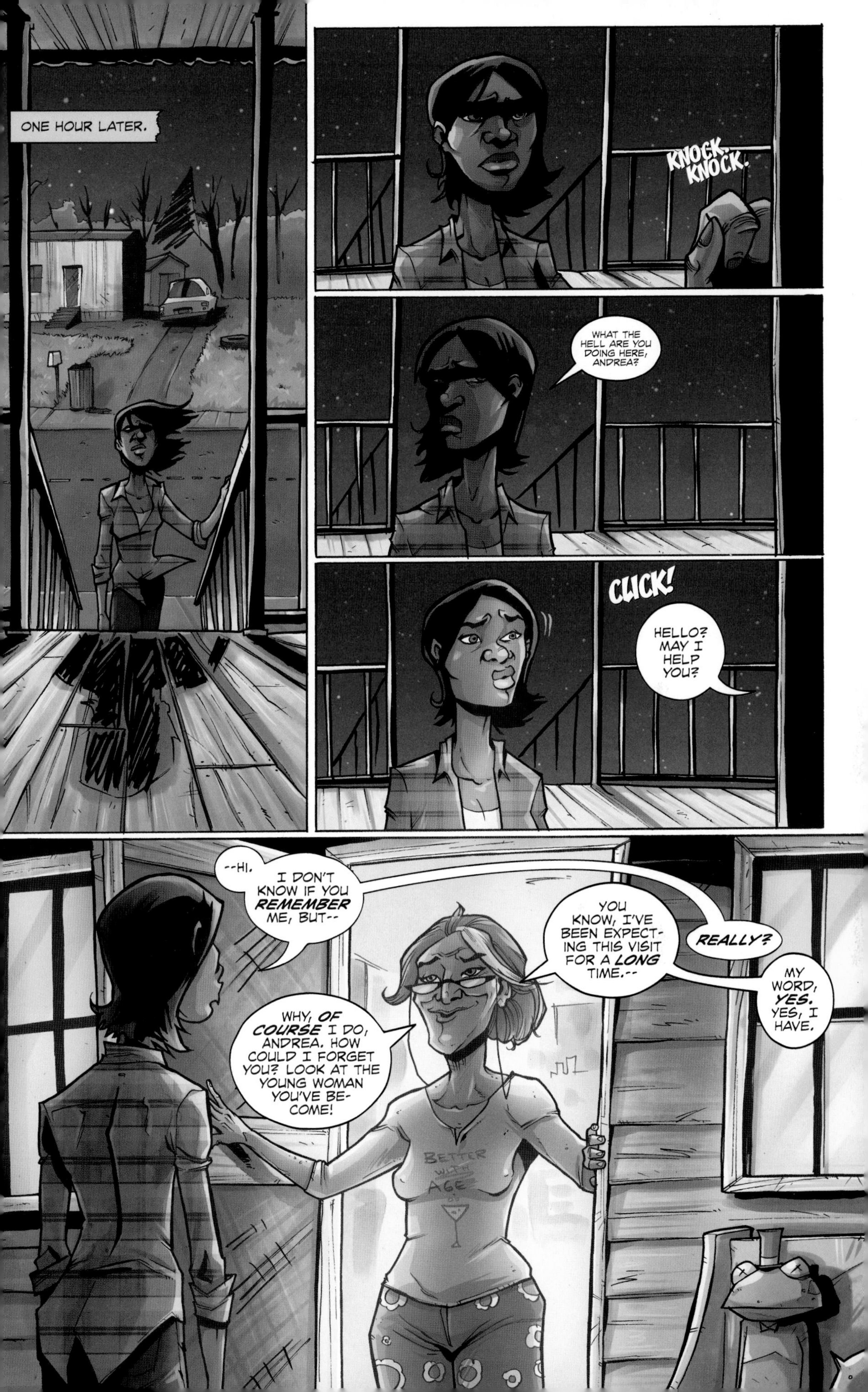

ONE HOUR LATER.
KNOCK. KNOCK.
WHAT THE HELL ARE YOU DOING HERE, ANDREA?
CLICK!
HELLO? MAY I HELP YOU?
--HI. I DON'T KNOW IF YOU **REMEMBER** ME, BUT--
WHY, **OF COURSE** I DO, ANDREA. HOW COULD I FORGET YOU? LOOK AT THE YOUNG WOMAN YOU'VE BECOME!
YOU KNOW, I'VE BEEN EXPECTING THIS VISIT FOR A **LONG** TIME.--
REALLY?
MY WORD, **YES.** YES, I HAVE.
BETTER WITH AGE

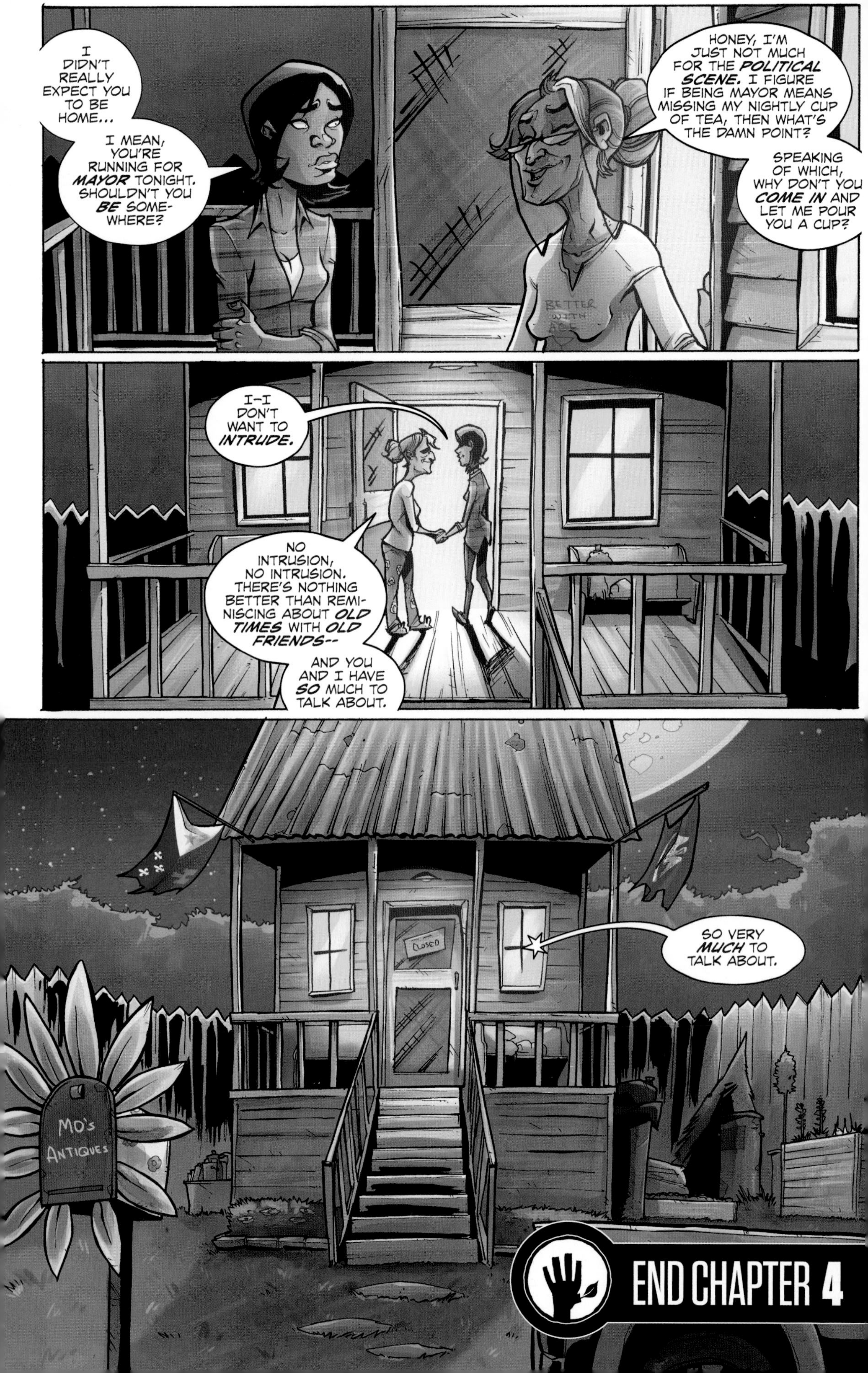
I DIDN'T REALLY EXPECT YOU TO BE HOME...
I MEAN, YOU'RE RUNNING FOR MAYOR TONIGHT. SHOULDN'T YOU BE SOME-WHERE?
HONEY, I'M JUST NOT MUCH FOR THE POLITICAL SCENE. I FIGURE IF BEING MAYOR MEANS MISSING MY NIGHTLY CUP OF TEA, THEN WHAT'S THE DAMN POINT?
SPEAKING OF WHICH, WHY DON'T YOU COME IN AND LET ME POUR YOU A CUP?
BETTER WITH AGE
I--I DON'T WANT TO INTRUDE.
NO INTRUSION, NO INTRUSION. THERE'S NOTHING BETTER THAN REMI-NISCING ABOUT OLD TIMES WITH OLD FRIENDS--
AND YOU AND I HAVE SO MUCH TO TALK ABOUT.
CLOSED
SO VERY MUCH TO TALK ABOUT.
MO's ANTIQUES
END CHAPTER 4

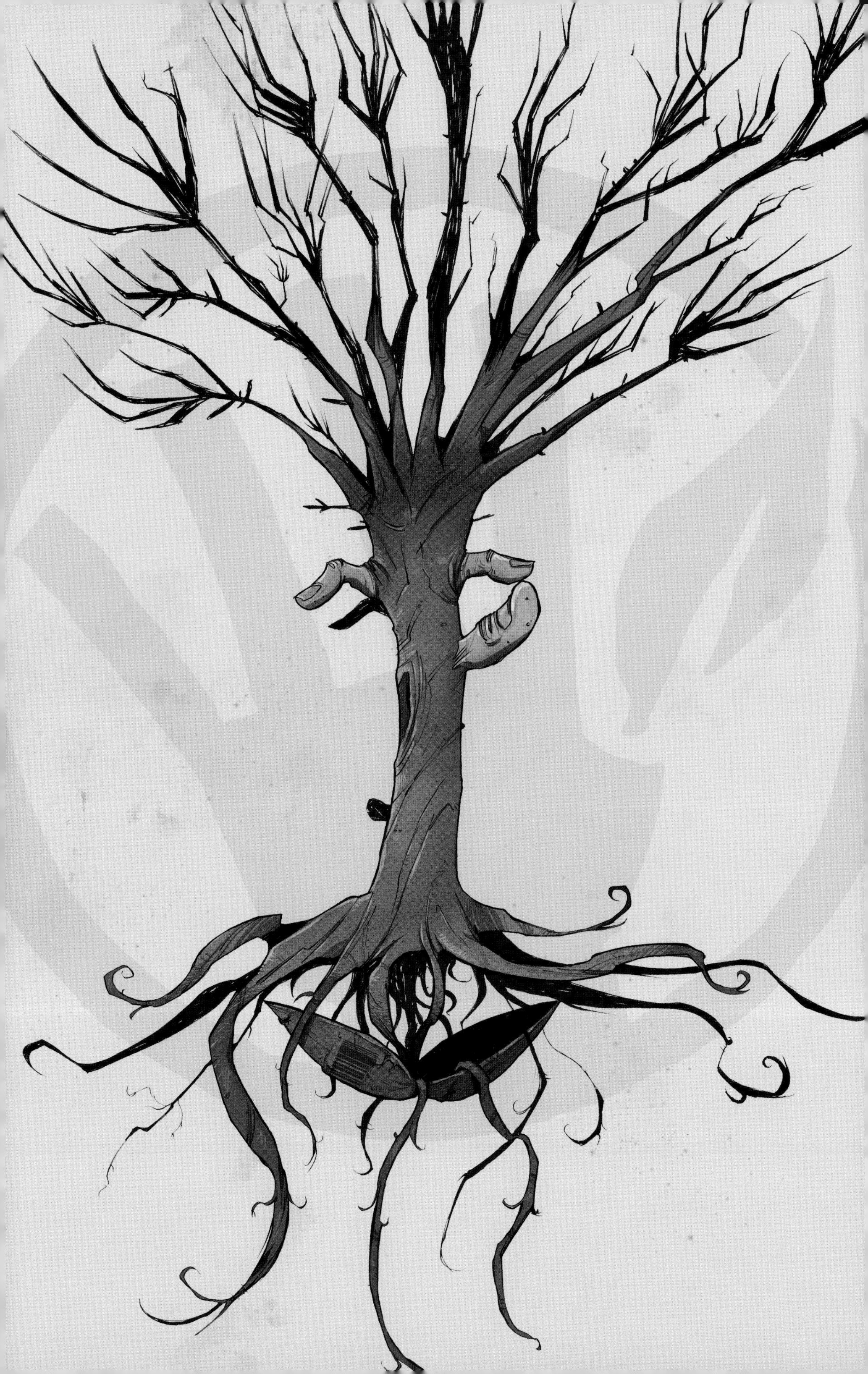

CHAPTER 5

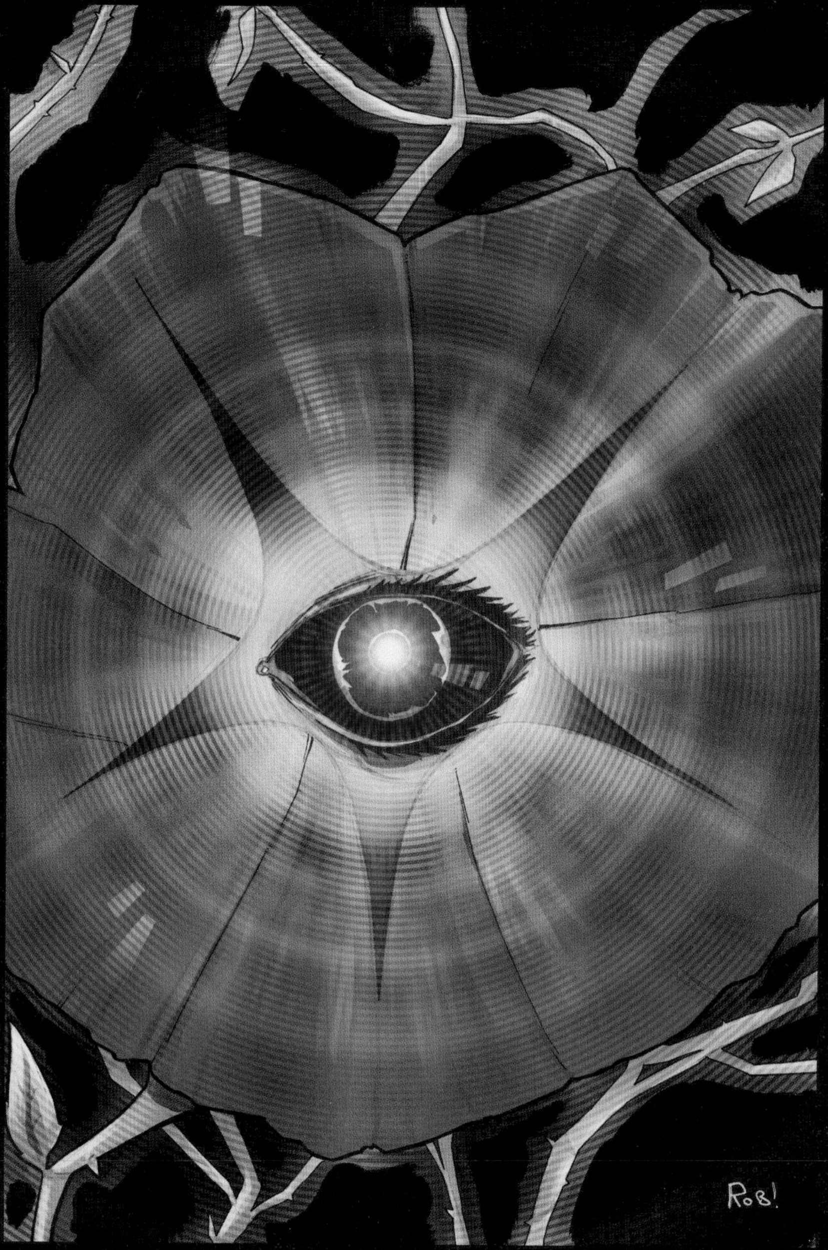
RoB!

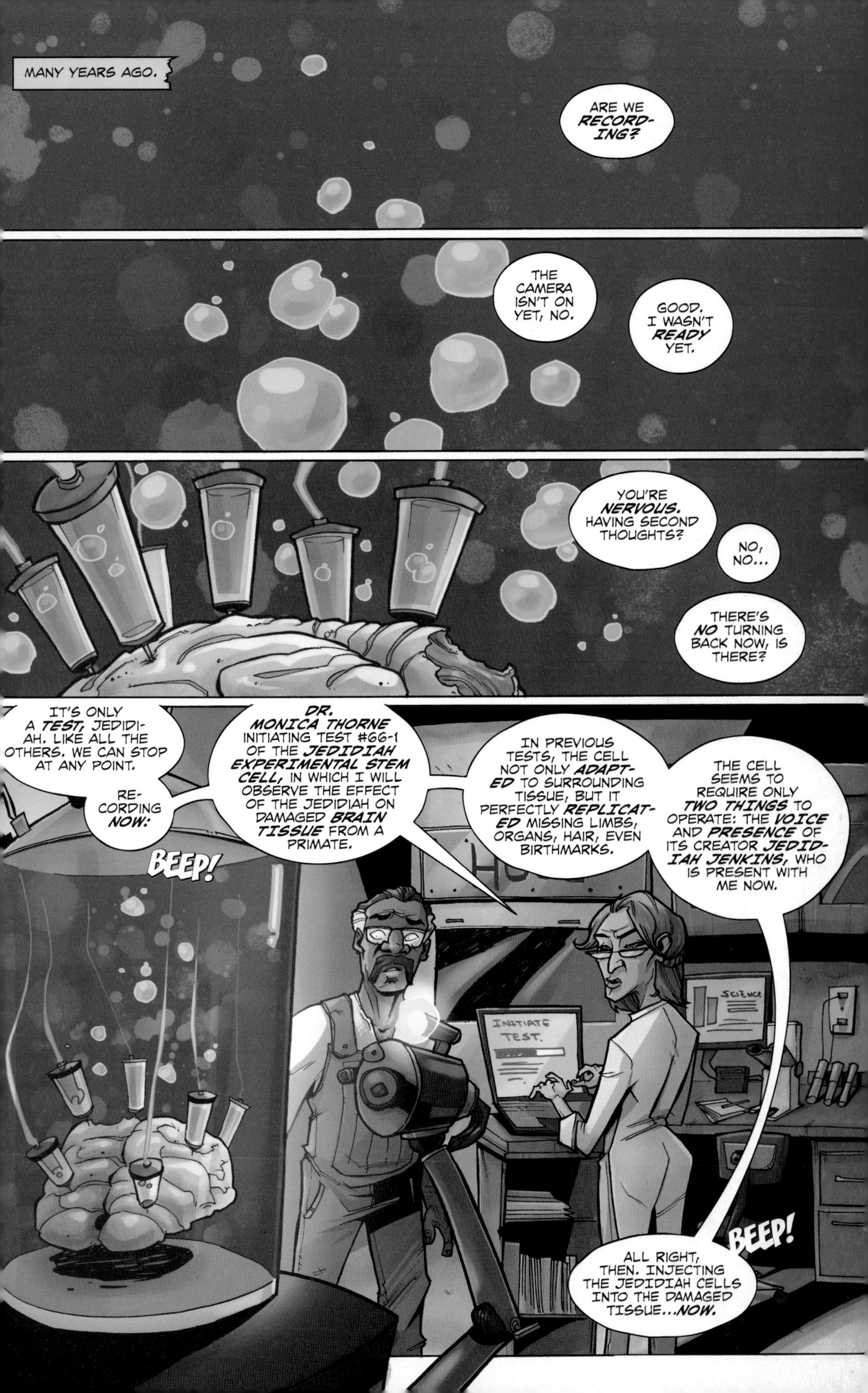
MANY YEARS AGO.
ARE WE RECORDING?
THE CAMERA ISN'T ON YET, NO.
GOOD. I WASN'T READY YET.
YOU'RE NERVOUS. HAVING SECOND THOUGHTS?
NO, NO...
THERE'S NO TURNING BACK NOW, IS THERE?
IT'S ONLY A TEST, JEDIDIAH. LIKE ALL THE OTHERS. WE CAN STOP AT ANY POINT.
RE-CORDING NOW:
DR. MONICA THORNE INITIATING TEST #66-1 OF THE JEDIDIAH EXPERIMENTAL STEM CELL, IN WHICH I WILL OBSERVE THE EFFECT OF THE JEDIDIAH ON DAMAGED BRAIN TISSUE FROM A PRIMATE.
IN PREVIOUS TESTS, THE CELL NOT ONLY ADAPTED TO SURROUNDING TISSUE, BUT IT PERFECTLY REPLICATED MISSING LIMBS, ORGANS, HAIR, EVEN BIRTHMARKS.
THE CELL SEEMS TO REQUIRE ONLY TWO THINGS TO OPERATE: THE VOICE AND PRESENCE OF ITS CREATOR JEDIDIAH JENKINS, WHO IS PRESENT WITH ME NOW.
BEEP!
INITIATE TEST.
SCIENCE
BEEP!
ALL RIGHT, THEN. INJECTING THE JEDIDIAH CELLS INTO THE DAMAGED TISSUE...NOW.

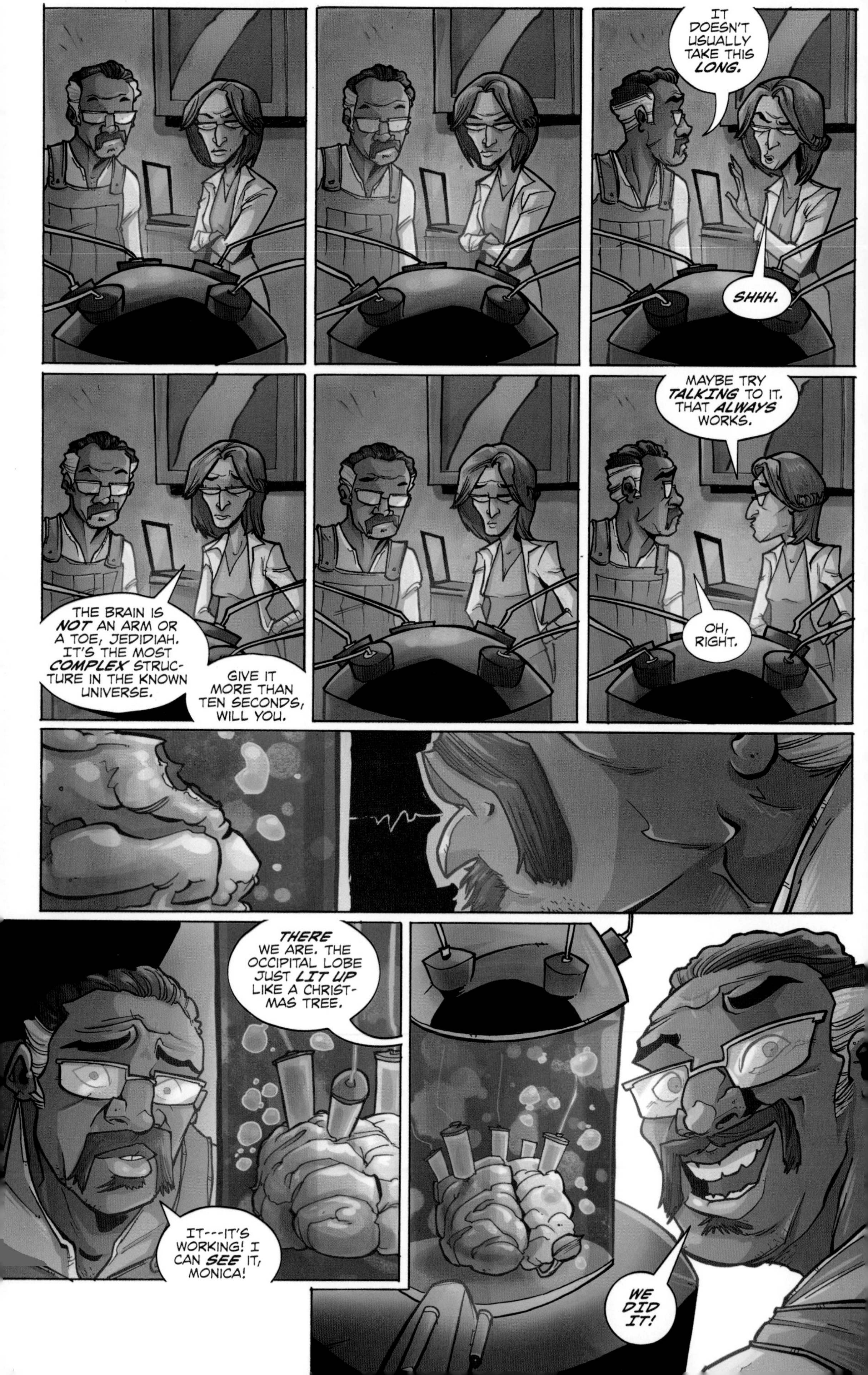
IT DOESN'T USUALLY TAKE THIS LONG.
SHHH.
MAYBE TRY TALKING TO IT. THAT ALWAYS WORKS.
THE BRAIN IS NOT AN ARM OR A TOE, JEDIDIAH. IT'S THE MOST COMPLEX STRUCTURE IN THE KNOWN UNIVERSE.
GIVE IT MORE THAN TEN SECONDS, WILL YOU.
OH, RIGHT.
THERE WE ARE. THE OCCIPITAL LOBE JUST LIT UP LIKE A CHRISTMAS TREE.
IT---IT'S WORKING! I CAN SEE IT, MONICA!
WE DID IT!

...NO.

NO, GOD, NO.

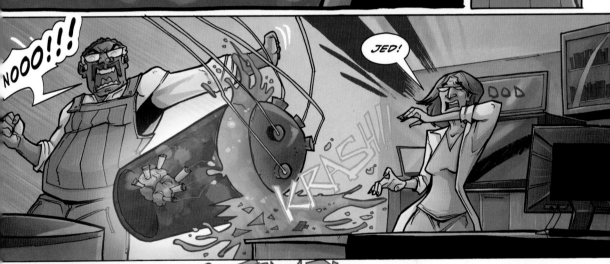

NOOO!!!

JED!

STOMP!
STOMP!!
STOMP!
STOMP!

NO!
NO! NO!
NO!

HUH. HUH. HUH... NO.

JED? IT'S OKAY, JED. IT'S OV--

WE DON'T-- TOUCH THE BRAIN--FROM HERE ON. YOU HEAR ME?

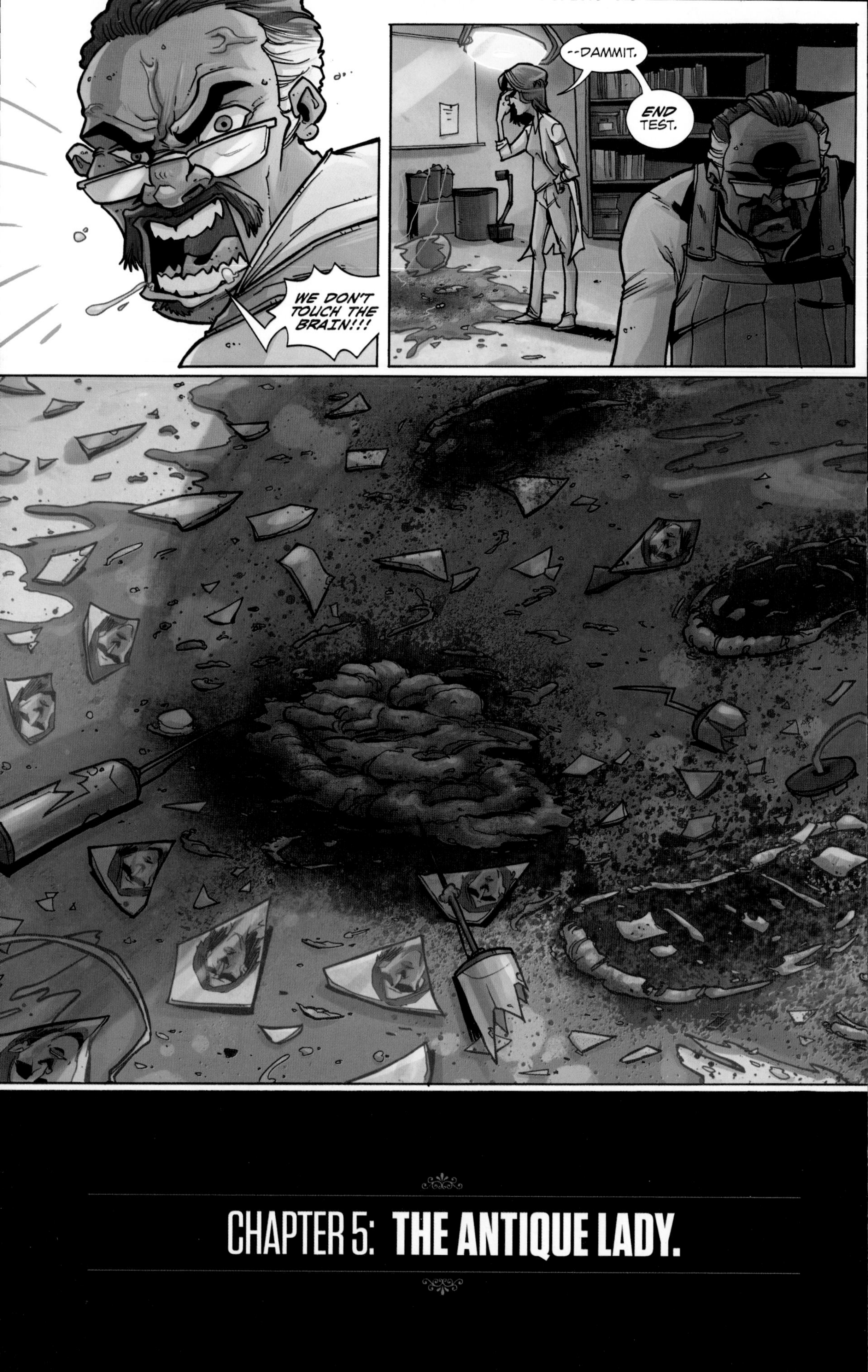
WE DON'T TOUCH THE BRAIN!!!
--DAMMIT.
END TEST.

CHAPTER 5: THE ANTIQUE LADY.

TODAY.

DAY AFTER THE ELECTION.

BANG!

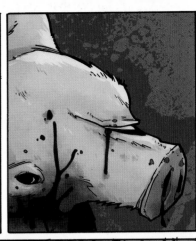

THE FREETOWN ANNUAL CAJUN *BOUCHERIE*.

A CELEBRATION OF THE FIRST ACADIAN IMMIGRANTS TO SOUTH LOUISIANA, THE *BOUCHERIE* (MEANING *BUTCHERY*) WAS A WAY LOCAL FAMILIES COULD SHARE IN THE BOUNTIES OF LOCAL WILDLIFE IN AN ERA BEFORE *REFRIGERATION*.

ONE HOG WAS MORE THAN ENOUGH MEAT FOR ONE FAMILY, SO FAMILIES CAME *TOGETHER* TO TAKE PART IN THE ANIMAL'S PREPARATION.

THEY MADE IT INTO A *PARTY*, AS CAJUNS TEND TO DO.

EVERY FAMILY PARTICIPATED. AND EVERYONE ATE. *TOGETHER*.

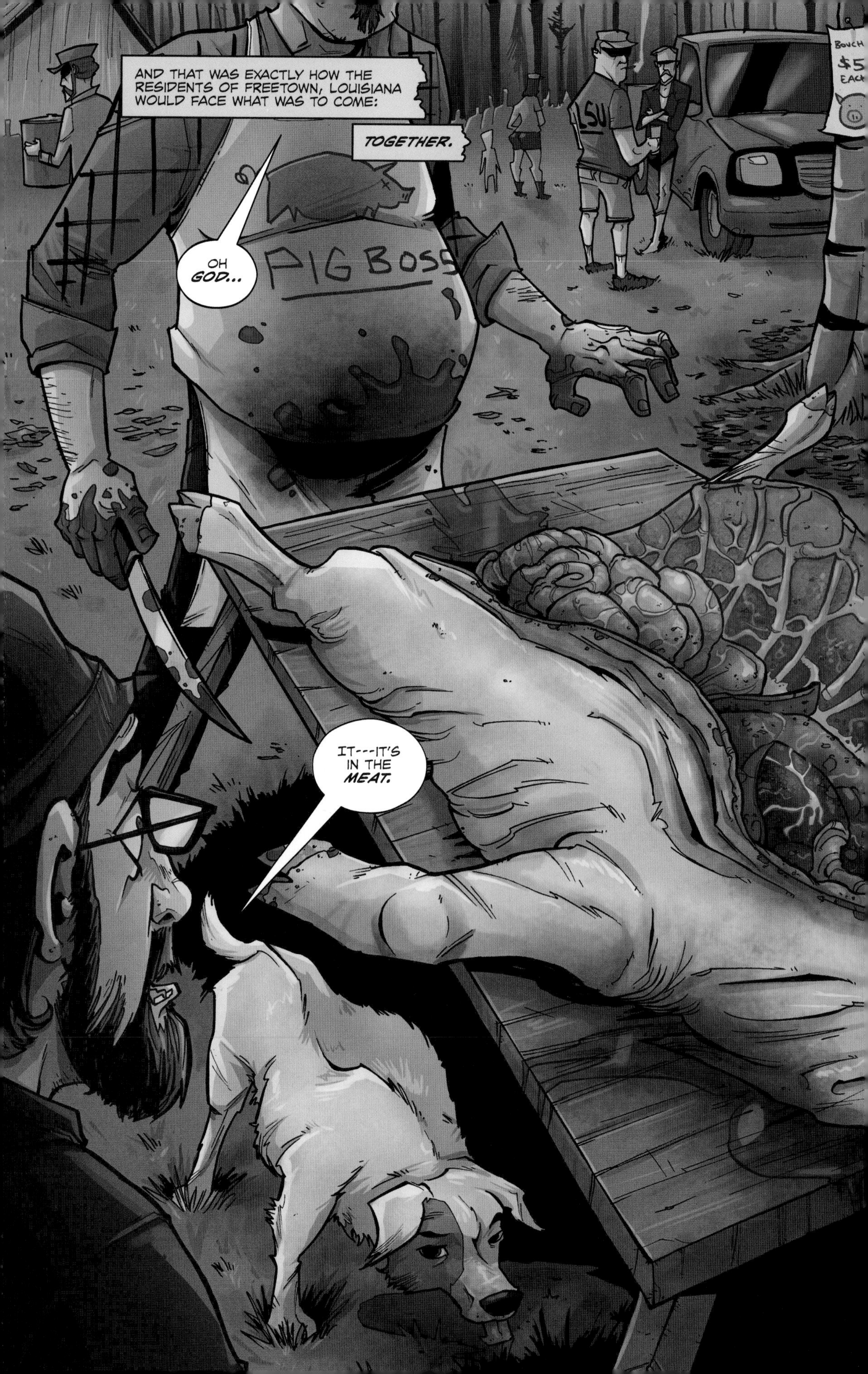
AND THAT WAS EXACTLY HOW THE RESIDENTS OF FREETOWN, LOUISIANA WOULD FACE WHAT WAS TO COME:
TOGETHER.
LSU
PIG BOSS
OH GOD...
IT---IT'S IN THE MEAT.

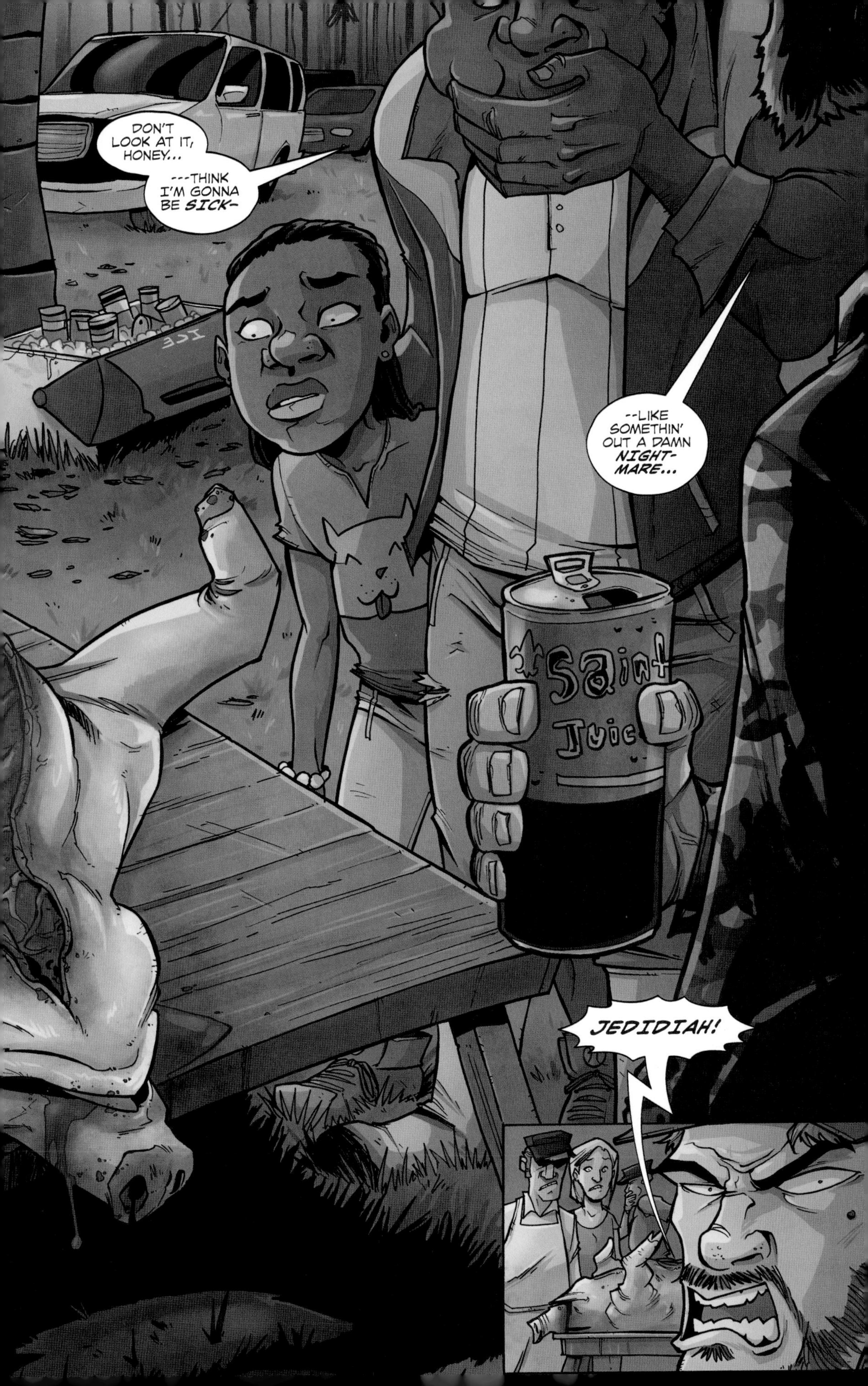
DON'T LOOK AT IT, HONEY...
---THINK I'M GONNA BE SICK-
--LIKE SOMETHIN' OUT A DAMN NIGHT-MARE...
Saint Juic
JEDIDIAH!

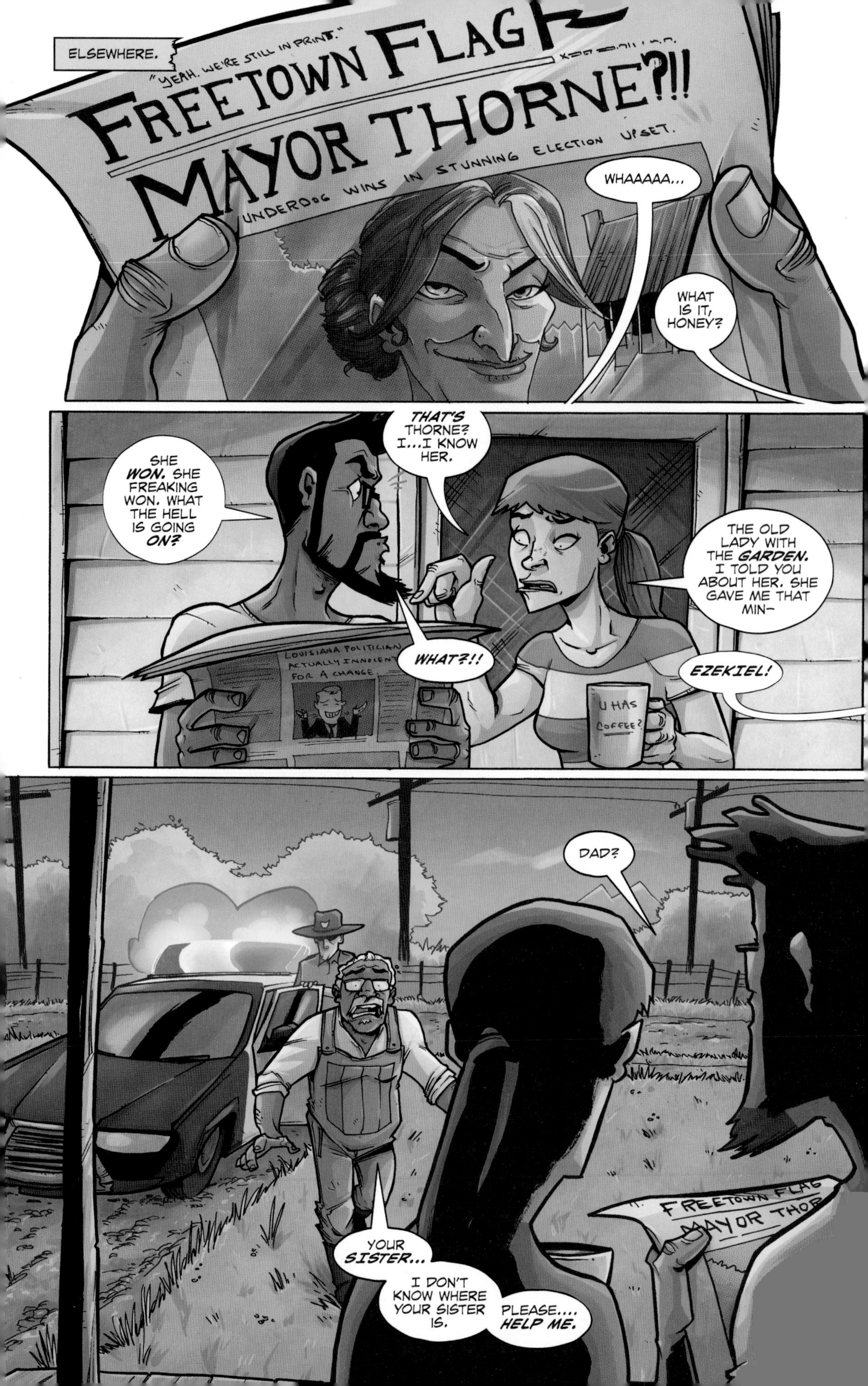
ELSEWHERE.
"YEAH. WE'RE STILL IN PRINT."
FREETOWN FLAG
MAYOR THORNE?!!
UNDERDOG WINS IN STUNNING ELECTION UPSET.
WHAAAAA...
WHAT IS IT, HONEY?
SHE WON. SHE FREAKING WON. WHAT THE HELL IS GOING ON?
THAT'S THORNE? I...I KNOW HER.
THE OLD LADY WITH THE GARDEN. I TOLD YOU ABOUT HER. SHE GAVE ME THAT MIN–
LOUISIANA POLITICIAN ACTUALLY INNOCENT FOR A CHANGE.
WHAT?!!
EZEKIEL!
U HAS COFFEE?
DAD?
FREETOWN FLAG
MAYOR THOR
YOUR SISTER...
I DON'T KNOW WHERE YOUR SISTER IS.
PLEASE.... HELP ME.

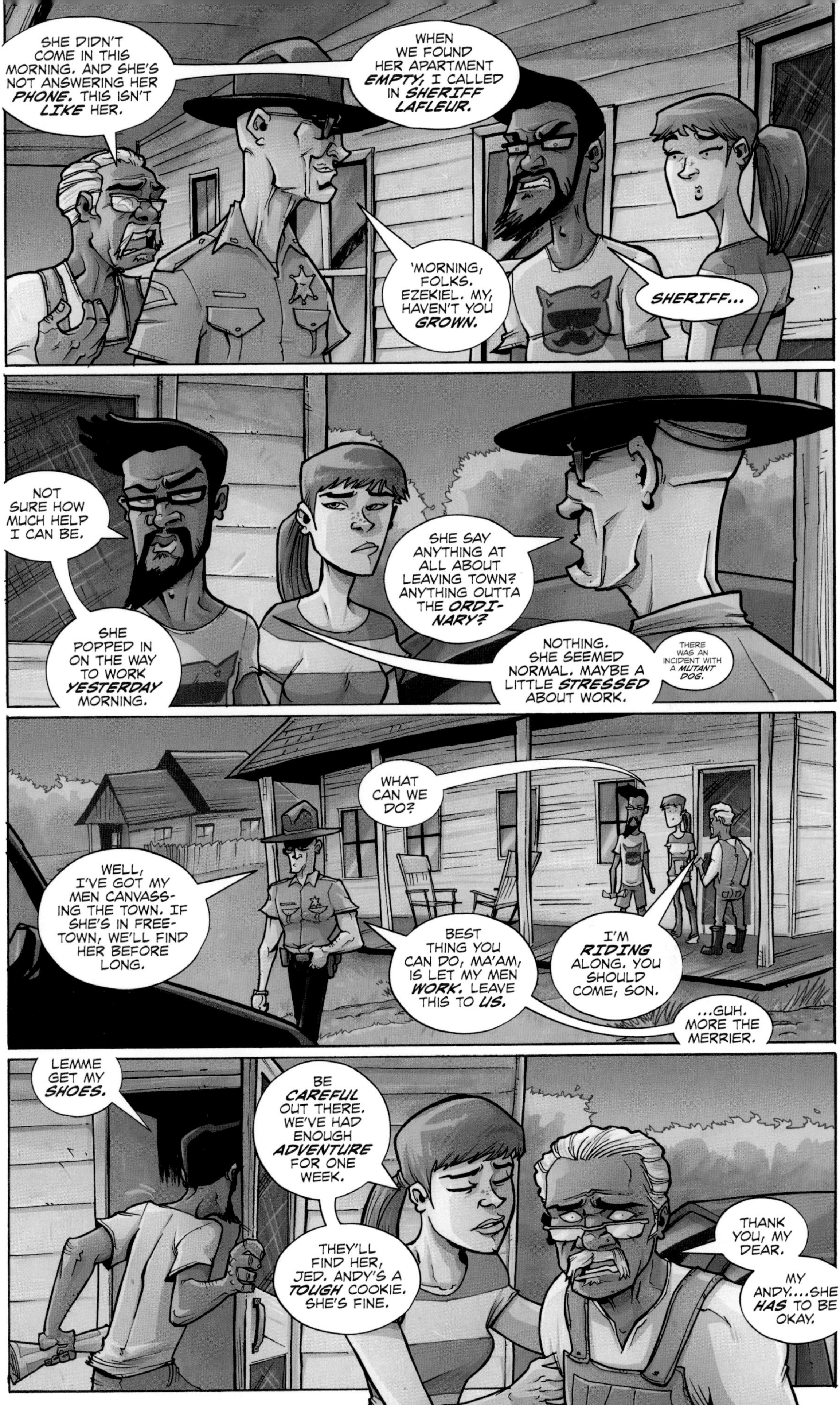
SHE DIDN'T COME IN THIS MORNING. AND SHE'S NOT ANSWERING HER PHONE. THIS ISN'T LIKE HER.
WHEN WE FOUND HER APARTMENT EMPTY, I CALLED IN SHERIFF LAFLEUR.
'MORNING, FOLKS. EZEKIEL. MY, HAVEN'T YOU GROWN.
SHERIFF...
NOT SURE HOW MUCH HELP I CAN BE.
SHE POPPED IN ON THE WAY TO WORK YESTERDAY MORNING.
SHE SAY ANYTHING AT ALL ABOUT LEAVING TOWN? ANYTHING OUTTA THE ORDI-NARY?
NOTHING. SHE SEEMED NORMAL. MAYBE A LITTLE STRESSED ABOUT WORK.
THERE WAS AN INCIDENT WITH A MUTANT DOG.
WHAT CAN WE DO?
WELL, I'VE GOT MY MEN CANVASS-ING THE TOWN. IF SHE'S IN FREE-TOWN, WE'LL FIND HER BEFORE LONG.
BEST THING YOU CAN DO, MA'AM, IS LET MY MEN WORK. LEAVE THIS TO US.
I'M RIDING ALONG. YOU SHOULD COME, SON.
...GUH. MORE THE MERRIER.
LEMME GET MY SHOES.
BE CAREFUL OUT THERE. WE'VE HAD ENOUGH ADVENTURE FOR ONE WEEK.
THEY'LL FIND HER, JED. ANDY'S A TOUGH COOKIE. SHE'S FINE.
THANK YOU, MY DEAR.
MY ANDY....SHE HAS TO BE OKAY.

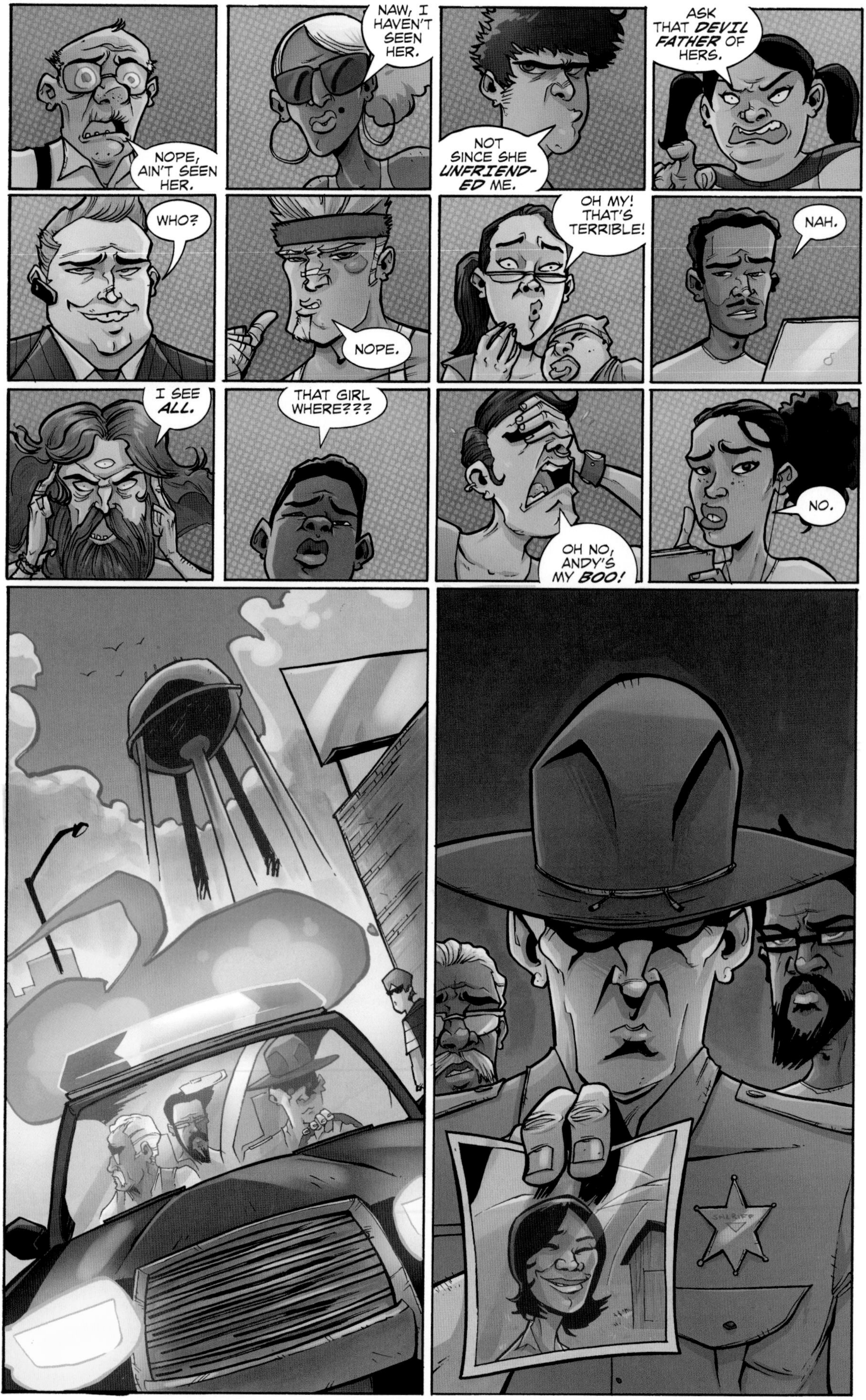
NOPE, AIN'T SEEN HER.
NAW, I HAVEN'T SEEN HER.
NOT SINCE SHE UNFRIENDED ME.
ASK THAT DEVIL FATHER OF HERS.
WHO?
NOPE.
OH MY! THAT'S TERRIBLE!
NAH.
I SEE ALL.
THAT GIRL WHERE???
OH NO, ANDY'S MY BOO!
NO.
SHERIFF

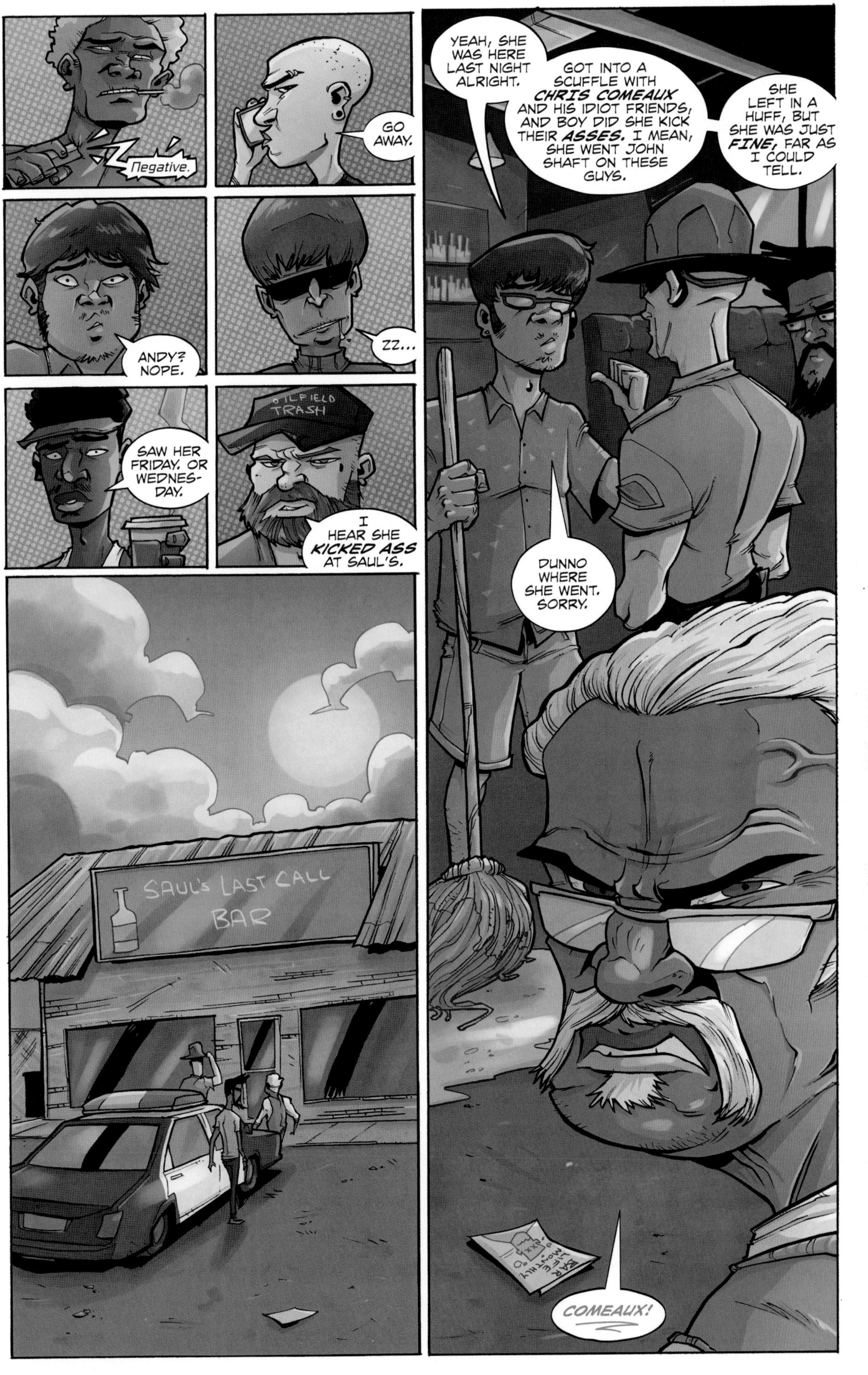
Negative.
GO AWAY.
ANDY? NOPE.
ZZ...
SAW HER FRIDAY. OR WEDNES-DAY.
OILFIELD TRASH
I HEAR SHE KICKED ASS AT SAUL'S.
SAUL'S LAST CALL BAR
YEAH, SHE WAS HERE LAST NIGHT ALRIGHT.
GOT INTO A SCUFFLE WITH CHRIS COMEAUX AND HIS IDIOT FRIENDS, AND BOY DID SHE KICK THEIR ASSES. I MEAN, SHE WENT JOHN SHAFT ON THESE GUYS.
SHE LEFT IN A HUFF, BUT SHE WAS JUST FINE, FAR AS I COULD TELL.
DUNNO WHERE SHE WENT. SORRY.
COMEAUX!

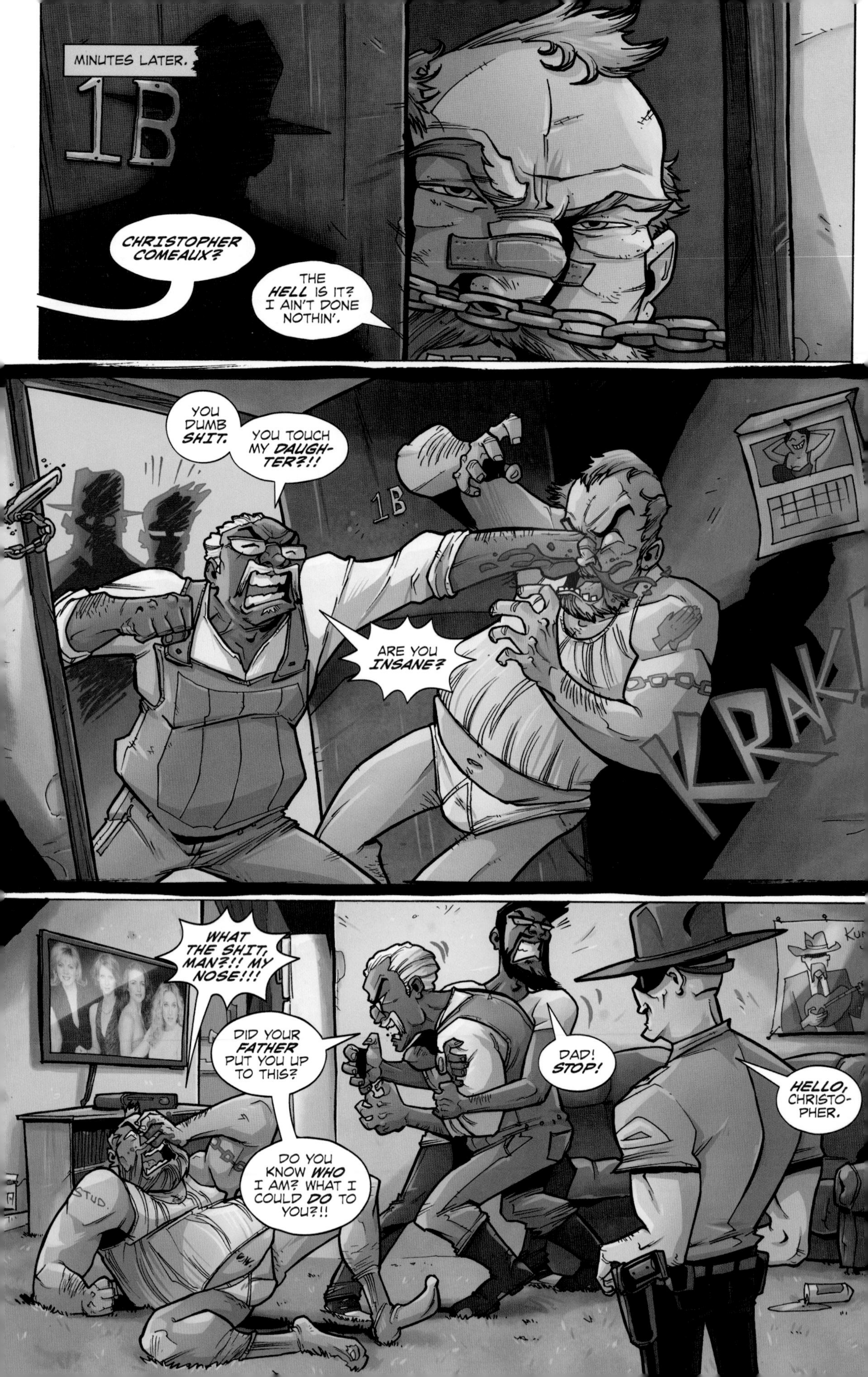
MINUTES LATER.
1B
CHRISTOPHER COMEAUX?
THE HELL IS IT? I AIN'T DONE NOTHIN'.
YOU DUMB SHIT.
YOU TOUCH MY DAUGHTER?!!
1B
ARE YOU INSANE?
KRAK!
WHAT THE SHIT, MAN?!! MY NOSE!!!
DID YOUR FATHER PUT YOU UP TO THIS?
DO YOU KNOW WHO I AM? WHAT I COULD DO TO YOU?!!
DAD! STOP!
HELLO, CHRISTOPHER.
STUD.

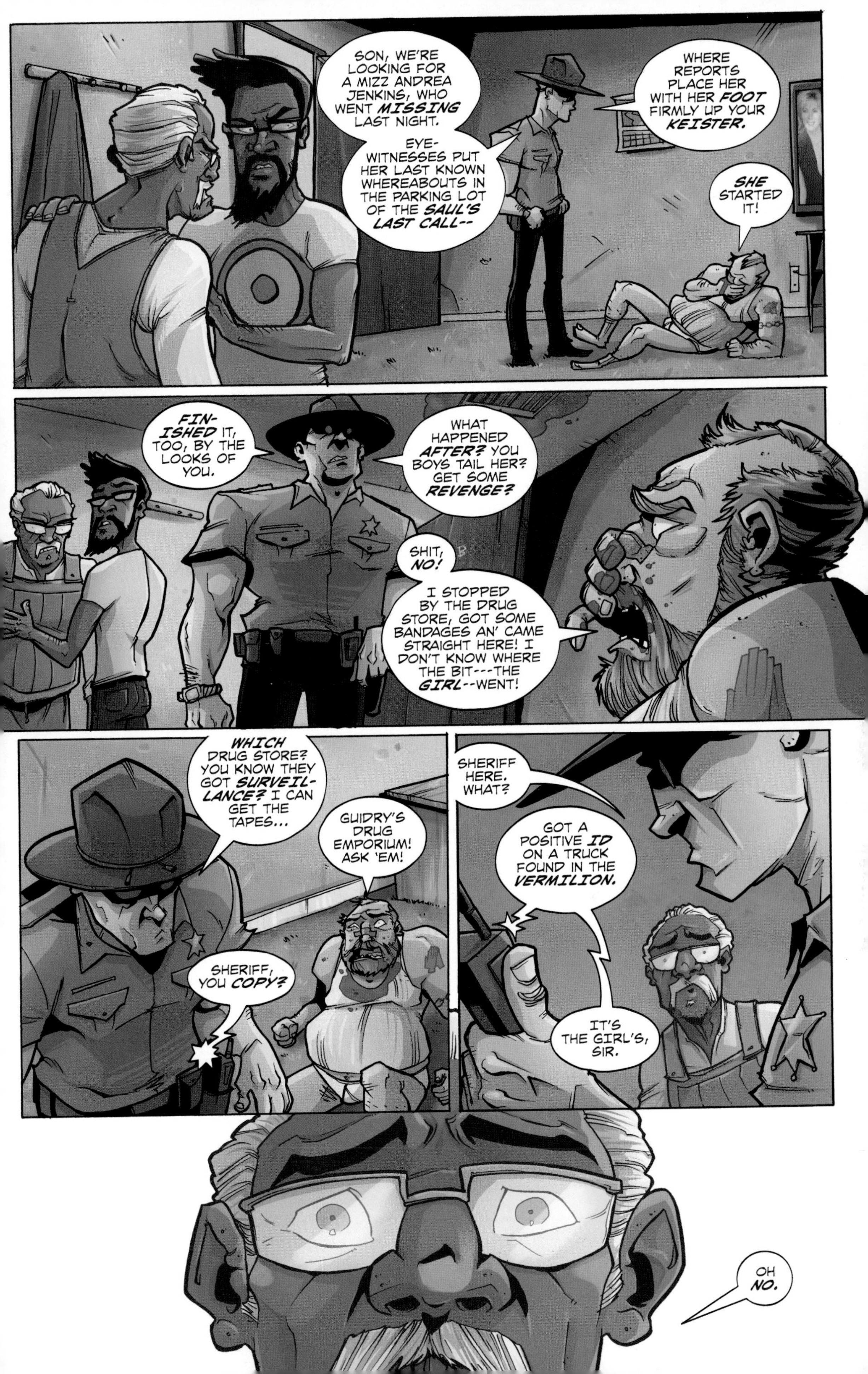
SON, WE'RE LOOKING FOR A MIZZ ANDREA JENKINS, WHO WENT MISSING LAST NIGHT.
EYE-WITNESSES PUT HER LAST KNOWN WHEREABOUTS IN THE PARKING LOT OF THE SAUL'S LAST CALL--
WHERE REPORTS PLACE HER WITH HER FOOT FIRMLY UP YOUR KEISTER.
SHE STARTED IT!
FIN-ISHED IT, TOO, BY THE LOOKS OF YOU.
WHAT HAPPENED AFTER? YOU BOYS TAIL HER? GET SOME REVENGE?
SHIT, NO!
I STOPPED BY THE DRUG STORE, GOT SOME BANDAGES AN' CAME STRAIGHT HERE! I DON'T KNOW WHERE THE BIT---THE GIRL--WENT!
WHICH DRUG STORE? YOU KNOW THEY GOT SURVEIL-LANCE? I CAN GET THE TAPES...
GUIDRY'S DRUG EMPORIUM! ASK 'EM!
SHERIFF, YOU COPY?
SHERIFF HERE. WHAT?
GOT A POSITIVE ID ON A TRUCK FOUND IN THE VERMILION.
IT'S THE GIRL'S, SIR.
OH NO.

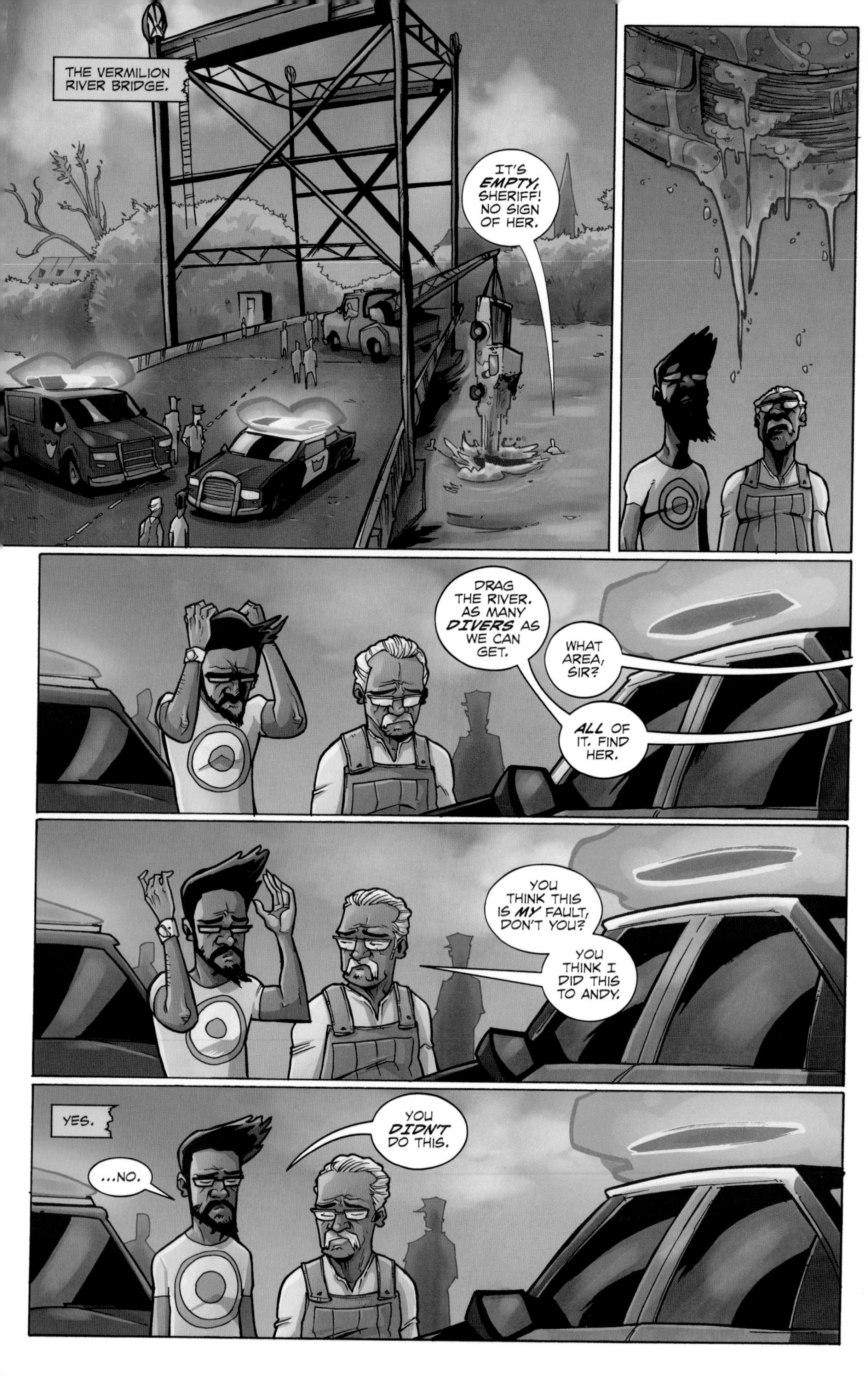
THE VERMILION RIVER BRIDGE.
IT'S EMPTY, SHERIFF! NO SIGN OF HER.
DRAG THE RIVER. AS MANY DIVERS AS WE CAN GET.
WHAT AREA, SIR?
ALL OF IT. FIND HER.
YOU THINK THIS IS MY FAULT, DON'T YOU?
YOU THINK I DID THIS TO ANDY.
YES.
YOU DIDN'T DO THIS.
...NO.

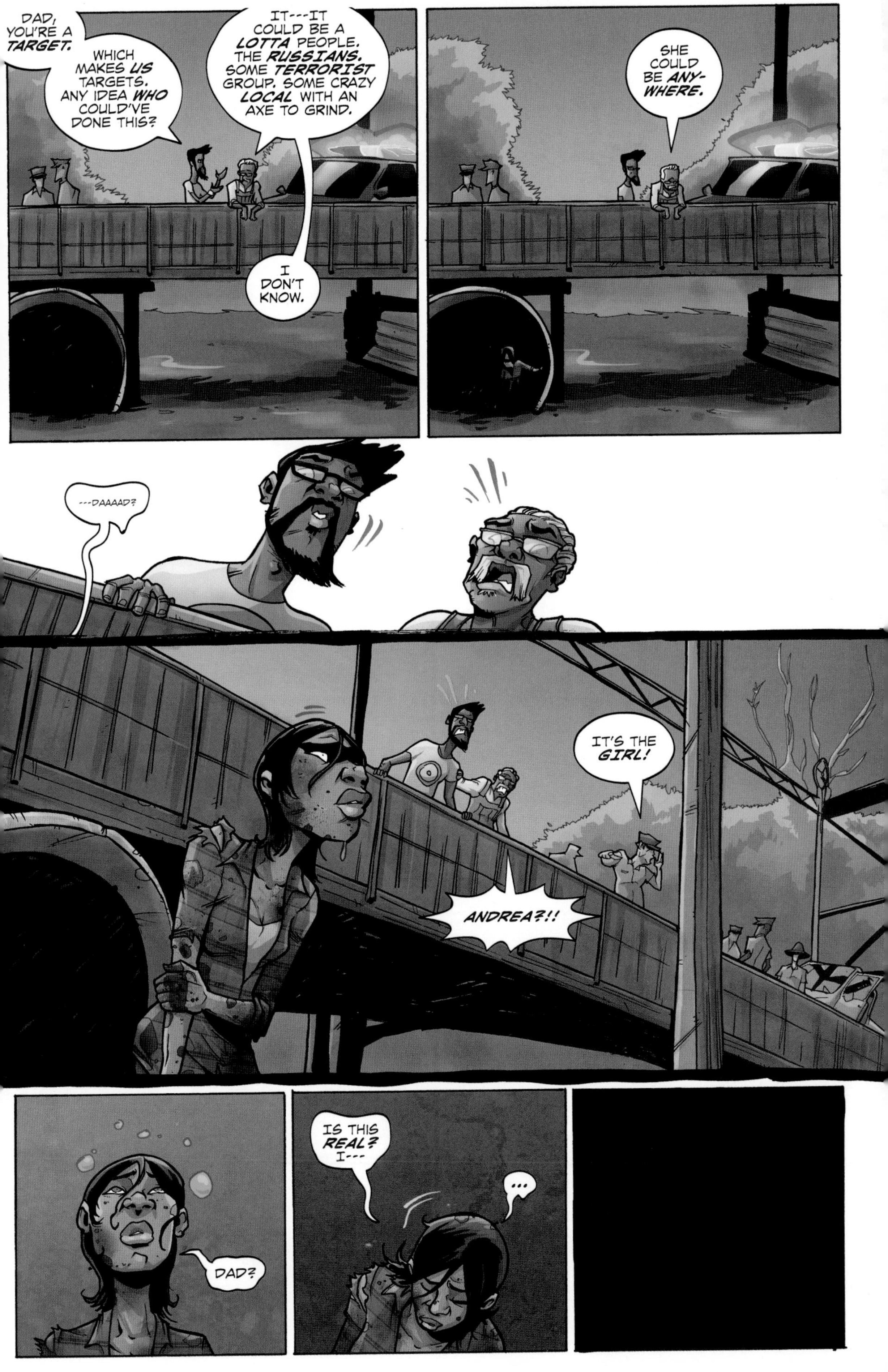
DAD, YOU'RE A TARGET.
WHICH MAKES US TARGETS. ANY IDEA WHO COULD'VE DONE THIS?
IT---IT COULD BE A LOTTA PEOPLE. THE RUSSIANS. SOME TERRORIST GROUP. SOME CRAZY LOCAL WITH AN AXE TO GRIND.
I DON'T KNOW.
SHE COULD BE ANY-WHERE.
---DAAAAD?
IT'S THE GIRL!
ANDREA?!!
DAD?
IS THIS REAL? I---
...

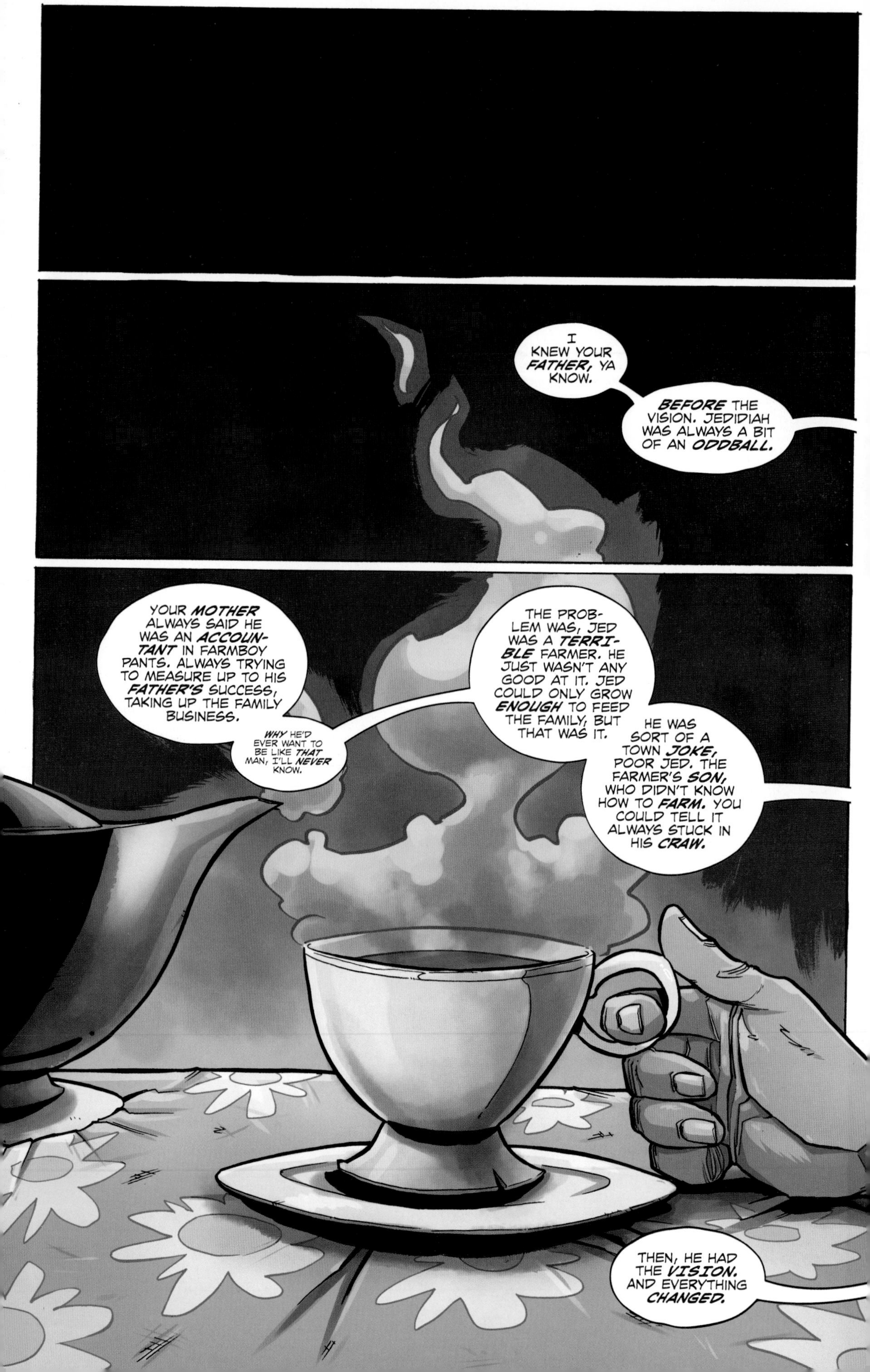
I KNEW YOUR FATHER, YA KNOW.
BEFORE THE VISION. JEDIDIAH WAS ALWAYS A BIT OF AN ODDBALL.
YOUR MOTHER ALWAYS SAID HE WAS AN ACCOUN-TANT IN FARMBOY PANTS. ALWAYS TRYING TO MEASURE UP TO HIS FATHER'S SUCCESS, TAKING UP THE FAMILY BUSINESS.
WHY HE'D EVER WANT TO BE LIKE THAT MAN, I'LL NEVER KNOW.
THE PROB-LEM WAS, JED WAS A TERRI-BLE FARMER. HE JUST WASN'T ANY GOOD AT IT. JED COULD ONLY GROW ENOUGH TO FEED THE FAMILY, BUT THAT WAS IT.
HE WAS SORT OF A TOWN JOKE, POOR JED. THE FARMER'S SON, WHO DIDN'T KNOW HOW TO FARM. YOU COULD TELL IT ALWAYS STUCK IN HIS CRAW.
THEN, HE HAD THE VISION. AND EVERYTHING CHANGED.

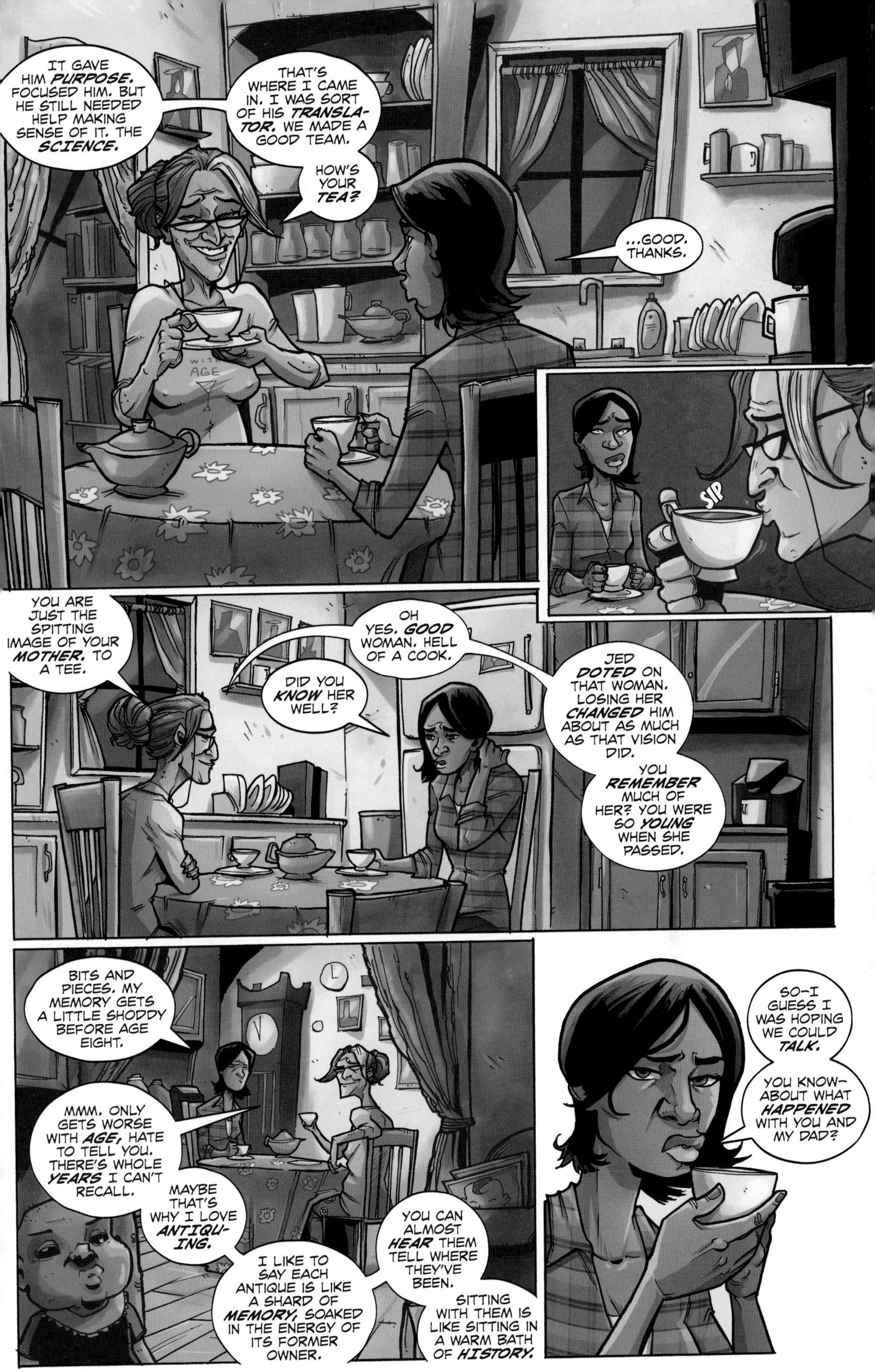
IT GAVE HIM *PURPOSE.* FOCUSED HIM. BUT HE STILL NEEDED HELP MAKING SENSE OF IT. THE *SCIENCE.*
THAT'S WHERE I CAME IN. I WAS SORT OF HIS *TRANSLATOR.* WE MADE A GOOD TEAM.
HOW'S YOUR *TEA?*
...GOOD. THANKS.
WITH AGE
SIP
YOU ARE JUST THE SPITTING IMAGE OF YOUR *MOTHER.* TO A TEE.
DID YOU *KNOW* HER WELL?
OH YES. *GOOD* WOMAN. HELL OF A COOK.
JED *DOTED* ON THAT WOMAN. LOSING HER *CHANGED* HIM ABOUT AS MUCH AS THAT VISION DID.
YOU *REMEMBER* MUCH OF HER? YOU WERE SO *YOUNG* WHEN SHE PASSED.
BITS AND PIECES. MY MEMORY GETS A LITTLE SHODDY BEFORE AGE EIGHT.
MMM. ONLY GETS WORSE WITH *AGE,* HATE TO TELL YOU. THERE'S WHOLE *YEARS* I CAN'T RECALL.
MAYBE THAT'S WHY I LOVE *ANTIQUING.*
I LIKE TO SAY EACH ANTIQUE IS LIKE A SHARD OF *MEMORY,* SOAKED IN THE ENERGY OF ITS FORMER OWNER.
YOU CAN ALMOST *HEAR* THEM TELL WHERE THEY'VE BEEN.
SITTING WITH THEM IS LIKE SITTING IN A WARM BATH OF *HISTORY.*
SO–I GUESS I WAS HOPING WE COULD *TALK.*
YOU KNOW–ABOUT WHAT *HAPPENED* WITH YOU AND MY DAD?

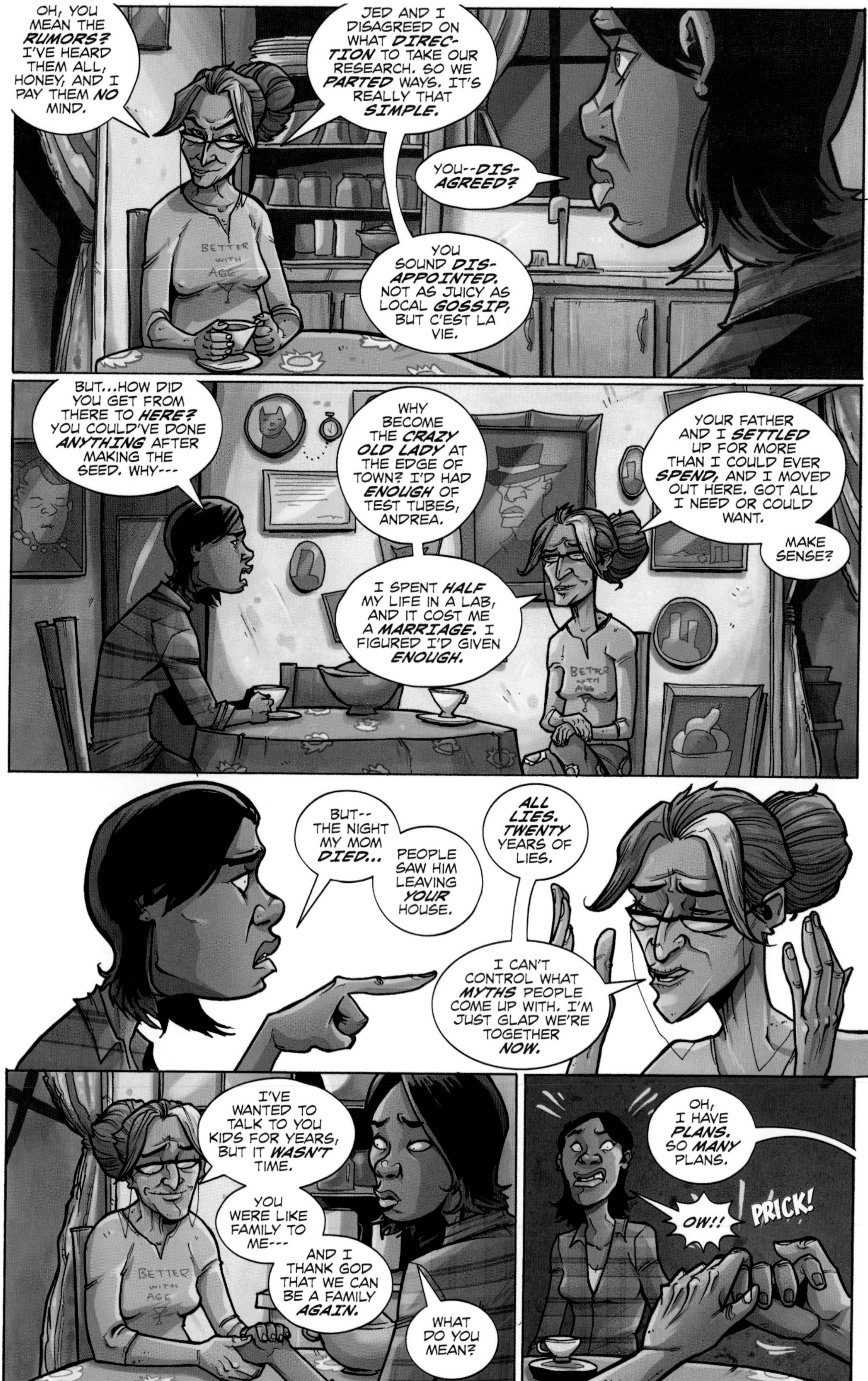
OH, YOU MEAN THE RUMORS? I'VE HEARD THEM ALL, HONEY, AND I PAY THEM NO MIND.
JED AND I DISAGREED ON WHAT DIREC-TION TO TAKE OUR RESEARCH. SO WE PARTED WAYS. IT'S REALLY THAT SIMPLE.
YOU--DIS-AGREED?
YOU SOUND DIS-APPOINTED. NOT AS JUICY AS LOCAL GOSSIP, BUT C'EST LA VIE.
BETTER WITH AGE
BUT...HOW DID YOU GET FROM THERE TO HERE? YOU COULD'VE DONE ANYTHING AFTER MAKING THE SEED. WHY---
WHY BECOME THE CRAZY OLD LADY AT THE EDGE OF TOWN? I'D HAD ENOUGH OF TEST TUBES, ANDREA.
I SPENT HALF MY LIFE IN A LAB, AND IT COST ME A MARRIAGE. I FIGURED I'D GIVEN ENOUGH.
YOUR FATHER AND I SETTLED UP FOR MORE THAN I COULD EVER SPEND, AND I MOVED OUT HERE. GOT ALL I NEED OR COULD WANT.
MAKE SENSE?
BUT-- THE NIGHT MY MOM DIED...
PEOPLE SAW HIM LEAVING YOUR HOUSE.
ALL LIES. TWENTY YEARS OF LIES.
I CAN'T CONTROL WHAT MYTHS PEOPLE COME UP WITH. I'M JUST GLAD WE'RE TOGETHER NOW.
I'VE WANTED TO TALK TO YOU KIDS FOR YEARS, BUT IT WASN'T TIME.
YOU WERE LIKE FAMILY TO ME---
AND I THANK GOD THAT WE CAN BE A FAMILY AGAIN.
WHAT DO YOU MEAN?
OH, I HAVE PLANS. SO MANY PLANS.
OW!!
PRICK!

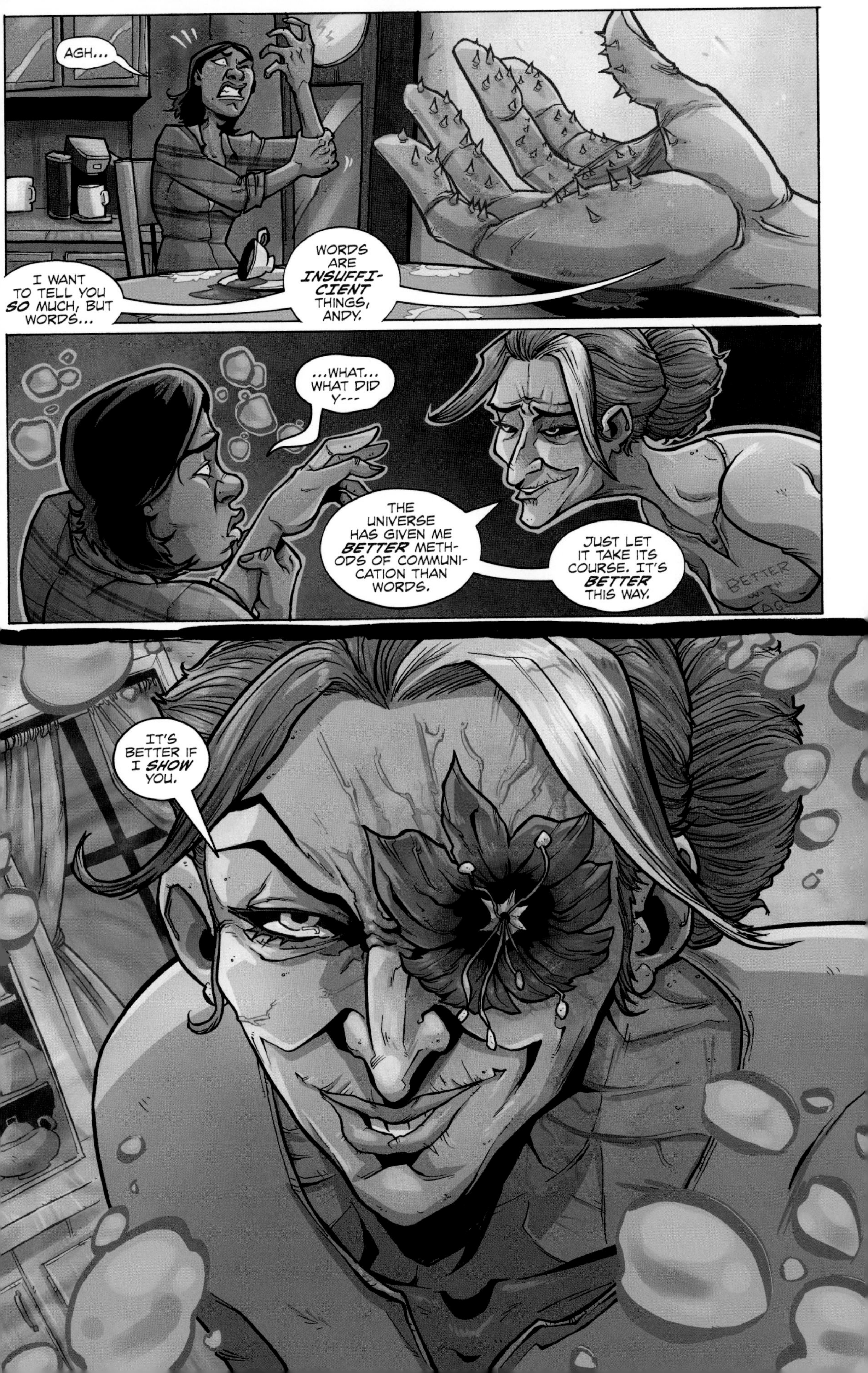
AGH...
I WANT TO TELL YOU **SO** MUCH, BUT WORDS...
WORDS ARE ***INSUFFICIENT*** THINGS, ANDY.
...WHAT... WHAT DID Y---
THE UNIVERSE HAS GIVEN ME ***BETTER*** METHODS OF COMMUNICATION THAN WORDS.
JUST LET IT TAKE ITS COURSE. IT'S ***BETTER*** THIS WAY.
IT'S BETTER IF I ***SHOW*** YOU.

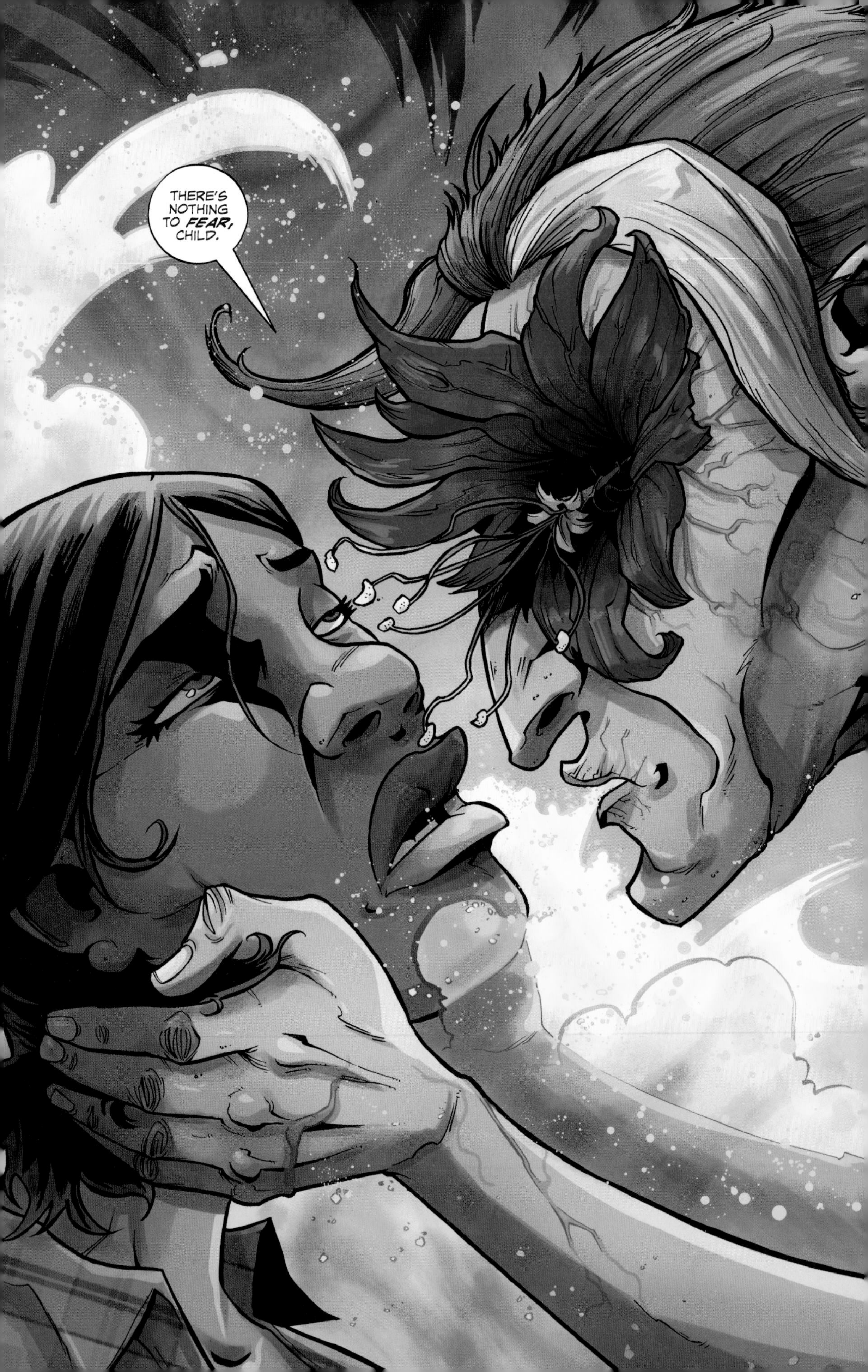
THERE'S NOTHING TO *FEAR*, CHILD.

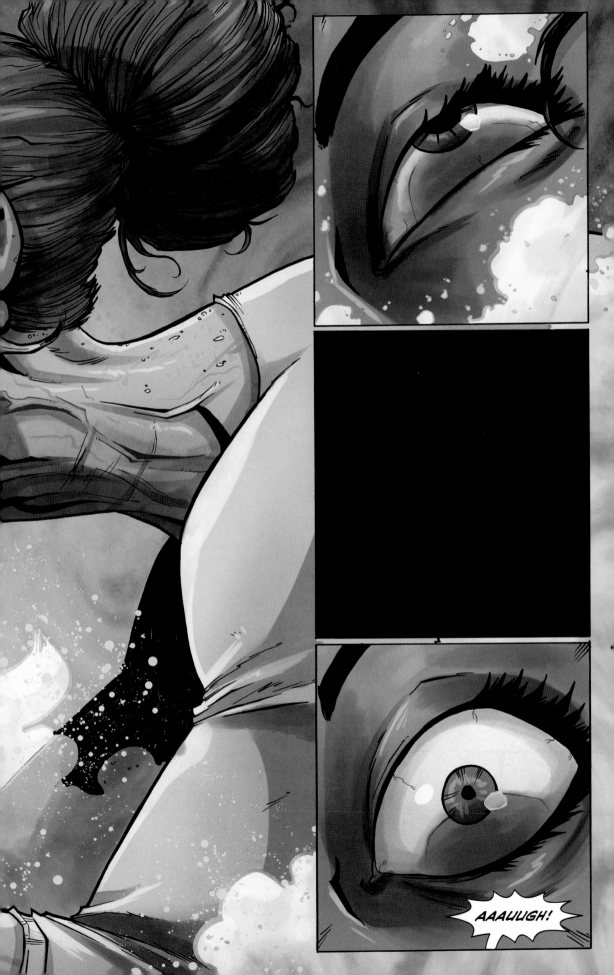

AAAUUGH!

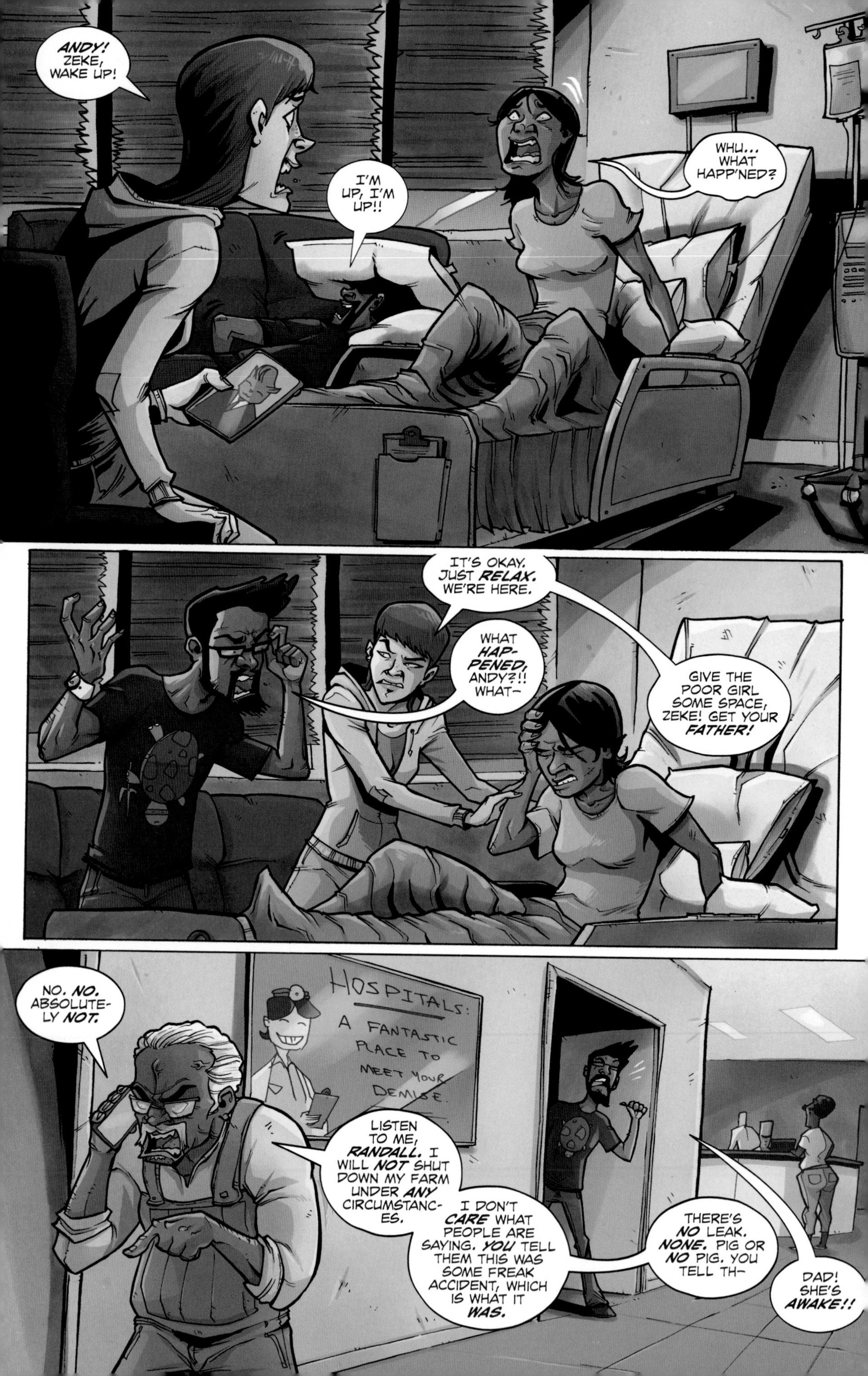
ANDY! ZEKE, WAKE UP!
I'M UP, I'M UP!!
WHU... WHAT HAPP'NED?
IT'S OKAY. JUST RELAX. WE'RE HERE.
WHAT HAP-PENED, ANDY?!! WHAT–
GIVE THE POOR GIRL SOME SPACE, ZEKE! GET YOUR FATHER!
NO. NO. ABSOLUTE-LY NOT.
HOSPITALS: A FANTASTIC PLACE TO MEET YOUR DEMISE.
LISTEN TO ME, RANDALL. I WILL NOT SHUT DOWN MY FARM UNDER ANY CIRCUMSTANC-ES.
I DON'T CARE WHAT PEOPLE ARE SAYING. YOU TELL THEM THIS WAS SOME FREAK ACCIDENT, WHICH IS WHAT IT WAS.
THERE'S NO LEAK. NONE. PIG OR NO PIG. YOU TELL TH–
DAD! SHE'S AWAKE!!

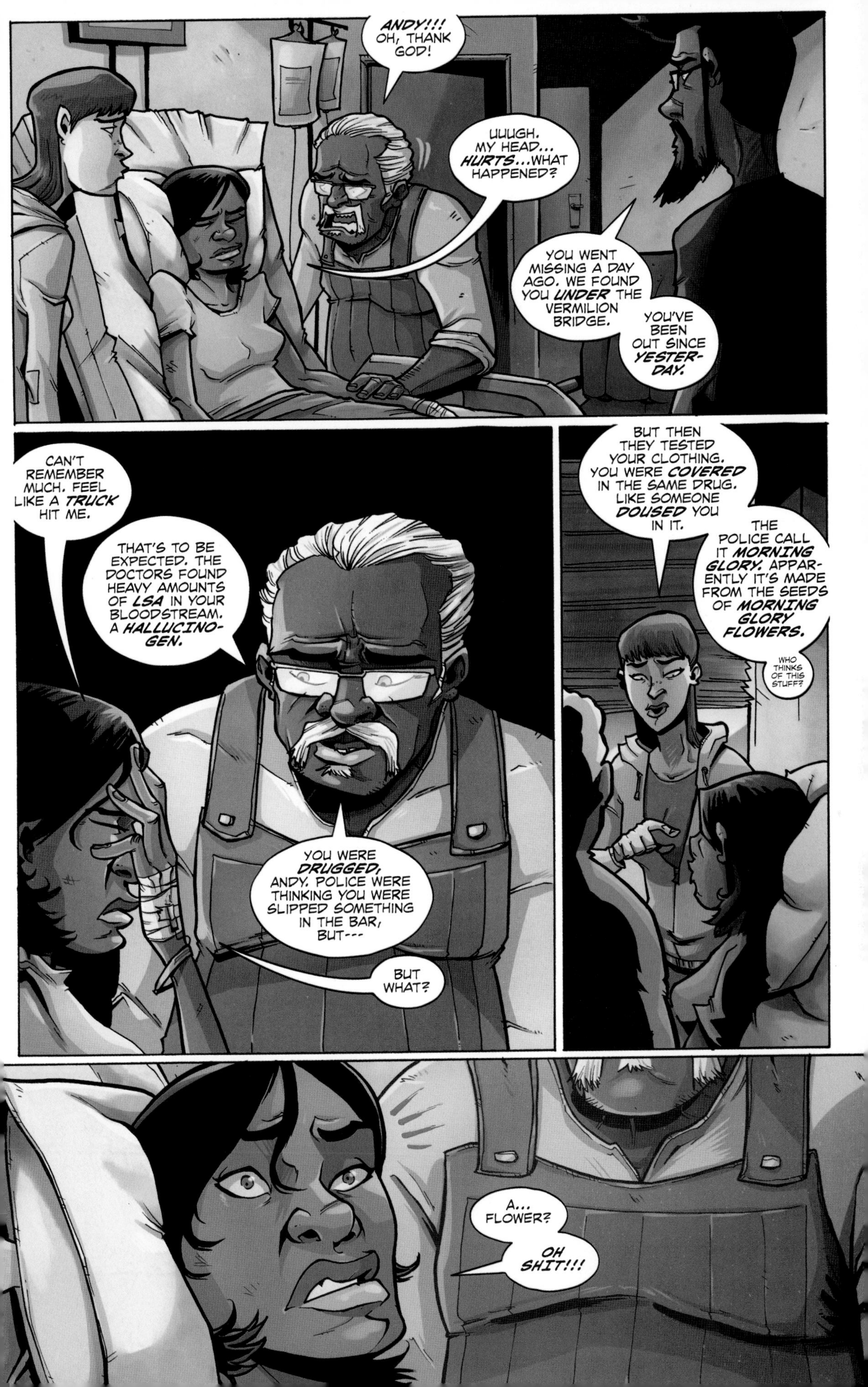
ANDY!!! OH, THANK GOD!
UUUGH. MY HEAD... HURTS...WHAT HAPPENED?
YOU WENT MISSING A DAY AGO. WE FOUND YOU UNDER THE VERMILION BRIDGE.
YOU'VE BEEN OUT SINCE YESTER-DAY.
CAN'T REMEMBER MUCH. FEEL LIKE A TRUCK HIT ME.
THAT'S TO BE EXPECTED. THE DOCTORS FOUND HEAVY AMOUNTS OF LSA IN YOUR BLOODSTREAM. A HALLUCINO-GEN.
YOU WERE DRUGGED, ANDY. POLICE WERE THINKING YOU WERE SLIPPED SOMETHING IN THE BAR, BUT---
BUT WHAT?
BUT THEN THEY TESTED YOUR CLOTHING. YOU WERE COVERED IN THE SAME DRUG. LIKE SOMEONE DOUSED YOU IN IT.
THE POLICE CALL IT MORNING GLORY. APPAR-ENTLY IT'S MADE FROM THE SEEDS OF MORNING GLORY FLOWERS.
WHO THINKS OF THIS STUFF?
A... FLOWER?
OH SHIT!!!

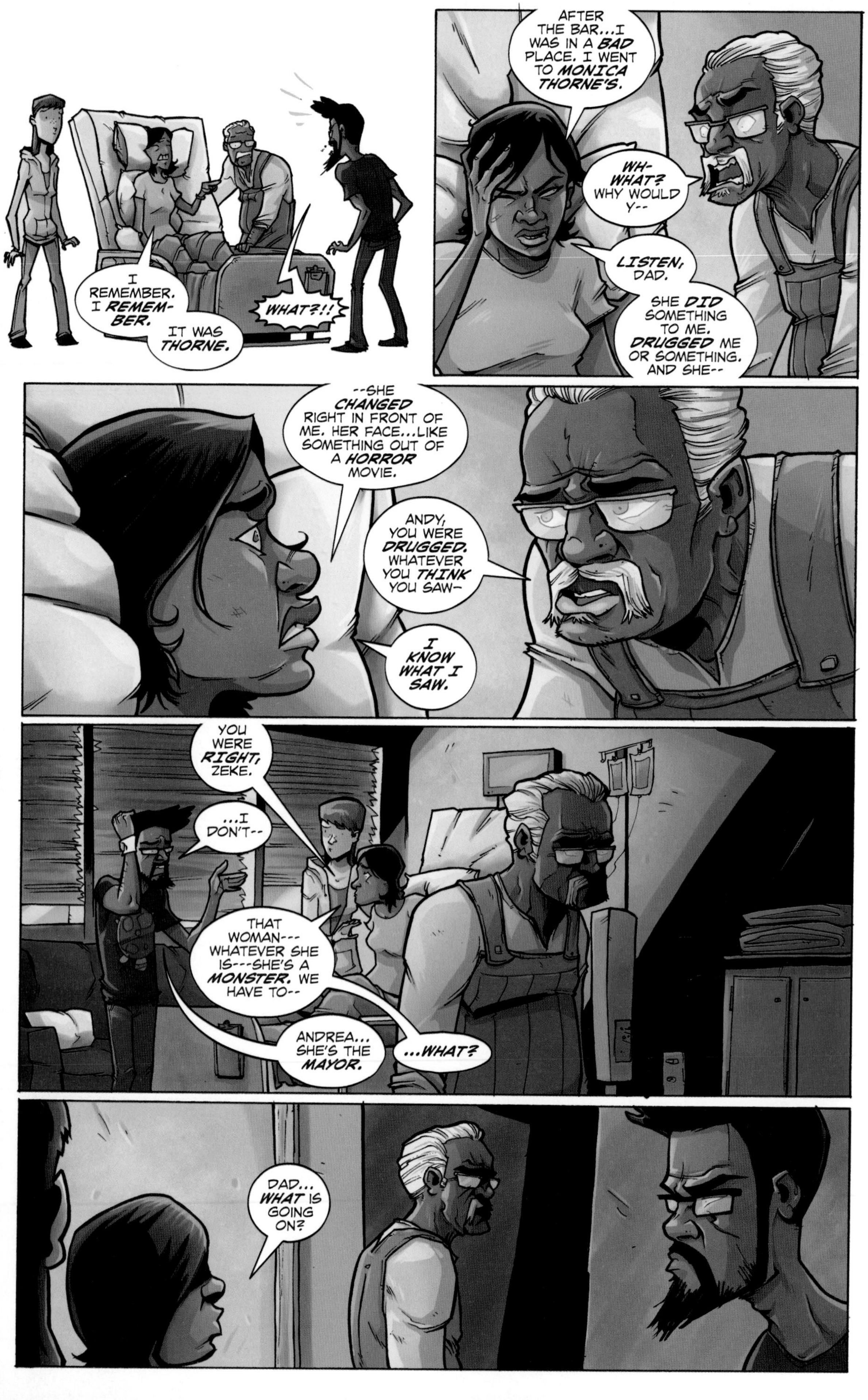
I REMEMBER. I REMEMBER.
IT WAS THORNE.
WHAT?!!
AFTER THE BAR...I WAS IN A BAD PLACE. I WENT TO MONICA THORNE'S.
WH-WHAT? WHY WOULD Y--
LISTEN, DAD.
SHE DID SOMETHING TO ME. DRUGGED ME OR SOMETHING. AND SHE--
--SHE CHANGED RIGHT IN FRONT OF ME. HER FACE...LIKE SOMETHING OUT OF A HORROR MOVIE.
ANDY, YOU WERE DRUGGED. WHATEVER YOU THINK YOU SAW-
I KNOW WHAT I SAW.
YOU WERE RIGHT, ZEKE.
...I DON'T--
THAT WOMAN---WHATEVER SHE IS---SHE'S A MONSTER. WE HAVE TO--
ANDREA... SHE'S THE MAYOR.
...WHAT?
DAD... WHAT IS GOING ON?

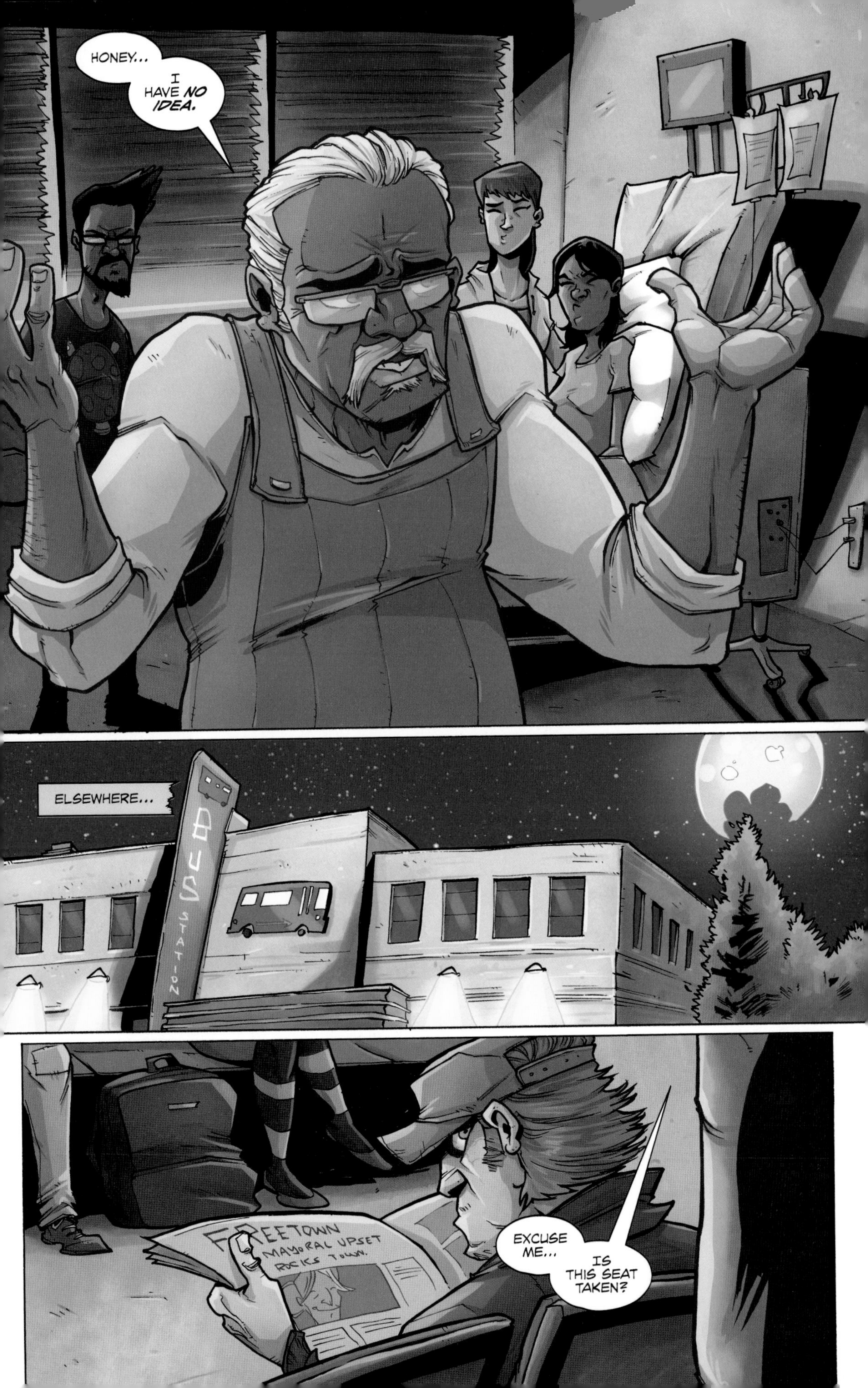
HONEY...
I HAVE NO IDEA.
ELSEWHERE...
BUS STATION
FREETOWN
MAYORAL UPSET ROCKS TOWN.
EXCUSE ME...
IS THIS SEAT TAKEN?

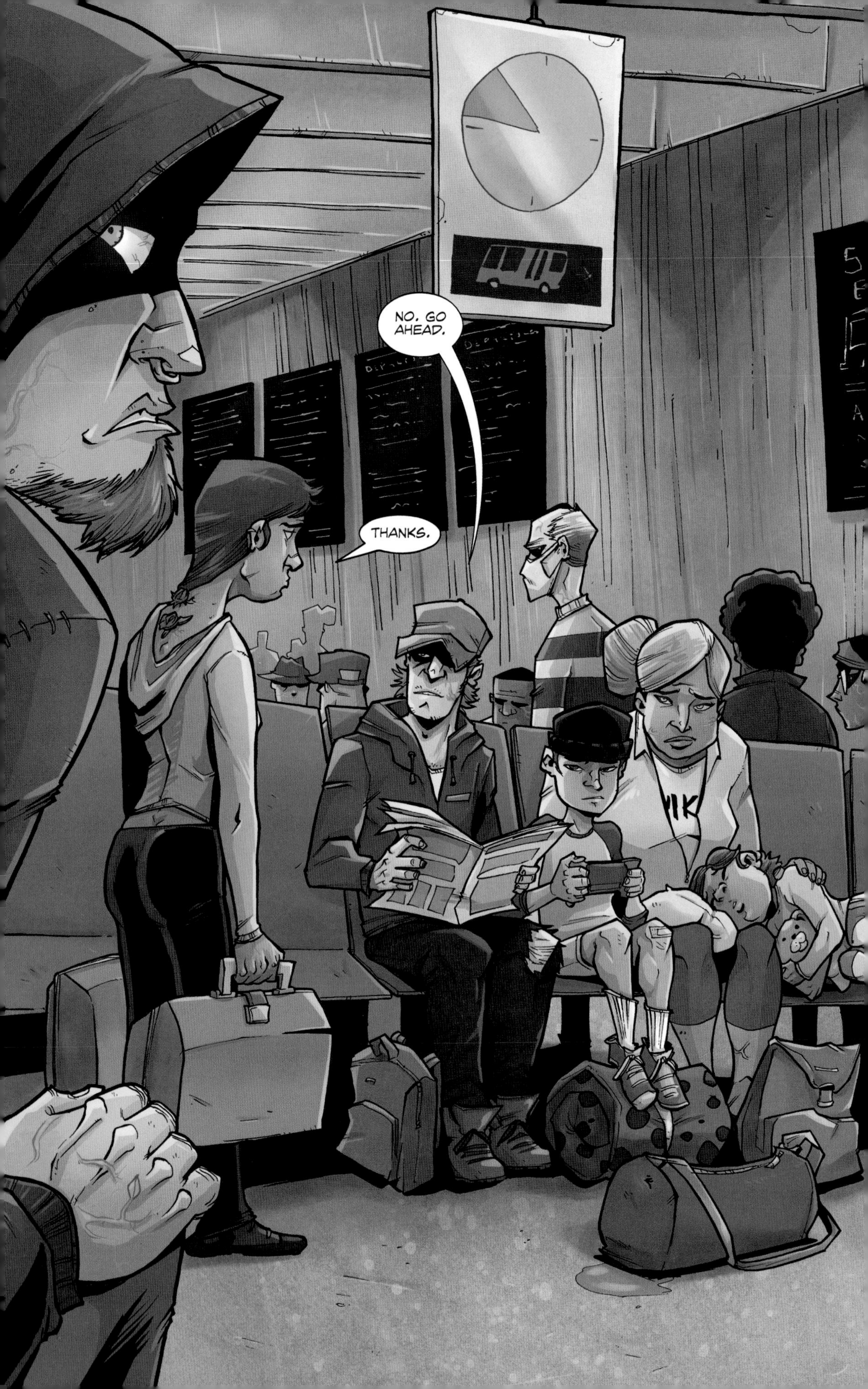
NO. GO AHEAD.
THANKS.

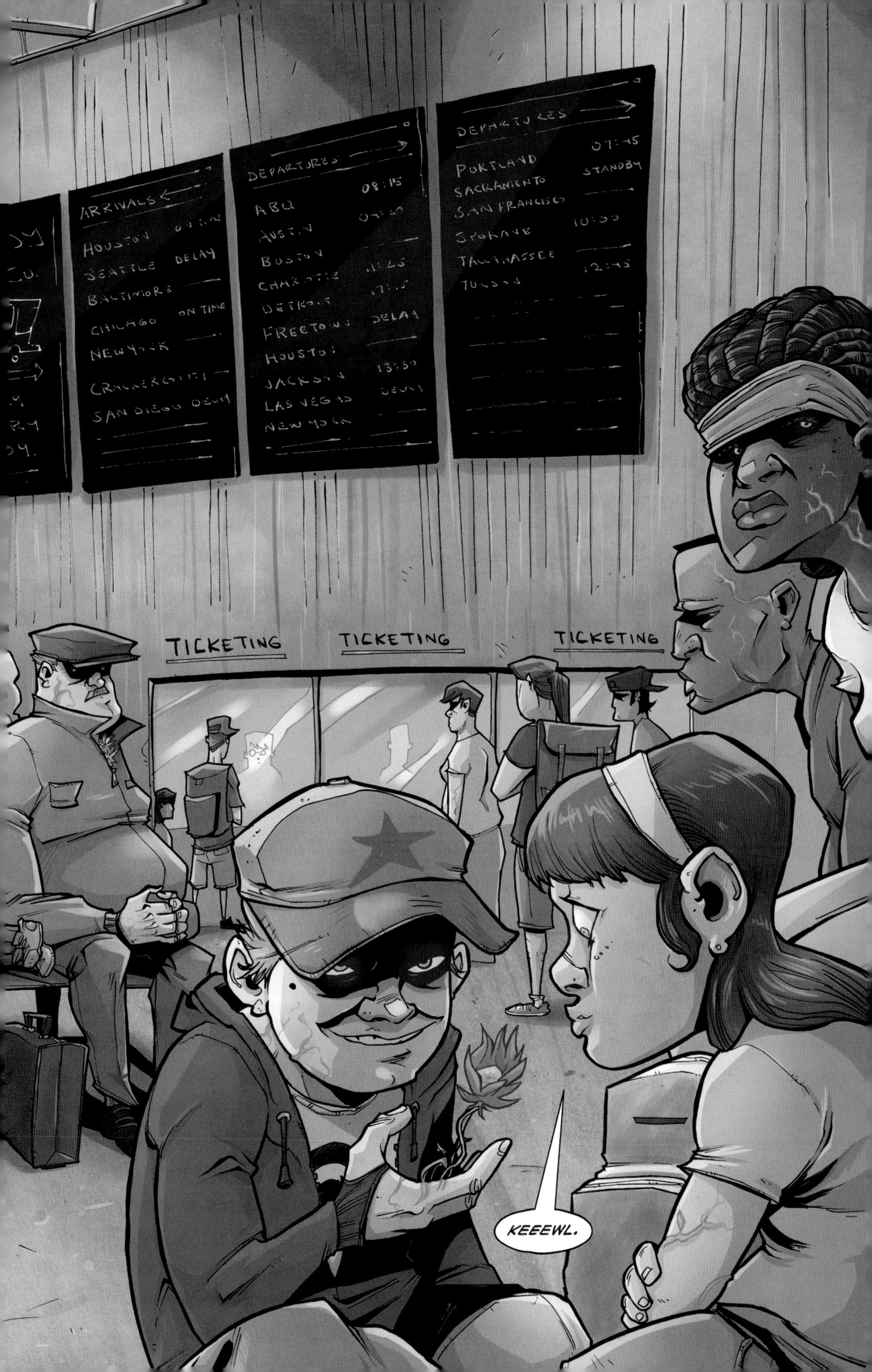
ARRIVALS
HOUSTON
SEATTLE DELAY
BALTIMORE
CHICAGO ON TIME
NEW YORK
SAN DIEGO
DEPARTURES
ABQ 08:15
AUSTIN
BOSTON
CHARLOTTE
DETROIT
FREETOWN DELAY
HOUSTON
JACKSON 13:50
LAS VEGAS
NEW YORK
DEPARTURES
PORTLAND 07:45
SACRAMENTO STANDBY
SAN FRANCISCO
SPOKANE
TALLAHASSEE 12:45
TUCSON
TICKETING
TICKETING
TICKETING
KEEEWL.

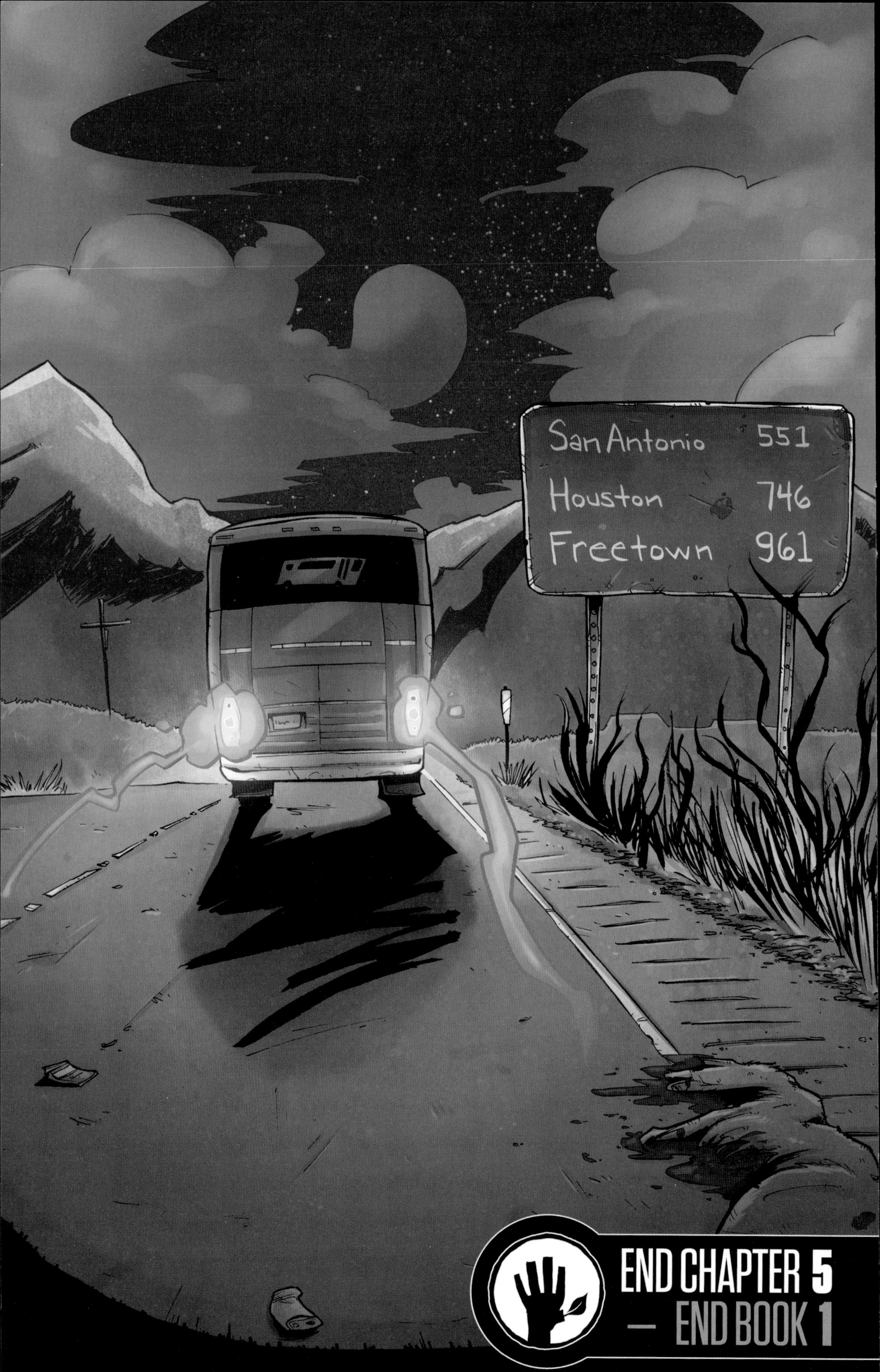
San Antonio 551
Houston 746
Freetown 961
END CHAPTER 5
— END BOOK 1

He told another story.

God's kingdom is like a farmer who planted good
seed in his field. That night, while his hired men
were asleep, his enemy sowed thistles all through
the wheat and slipped away before dawn.
When the first green shoots appeared and the grain
began to form, the thistles showed up, too.

The farmhands came to the farmer and said,
'Master, that was clean seed you planted, wasn't it?
Where did these thistles come from?'

He answered,
'Some enemy did this.'

Matthew 13:24-30 MSG

FARMHAND CONCEPT ART

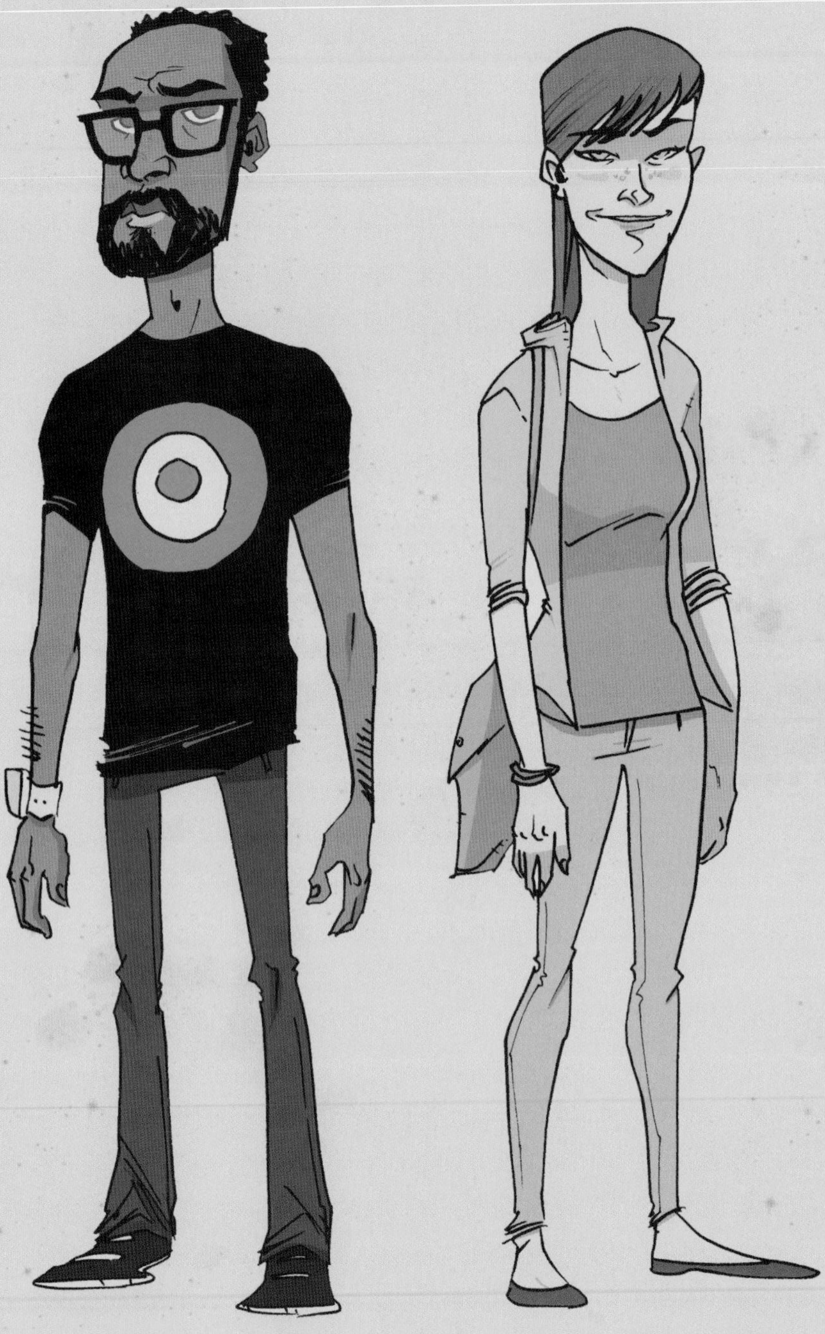

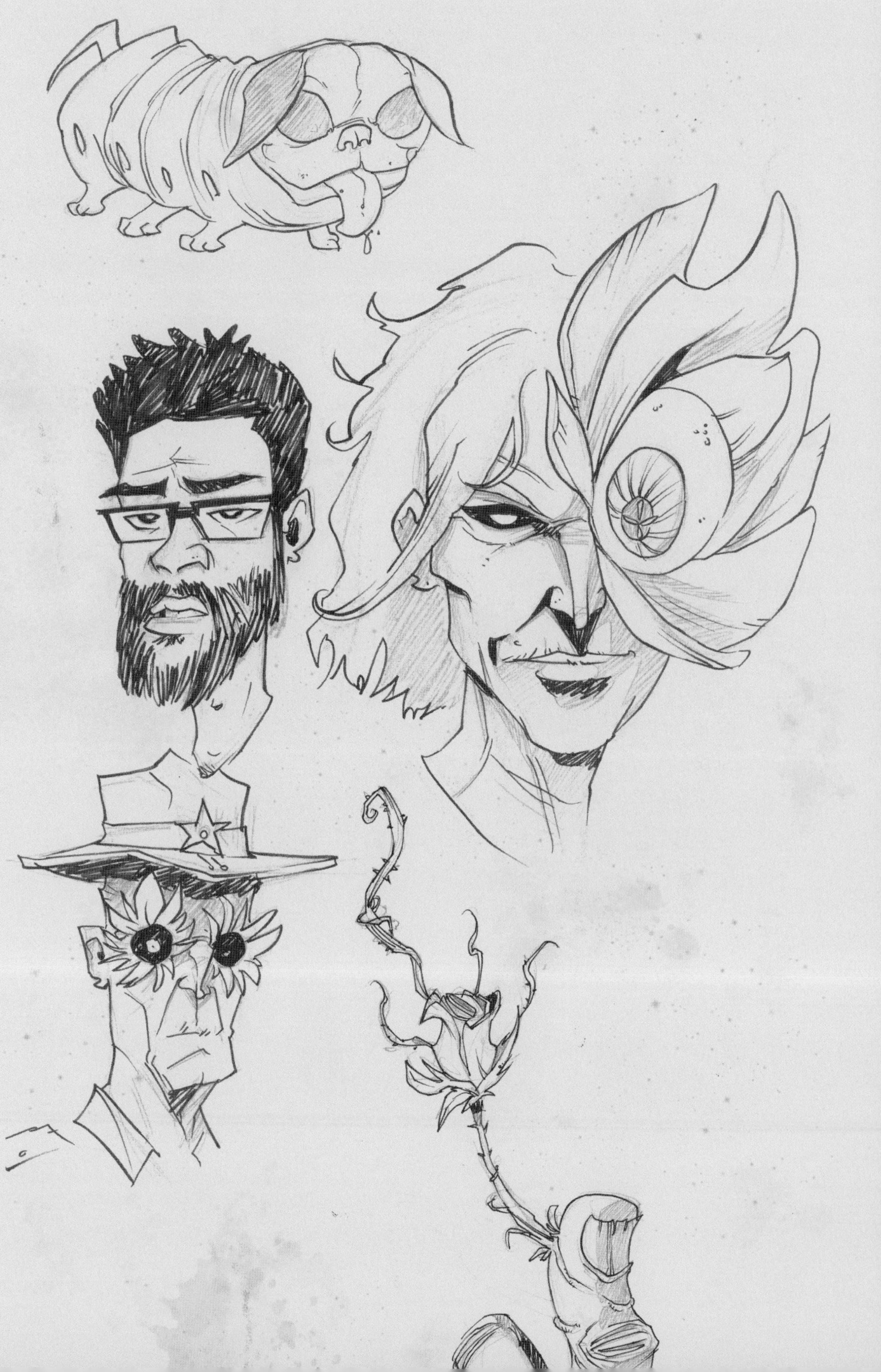

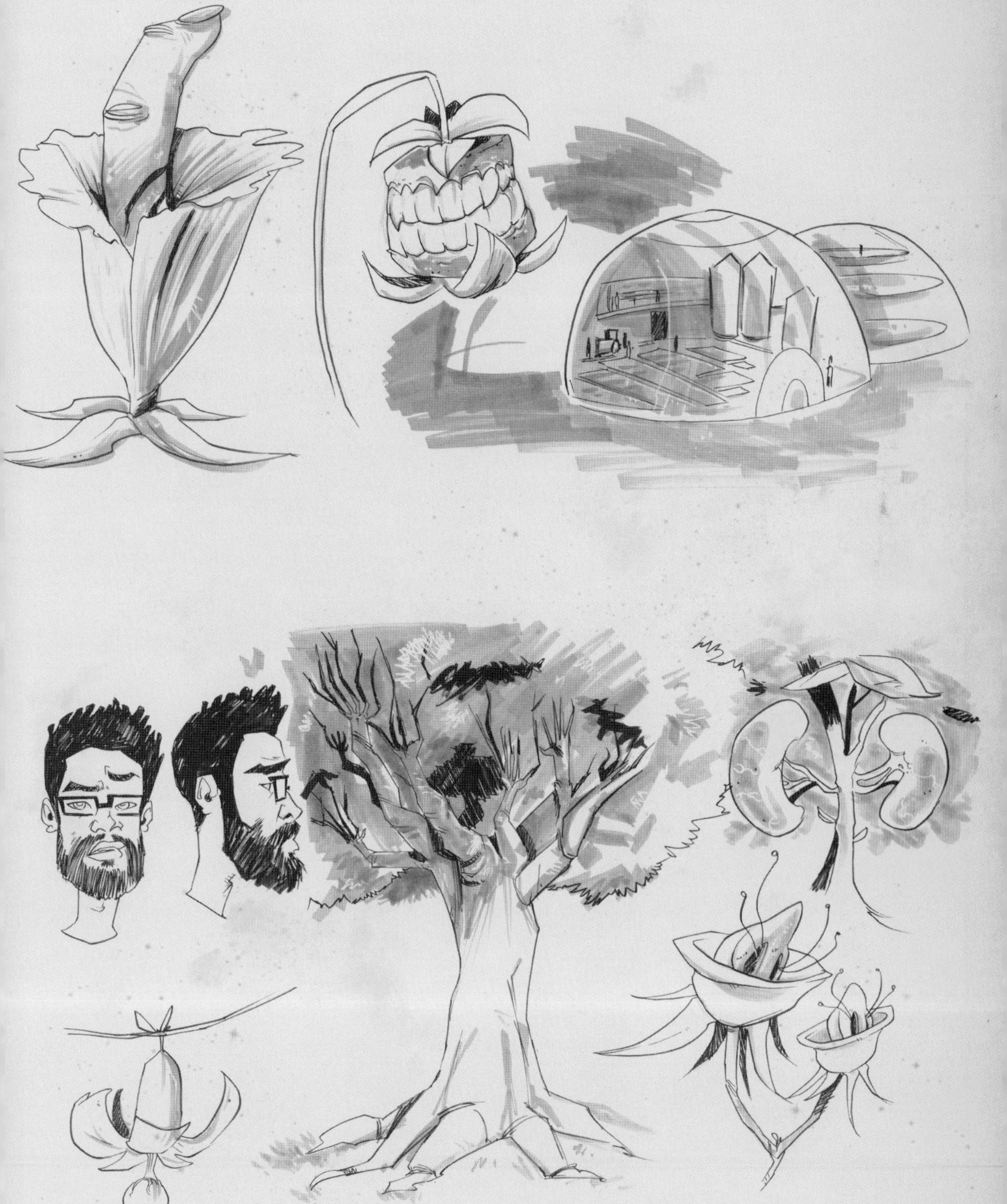

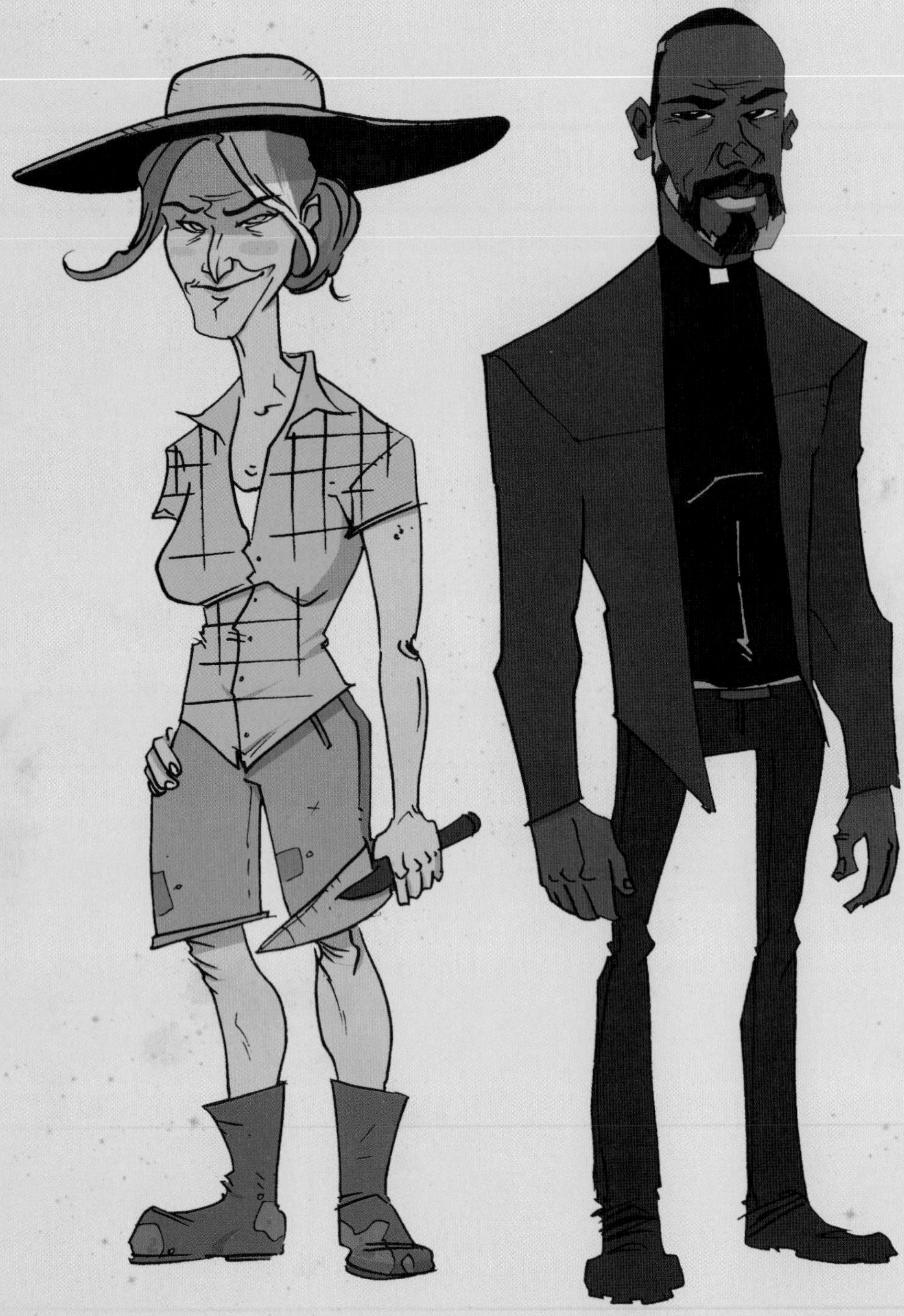

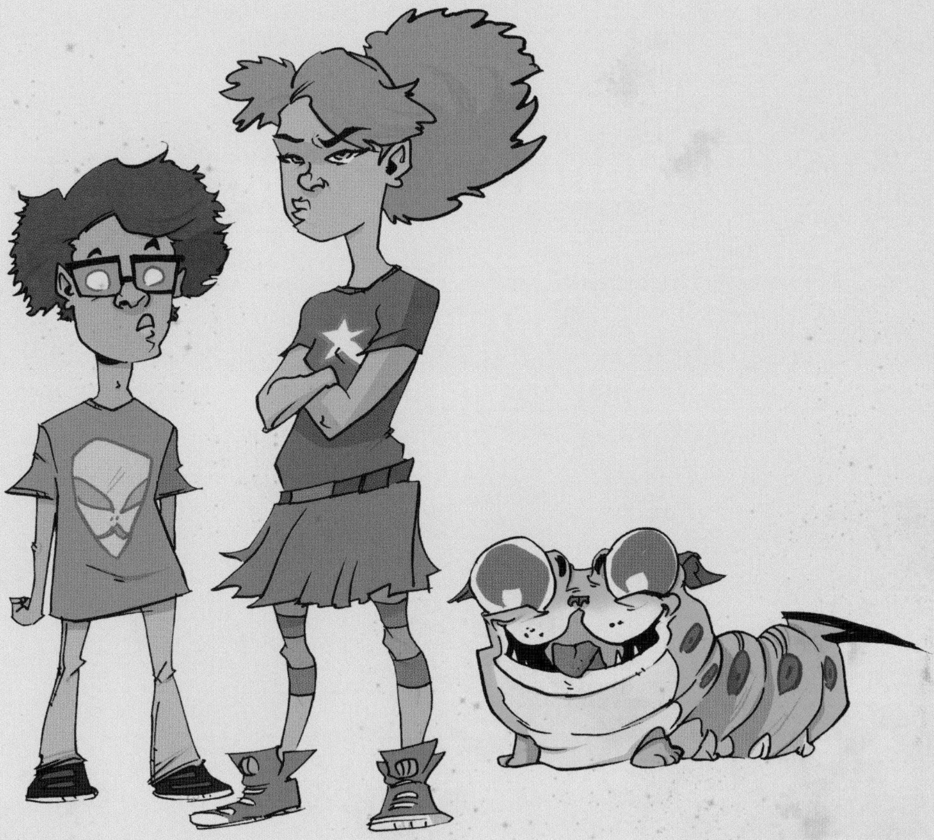

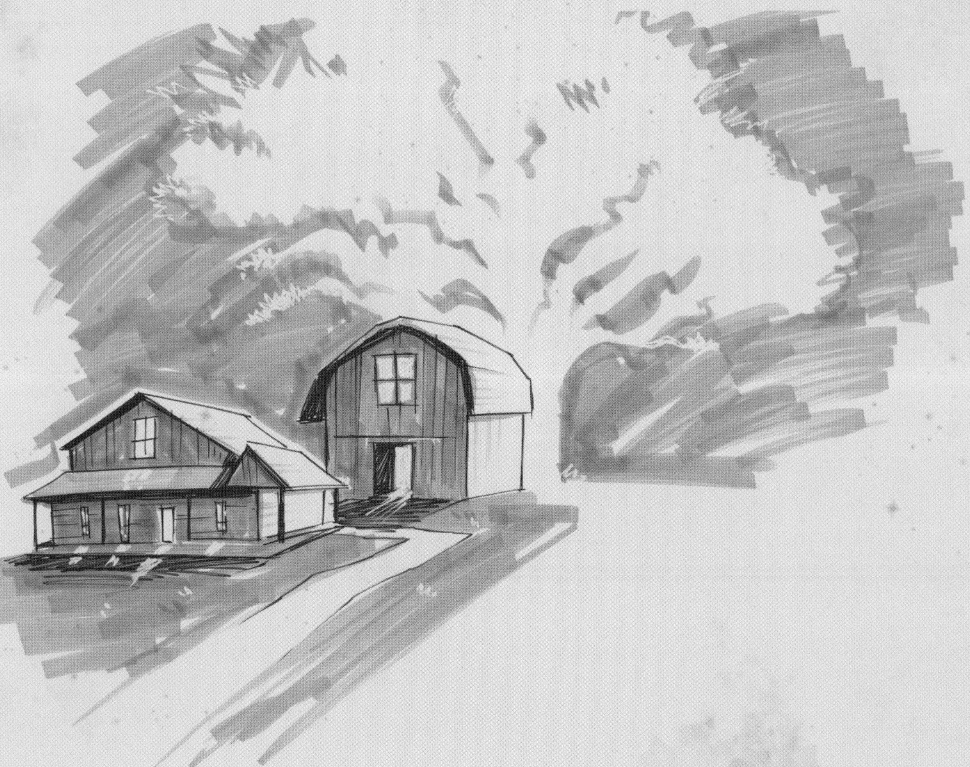

RobGuillory.com

Original Art
Merch
Signed Books